"PENMAN IS A SUPERB STORYTELLER."
—*The Miami Herald*

"Penman manages to illuminate the alien shadowland of the Middle Ages and populate it with vital characters whose politics and passions are as vivid as our own."
—*San Francisco Chronicle*

"[Penman's] many fans will welcome this new foray into territory she knows well. . . . The first in what promises to be a rousing series."
—*The Orlando Sentinel*

"It is through the characters created from her imagination that Penman manages to create a believable twelfth-century environment."
—*Chicago Tribune*

"[Penman] has made quite a niche for herself in the historical genre: novels based on historical fact, embroidered with lively imagination to breathe life into her characters and their times."
—*The Knoxville News-Sentinel*

*Please turn the page
for more reviews. . . .*

By Sharon Kay Penman
Published by Ballantine Books:

THE SUNNE IN SPLENDOUR
HERE BE DRAGONS
FALLS THE SHADOW
THE RECKONING
WHEN CHRIST AND HIS SAINTS SLEPT
CRUEL AS THE GRAVE

THE QUEEN'S MAN

A Medieval Mystery

Sharon Kay Penman

FAWCETT CREST • NEW YORK

A Fawcett Book
Published by The Ballantine Publishing Group
Copyright © 1996 by Sharon Kay Penman

http://www.randomhouse.com

Library of Congress Catalog Card Number: 00-190372

ISBN 0-345-42316-X

This edition published by arrangement with Henry Holt and Company, Inc.

Manufactured in the United States of America

First Ballantine Books Edition: April 1998
First Fawcett Edition: July 2000

10 9 8 7 6 5 4 3 2 1

TO EARLE KOTILA

1

THE BISHOP'S PALACE, CHESTER, ENGLAND

December 1192

"Do you think the king is dead?"

Aubrey de Quincy was caught off balance and furious with himself for his negligence; he ought to have expected this. Throughout their meal, the sole topic had been King Richard's disappearance. All of England—and indeed, most of Christendom—talked of little else this Christmastide, for more than two months had passed since the Lionheart had sailed from Acre. By December, other crusaders had begun to reach English ports. But none had word of the king.

Had the query been posed by one of his other guests, Aubrey would have taken it for natural curiosity. Coming from Hugh de Nonant, it was neither random nor innocent. Coventry's worldly bishop had few peers when it came to conversational ambushes, laying his verbal snares so deftly that his quarry rarely sensed danger until it was too late.

Aubrey had no intention, though, of falling heedlessly into the other bishop's trap. Stalling for time, he signaled for more wine; he prided himself upon his hospitality, so much so that men said none in the Marches set a finer table than His Grace, the Bishop of Chester. The servers were bringing in the next course, a large peacock afloat in a sea of gravy, bones strutted and skin and feathers painstakingly refitted, a sight impressive enough to elicit admiring murmurs from the guests. Aubrey's cooks had labored for hours to create this culinary masterpiece. Now he gazed at it with indifferent eyes, for the shadow of treason had fallen across the hall.

1

Was King Richard dead? Many men thought so, for certes. In alehouses and taverns, they argued whether his ship had been sunk in a gale or attacked by pirates. The credulous speculated about sea monsters. But as the weeks went by, more and more of the missing king's subjects suspected that he was dead, must be dead. And none willed it more passionately than the man Hugh de Nonant served.

The Crusade had been a failure; not even so fine a soldier-king as Richard had been able to reclaim Jerusalem from the infidels. But to Aubrey, the Lionheart's greatest failure was that he'd not sired a son. He'd named his young nephew Arthur as his heir, but Arthur was a child, dwelling with his mother in Brittany. There was another royal rival, one much closer at hand, Richard's younger brother, John, Count of Mortain. No one doubted that John would seek to deny Arthur the crown. What none could be sure of, however, was what the queen mother would do. All knew that Queen Eleanor and John were estranged. Yet he was still her son. If it came to war, whom would she back: John or Arthur?

Aubrey doubted that John would make a good king, for if the serpent was "more subtle than any beast of the field," so, too, was Queen Eleanor's youngest son, unfettered by scruples or conscience qualms. But he did not doubt that John would prevail over Arthur—one way or another. And so he'd concluded that if he were ever faced with that choice, he'd throw his lot in with John.

But this was far more dangerous. The Bishop of Coventry's deceptively innocuous question confirmed Aubrey's worst fears. John was not willing to wait for word of Richard's death. John had never been one for waiting. But what if Richard was not dead? What if he returned to reclaim his crown? If Arthur was no match for John, neither was John a match for Richard. His wrath would be terrible to behold. And even if he eventually forgave John, there would be no forgiveness for the men who'd backed him.

But Aubrey knew that if he balked at supporting John's coup and Richard was indeed dead, he'd be squandering his one chance to gain a king's favor. For John nursed a grudge to the grave, and he'd not be forgetting who stood with him . . . and who had not.

"Well?" the Bishop of Coventry prodded, smiling amiably as if they were merely exchanging pleasantries. "What say you? Is he dead?"

Aubrey's own smile was as bland as almond milk. "If I knew the answer to that question, my lord bishop, I'd be riding straightaway for London to inform the queen."

"I fear the worst, alas," Hugh confided, though with no noticeable regret. "If evil has not befallen him, surely his whereabouts would be known by now."

"I'm not ready to abandon all hope," Aubrey parried, "and for certes, the queen is not."

"It is to be expected that a mother would cling to the last shreds of hope, no matter how meagre or paltry. But the rest of us do not have that luxury, for how long can England be without a king?" Hugh had a pleasant voice, mellow and intimate, ideal for sharing secrets, and his words reached Aubrey's ear alone. "How long dare we wait?"

Aubrey was spared the need to reply by the sudden appearance of his steward on the dais. "My lord bishop, may I have a word with you?"

"What is it, Martin? Is something amiss?"

"It is Justin, my lord. He rode in a few moments ago, is insisting that he must see you at once."

"Justin?" Aubrey was startled and not pleased. "Tell him I will see him after the meal is done and my guests have gone to their beds. Have the cooks see that he is fed." To Aubrey's surprise, the steward made no move to withdraw. "Well?"

The man shifted uncomfortably. "It is just that . . . that the lad seems sorely distraught, my lord. In truth, I've never seen him like this. I do not think he's of a mind to wait."

Aubrey kept his temper in check; he had contempt for men who were ruled by emotion and impulse. "I am not offering him a choice," he said coolly. "See to it."

He was vexed by Justin's unexpected and ill-timed arrival, and vaguely uneasy, too, with that peculiar discomfort that only

Justin could provoke. Nor was his mood improved to realize that Hugh de Nonant had overheard the entire exchange.

"Who is Justin?"

Aubrey gave a dismissive shrug. "No one you know, my lord . . . a foundling I took in some years back."

He'd hoped that Hugh would take the hint and let the matter drop. But the Bishop of Coventry had an eerie ability to scent out secrets. Like a pig rooting after acorns, Aubrey thought sourly, finding himself forced by the other's unseemly and persistent curiosity to explain that Justin's mother had died giving him birth. "The father was known but to God, and there were none to tend to the babe. It was my parish and so when his plight was brought to my attention, I agreed to do what I could. It is our duty, after all, to succor Christ's poor. As Scriptures say, 'Suffer the little children to come unto me.' "

"Very commendable," Hugh said, with hearty approval that would not have been suspect had the speaker been anyone else. He was regarding Aubrey benevolently, and Aubrey could only marvel at how deceptive outer packaging could be. The two men were utterly unlike in appearance: Aubrey tall and slim and elegant, his fair hair closely cropped and shot through with silver, and Hugh rotund and ruddy and balding, looking for all the world like a good-natured, elderly monk. But Aubrey knew this grandfatherly mien camouflaged a shrewd, cynical intelligence, and Hugh's curiosity about Justin was neither idle nor benign. Ever on the alert for weaknesses, the good bishop. And Aubrey was suddenly very angry with Justin for attracting the notice of so dangerous a man as Hugh de Nonant.

"It may be, though, that you've been too indulgent with the lad," Hugh remarked placidly. "It does seem rather presumptuous of him to demand an audience with you."

Aubrey declined the bait. "I've never had reason to complain of his manners . . . until now. You may be sure that I'll take him to task for it."

A loud fanfare of trumpets turned all heads toward the door, heralding the arrival of the meal's pièce de résistance: a great, glazed boar's head on a gleaming silver platter. Men leaned forward in their seats to see, Aubrey's minstrels struck up a carol, and in the flurry of the moment, the bishop's foundling was forgotten.

Aubrey began to relax, once more the gracious host, a role he played well. The respite gave him the chance, too, to consider his options. He must find a way to intimate—without actually saying so—that he was indeed sympathetic to John's cause, but not yet ready to commit himself, not until there was irrefutable proof of King Richard's death.

It was the sharp-eyed Hugh who first noticed the commotion at the far end of the hall. In the doorway, the steward was remonstrating with a tall, dark youth. As Hugh watched, the younger man pulled free of the steward's restraining hold and stalked up the center aisle toward the dais. Hugh leaned over and touched his host's sleeve. "May I assume that angry young interloper is your foundling?"

Oblivious to the intruder bearing down upon them, Aubrey had been conversing politely with the seatmate to his left, the venerable abbot of Chester's abbey of St Werburgh. At Hugh's amused warning, he stiffened in disbelief, then shoved his chair back.

Striding down the steps of the dais, he confronted Justin as he reached the open hearth, trailed by the steward. "How dare you force your way into my hall! Are you drunk?"

"We need to talk," Justin said tersely, and Aubrey stared at him incredulously, unable to believe that Justin could be defying him like this.

He was acutely aware of all the curious eyes upon them. The steward was hovering several feet away, looking utterly miserable—as well he ought. Martin had always been friendly with Justin, too friendly, it now seemed. "I told you that you must wait, Justin!"

"I have been waiting—for twenty years!"

Aubrey hesitated no longer. As bad as this was, it was about to get worse. Justin was a smoldering torch; God only knew what damage would be done if he flared up there in the hall. "Come with me," he said abruptly. "We'll talk above-stairs."

* * *

Aubrey could have led Justin up to his chambers above the hall. He chose, instead, to enter his private chapel, for that was his own province, and the familiarity of the surroundings might give him an edge. He was going to need every advantage he could get.

Two tall candles were lit upon the altar, and glowing between them was the silver-gilt crucifix that was Aubrey's particular pride, both as a symbol of faith and as a work of art. Reaching out, he ran his fingers lightly over the smooth surface while bracing himself for what was to come.

Justin had followed him toward the altar. "Were you ever going to tell me?"

"Tell you what?"

"That I'm your son."

There was no surprise. He'd known as soon as their eyes met in the hall. What else could have gotten Justin so agitated? His mouth was dry, but he still managed to summon up a thin, ironic smile. "Surely you are not serious?"

Justin was close enough now to touch, close enough for Aubrey to see the muscles tighten along his jaw. "I've come from Shrewsbury," he said. "I tracked down Hilde, the cook at St Alkmund's rectory. She told me about you and my mother."

"And you took an old woman's ramblings as gospel?"

"You deny it?"

"Yes," Aubrey said emphatically, "I do."

Justin looked at him, saying nothing. The silence seemed to fill every corner of the chapel, every corner of their lives. When Aubrey could endure it no longer, he said, "This night never happened. We need not refer to it again."

"How generous of you." Justin's voice was toneless, impossible to read. Turning away, he stood motionless for a moment before the altar, and Aubrey dared to think he had won. But then Justin swung around, holding out the silver-gilt crucifix.

"Swear it," he challenged. "Swear upon Our Lord Christ that you are not my father!"

Aubrey opened his mouth. But no words came out. It was so quiet that he could hear his own breathing, uneven and much too rapid. Or was it Justin's? After an eternity, Justin lowered the crucifix, replacing it upon the altar.

"Well," he said, "at least you'll not lie to God."

Aubrey found it unexpectedly difficult to meet Justin's gaze. "There was no need for you to know," he said at last. "What mattered was that I did right by you, and you cannot deny that I did. I did not shirk my duty. You always had food for your belly, a roof over your head——"

"What are you saying? That I ought to thank you for not letting me starve?"

"I did more than that for you," Aubrey snapped, "and well you know it! I saw to your schooling, did I not? Nor did I turn away once you were old enough to fend for yourself. If not for me, Lord Fitz Alan would never have taken you on as a squire. You have nothing to reproach me for, Justin, nothing!"

"A pity my mother could not say as much!"

Aubrey's mouth hardened. "This serves for naught. The woman is twenty years dead. Let her lie in peace."

Justin's eyes were darker than Aubrey had ever seen them, a storm-sky grey. "Her death was convenient, was it not? How disappointed you must have been that I was not stillborn, for then you could have buried all your sins in one grave."

Aubrey lost color. "That is not true. You are not being fair, Justin."

"Fair? What fairness did you ever show my mother, even in death? Have you forgotten what you told me? I was fourteen, had finally gotten up the courage to ask you about her. You said that any woman bearing a child out of wedlock was a wanton, and I should put her out of my thoughts."

"I thought it was for the best."

"Best for you," Justin said scathingly, and then stunned Aubrey by starting toward the door.

"Justin, wait!"

Justin halted, his hand on the door latch, and then slowly turned around. "What more is there to say?"

"A great deal," Aubrey insisted. "We must decide how to deal with this. Do you mean to go back to Lord Fitz Alan? I think it best if I find you another position. You need not fret, for you'll not be the loser for it. I will write on your behalf to Walter de Fauconberg,

Lord of Rise in Holderness up in Yorkshire, ask him to take you into his service."

"Will you, indeed?" Justin's face was in shadow, for he'd moved out of candle range. "Is Yorkshire far enough for you? Are you sure you'd rather not send me up into Scotland?"

Aubrey sucked in his breath. "Damnation, lad, I am trying to help you!"

"Are you truly as blind as that?" Justin asked huskily. "I do not want your help. If I were drowning, I'd not want you to throw me a lifeline!"

Aubrey stared at his son. "As you will. You may be sure that I'll not offer again. But I want your word that you'll say nothing of this to Lord Fitz Alan."

"I have no intention of telling Lord Fitz Alan that you're my father." Justin jerked the door open, then paused. "You see," he said, "you're nothing to boast about."

Aubrey's face flamed. Clenching and unclenching his fists, he stood before the altar, watching as the candles guttered in the sudden draft. Only gradually did he become aware of the cold. A pervasive chill seemed to have seeped into the stone walls of the chapel, as damp and icy and desolate as the December night.

It was a wretched January night, the air frigid, the sky choked with billowing clouds, the wind snarling at shuttered windows, chasing all but the most foolhardy of Winchester's citizens from its iced, empty streets. Most were huddled before their own hearths. But for Justin, who had neither hearth nor home, shelter on this dismal Epiphany Eve was a seedy, squalid alehouse on Tanner Street, in one of the city's poorest quarters.

The alehouse was drafty and dimly lit, reeking of sweat and smoke and the acrid odor of burning tallow. The company was as cheerless as the surroundings. The burly, taciturn owner inspired no tipsy confidences and tolerated no tomfoolery, serving his customers curtly and grudgingly, as if they were un-bidden guests who'd overstayed their welcome. In the corner, a noisy drunkard was bullying the serving maid and bragging to all within earshot of his success in foisting off sacks of worm-eaten flour upon the lepers of St Mary Magdalen's. Across from

Justin was a shabbily dressed man of middle years, grey haired and sad eyed, nursing a tankard of ale to last till closing. There were two tanners dicing by the hearth, being cheered on by a buxom harlot. And then there was Justin, brooding over the bad luck that seemed to be stalking him so relentlessly in the last fortnight.

Lord Fitz Alan had dismissed him, angered by his stubborn refusal to explain why he'd not returned from Shrewsbury straightaway as instructed. Justin was not entirely sorry to go, for Fitz Alan was part of a past he wanted only to repudiate. His one regret was that when his father learned of this, he'd think Justin had kept quiet for his sake. The truth was that the wound was still too raw. Nothing could have induced Justin to let Fitz Alan know how badly he was bleeding.

Riding away from Fitz Alan's Shropshire manor with meagre savings and uncertain prospects, he'd not despaired, though, for he was not friendless. Deliverance had come from an unlikely source: his father's steward.

Martin had been a member of the bishop's household for as long as Justin could remember, and had often gone out of his way to show kindness to the solitary, wary child who bore a double stigma: illegitimate and orphaned. Justin had been grateful for the attention, and at last understood why the steward had been so protective. Martin had known or suspected the truth. How else explain what he'd done after that bitter scene in the bishop's chapel? Following Justin out to the stables, he'd given him the name of a kinsman, a Hampshire knight who might offer him employment should he have need of it.

Since he could expect no reference from Fitz Alan, Martin's recommendation was a godsend, and Justin had taken the road south, heading for the town of Andover. But the journey ended in disappointment: Martin's kinsman was in Normandy, not expected back until the spring. At a loss, Justin had continued on to Winchester, simply because he had nowhere else to go.

His ale cup was almost empty. Could he spare enough for a second ale? No . . . not unless he expected to find a miraculous windfall on his way back to his inn. The door banged open, admitting two new customers. They were better dressed than the other patrons, and in better spirits, too, boisterously demanding service from the serving maid even before they laid claim to a nearby table. They were soon haggling with the prostitute over her price, so loudly that the others in the alehouse had no choice but to listen.

Involuntary eavesdropping was not Justin's idea of fun, and he was starting to rise when he was jolted by a braying cry of "Aubrey!" A third man had stumbled into the alehouse, weaving his way toward his beckoning companions. Justin sat back again and drained the last of his ale. The name Aubrey was a common one. Was he going to flinch every time he heard it uttered? His own name was far more unusual, and he'd often been called upon to explain that it was the name of an early Christian martyr. He wondered why his father had chosen it, if it held ironic undertones. What would his mother have named him had she lived? He knew nothing about her, not even her name. Nor would he ever know now, for the only person who could answer his questions was the last one he'd ask.

Another name now intruded into his awareness, catching his attention no less fully than "Aubrey" had done. His raucous neighbors were joking about King Richard's disappearance. The jests were lame, and Justin had heard them before. What intrigued him was the mention of the king's brother.

"I tell you," the man called Aubrey was insisting, "that the king's brother must be planning to do the Devil's work. One of the serjeants at the castle says he heard that John is hiring men as fast as he can find them. You two lackwits ought to give it some thought, for he's not particular. If a man has a pulse and can wield a sword, he'll be taken into John's service!"

Inn guests were expected to share beds, for privacy was an unknown luxury in their world. Sandwiched between two snoring strangers, Justin got little sleep. Rising at dawn, he discovered that it had snowed in the night.

Winchester was beginning to stir. A sleepy guard waved Justin on through the East Gate, and he headed out of the city on the Alresford Road. The sky was leaden. Justin had ridden less than a mile before it started to snow again. There were no other travelers, only a lone figure huddled by the side of the road. Justin wondered what dire need could send a man out to beg in the snow, and as he drew nearer, he had his answer in the latten clappers leaning against the beggar's alms bowl—used by lepers to warn people of their approach.

Justin had great pity for lepers, forsaken by all but God. Embarrassed and regretful that he could not afford to give alms, he drew rein and said politely, "Good morrow, friend."

The man's face was shadowed by his leper's cloak. Whether it also hid the ravages of his disease, Justin could not tell, but he did get a glimpse of the leper's mutilated hand, with stumps where fingers ought to have been. His own plight suddenly seemed less perilous, and Justin fumbled for his money pouch, leaned over, and dropped a farthing into the alms bowl, ashamed that he could spare so little. The leper had learned, though, to be thankful for the most meagre offering, even courtesy, and wished Justin "Godspeed."

The road was half hidden by snow and icy in patches. Fortunately, Justin's big chestnut was as surefooted as a mule. But it would be slow going, for he'd not risk the stallion's safety. Copper was his pride and joy; he knew how lucky he was to own a horse, especially one of Copper's calibre. He'd been able to buy the stallion only because the animal had gone lame and he'd offered more than the butcher would. It had taken months to nurse the chestnut back to health, but well worth the time and trouble. Reaching out, he gave the horse a pat on the neck, and then blew on his hands to warm them, for his fingers were beginning to cramp with the cold.

The innkeeper had told him that the village of Alresford was just seven miles from Winchester, and the village of Alton another eight miles or so. If this were summer, he could reasonably have expected to cover thirty miles before nightfall. Today he'd be lucky to reach Alton by dusk. From there it was another twenty miles to Guildford and a final thirty to his destination: London. That meant four or five days on the road, depending on the weather. It was a long way to go on a hunch.

Slackening the reins, Justin gave Copper a brief respite. The leper hospital of St Mary Magdalen had receded into the distance some time ago. The ground had leveled off, for St Giles's Hill was now far behind him. It was like a ghost road, though; the only other soul he'd seen was the leper.

Was this a fool's mission, riding for London? Lying awake last night in that forlorn, flea-infested inn, he'd thought long and hard about his future and his survival skills. During his years in Lord Fitz Alan's service, he'd been taught to handle a sword. And he knew how to read and write. He'd been well educated for a "harlot's bastard." At least now he understood why: not Christian charity, a sop to a guilty conscience.

But that education might well be his salvation. He'd heard that London scribes set up booths in the nave of St Paul's Cathedral, writing letters and legal documents for a price. If he could hire out as a scribe, mayhap he could buy himself some time, a chance to decide what he should do next.

Or he could take another fork in the road. He could offer his sword to the king's brother. If that lout in the alehouse had spoken true, John was not asking for references. Justin did not know whether he wanted to fight to make John King of England. But he suspected that hunger would banish such qualms right quick.

The road had begun to narrow, for he was well into the woods now. Bare, skeletal branches stabbed the sky over his head. Ice-glazed ash swayed in the wind and the starkly graceful silhouettes of silver birch rose up behind him. The underbrush was thick and tangled with elder shrubs, holly, and hawthorn hedges, and the glistening, unsullied snow was occasionally smudged by deer tracks and paw prints of marten and fox. A rabbit sprinted for cover and an inquisitive red squirrel followed Justin for a time, sailing from tree to tree with acrobatic ease. There was an austere beauty about this frozen, snow-drifted landscape, but Justin would have appreciated it better had he not been half-frozen himself.

"Now?"

"No, it's not him."

Startled by the sudden sound of voices, so utterly out of place in this quiet, sylvan setting, Justin swung around in the saddle, reaching for the hilt of his sword. Off to his left, several fallen trees had formed a covert, screened off by glossy, green holly boughs. To a lost traveler, this sheltered lair offered sanctuary. To an outlaw, ideal camouflage for an ambush.

Justin spurred Copper forward and the stallion responded like a launched arrow, sending up a spray of snow as he lengthened stride. Within moments, they were in the clear. Glancing over his shoulder, Justin saw no movement, suspicious or otherwise. It was easy to doubt his own senses, to wonder if he'd imagined those disembodied woodland whispers. "Fool," he jeered aloud. "I'll be seeing forest phantoms next, Copper, with a few horned demons thrown in for good measure!"

But there had been something very disquieting about those eerie whispers, and his unease lingered. "We ought to be at Alresford soon," he told his stallion, and the horse twitched his ears at the sound of his voice. So far the snowfall had been light and powdery and the wind seemed to be dying down. God Willing, the rest of his journey would be trouble free. What would London be like? He'd been told that more than twenty-five thousand souls dwelled within its walls, but he could not imagine a city so huge. He was no stranger to towns, having passed his childhood in Shrewsbury and Chester, and he'd been to Oxford and now Winchester. None of them could compare, though, to London in size or significance.

The first shout was muffled, indistinct. Justin reined in, straining to hear. It came again, and this time there was no mistaking what it was: a desperate appeal for help. Later—much later—Justin would marvel at his reckless response. Now, though, he reacted instinctively, drawn irresistibly by the haunting echoes of that urgent, despairing cry.

Backtracking through the snow, he turned a bend in the road and nearly collided with a runaway, riderless horse. Swerving just in time to avoid the panicked animal, he unsheathed his sword, for any doubts he'd had about what he might find had been dispelled.

The sounds of strife had gotten louder. Responding gamely to Justin's urging, his stallion skimmed over the snow, reaching a dangerous level of speed for such treacherous terrain. Up ahead, a horse neighed shrilly. There was another choked cry for help, a burst of cursing. By then Justin was within sight of the covert. A figure lay prone in the middle of the road, groaning. Nearby, two men were struggling fiercely, while a third man sought to hold on to the reins of a plunging roan stallion. But although Justin was now close enough to see what was occurring, he was not yet close enough to prevent what happened next. One of the men suddenly staggered, then slumped to the ground at his assailant's feet. The outlaw never hesitated. Bending over his victim, blood still dripping from his dagger, he stripped rings from the man's fingers, then began a hasty search of the body.

"Did you find it?" Getting a grunt in reply, the second outlaw tried to lead the horse over, swearing when the animal balked. "Mayhap he hid it in his tunic. He—Christ's Blood! Gib, beware!"

Gib spun around, saw Justin racing toward them, sword drawn, and lunged to his feet. In three strides, he reached the roan stallion, vaulting up into the saddle. "What are you waiting for, you dolt!" he snarled at his partner, who'd yet to move, continuing to gape at Justin's approach. Coming to his senses, the laggard grabbed for the outstretched hand and scrambled up behind his companion. By the time Justin reached the ambush scene, the outlaws were in flight.

Justin had no intention of pursuit. They would have horses hidden close by, and they knew these woods far better than he. As he reined in his mount, he almost came to grief, for Copper shied without warning, nearly unseating him. From the corner of his eye, he caught a slithering, sideways movement, and somewhere in the back of his brain, he noted it, a puzzle to be resolved later, for snakes usually denned up in burrows during the winter months. At the moment, though, his only concern was in calming his horse. Once he had, he dismounted swiftly, anchored Copper to a nearby bush, and turned his attention toward the men.

The closer of the two was a strapping youth about Justin's own age. His face was as colorless as the snow, his hair matted with blood, and he looked dazed and disoriented. But he'd managed to sit up, and Justin bypassed him in favor of the second man, who lay ominously still, a crimson stain spreading beyond him into the snow. Kneeling by his side, Justin caught his breath, for he knew at once that he was looking death in the face.

The man was well past his youth, fifty or so to judge by the grey generously salted throughout the walnut-brown hair and neatly trimmed beard. His mantle was of good quality wool, his boots of soft cowhide, and from what Justin had seen of his stolen roan stallion, he'd been riding an exceptionally fine animal. A man very prosperous, for certes, wealthy enough to be traveling with a servant, dying now in trampled, bloodied snow, unshriven and alone, with only a stranger to hold his hand.

Never had Justin felt so helpless. He attempted to staunch the bleeding with that costly wool mantle, but soon saw it was futile. Cradling the man's head in the crook of his arm, he unhooked the wineskin from his belt, murmuring words of comfort and hope that he knew to be lies. A life was ebbing away before his eyes, and he could do nothing.

The man's lashes quivered. His pupils were dilated, glassy, and unseeing. When Justin tilted the wineskin to his lips, the liquid dribbled down his chin. By now the other man had stumbled over, sinking down in the snow beside them. From him, Justin learned that the dying man was an affluent Winchester goldsmith, Gervase Fitz Randolph, on his way to London on a secret matter that he'd confided to no one, when they'd been set upon by bandits who'd somehow spooked their horses. "I was thrown," the youth said, stifling a sob. "I am sorry, Master Gervase, so sorry . . ."

The sound of his name seemed to rouse Gervase from his stupor. His gaze wandered at first, then slowly focused upon Justin. His chest heaved as he sought to draw air into his laboring lungs, but he had a need no less pressing than his pain, and he ignored Justin's plea to lie still.

"They . . . did not . . . not get it . . ." His words were slurred, soft as a sigh, yet oddly triumphant, too.

Justin was puzzled, for he'd seen the outlaw steal Gervase's money pouch. "What did they not get?"

"Her letter . . ." Gervase gulped for air, and then said with surprising clarity, "I cannot fail her. You must promise me, promise . . ."

"Promise you what?" Justin asked warily, for a deathbed promise was a spiritual spider's web, sure to ensnare.

Blood had begun to trickle from the corner of Gervase's mouth. When he spoke again, Justin had to bend down to hear, so close that he could feel Gervase's faltering breath on his face. Unable to believe what he'd just heard, he stared incredulously at the mortally wounded goldsmith. "What did you say?"

"Promise me," Gervase repeated, and if his voice was weak, his eyes burned into Justin's with mesmerizing fervor. "You must deliver this letter to her . . . to the queen."

2

LONDON

January 1193

Reining in on Old Bourn Hill, Justin gazed down at the city below. Never had he seen so many rooftops, so many church steeples, such a tangled maze of streets and alleys. The partially completed tower and spire of St Paul's Cathedral seemed to soar halfway to Heaven, and in the distance the whitewashed keep of the Tower gleamed through the dusk. The River Thames had taken on a dull-gold sheen, spangled with flickering lights as lantern-lit boats bobbed on the current. Justin sat his horse as the daylight began to fade, awed by his first glimpse of London.

Up close, the city was even more daunting, exciting and crowded and chaotic. The streets were narrow, unpaved, and shadowed by overhanging timbered houses painted in vivid shades of red and blue and black. The sky was smudged with the smoke from hundreds of hearth fires, and flocks of sea gulls wheeled overhead, adding their raucous cries to the clamor of river traffic. Ferrymen shouted "Westward ho!" as they steered toward Southwark, "Eastward ho!" for those wanting to cross over to the London bankside. Some peddlers hawked "Hot pies!" along the Cheapside; others sought to entice customers with bellowing boasts about the fine quality of their needles and pins, their miraculous salves and healing balms, their ribbons and wooden combs and wrought-iron candlesticks. Justin did not doubt that if he asked one of them for the Holy Grail, the man would promise to produce it straightaway.

Weaving his way along the Cheapside, Justin had to check his stallion frequently, for the street was thronged with pedestrians, darting between lumbering carts and swearing horsemen with the aplomb of the true city dweller. They seemed equally

17

indifferent to the dogs and geese and stray pigs wandering about, and were not fazed even when a woman opened an upper-story window and flung the contents of a chamber pot down into the street's central gutter. The Londoners scattered in the nick of time, a few pausing to curse upward, most continuing on their way without losing a stride. Marveling at this urban insouciance, Justin rode on.

Theirs was a world constantly echoing with the chiming of church bells, for they were rung for festivals, for funerals, for marriages, for royal coronations and city elections, for processions and births and to elicit prayers for dying parishioners, to call Christ's faithful to Mass and to mark the canonical hour. Like most people, Justin had learned to be selectively deaf, so that the incessant pealing faded into the background noises of daily life. But never before had he been in a city with more than a hundred churches, and he found himself engulfed in waves of shimmering sound. The sun had slid below the horizon, and he hastily stopped a passerby, asking about lodgings. Directed to a small, shabby inn off the Cheapside, he engaged a bed for himself and a stall for Copper in the stables. The inn offered no meals; Justin was told brusquely that if he was hungry, there was a cookshop down by the river.

Justin was indeed hungry, but even more exhausted. He'd gotten little sleep since the Epiphany ambush on the Alresford Road. He and Gervase Fitz Randolph's groom, Edwin, had taken the goldsmith's body to Alresford, where the village priest had promised to alert the sheriff of Hampshire and to break the sad news to the Fitz Randolph family. Justin had then continued on toward London, but he was trailed by memories of the killing, and the letter he'd hidden within his tunic was heavier than any millstone.

According to the innkeeper, Justin would be sharing a chamber with two Breton sailors, but they were out. The room was scantily furnished, containing only three pallets covered with moth-eaten woolen blankets and a few stools, not even a chamber pot. Sitting down on the closest bed, Justin set his candle upon one of the stools and then drew out the letter.

Gervase had secreted it in a leather pouch around his neck, a pouch so soaked with his blood that Justin had discarded it at the murder site. The parchment was folded, threaded through with a thin, braided cord, the ends sealed with wax. The signet was still intact, although it meant nothing to Justin. No matter how many times he examined it, the letter offered no clues. As evidence of a man's violent death, it was compelling. But was it truly meant for England's queen?

A dozen times he'd been about to break the seal; a dozen times he'd checked the impulse. Was it the dried blood mottling the parchment that gave him such a sense of foreboding? What in God's Name had he gotten himself into? How was he supposed to deliver a dead man's letter to Eleanor of Aquitaine?

He knew of Eleanor's remarkable history, of course, as who in Christendom did not? In her youth, she'd been a great beauty, an even greater heiress, Duchess of Aquitaine in her own right. At age fifteen, she'd become Queen of France. But the marriage had not prospered, for wine and milk were not meant to mix. The pious, painfully earnest Louis was as baffled as he was bewitched by his high-spirited young wife, while his advisers whispered that she was too clever by half, more strong-willed and outspoken than any woman ought to be. There had been rumors and hints of scandal as the years went by, a disastrous crusade to the Holy Land, a public estrangement and reconciliation, at the Pope's urging. Few were surprised when the French king and his controversial queen were eventually divorced, for however much Louis still loved her—and he did—she'd failed to give him a son, and that was the one sin no queen could be forgiven.

Eleanor had then returned to her own domains in Aquitaine, and it was expected that after a decorous interval, Louis and his council would choose another husband for her, a man deemed acceptable to the French Crown. What Eleanor might want, no one even considered. And so the shock was all the greater when word got out of her sudden, secret wedding two months after the divorce to Henry Fitz Empress, Duke of Normandy.

If Eleanor and Louis had been grievously mismatched, she and Henry were almost too well matched, two high-flying hawks soaring toward the sun. Eleanor was nigh on thirty, Henry just nineteen, but they were soulmates in all the ways that mattered, lusting after empires and each other, indifferent to scandalized public opinion and the wounded outrage of the French king. Henry soon showed the rest of Christendom what Eleanor had seen in him. When Louis was goaded into a punitive expedition against the newlyweds, Henry sent the French army reeling back across the border in six short weeks. He then turned his attention to England. His mother had fought a long and bloody civil war with her cousin over the English throne. Henry avenged her loss, claiming the crown she'd been denied. Barely two years after their marriage, Eleanor was once more a queen, this time Queen of England.

Her marriage to Henry had proved to be a passionate and tumultuous and, ultimately, doomed union. The "barren queen" bore him eight children, five sons and three daughters. They loved and quarreled and reconciled and ruled over a vast realm that stretched from Scotland to the Pyrenees. But then Henry committed an unforgivable sin of his own, giving his heart to a younger woman. In their world, a wife was expected to overlook a husband's infidelities, no matter how flagrant. Eleanor was not like other women, though, and Henry was to pay a high price for his roving eye: a rebellion instigated by his queen, joined by his own sons.

But Eleanor paid a high price, too. Captured by Henry's soldiers, she was held prisoner for sixteen years, freed only by Henry's death. Such a lengthy confinement would have broken most people. It had not broken Eleanor. The passionate young queen and the embittered, betrayed wife were ghosts long since laid to rest. Now in her seventy-first year, she was acclaimed and admired for her sagacity and shrewd counsel, reigning over England in her son's absence, fiercely protective of his interests, proud matriarch of a great dynasty. A living legend. And this was the woman expecting a letter from a murdered goldsmith? Justin thought it highly unlikely.

Sounds in the stairwell roused Justin from his uneasy reverie, reminding him that his privacy was fleeting; the Breton sailors might return at any moment. It was time. Jerking the cords, he broke the seal and unfolded the parchment. There were two letters. Justin picked one up, catching his breath when he saw the salutation: *Walter de Coutances, Archbishop of Rouen, to Her Grace, Eleanor, Queen of England, Duchess of Aquitaine, and Countess of Poitou, greetings.* So the goldsmith had spoken true! Scanning the page, he read enough to make him reach hastily for the second letter.

Henry, by the grace of God, Emperor of the Romans and ever august, to his beloved and special friend, Philip, the illustrious King of the French, health and sincere love and affection. Justin brought the parchment closer to his candle's shivering light, his eyes riveted upon the page. When he was done, he sat very still, stunned and chilled by what he'd just learned. God help him, what secret could be more dangerous than the one he now possessed? For he had the answer to the question being asked throughout Christendom. He knew what had befallen the missing English king.

Queen Eleanor had held her Christmas court at Westminster, but she was currently in residence at the Tower, occupying the spacious second-floor quarters of its great keep. The first-floor chambers had been crowded all day with petitioners, vying with one another to persuade Peter of Blois, the queen's secretary-chancellor, that they deserved a brief audience. Peter was not easily impressed by tales of woe, and most petitioners would be turned away. One who steadfastly refused to go eventually attracted the attention of Claudine de Loudun, a young widow who was a distant kinswoman and attendant of the queen. She was curious enough to investigate and by the time she went back above-stairs, she had determined to thwart the imperious Peter's will.

The men in Eleanor's great hall were gathered in a circle near the hearth. Claudine was not surprised to find Sir Durand de Curzon holding court again, for he seemed to crave an audience as much as he did wine and women and good living. His current joke involved a highwayman, a nun, and a befuddled innkeeper, and reaped a harvest of hearty laughter. Lingering just long enough to hear the predictable punch line, Claudine crossed the hall and entered the queen's great chamber.

It was quieter than the hall, but even there the queen was rarely alone. Another of Eleanor's ladies was sorting through a coffer overflowing with bolts of silk and linen, a servant was tending to the hearth, and the queen's pampered greyhound was gnawing contentedly on a purloined cushion. Claudine didn't have the heart to deprive the dog of his booty and pretended not to see, hers the complicity that one rebel owed another.

Nearby, the queen's chaplain was discussing falconry with William Longsword, a bastard-born son of Eleanor's late husband. Claudine would usually have joined the conversation, for she loved hawking and both men were favorites of hers. She enjoyed teasing the courtly, debonair chaplain that he was far too handsome to be a priest, and Will, an affable, stocky redhead in his mid-thirties, was that rarity: a man of influence without enemies, so good-hearted that even the most cynical could not doubt his sincerity. She flashed them a playful smile as she passed, but did not pause, for she was intent upon finding the queen.

The door at the south end of the chamber led to the Chapel of St John the Evangelist, but Claudine had no qualms about entering, for she knew Eleanor well enough to be sure that the queen was seeking solitude, not spiritual comfort. Pale January sun spilled into the chapel from so many windows that the stone walls and soaring pillars seemed to have been sculpted from ivory. To Claudine, the stark simplicity of this small Norman chapel was more beautiful than the grandest of God's cathedrals. Claudine's piety had strong aesthetic underpinnings; in that, she was very like her royal mistress.

As she expected, she did not find Eleanor in prayer. The queen was standing by one of the stained glass windows, gazing up at the cloud-dappled sky. Few people ever reached their biblical threescore years and ten, but Eleanor carried hers lightly. She was still willow-slim, her step sure and quick, her will as indomitable as ever. She was aging as she'd lived, in defiance of all the rules. The one foe she could not defeat, though, was death. She was no stranger to a mother's grieving; she'd buried four of her children so far. But none were so loved as Richard.

Eleanor turned from the window as the door opened. The white winter light robbed her face of color, deepening the sleepless shadows that lurked like bruises under her eyes. But she smiled at the sight of Claudine, a smile that belied her age and defied her cares. "I was wondering where you'd gotten to, Claudine. You have that cat-in-the-cream look again. What mischief have you in mind this time?"

"No mischief, madame, a good deed." Claudine added a "truly" in mock earnest. "I have a favor to ask of you, my lady. Peter told me he means to tell the remaining petitioners that they must come back on the morrow. Ere he does, can you spare a few moments for one of them? He has been here since first light, and I do believe he is willing to wait till Judgment Day if he must."

"If his need is so urgent, why has Peter not admitted him?"

"I daresay because he balked at telling Peter why he seeks an audience with you." Claudine did not point out that there was no quicker way to vex Peter than to deny him pertinent information. She did not need to, for Eleanor had a comprehensive understanding of all in her service; she made sure of that.

"How lucky for this young man that you are willing to speak up for him," Eleanor said dryly. "He is young, is he not? And pleasing to the eye?"

Claudine grinned, quite unabashed at being caught out. "Indeed he is, my lady. Tall and well made, with hair darker than sin, smoke-color eyes, and a smile like the sunrise. He was no more forthcoming with me than he was with Peter, but his manners were good and he has a fine sword at his hip." This last bit of information was meant to assure Eleanor that the stranger was one of their own, not baseborn.

Eleanor's eyes held an amused glint. "Well, we can hardly turn away a man with such a fine sword, can we?"

"My sentiments exactly," Claudine said cheerfully, and headed for the door. Widowhood had proved to be unexpectedly liberating, expanding horizons far beyond the boundaries of her native Aquitaine. Among her many newfound liberties, she enjoyed the freedom to flirt and even to indulge in an occasional discreet dalliance. She supposed that eventually she'd wed again, but she was in no hurry. What husband could match what the Queen of England had to offer?

*   *   *

Justin was as taut as a drawn bow. He dreaded the thought of another night as custodian of the queen's letter. Logic told him that none could know he had it, but there was nothing remotely logical about his predicament. His hopes had briefly flared up after his conversation with a young woman who claimed to be one of the queen's attendants. She was very pretty, with wide-set dark eyes and deep dimples, and she'd promised to see if she could get him admitted. She'd not returned, though, and now the queen's secretary had begun to usher people out.

Seeking a royal audience was not for the fainthearted, and most of the dismissed petitioners tried to argue or plead. Peter brushed aside their objections, and the knight assisting him was even more brusque. He was a big man, so fashionably dressed he might have been taken for a court fop, the sleeves of his tunic billowing out at the wrists, his leather shoes fastened at the ankles with gleaming bronze buckles, his dark-auburn hair brushed to his shoulders in burnished waves. But it would have been a great mistake to dismiss him as a mere coxcomb. He had the insolent bearing of a highborn lord and the swagger of a soldier, with blue-ice eyes and a wide, mobile mouth that seemed set in a sneer. Justin needed no second glance to recognize that this was a dangerous man, one he instinctively disliked and mistrusted.

He tensed as Peter now looked his way. He had no intention of going quietly, but neither did he expect to prevail; orphans are rarely optimists. The knight had just shoved a protesting merchant toward the door, ignoring the man's indignant claim of kinship to the city's mayor. Justin's turn would be next. But it was then that the queen's lady-in-waiting emerged from the stairwell.

The knight lost interest in evicting petitioners. Moving swiftly, he backed her against the wall, barring her way with an outstretched arm. Leaning down, he murmured intimately in her ear, his fingers sliding suggestively up her arm. She shook his hand off, slipping under his arm with an impatient "By the Rood, Durand, do you never give up?"

Durand did not take the rebuff with good grace, scowling at

Claudine with simmering anger. She shrugged off his ill will as easily as she had his hand and crossed the hall to Justin.

Her smile was dazzling. "The queen," she said, "will see you now."

Eleanor of Aquitaine had been blessed with the bone structure that age only enhances, and it was easy to see in the high cheek-bones and firm jawline evidence of the youthful beauty that had won her the hearts of two kings. She was elegantly clad in a gown of sea-green silk, her face framed in a delicate, white wimple. As he knelt, Justin caught the faintest hint of summer, a fragrance as intriguing as it was subtle, one sure to linger in a man's memory. Her throat was hidden by the softly draped wimple, and only her hands testified to her seven decades, veined by age, but also adorned with the most magnificent gem-stones he'd ever seen, rings of emerald and pearl and beaten gold. But what drew and held his gaze were her extraordinary eyes, gold flecked with green, candle lit and luminous and quite inscrutable.

"I thank you for seeing me, madame." Justin drew a bracing breath, then said in a rush, before he could lose his nerve, "For-give me if this sounds presumptuous, but would it be possible for us to talk in greater privacy?" Dropping his voice, he said ur-gently, "I have a letter for you. I believe it has already cost one man his life, and I'd not have it claim any more victims."

She studied him impassively, but Claudine gave him a re-proachful look, letting him know that thwarting her curiosity was poor repayment for her kindness. Whatever Eleanor saw in Justin's face was convincing, though, and she signaled to Peter, who was hovering a few feet away, bristling at such an audacious request. Within moments, the chamber had been cleared of all but Eleanor, Justin, Will Longsword, and her chaplain.

"This," Eleanor said coolly, "is as private as it gets. Now . . . what would you say to me?"

"Your son is alive, madame. But King Richard is in peril, for he has been taken by his enemies."

Her control was impressive; only the twitch of suddenly clenched fingers gave her away. The men were not as disciplined, their shocked questions and challenges cut off when Eleanor raised a hand for silence. "Go on," she said, and Justin did.

"The king was shipwrecked, madame, not far from Venice. He was not hurt, but soon thereafter, he was captured by a vassal of the Duke of Austria and turned over to the Holy Roman Emperor."

There were smothered exclamations at that from Will and the chaplain. Richard had made many enemies in his thirty-five turbulent years, but only the French king Philip hated him more than the emperor and Austria's duke. Again Eleanor stilled the clamor. "How do I know this is true? Have you any proof?"

Justin drew the letters from his tunic. "Three days after Christmas, the emperor wrote to the French king, informing him of King Richard's capture. The Archbishop of Rouen learned of this letter and somehow had it copied. He entrusted it to a Winchester goldsmith named Gervase Fitz Randolph, fearing to send it by agents known to the French Crown." Holding out the letters, Justin said quietly, "This is Fitz Randolph's blood, madame. I cannot swear that the letter is genuine. I can attest, though, that Fitz Randolph died believing it to be so."

There was not a sound in the chamber as Eleanor read. The others scarcely seemed to be breathing, so still was it. When she at last looked up, she was very pale, but in command of her emotions. Seeing Will's stricken expression, she said, "No, Will, no grieving. Richard is alive and that is what matters. No one has ever come back from the bottom of the Adriatic Sea, but men do get out of Austrian dungeons." Justin was still kneeling and she gestured for him to rise. "How did you come by this letter?"

Justin told her, as succinctly as possible. She listened intently, her eyes never leaving his face. When he was done, she said, "What we have learned here must not go beyond this chamber, not until I've been able to consult with the archbishop and the other justiciars. Now I would speak with this young man alone."

They were reluctant, but they obeyed. Once they were gone, Eleanor motioned for Justin to take a seat. She was fingering the broken seal. He'd planned to claim it had happened when Gervase was struggling with the outlaws, but as his eyes met Eleanor's, he found that he could not lie to her. "If I was to get killed because of that letter, I did not want to go to my grave with my curiosity unsatisfied." He held his breath then, hoping that his candor had not offended.

"If you'd brought this letter to me unread, I'd have been impressed by your honour, but I'd have wondered about your common sense."

Justin looked up, startled, in time to catch the glimmer of a smile. When he smiled back, he shed anxiety and years, and she realized for the first time how young he really was. "What is your name, lad?"

"Justin, my lady." She was waiting expectantly. But he had no family name, no family at all—only a father who had refused to acknowledge him. "Justin of Chester," he said at last, for he'd passed much of his childhood in that unruly border town.

"You said the goldsmith was slain by outlaws. What makes you think this was not just a robbery gone wrong? Have you reason to believe they were after the letter?"

"Gervase thought so, madame. I cannot say, for certes, that he was right. I do believe it was no random robbery. They were lying in wait for him, that I know. I'd passed by earlier and heard them whispering. I did not understand at the time, but I do now. 'No, it's not him.' And when I came upon the attack, one of the men was searching his body and the other called out, 'Did you find it?' He was not referring to Gervase's money pouch, for the outlaws already had that. Mayhap Gervase had something else of value, but the letter might well have been what they sought. The Archbishop of Rouen had spies at the French court, for how else could he have gotten a copy of the French king's letter? So who is to say that the French king did not have spies, too?"

"From what I know of Philip, you may be sure that he has far more spies than he has scruples." Eleanor was silent for several moments, absorbed in her own thoughts. When Justin had begun to wonder if she'd forgotten him altogether, she said, "You have done me a great service, Justin of Chester. Now I would have you do me another one. I want you to find out who murdered Gervase Fitz Randolph . . . and why."

Justin stared at her. Surely he could not have heard right? "Madame, I do not understand. The sheriff of Hampshire is far more capable of tracking down the killers than I am!"

"I disagree. I think you are uniquely qualified for the task at hand. You are the only one who saw the killers, the only one who can recognize them on sight."

Eleanor paused, watching him attentively. "Moreover, it would seem perfectly natural for you to return to Winchester to find out if the culprits had been caught and to offer your condolences to the Fitz Randolph family. No one would think to question that. To the contrary, the family would surely welcome you with gratitude, for you tried your best to save the man's life and you did save his servant."

"I suppose so," Justin conceded. "But why, my lady? Why would you have me do this?"

Eleanor's brows arched. "To see justice done, of course."

Justin glanced away lest she notice his perplexity. It made sense that the queen should want to see the killers punished. The king's roads must be safe for travel; that was part of the covenant between a sovereign and his subjects. And it could be said that the goldsmith had died in the queen's service. Yet there was more to Eleanor's request, much more. He could not have explained why he was so sure of that, but he had no doubts whatsoever that it was so.

"And if I am able to discover the identities of the killers? Should I turn that information over to the sheriff?"

"No," she said swiftly. "Say nothing to anyone. Report back to me, and only to me."

He had confirmation now of his suspicions, but what of it? Whatever Eleanor's private motives, there was no question of refusal. A queen was not to be denied, especially this queen. "I will need a letter of authorization, madame, stating that I am acting on your behalf. If I am going to be venturing into deep waters, I'll want a lifeline."

Eleanor smiled. "Clever lad," she said approvingly. "That bodes well for your success. Now . . . pour us some wine and then fetch me that ivory casket on the table."

Justin did as bidden, and a few moments later, he was holding a leather pouch in the palm of his hand. He thought it would be rude to count it in her presence, but was reassured by its solid weight, proof that the sum was a generous one.

He could not ask her the real reason why she was so intent upon solving the goldsmith's murder. But he could ask, "Why me?" He had the right to know that much, for the task she'd given him held as many risks as it did rewards. "I am honoured, madame, by your faith in me. Yet I am puzzled by it, too. I am a stranger to you, after all."

"I know more about you than you realize, lad. You have rare courage. You are no man's fool, for you do not trust easily. You are resourceful and personable."

She stopped to take a swallow of her wine. "You own a horse, which is more than most men can say. You can handle a sword, not a skill easily mastered. And you could read these letters, proof indeed that you've had an uncommonly good education, Justin of Chester. All you seem to lack is a surname."

Justin stiffened, but she ignored his sudden tension, continuing to regard him pensively. "An intriguing mystery. Why should a young man with so many admirable attributes be adrift, utterly on his own? You are too well educated to be lowborn. A younger son having to make his own way in the world? Possibly, but why would you disavow your surname? A black sheep, cast out by his family? I think not, for most men would take great pride in a son such as you. But what of a son born out of wedlock?"

Justin said nothing, but he could feel his face getting hot. Eleanor took another sip of wine. "Even if you were bastard-born, though, why would your father not claim you? My husband freely acknowledged his by-blows; most lords do. Adultery is more often held up as a female sin, not a male one. But the Church . . . now she is a far more jealous mistress than a wronged wife."

"Jesú!" Justin hastily gulped down the contents of his wine cup, much too fast. Coughing and sputtering, he blurted out, "Do you have second sight?"

Eleanor smiled faintly. "Oddly enough, witchcraft is the one sin my enemies have not accused me of. It was easy enough to guess. The Church preaches celibacy, but how many of her priests practice it? They no longer can take wives, but hearth-mates to tend their houses and warm their beds . . . well, what harm in that? At least not for a village priest. But for a man who aims higher, a bastard child is an embarrassing encumbrance, one to be shunted aside, hidden away to keep scandal at bay. Was that how it was for you, Justin?"

He nodded, and she said softly, "Who is your father, lad?"

It never occurred to Justin not to answer. "The Bishop of Chester."

He was half expecting disbelief. But Eleanor showed no surprise whatsoever. "Aubrey de Quincy? I know him, although not well."

"I can say the same."

There was too much bitterness in Justin's voice for humor. Eleanor gave him a curious look. "He did assume some responsibility for you, did he not?"

"Yes," Justin said grudgingly. "I grew up believing I was a foundling. It was no secret that the bishop was my benefactor, for I was often told how lucky I was that he'd taken pity on me. When I was a babe, he placed me with a family in Shrewsbury. Later— he was an archdeacon by then—he had me brought to Chester. I saw him but rarely. I would occasionally be summoned into his presence, and he'd lecture me about my studies and the sinful state of my soul, then berate me for my misdeeds, even those I had not committed yet." Justin's mouth tightened. "It was like being interrogated by Almighty God Himself."

Eleanor was not yet convinced that he had cause for complaint. "He did see that you had food and shelter and an excellent education."

"He was quick to remind me of that, too, madame. But he owed me more than bread or even books. If nothing else, he owed me the truth about my mother!"

That hit home for Eleanor. After she'd wed Henry, the French king had done what he could to turn their two young daughters against her; she'd not seen either one for years, not until they were both grown, with husbands of their own. "How did you find out the truth?"

"When I asked him about her, he told me that she was a woman of low morals. And I'd have gone to my grave believing his lies. But by chance, Lord Fitz Alan sent me to Shrewsbury last month, and it occurred to me that there might be people who remembered my birth, remembered my mother. I started at St Alkmund's, his old parish church, and eventually I tracked down an elderly woman who'd been the cook at the rectory. She did indeed remember my mother, not a slut as he'd claimed, a young village girl bedazzled and seduced by a man of God."

"I assume that you then confronted your father?"

He nodded again, grimly. "He did not think he'd wronged me, insisting that he'd been more than fair. He could not understand that I might have forgiven him for denying his paternity, for letting me be raised by strangers, but not for lying about my mother. Never for that."

It was quiet then. Justin slumped back in his chair, drained by his outburst and disquieted, too. How could he have revealed his soul's deepest secret to this woman he barely knew? What would the Queen of England care about the griefs and grievances of a bishop's bastard? "I am sorry, madame," he said stiffly. "I do not know why I told you all this—"

"Because I asked," she said, holding out her wine cup for a refill. "If you return on the morrow, I'll have that letter ready for you, the one that identifies you as the queen's man. I trust you will be discreet in its use, Justin. No flaunting it in alehouses to get free drinks, no whipping it out at opportune moments to impress young women."

Justin's surprise gave way almost at once to amusement. He opened his mouth to ask if he could at least use it to gain credit with local merchants, then thought better of it, not sure if it would be seemly for him to jest, too. She'd been remarkably kind to him so far, and she was not a woman renowned for her kindness. But she was England's queen and he dared not forget that, not even for a heartbeat.

She'd not relinquished the letters, still holding them on her lap. Justin felt a sudden rush of sympathy. She was more than Christendom's most celebrated queen. She was a mother, and the captive king her favorite son. "I am sorry, madame," he said again, "sorrier than I can say that I must bring you such dire news . . ."

"Ah, no, Justin. You brought me hope. For the first time in many weeks, I will go to sleep tonight knowing that my son still lives."

"My lady . . ."

She knew what he was reluctant to ask. "Will the emperor free Richard? He may, if it is made worth his while to do so. As much as he detests my son, he craves money more than vengeance. The greatest danger is that the French king may bid for Richard, too. If he ever ended up in a French dungeon, he'd not see the sun again, no matter how much was offered for his ransom. Philip and Richard were friends once, but they quarreled bitterly during the Crusade, and since Philip's return to Paris, he has done whatever he could to give Richard grief, ensnaring—"

She cut herself off so abruptly that Justin was able to guess what she was so loath to say: the name of her son, John, who was rumored to have been conniving with Philip for the past year, plotting to cripple Richard's kingship. It seemed all the more baffling to Justin that a queen beset with such troubles should give so much attention to the killing of a Winchester goldsmith. Wishing he had more comfort to offer, he said, "I will pray for the king's safe release, madame."

"Do so," she said, "for he will need our prayers. But do more than that. You look after yourself in Winchester, Justin de Quincy. Watch your back."

"I will . . ." His reassurance trailed off as he realized the significance of what she'd just said. "I have no right to that name, my lady. My father would be outraged if I claimed it."

"Yes," Eleanor agreed, "indeed he would," and when she smiled, it was not the smile of a venerable dowager queen, but the smile of the royal rebel she'd always been, a free spirit who'd dared to defy convention, husbands, and the Church, blazing her own path with a devil-be-damned courage and a capricious, beguiling charm.

Justin did not offer even token resistance; it was unconditional surrender. In that moment, he, too, joined the ranks of all who'd fallen under Eleanor of Aquitaine's spell. "I will not fail you, my lady," he promised recklessly. "I will find Gervase Fitz Randolph's killers for you, that I swear upon the surety of my soul."

3

WINCHESTER

January 1193

The cold spell continued without letup, but the skies stayed clear, and Justin made good time. At midday on the fourth afternoon since leaving London, he was within sight of Winchester's walls.

He'd used those days on the road to plot a strategy. He meant to seek out the sheriff and the Fitz Randolph family. If Eleanor was right—and he suspected she usually was—the slain goldsmith's kindred would make him welcome. But what then? Mayhap the sheriff had already captured the outlaws. He knew, though, what a frail hope that was. Even if he found the men chained up in Winchester Castle's dungeon, how could he root out the truth about the ambush? Were they hired killers or just bandits on the prowl for prey? If they had indeed been lying in wait for Gervase, who had paid them? And why? Was it for the queen's bloodstained letters? Or for reasons he knew nothing about? Had the goldsmith been struck down by King Richard's enemies? Or did he have enemies of his own?

The more Justin tried to sort it out, the more disheartened he became. Questions he had in plenitude, answers in scant supply. Yet as daunting as his task was, he had to try. He owed the queen his best efforts. He owed Gervase that much, too. He'd never watched a man die before, and pray God, never again. The goldsmith's death had not been an easy one; he'd drowned in his own blood.

Admitted into the city through the East Gate, Justin hailed a passing Black Monk. "Brother, a moment, if you will. Can you tell me how to find the shop of Gervase Fitz Randolph, the goldsmith?"

The man frowned. "Are you a friend of Master Gervase?" When Justin shook his head, the man's face cleared. "Just as well. Master Gervase is dead. May God assoil him, but he was foully murdered ten days ago."

"Yes, I know. Have the killers been caught?"

"The sheriff is off in the western parts of the shire. I doubt if he even knows yet."

"There has been no investigation, none at all? By the time the sheriff gets back, the trail will be colder than ice!"

"The killing was reported to the under-sheriff, Luke de Marston. I assume he has been looking into it."

Somewhat mollified, Justin asked where he could find this Luke de Marston, only to be told that he was in Southampton, not expected back till the morrow. The local authorities did not seem afire with zeal to solve the goldsmith's murder. Justin could imagine their response all too well: murmured regrets, then a shrug, a few perfunctory comments about bandits and the perils of the road. He was suddenly angry; Gervase deserved more than this official indifference. "The goldsmith's shop?" he reminded the monk, and got a surprising answer in return.

"Is it the shop you want, friend, or the family dwelling?"

The vast majority of craftsmen lived above their workshops. Gervase must have been very successful, indeed, to afford a separate residence. Justin hesitated. Most likely Gervase had retained at least one apprentice, and a journeyman, too. But even if the shop was still open, it was the family he needed to see. "Their home," he declared, and the monk gave him detailed directions: south of Cheapside, on Calpe Street, past St Thomas's Church.

The Fitz Randolph house was set back from the street, a two-story timber structure of substantial proportions, brightly painted and well maintained. Further proof of Gervase's affluence lay within the gate: his own stable, hen roost, and a well with a windlass. Justin already knew Gervase had thrived at his craft; on that bleak trek to Alresford with the goldsmith's body, the groom, Edwin, had confided that Gervase had just delivered a silver-gilt crozier and an enameled chalice to the Archbishop of Rouen. But even for a man who'd counted an archbishop among his customers, this house was an extravagance. Gazing upon Gervase Fitz Randolph's private, hard-won Eden, Justin felt a muted sense of sadness, pity for the man who'd had so much—family, a respected craft, this comfortable manor—only to lose it all to the thrust of an accursed outlaw's blade. Where was the fairness in that?

But he also found himself wondering if Gervase's high living might have played a part in his death. A man so lavish in his spending might well have incurred dangerous debts. He could have stirred envy, too, in the hearts of his less fortunate neighbors. Had someone resented Gervase's conspicuous prosperity—enough to kill him for it?

"Can it be?" Emerging from the stable, Edwin stood gaping at Justin. "By Corpus, it truly is you!" Striding forward eagerly, he reached up to help Justin dismount. "I never thought to see you again. But you'll be in my prayers for the rest of my born days, that you can rely upon!"

"I'll take prayers wherever I can get them," Justin said with a smile. "But you owe me nothing."

"Only my life." Edwin was not quite as tall as Justin, but more robust, as burly as Justin was lean. He had the reddest hair and beard Justin had ever seen, brighter than blood, with very fair skin that must burn easily under summer suns, but without the usual crop of freckles to be found on a redhead's face. His grin was engaging, revealing a crooked front tooth and a vast reservoir of goodwill. "If not for you, those hellspawn would have slit my throat, for certes. I have a confession of sorts, one that will make me sound a right proper fool. I daresay you told me your name, but I was so distraught that I could not remember it afterward to save my soul."

"That is easily remedied. I am Justin de Quincy." It was the first time that Justin had said the name aloud. He liked the sound of it, at once an affirmation of identity and an act of defiance.

The young groom's grin widened. "I am Edwin, son of Cuthbert the drover. Welcome to Winchester, Master de Quincy. What brings you back?"

"I had business to tend to in London, but once it was done, I found myself brooding upon the killing. I would see those brigands brought to justice. It is my hope that I can aid the sheriff in his hunt, for I got a good look at them."

"Better than me," Edwin conceded. "About all I saw was the ground rushing up to meet me! I still have not figured out how they spooked our horses so easily . . . But no matter. I am right pleased that you've come back, and I know Mistress Ella will be, too."

Justin assumed that was Gervase's widow. "I'd like to pay my respects to her," he said, and had confirmation of her identity when Edwin nodded.

"Indeed," he said, "but she is not at home now and will not be back till later. Whilst you are waiting, why not let me take you to the shop? Master Gervase's son will be there."

Justin gladly accepted the offer. "What about my horse? Is there room in the stable for him?"

"I can put him in Quicksilver's stall. You remember Master Gervase's stallion, the one the bandits stole?"

Justin did. "The pale roan, right? A handsome animal."

"A rare prize." Edwin sighed. "I miss him sorely, for Master Gervase would let me exercise him on those days when he had not the time. That horse could outrace the wind, God's Truth, a sight to behold, with that silver tail streaming out like a battle banner and his hooves barely skimming the ground!"

Justin warmed to the groom's enthusiasm; he had the same pride in Copper. But when Edwin bragged that Gervase had paid ten marks for the stallion, he whistled, for that was still more evidence of Gervase's lavish living. Was it significant that the goldsmith had been a spendthrift? Could he have been borrowing from moneylenders? Making a mental note to try to find out more about the slain man's finances, Justin followed Edwin into the stable.

A short time later they were walking briskly up Calpe Street. Outgoing and exuberant, the young groom was more than willing to enlighten Justin about Gervase Fitz Randolph and his family. By the time they reached the High Street, Justin had learned that Gervase had taken his younger brother, Guy, into the business, that they employed a journeyman, Miles, who'd lacked the funds to set himself up as a craftsman once his apprenticeship was done, and that Gervase's son, Thomas, was presently laboring as an apprentice, although not by choice. "Thomas never had an interest in goldsmithing," Edwin explained, "but it was Master Gervase's wish that he learn the craft."

"Is the brother at the shop with Thomas?"

Edwin shook his head. "Master Guy is back at the house, abed. He has been poorly all week, suffering from bad headaches. If you ask me, I think he has sickened on his grieving."

"The brothers were close, then?"

"No . . ." Edwin's brow furrowed. "If truth be told, they squabbled like tomcats. But I do believe Master Guy is taking the death hardest of all."

"Mayhap he feels guilty," Justin said, as noncommittally as he could, but the words left a sour aftertaste in his mouth. He'd not fully realized that to find a killer, he'd have to wade through other people's pain.

Deciding that he needed to put the murder aside, if only for a brief while, he cast about for a more innocuous topic. Edwin and Cuthbert, Saxon names both. Many of Saxon birth took fashionable Norman-French names, but the reverse was rarely true. And as serviceable as Edwin's French was, it was not his native tongue, not as it was for Justin.

Growing up in the Marches, Justin had learned to speak both languages, even a little Welsh. He'd not often thought about the bilingual barriers separating Saxons and Normans, accepting them as a burdensome fact of life. French was the language of the royal court, the language of advancement and ambition and culture, English the tongue of the conquered. And yet it still endured, more than a hundred years after England had come under the mastery of the Norman duke, William the Bastard. Saxons stubbornly clung to their own speech, and the river ran both ways. Justin doubted that King Richard spoke any English. But he was sure that Gervase had been fluent in the Saxon tongue; commerce and convenience demanded as much.

"Your French is quite good," he told Edwin, "much better than my English!"

Edwin looked so pleased that Justin guessed few compliments

ever came his way. "I've been working for Master Gervase for nigh on five years," he said, "since I was about fourteen. Master Thomas was the same age, and he agreed to help me with my French. Thomas likes to instruct others," he added, wryly enough to make Justin suddenly curious about the goldsmith's son.

"What sort of a master was Gervase, Edwin?"

"I had no complaints. He could be hard, but always fair. He was a gifted goldsmith, and he knew it—no false pride there. Ambitious, with a liking for his comforts, and generous to a fault. Not just for his own needs or wants, either. He denied Mistress Ella and Mistress Jonet nothing; they dressed like ladies of quality. He never passed a beggar without tossing a coin and gave alms every Sunday at church. But he was not one for listening. So sure that his way was best. Unable to compromise. I daresay you have known men like that?"

"Yes," Justin said tersely, trying not to think of his father. "Who is Jonet?"

"His daughter. They had only the two, Thomas and Jonet. Mistress Ella lost several, one in the cradle and two stillborn, so they doted on those they had left. Master Gervase had high hopes for them both. Thomas was to follow in his footsteps and Jonet was to wed a baron. He dared to dream, did Master Gervase. It does not seem right that two misbegotten churls could take it all away like that."

"No," Justin agreed, "it does not." They were drawing near a crippled, legless beggar, wheeling himself along on a small wooden platform. Reaching into his pouch, Justin dropped several coins into the man's alms cup, getting a startled "God bless you" for his generosity. "Gervase was seeking a baron for his daughter? Surely that was not very likely? The marriage portion would have to be huge to tempt a lord into marrying out of his class."

"You have not yet seen Mistress Jonet."

Justin's smile was faintly skeptical. "Is she as fair as that?"

"Fairer than one of God's own angels," Edwin said, but without any enthusiasm, and Justin gave him a curious glance. Was it that Edwin liked Mistress Jonet not at all—or too much?

"There it is," Edwin said, pointing up Alwarne Street. As they got closer, Justin recognized the crude unicorn sketched into the wood of an overhanging sign, the universal emblem of goldsmiths. "I hope Thomas is back from dinner."

"He takes two full hours for dinner?" Thomas was beginning to sound like some of the spoiled young lordlings Justin had known in Lord Fitz Alan's service, wellborn youths more interested in dicing and whoring than in learning the duties of a squire. "So Thomas likes to visit the alehouses and bawdyhouses?"

"Thomas?" Edwin chortled. "That will be the day!"

Justin wanted to ask more questions about the mysterious Master Thomas, but thought better of it. He'd been fortunate to find such a source in Edwin, did not want to risk poisoning the well by pushing too hard. Nor was he completely comfortable with this oblique interrogation. Good intentioned or not, he felt as if he were somehow taking advantage of Edwin's trust. "How is it that you know so much about the family secrets?" he joked, instead. "Are you a soothsayer in your spare time?"

Edwin grinned. "Nay, I merely befriended the cook. Not only does she save me extra wafers and bone-marrow tarts, she serves up ample helpings of family gossip, too. God love them, for cooks always know where the bodies are buried!"

Justin's face shadowed, for he could not help thinking of another gossip-prone cook, this one in a Shrewsbury rectory, watching as a priest seduced an innocent. Pushing the memory away, he groped for something to say. But there was no need to dissemble. They'd reached the goldsmith's shop.

Horizontal shutters that opened upward and downward protected shops at night. During the day, the top half of the shutter was propped up, acting as a canopy to shelter customers, while the lower shutter extended out toward the street, serving as a display counter. Inside was a small room, lit with cresset lamps. Justin could distinguish the outlines of a workbench, an anvil, and a table covered with clay; he had watched other goldsmiths at work, knew the clay was used to sketch out designs. But there was no sign of life.

Leaning over the counter, Edwin peered into the shadows. "Now where in blazes are they? Thomas might wander off on a whim; God knows he has done it often enough. But what of Miles? Look at those amethysts and moss agates spread out on the workbench. A thief could vault over the counter, snatch up a handful, and be off in a trice! I do not like this, Master Justin," he muttered, "not at all . . ."

Neither did Justin. Goldsmiths were known to keep silver and gemstones on hand, even a small supply of gold. Had Gervase's killers struck again? "Where does yonder door lead, Edwin? Can we get in that way?"

"There is a second room beyond, where Master Gervase keeps—kept—his forge and bellows and heavier anvils. Miles sleeps there at night. There is an outer door in the alley, but it is locked and I lack the key."

With that, Edwin swung up onto the counter and over. Justin followed swiftly. A charcoal brazier was burning in a corner, still smoldering. A hammer lay in the floor rushes, as if dropped in haste. A wooden trencher had been left on the bench; it held a half-eaten chunk of goat's cheese and the remains of a small loaf of bread. Justin and Edwin exchanged uneasy glances. What had happened here? Their nerves were taut, and they both jumped when a muffled sound came from the inner room. Justin swept his mantle back, his hand closing around the hilt of his sword. Edwin was unarmed, but he stooped and grabbed the hammer. Communicating by gestures and nods, they moved stealthily forward and then hit the door together, Justin kicking at the latch and Edwin slamming a muscular shoulder against the aged wood.

The door was in better shape than they'd expected. Had it been latched, it would have held. But it was not, and it burst open under their joint assault. Justin's boot slipped in the floor rushes and he almost lost his balance, while Edwin's wild rush catapulted him headfirst into the room. Justin heard—simultaneously—a woman's scream, a garbled curse, and a loud crash. His sword clearing its scabbard, he plunged through the doorway, only to come to an astonished halt at the sight meeting his eyes.

Edwin was on his hands and knees, an expression of shocked dismay on his face. A man with flaxen hair was straddling a workbench, flushed and disheveled and blinking in bewilderment. On his lap was a vision. Her hair was a lustrous silver blonde, spilling out of its pins in silken disarray. Her clothes were equally askew. Her bodice was unlaced, offering Justin an inadvertent but provocative glimpse of her cleavage with every breath she drew, and her skirts were hiked up to reveal very shapely legs. With eyes bluer than cornflowers and skin whiter than Madonna lilies, she could have been conjured up from a minstrel's song, so perfectly did she embody their society's ideal of feminine beauty. But that illusion lasted only as long as it took her to scramble off her lover's knee.

"You lowborn, half-witted, wretched . . ." Sputtering in her fury, she nearly choked on her own indignation. "How dare you spy on me! I'll see you fired for this, by God, I will!"

"That is not fair, Mistress Jonet! I feared something was wrong—"

"Something is wrong, indeed! Sneaking around, meddling, prying into my private life! Well, no more, for I've had enough—"

So had Justin. Sheathing his sword, he said coolly, "If you have a grievance, demoiselle, it is with me, not Edwin. I told him to breach the door."

The girl's angry tirade was stopped in midcry. "Oh!" Her pretty mouth hung ajar, blue eyes widening as she took in the sword at Justin's hip, his demeanor, that deliberate use of "demoiselle," all unmistakable indications of rank.

Taking advantage of her momentary consternation, Edwin got to his feet. "Mistress Jonet, I'd have you meet Justin de Quincy." He paused before adding with malicious satisfaction, "He is the man who sought to save your father from those outlaws."

"Oh," she said again, this time in a soft, quavering tone of chagrin. Blushing for Justin as she had not for Edwin, she hastily began to relace her gaping bodice. Justin did what he could to intensify her embarrassment by stepping forward and kissing her hand in his most courtly manner. He suspected that she was rarely so tongue-tied; any girl who looked like this one did would have learned at an early age how to make the most of her assets. Enjoying her discomfiture as much as Edwin, he said, "We feared that something was amiss, what with the shop open and unattended . . . If we jumped to the wrong conclusion, I am indeed sorry."

Jonet's blush deepened. Bending over, she hastily retrieved her veil from the floor rushes. "I stopped by to see Thomas. You do not know my brother, but he can be very irresponsible. He just took off, leaving Miles with orders to complete and repairs to make and customers to tend to."

Justin had a diabolic urge to point out that Jonet had certainly done her best to make it up to Miles, but he managed to resist the temptation. He could not help glancing toward the journeyman, though. Justin guessed him to be in his early- or mid-twenties, undeniably good looking in a bland sort of way, and apparently blessed with an abundance of self-confidence, for he seemed unperturbed by this sudden exposure of his love affair with his employer's daughter. Brushing aside a bright forelock, he said amiably, "Tom has always been a bit flighty, but he's a good lad. I do not mind pitching in to do his share."

Justin was sure that no one called the missing apprentice "Tom" except Miles. Nor did he doubt that if he became friendly with the journeyman, he'd soon be "Jus." "I believe this is yours," Justin said, reaching down and plucking a rabbit's foot from the rushes. He knew it was used by goldsmiths to polish silver and gold, but from the way Jonet blushed anew, he'd wager they'd been putting it to more creative use. "Well, I've been enough of a disruption," he began, but Jonet contradicted him quickly.

"No one could be more welcome than you, Master de Quincy," she insisted, turning upon him the full power of her most coquettish smile. "I know my mother will want you to take supper with us. Our servant will get you back to our house. I trust you can do that, Edwin, without going astray?"

Edwin dared not ignore her, but he could not bring himself to acquiesce in his own humiliation, and he grunted something that might have been either assent or denial. Justin bent over Jonet's hand again, this time making the gesture perfunctory, not gallant. Jonet realized that she'd done something to earn his disapproval, but she did not know how she'd offended. "Wait," she cried as Justin turned to go. "I do not want you to misunderstand, Master de Quincy. Miles and I . . . we are plight trothed."

That was obviously news to Edwin, for he gave Jonet a startled glance that, under other circumstances, might have been comical. There was an awkward silence, finally broken by Justin. "I wish you both well," he said politely. It was a tepid response, but it seemed to satisfy Jonet and Miles. They followed him out to the street, smiling.

Justin and Edwin walked without speaking for a time, detouring around a hissing goose and a pig foraging in a pile of rotting garbage. "Well," Justin said at last, "she may have the face of one of God's angels, but she has the Devil's own temper."

Edwin laughed, without much humor. "You do not know the half of it! There is no pleasing that one. You could give her Queen Eleanor's royal crown and she'd just bemoan the fit!"

"Am I safe in assuming that Master Gervase knew nothing of this plight-troth?"

Edwin snickered. "His precious daughter and his hired man? When pigs sprout wings!"

"Are you sure he did not know, Edwin?"

"Miles is still employed, is he not? What more proof do you need than that? As I told you, Master Gervase had his heart set upon snaring a highborn husband for his lass—Sir Hamon de Harcourt. He is fifty if he is a day, paunchy and bald as an egg, but he has a fine manor outside Salisbury and another one at Wilton, as well as rental property here in Winchester—or so Berta the cook claims! Sir Hamon has grown sons who were objecting to his marrying a craftsman's daughter, even one who'd bring a goodly marriage portion. But I think the marriage would have come about in time. Hell and furies, he could not look at Jonet without drooling! You think Master Gervase would pass up a baron for a hireling who sleeps in his shop?"

Justin had the answer he needed, if not the one he wanted. He'd never truly expected to find clues to Gervase's killing in the man's own home. And yet he could not deny that Jonet and Miles had a convincing motive for murder.

They had turned onto Calpe Street when Edwin gave a sudden exclamation. "Up ahead, that is Mistress Ella and Edith!" He lengthened his stride and Justin had to hasten to keep pace. Hearing the hurrying footsteps behind her, Ella Fitz Randolph looked over her shoulder. At the sight of her groom, she halted, waiting for them to catch up.

Justin had cast Gervase's widow in a matronly mold, assuming that a longtime wife and mother would naturally be plump and pleasant in appearance, comforting in manner. Had he given it much thought, he'd have seen the error of his assumptions, for Queen Eleanor was a wife and mother, too, and she was about as maternal and nurturing as Cleopatra. He did not realize how his limited experience with motherhood had led him astray until he found himself face-to-face with Ella Fitz Randolph.

By his calculations, she had to be past forty, for Edwin had told him she and Gervase had been wed more than twenty years, but if she was losing the war with age, she was not yet ready to concede defeat. In her youth, she had probably been as striking as her daughter. She was still slender, almost gaunt, for now it was the result of willpower, not nature. She had Jonet's blue eyes and the same fair skin, stretched too tightly across her cheekbones. Her mouth was carefully rouged, but the corners were kissed by shadows, while her cares were etched like cobwebs across the high, white brow. She was a handsome woman, but hers was a fading, brittle beauty, as fragile as finely spun glass, to be admired safely only from a distance. She aroused Justin's protective instincts at the same time that she made him feel vaguely uncomfortable, for she seemed both vulnerable and aloof, and he did not know which signal to heed.

"Why are you not at the stable, Edwin?"

Ella was questioning, not accusing. Even after encountering her groom roaming about the town, she would not judge him until she'd heard his explanation, and Justin liked her for that. He remembered Edwin's saying that Master Gervase had been fair. So, it seemed, was his widow, which was more, Justin thought, than could be said for his daughter.

"We've come from the shop, Mistress Ella. This is the man I told you about, the one who tried to save Master Gervase on the Alresford Road!"

Ella swung around to stare at Justin, then reached out and

took his hands in hers. "I am glad you've come back, glad I have this opportunity to express my gratitude for what you did for my husband."

"If only I could have gotten there in time," Justin said, with such heartfelt regret that she gave him a sad smile.

"The Almighty chose to call him home, and even if we do not understand, we must accept. Now . . . I hope you will stay with us whilst you are in Winchester."

"Mistress Fitz Randolph, that is most kind, but—"

"I insist," she said firmly, and it was as easy as that for Justin to gain access to the Fitz Randolph home. But his triumph was short-lived. The serving maid, Edith, now joined her mistress, and the sight of the bolts of black cloth in her basket robbed him of any satisfaction in his success, reminding him that he'd be infiltrating a household in mourning.

Supper that evening was not an enjoyable meal. The Friday fish menu would have tempted only the starving, and the tension in the hall was oppressive. Justin detested salted herring and he pushed the fish around on his trencher to be polite, then filled up on a thick pottage of onions and cabbage. While both Thomas and Jonet were eating heartily, neither Gervase's widow nor his brother seemed to have an appetite. She was gazing off into space, while Guy confined himself to an occasional swallow from the wine cup at his elbow.

Reaching for a chunk of bread, Justin studied Guy covertly. He was much younger than Gervase, for he appeared to be no more than thirty-five. He had his brother's brown hair and beard; the resemblance was pronounced. Whether he also had Gervase's dark eyes, Justin could not tell, for Guy had yet to meet his gaze. Justin would not have needed to be told that he was ailing. His skin had a greyish cast, and a vein was throbbing in his temple. Nor were his hands all that steady. He had a solicitous young wife, a baby daughter in her cradle, and a far greater voice now in the running of the family business. But to Justin, he looked haunted.

Guy was not the only one on edge. As the meal progressed, Thomas was growing increasingly restless, fidgeting in his seat, glancing surreptitiously at his mother whenever she wasn't looking. But Justin thought he seemed more expectant than anxious, like a child eager to share a secret. Absently crumbling his bread, Justin regarded Thomas critically. His curly fair hair and delicate bone structure made him seem younger than his nineteen years, but his appearance was deceptive. He may have looked almost angelic, but throughout supper, he'd been displaying a prickly disposition and a waspish tongue, snapping at the serving maid, sparring with his sister, interrogating Justin with a brusqueness that bordered on rudeness. Was he always so belligerent? Justin had been prepared to sympathize fully with Gervase Fitz Randolph's bereaved children. It was disconcerting to find himself disliking them instead.

The conversation was flagging again. Becoming aware of the silence, Ella roused herself from her lassitude. "I saw Sir Hamon's steward in town today, Jonet. He said that Sir Hamon will be in Winchester next week. I think we ought to invite him to dinner whilst he is here."

Jonet did not reply, but she did not need to; she had an expressive face. In their world, women were given no voice in deciding their own destinies, and few would have sympathized with Jonet's plight. Justin did, though, for he had a foundling's instinctive sympathy for the powerless and downtrodden. He might not like Jonet, but he did not think it fair that she would have been compelled to wed the man of her father's choosing, despite the fact that she'd given her heart—and probably her maidenhead—to Miles. Watching Jonet's squirming at the mere mention of Sir Hamon's name, Justin could not help identifying with her rebellious spirit. If only her clandestine love affair did not give her such an excellent motive for murder!

Oblivious to her daughter's discomfort, Ella was continuing to speak glowingly of Jonet's wellborn suitor: his piety, his honesty, his standing in the community. By now, Justin was squirming, too, burdened by his knowledge of Jonet's guilty secret. He was almost as grateful as Jonet when Guy finally intervened.

"I know you want to see Jonet wed to Sir Hamon, Ella. But I think we'd best face facts. Gervase's death changes everything."

Jonet gave her uncle a look of wholehearted devotion, Ella

gave him one of reproach. "No," she insisted, "we must still find the money for her marriage portion, for that was what Gervase would have wanted."

Guy and Jonet exchanged glances, and he shook his head, almost imperceptibly. Justin observed their byplay with extreme interest; so they were allies as well as kin? This household was awash in undercurrents. Who knew what else was going on beneath the surface?

Thomas speared a piece of herring. "Do not give up hope yet, Mama. Mayhap Sir Hamon would be willing to accept a smaller marriage portion."

That did seem to cheer Ella, but Jonet looked as if she yearned to impale her brother on his own eating knife. She did not strike back at once, though. Helping herself to more bread, she nibbled daintily around the crust before saying sweetly, "I stopped by the shop to see you this afternoon, Thomas, and was so surprised to find you gone. I waited and waited, but you never did come back. Where did you go?"

"Oh, Thomas!" Ella was staring at her son in dismay. "How could you shirk your responsibilities like that, with your poor father only ten days dead? I must depend upon you more than ever now. Miles cannot manage on his own, so—"

"Why not?" Jonet rushed loyally—if rashly—to her lover's defense. "Miles is very skilled at his craft. Even Papa was pleased with his work, and you know how demanding he could be!"

"I was not finding fault with Miles, Jonet. I do think he is a good worker. But he is not family, dearest. That is what I meant."

"Since when do you speak so kindly of the hired help, Jonet?" Thomas asked snidely. "I never heard you lavishing praise on Berta's custard or telling Edwin what a good hand he was with the horses."

Jonet betrayed herself with a deep blush, but fortunately for her, Ella was too accustomed to their bickering to pay it any heed. Glancing from face to face, Justin decided that Guy knew about Miles and Jonet. He doubted, though, that Thomas knew, for he was too self-absorbed to ferret out other people's secrets; his gibe had been a random shot that just happened to hit its target. Jonet had reached that same conclusion; her blush was fading. For a few moments, it seemed as if the remainder of the meal would be passed in a semblance of peace.

Guy was rubbing his aching temples, all the while regarding his nephew with unconcealed disapproval. "Well, Thomas? Just where were you this afternoon?"

Thomas set his wine cup down, looking first at his mother and then his uncle. "I was going to wait, but I think it best to tell you here and now. I went to Hyde Abbey to meet with Abbot John."

Justin thought that, as excuses went, this was a good one, a much more respectable reason for playing truant than stopping off at the closest alehouse. He did not understand, therefore, why Ella and Guy looked so upset, Jonet so pleased.

"Thomas!" Ella sounded stricken. "It was agreed that we'd talk no more of this—"

"You and Papa agreed, I did not! I have had a candid talk with Father Abbot and he has agreed to accept me as a novice in the Benedictine order, with the intent of taking holy vows once I have proved myself worthy."

"It was your father's dearest wish that you become a goldsmith!"

"What is Papa's wish when compared with God's Will?"

"You had no right to do this!"

"I am doing Almighty God's bidding, Uncle Guy! And I'll not let Mama and you thwart me as Papa did, that I swear by the Blessed Cross!"

Justin shoved his bench out. As rude as it would be to leave in the middle of the meal, it would be worse to remain, an unwilling eavesdropper to this family breach. "My horse picked up a pebble on the road . . . I need to make sure the hoof is not bruised . . ." Mumbling whatever came to mind, he backed away from the table.

His departure went unnoticed. By the time he reached the door, the hall was in utter turmoil: Guy and Thomas were trading heated accusations, Ella wiping away tears with a napkin, Guy's anxious wife wavering between her white-faced husband and the baby now wailing in her cradle, Berta and Edith drawn by the uproar. Only Jonet remained calm, elbows propped on the table, chin resting on her laced fingers, watching with alert interest and the faintest inkling of a smile.

* * *

The night sky was adrift in stars, but a gusting wind sent Justin hastening toward the shelter of the stable. Within, a wick floated in the oil of a cresset lamp, sputtering fitfully. Copper and two bay rounceys stretched their necks over their stall doors, nickering. Edwin was sprawled on a blanket, an empty trencher beside him in the straw. "What brings you out here?" he asked in surprise.

"I'm in need of a safe haven. How would you like to show me your favorite alehouse?"

Edwin was already on his feet. "It is right up the road. And wait till you see Avis, the serving maid! But what are you fleeing from?"

"A family bloodletting. Thomas announced that he means to become a monk and they did not take it well."

"I was wondering when he'd spring that on them. I half expected him to do it at graveside as they were burying his father!"

"You knew, then, about this?"

"Me and half of Winchester!"

Out on the street, it was too cold to talk. The wind blew back the hoods of their mantles, soon set their teeth to chattering. Fortunately, Edwin had not exaggerated the alehouse's proximity, and they raced each other for that beckoning doorway. Inside, it was crowded and noisy and hazy with hearth smoke, and looked far more welcoming to Justin than the Fitz Randolphs' spacious great hall.

Much to Edwin's disappointment, Avis had gone home with a toothache. He cheered up, though, when Justin paid for their ale, and was quite willing to tell all he knew about the goldsmith's son and his zeal to become a Black Monk.

"Thomas never made a secret of his belief that God had called him to serve. He has been set upon the religious life since he was sixteen, but his father balked and would not give his consent. A baron's family can afford to spare a younger son for the Church, not a craftsman with but one son and heir. Master Gervase hoped that it was a youthful whim, one Thomas would outgrow in time. He never understood that Thomas truly believes he is one of The Chosen and it would be a mortal sin not to obey God's Holy Word."

When Edwin paused to drink, Justin did, too, needing something to dispel a chill that had nothing to do with the cold. Could love of God have led to murder? It was such an unholy thought that he wanted to reject it out of hand. It was not that easy, though. Thomas's strident voice was echoing in his ears. *What is Papa's wish when compared with God's Will?*

Making an effort, he banished his suspicions back into the shadows, to be scrutinized in the reassuring light of day. "You said that Gervase and Guy were often at odds. What did they fight about, Edwin—money?"

"Yes." Edwin's smile was curious. "How did you guess?"

"Guy objected to putting up a large marriage portion for Jonet. So it only makes sense that he'd have objected, too, to Gervase's openhanded spending."

"That he did, loudly and often. It availed him naught, of course. In Gervase's eyes, he was still the little brother. Where Master Gervase saw opportunity, Master Guy saw risks, and so they could not help but clash. Especially since the more successful Master Gervase became, the bigger his dreams got. Master Guy even accused him once of aping his betters and trying to live like a lord!"

"That sounds like more than a mere squabble. Did they often quarrel that hotly?"

"No . . . not often. Just whenever Master Gervase would do something truly extravagant—like when he bought Quicksilver and gave the cottage to Aldith and sought to buy Jonet a highborn husband. Now, those quarrels were hotter than a baker's oven!"

"Who is Aldith and why was he giving her a cottage?"

Edwin winked. "Now, why do you think?"

Justin sat up straight on the bench. "He kept a whore?"

"It depends on who you ask. I'd call her a concubine, a paramour, mayhap even a leman, for Master Gervase was right fond of her. Thomas did call her a whore, and his father backhanded him across the face for it. I saw it all, there in the stable. Blood spurting from Thomas's nose and Master Gervase sorry afterward, almost apologizing, but Thomas having none of it, just one more grievance to hold fast."

"Did Gervase's wife know?"

"You think Thomas did not make sure of that? She knew. She'd have had to be blind, deaf, and dumb not to know, for it lasted nigh on ten years. Master Gervase did not flaunt Aldith, but neither did he make a secret of her. It was not unusual for him to dispatch me on an errand for her, and whenever she was taken ill, he'd have Berta cook a special soup that Aldith fancied. She was part of his life, you see. The priest could rail against adultery in his Sunday sermons, but I'd wager Master Gervase still saw it as a venial sin, one hardly worth bothering the Almighty with!"

"It could not have been easy, though, for Mistress Ella." This had been a day of surprises, for certes. "What is she like, Gervase's concubine?"

"Remember what Scriptures say about Eve tempting Adam with that fruit? Well, if Adam had been in Eden with Aldith instead of Eve, he would not have minded being cast out of Paradise, not as long as she went with him!"

Justin grinned. "Edwin, you sound downright smitten."

Edwin grinned back. "You'd be just as besotted if you ever laid eyes on her!"

"Can you tell me how to find her cottage?"

"Yes . . . but why?"

Justin could not think of a plausible reason why he should be seeking out Gervase's mistress. The best he could offer was a half-truth. "Let's say that Aldith has aroused my curiosity."

Edwin burst out laughing. "Mistress Aldith is right good at that, at arousing a man's . . . curiosity, was it? I'll give you directions. Do not say, though, that you were not warned!"

Justin signaled for more ale; not only was Edwin a good source, he was good company, too. They passed an agreeable half hour in easy conversation, but then the groom pushed reluctantly away from the table, saying that he ought to get back ere he was missed. Justin lingered to finish his drink, and to think upon what he'd discovered this day.

The truth was that he was rather disheartened by his sojourn in the Fitz Randolph household. The slain goldsmith had been a decent, God-fearing soul, mayhap stubborn and stiff necked, yet a good man, withal. A husband, father, brother: his death ought to have left a great, gaping hole in his family. But it barely seemed to have made a dent. This was not how Justin had envisioned family life. To an orphan, that was the Grail of legend and myth: a castle high on a hill, a safe refuge against a hostile world. It was disillusioning to learn that Gervase's castle had held so much dissension and so little harmony.

His cup was empty. Justin got to his feet, fumbling for a coin and then heading for the door. The cold took his breath away. Lacking a lantern, he had only starlight to guide him. The street was deserted, icy in patches, and deeply rutted. When a ghostly pale streak darted across his path, he recoiled in haste. But then he smiled. No imp of Satan, merely a stray cat. He half turned to watch the creature's skittering flight and caught a blurred movement behind him, quickly stilled.

Justin's pulse speeded up again, this time in earnest. Frowning, he surveyed the dark, silent street. Nothing seemed amiss—now. The hooded figure was gone. Had he conjured up a phantom spirit, seen someone who was never there? He'd have liked to believe that, but he knew better. As brief as his glimpse had been, it was enough. A man had been trailing after him, swiftly fading back into the shadows when he'd turned. Justin slowly loosened his sword in its scabbard, searching the blackness. But the night gave up no secrets.

The following morning, Justin accompanied the Fitz Randolph family to All Saints Church to hear a Requiem Mass for the soul of the murdered goldsmith. In midafternoon, he went to the castle. But his visit was unproductive. The sheriff was still absent from the town, and his deputy, Luke de Marston, was not expected back from Southampton until later in the day.

And so it was late when Justin was finally able to set out to find Aldith Talbot. According to Edwin, the house was in an open area near the city walls, not far from the North Gate. As the light faded, Justin's steps quickened, for last night's memory was still too vivid for comfort. Had someone truly been stalking him? Or had his imagination played him false? Logic argued for the latter. But instinct stronger than reason warned that the danger had been real, and daylight had done nothing to dispel his certainty.

Dusk was falling by the time he saw the cottage, a thin plume of pale smoke curling above its thatched roof, light glinting through chinks in the wooden shutters. It was small but well kept, newly whitewashed. He hesitated as he neared the door, for he had not yet come up with an excuse to explain his presence here. Hoping for inspiration to strike at the final moment, he reached for the metal door knocker. There was a roar from within, such a booming bark that he flinched. What did she have in there, a wolf pack?

The opening door blocked out most of the light. The woman was in shadows, her features hidden. The dog was the one to claim Justin's attention: blacker than coal, the largest mastiff he'd ever seen. Fortunately, she appeared to have a firm grip on the beast's collar.

"Yes?" Her voice was low for a woman, with a distinctive husky tone; it made Justin want to hear it again.

"Mistress Talbot? I know it is presumptuous of me to show up at your door like this. But I was hoping you could spare me a few moments. My name is Justin de Quincy. I was with Master Fitz Randolph when he died."

"Come in."

When she opened the door wider, Justin carefully edged inside, keeping a wary eye on the mastiff. "You need not worry about Jezebel," she said, sounding amused. "She has eaten already."

Jezebel? At least the woman had a sense of humor. And the dog was further proof of Gervase's devotion, for purebreds were outrageously expensive and mastiffs practically worth their weight in gold.

As she turned to close the door, Justin glanced curiously about the cottage. There was a fireplace against the far wall, a canopied bed partially screened off, a cushioned settle, an oak trestle table, several stools and coffer chests, and a woven wall hanging, dyed in bright shades of red and yellow. It was a comfortable room, and it was easy to imagine Gervase hastening here after another squabble with his brother, a spat with his son.

He had not realized that his scrutiny was so conspicuous until Aldith murmured, "Did you miss the fur-lined coverlet on the bed?"

Justin smiled apologetically. "I suppose I was staring, but—" He got no further, for Aldith Talbot quite literally took his breath away. She could not be considered beautiful in the strictest sense of the word, for her mouth was too large, her chin too pointed, her cheekbones too wide. But the result was somehow magical. Her hair was a rich, deep auburn, lustrous and gleaming wherever the firelight caught it, and it was loose about her shoulders, which had an erotic impact in and of itself, for women kept their hair covered in public, unbound only in the privacy of their homes. She had slanting cat eyes, a vibrant shade of blue-green, and Justin was sure that one lingering look would melt most men like candle wax. No wonder Gervase had thought her well worth a mortal sin!

"Are you done, Master de Quincy?"

Justin flushed, feeling like a grass-green stripling undone by his first glimpse of a trim female ankle. "Almost," he said sheepishly. "All I need to do now is to trip over your dog and spill some wine on your skirt."

"You might want to break a cup, too," she suggested, but he could see the laughter shimmering in the depths of those turquoise eyes, like sunlight on seawater. "I shall share a secret with you," she said. "There is not a woman alive who does not appreciate a compliment now and then, and yours was the most flattering tribute of all—the involuntary kind!"

Taking his arm, she steered him toward the settle. But once they were seated, Justin became aware of a savory aroma wafting from the hearth, where a cauldron was bubbling over an iron trivet. Glancing around the cottage, he focused for the first time on the table and its contents: the white cloth, the wrought-iron candlesticks, twin wine flagons and cups, a freshly baked loaf, two trenchers carved from stale bread, spoons and knives neatly aligned. "I am intruding," he said, starting to rise. "You are expecting company . . ."

"Sit," she urged. "We have time to talk. I would like you to tell me about Gervase's dying. Did he suffer much?"

She was the first one to ask him that. "He was in pain, Mistress Talbot, but not for long. Death came quickly."

"Thank God Almighty for that," she said somberly, and under her unwavering blue-green gaze, he told her how Gervase had died, omitting any mention of the queen's letter and his own rash promise to the goldsmith. When he was done, she sighed, daubed unself-consciously at her eyes with the flowing sleeve of her gown, and then insisted upon fetching him a cup of wine. "I am glad you sought me out so we'd have this chance to talk. And I am very glad, indeed, to be able to thank you, Master de Quincy, for all you did for Gervase—and for Edwin, too."

He'd had this same conversation once before—with Gervase's wife. Except that she had not thought to include Edwin. He hadn't expected Aldith to be so warm . . . or so guileless. She ought not to open her door to strangers like this, or to take what she was told on faith. He managed to rein in this newborn protective urge, at least long enough to ask her a few casually calculated questions about Gervase, questions she answered readily.

Yes, she confirmed, Gervase had been off on a business trip to Rouen. After his ship had docked at Southampton on Epiphany Eve, he had continued on to Winchester. Later that evening, he'd stopped by to let her know he was back and to explain that he must depart again on the morrow for London. He'd stayed only an hour or so, for he was weary and wanted to sleep in his own bed. That was the last time she'd seen him, alive or dead, for she had not been invited to the funeral. And no, he'd told her very little about his business in London.

"He hinted that he'd be able to tell me all about it on his return. It was the opportunity of a lifetime, he said, a chance to gain a king's favor. I did not understand, but when I asked what he meant, he just laughed and promised to bring me back a trinket from London."

She sighed again, and Justin resolutely kept his eyes on her face, not letting his gaze follow the rise and fall of her bosom. He ought not to be having lustful yearnings for a woman so recently bereaved. But she was sitting so close that he was having trouble keeping his thoughts from wandering into forbidden territory. Her perfume was scenting his every breath, her mouth as soft and ripe as summer strawberries. She was too trusting, not even realizing she was being interrogated.

"Poor Gervase . . ." A tear trembled on her lashes, and Justin watched in unwilling fascination as it trickled down her cheek, onto the soft skin of her throat. "I did not love him," she said with unexpected candor, "but I was very fond of him, I truly was. He was always right good to me. He deserved a far better death than the one he got. How much worse it might have been, though, if not for you, Master de Quincy . . . Justin. You cradled him as he lay dying, you sought to comfort him, you prayed over him, and for that, you will have my eternal gratitude." And leaning over, she kissed him on the cheek, a kiss feather-light and honey-sweet.

Drawing back then, she began to laugh. "Ah, look what I've done to you—smeared lip rouge all over your face! Here, let me repair the damage . . ." Licking her forefinger, she touched the smudge and began to rub gently. Justin reminded himself that she was a woman of dubious morals, a woman at least ten years older than he, a woman in mourning. But it was not his brain he was heeding at the moment, and when she smiled at him, the urge to kiss her was well-nigh irresistible.

But Justin was never to know if he would have yielded to the temptation. There was no warning whatsoever. He heard nothing until the shout, a hoarse "Christ on the Cross!" that seemed to fill the room like thunder. He spun around on the settle so fast that he spilled some of his wine, staring at the man framed in the doorway.

He had only a fleeting glimpse of the intruder—tall, tawny haired, and enraged—before the man lunged forward, crossed the cottage in three giant strides, and knotted a fist in the neck of Justin's tunic. Reacting with fury, not thought, Justin flung the contents of his wine cup into his assailant's face. The man gasped, his grip slackening enough for Justin to break free. Sputtering and swearing, he seemed ready to renew his attack. But by then Justin was on his feet, and Aldith had planted herself firmly between them.

"Have you gone stark mad? You're lucky I did not set Jezebel on you!" she scolded the interloper, although the threat would have been more impressive had the mastiff not been leaning her huge head against the man's leg, her tail beating an eager tattoo in the floor rushes.

The man paid no more heed to Aldith than he did to her dog. Never taking his eyes from Justin, he snarled, "I suppose I ought to get your name so I'll know what to tell the coroner! Who in hellfire are you?"

"I would ask you the same thing," Justin shot back, "except that it is obvious who you are—the town lunatic!"

"A bad guess, whoreson! I'm the under-sheriff for Hampshire!"

Justin was stunned. "You? You are Luke de Marston?"

"Yes, I am sorry to say that he is!" Aldith was glaring at the deputy. "Had you not burst in here, raving and ranting, you'd have found out that this is Justin de Quincy, the man who came to Gervase's rescue on the Alresford Road."

Luke's eyes narrowed, flicking from Aldith to Justin. His face grew guarded, impossible to read. "On another mission of mercy?" he asked Justin. "You cannot stop doing good deeds, can you?"

Justin ignored him, turning toward the settle to retrieve his mantle. "I will be going now, Mistress Talbot."

"Yes," she agreed, "I think that would be best." Following Justin to the door, she gave him an intimate, regretful smile. "I am so sorry . . ."

"Yes," Justin said coldly, "so am I." As their eyes met, she had the grace to blush a little. She started to speak, then stopped herself, but stood watching in the doorway until Luke's voice summoned her back inside.

The temperature had plunged once the sun set, but Justin was indifferent to the cold. His brain was whirling with half-formed thoughts. Yet one fact stood out in unsparing clarity. He had been set up. He had no doubts whatsoever that Aldith had contrived that compromising scene for Luke's benefit. He just did not understand why. Was she one of those women who enjoyed baiting men into fighting over her? Or was there a more specific intent to her mischief—a deliberate ploy to make Luke de Marston jealous?

But a moment later, Justin had forgotten about his bruised pride, halting abruptly on the darkened street in a belated, troubled understanding of what he'd witnessed. Aldith's dog had not barked at Luke's entrance. Nor had he knocked. The sheriff's deputy had a key to Aldith Talbot's cottage.

4

TOWER OF LONDON

January 1193

The groom took Copper's reins, then glanced inquiringly over his shoulder. "You want me to unsaddle him?"

Justin shook his head. "No need to bother." He did not think he would be long at the Tower. Once he'd confessed to the queen that he could not solve the goldsmith's murder, what further use would she have for him?

He was nearing the keep when he noticed the couple standing by the stairs. He recognized the woman at once: the queen's lady and his good angel. Even if she had not been so helpful to him, she was far too pretty to be forgotten. The man was unfamiliar, but Justin knew at once that this stranger was someone of significance, for he was richly dressed in a fur-lined mantle, and when he reached out to touch her cheek, an emerald ring glowed like fox fire. She did not appear to welcome the caress, but she did not rebuff it, either, showing a diffidence that Justin found surprising. She'd impressed him as a born flirt, and a sleekly self-confident one at that. She'd had no trouble spurning Durand's unwanted advances, for certes. Now, though, she seemed flustered. Justin waited to make sure she did not need a distraction, for he owed her a favor and would like nothing better than to repay it.

But their conversation was already ending. She backed away, smiling politely as the man began to climb the stairs. By the time he'd disappeared into the keep, Justin had reached her. She turned with a sudden smile, this one much more spontaneous. "Master de Quincy! I thought you'd gone off on a clandestine mission for the queen."

Justin was flattered to be remembered, but startled that she knew so much about him. "What makes you think that, demoiselle?"

"I asked Peter about you," she said forthrightly. "He said the queen had given him a letter for you, but I could not get much more out of him. Peter takes his duties entirely too seriously." She had an appealing grin, at once mischievous and coquettish. "I hope you do not mind my prying. Alas, curiosity has always been an abiding sin of mine."

"I'd forgive you far greater sins than that, demoiselle," Justin said gallantly. He at once felt rather foolish, for that sounded like something out of a minstrel's tale. It seemed to please her, though, and that was well worth a little embarrassment. She introduced herself now as Claudine de Loudun, and he seized the opportunity to kiss her hand. But when he ventured a discreet query about the one-sided flirtation he'd witnessed, he was jolted by her response.

"You were going to rescue me?" Her eyes widened. "You are either the bravest man I've ever met or the craziest, mayhap both! Unless . . . you do not know who he is, do you?"

"Obviously someone of importance," Justin said, somewhat defensively, for she sounded astonished, as if he'd failed to recognize the Son of God.

"Important? I'd say that is as good a way as any to describe a future king. That was the queen's son. John, the Count of Mortain." Claudine's amusement was waning. Glancing around, she lowered her voice. "I've heard that he has been asking about you."

Justin was dumbfounded. "Are you sure? How would the Count of Mortain even know I'm alive?"

"He may not know you personally, but he seems very interested in that letter you brought to the queen." She dropped her voice still further, brown eyes very serious. "And if John is interested in you, Master de Quincy, better that you know it."

Eleanor gazed searchingly into eyes very like her own, a golden hazel, utterly opaque, eyes that gave away no secrets. How little she knew him—this stranger, her son. For years he'd been on the outer reaches of her life. The last of their eaglets, the child she'd never wanted, born in the twilight of a dying marriage. A hostage to the impassioned enmity of a love gone sour. He'd been just six when she'd become Henry's captive, seventeen when next she saw him, and twenty-two when she was finally set free. He was six and twenty now and still he eluded her. She and Richard needed no words between them, so easy and instinctive was the understanding that had always been theirs. But with John, all the words in Christendom did not seem enough.

Would an outright challenge be best? Or nuance and equivocation? She was not usually so irresolute. But with John, she was always following unfamiliar trails, never sure what lay around the bend.

"I've been told that alarming rumors are circulating about Richard," she said abruptly, making up her mind to try a frontal assault. "Men are claiming that he is dead, shipwrecked on his way back from the Holy Land. Such talk is not new. It began when Richard's ship did not reach Brindisi. But these rumors are rather specific and remarkably widespread, almost as if they were deliberately sown. I would hate to think you had a hand in that, John."

"I'll not deny that I think hope has faded. But you cannot blame me because other men think so, too."

"Why are you so sure that Richard is dead?"

"Why are you so sure," he countered, "that he is not? I do not mean to be cruel, Mother, but I must be blunt. Richard has been missing for more than three months. If evil has not befallen him, why have we not gotten word of his whereabouts by now? Unless . . . you *have* heard from him?"

"No . . . I have heard nothing from Richard. Why would you ask that?"

He shrugged. "I suppose I was remembering the gossip I heard—talk of a mysterious letter delivered by an equally mysterious messenger. Naturally I was curious, and since Richard is so often in my thoughts these days, he came at once to mind."

Behind her, Eleanor heard a smothered cry, quickly broken off, as William Longsword half rose from his seat. Ignoring Will's distress, she smiled at her son. "I'd give little credence to gossip, John. You, of all men, ought to appreciate how unreliable it is. For the past twelvemonth, rumor has had you conspiring with the French king to usurp Richard's throne. But we both know that to be an outrageous falsehood . . . do we not?"

"The worst sort of defamation," he agreed gravely, but his eyes gleamed in the lamplight. One of his saving graces was his ability to laugh at himself. In Eleanor's eyes, that was no small virtue, for she had long ago concluded that if a lack of humor was not a sin, it ought to be. But this was what she too often found herself doing with John—sorting through all the weeds for that one flowering sprig.

Turning toward the table, John picked up a flagon of wine. When she shook her head, he poured for himself and Will. Eleanor had dismissed all the others from the chamber, for her son had a tendency to play to an audience. She'd often thought he'd have made a fine actor, with a particular talent for righteous indignation and bemused innocence.

Taking but a single sip of his wine, John then set it on the table. "I've matters still to tend to," he said, "so I'd best be off." Coming forward, he kissed Eleanor's hand, and as always, his gallantry bore the faintest hint of mockery. With John, even his kindnesses were slightly suspect. Or was she being unfair to him, this youngest and least known of all her children? Her every instinct urged wariness, warned that he could not be trusted. And yet he was still hers, flesh of her flesh, impossible to disavow.

"John!" He'd been reaching for the door latch, but stopped in midmotion, halted by her sudden vehemence. Coming swiftly across the chamber, Eleanor put her hand upon his arm. "Listen to me," she said, her voice low and intent. "In the days to come, watch where you tread. A misstep could bring your world tumbling down around you. I would borrow some of your 'bluntness' now. I know you love Richard not. I know, too, how much you covet his crown. But do not plot against him, John. For your own sake, do not. If it came to war, I do not think you could measure up to Richard."

His eyes took on a hard, greenish glitter. "You've already made that abundantly clear, madame," he said bitingly, "for most of my life!"

As the door closed behind John, his half-brother shot from his seat. "I did not tell John about the letter, madame. He asked, but I said nothing, I swear it is so!"

"I know that, Will." Turning, Eleanor found a smile for him, but all the while, her thoughts were following John, plunging after him into the shadows of the stairwell. Will was continuing to protest his innocence, needlessly, for his open, freckled face was like a window to his soul. He could no more lie convincingly than he could fly. Passing strange, that he was so like his father in appearance, so unlike him in temperament. He had Henry's reddish-gold hair, his high color, even his grey eyes. But he'd gotten none of Henry's fire or sardonic charm, and nothing whatsoever of his ruthless royal will.

Eleanor was genuinely fond of Will, and she sympathized with his plight. He disapproved utterly of the man John had become—a cynical opportunist willing to make any devil's deal that might gain him the English crown. But Will had fond memories of another John, the young brother in need of his guidance. Will had cast a protective eye upon that solitary little boy, and their childhood affection had endured even after they'd both grown to manhood. Eleanor could not help wondering if her family's harrowing history might have been different had Richard and John been able to forge such a brotherly bond, too. But her sons had never learned to love one another. That was a lesson she and Henry had failed to teach them.

"I would never betray your trust, madame—never!"

"I know, Will," she said again, with a patience she rarely showed to others. "A number of people heard Justin de Quincy mention a letter that had cost one life already. Any of them could have told John, inadvertently or otherwise. Most likely it was Durand. He and John share a fondness for dicing and whoring, for all that they barely acknowledge each other in my presence."

Will was shocked, both by the suggestion that John might plant a spy in his mother's household and by Eleanor's matter-of-fact acceptance of it. "My lady . . . do you think John knows that King Richard is being held prisoner in Austria?"

"I am not sure, Will." Just how much did John know? Had Philip shared his secret? If they were as deeply entangled as she feared, Philip would have sent word straightaway, days before the Archbishop of Rouen was able to obtain his covert copy of the Holy Roman Emperor's gloating letter. And if John had known of Richard's capture and kept silent, that in itself would be an admission of sorts. For silence under such circumstances was suspicious at best, sinister at worst. How far was John willing to go in his quest for his brother's crown?

"Madame?" Peter de Blois was standing in the doorway. "Master de Quincy is here. Shall I admit him?"

Eleanor was taken aback; Justin had been gone barely a week. "Yes, I will see him." When he was ushered into the chamber, she was not reassured by his appearance, for he looked fatigued and uneasy.

"I did not expect you back so soon," she said, once they were alone. "What did you find out?"

"I cannot solve this crime for you, madame. It grieves me that I must fail you, but—"

The door banged open without warning, startling them both. Striding into the chamber, John smiled at his mother, quite nonchalantly, as if their recent clash had never been. "I forgot to ask you, Mother . . ." He paused, his gaze coming to rest upon Justin. "Do I know you? You look most familiar."

Eleanor started to speak, but Justin was quicker, introducing himself before she could intervene. Watching John closely, she understood then why Justin had not wanted her to lie—John already knew his identity. He was regarding Justin now with a quizzical smile. "Have you brought my lady mother another vital letter, Master de Quincy?"

"A vital letter, my lord?" Justin echoed, with a quizzical smile of his own. "I am here on behalf of the abbot of St Werburgh's in Chester, but it is a routine matter, of no urgency."

Saying nothing, John glanced down at Justin's muddied boots and mantle. No man would come into the queen's presence in such travel-stained dishevelment for "a routine matter, of no urgency." John let his eyes linger upon those mud-caked boots long enough to convey his message: that Justin had lied and he knew it.

Eleanor moved between them. "John? What did you come back to ask me?"

"Well . . . to tell you true, Mother, it has gone right out of my head. Strange, is it not?"

"Not really," she said dryly. "Memory is a will-o'-the-wisp, unpredictable and wayward."

"Are you talking about memory, weather, . . . or sons?" And although it was said as a jest, it held one of John's buried barbs.

As soon as John had gone, Justin said, "Downstairs, Lord John was about to depart when he heard Master Peter call out my name. He seems much too curious about me for my peace of mind, my lady. Does he . . . does he . . . know about the French king's letter?"

"I've told him nothing." Which was true as far as it went. If sins of omission were still sins, did that apply as well to lies of omission? Eleanor had no qualms about lying when necessity demanded it; she'd always thought that honesty was an overrated virtue. But she owed Justin more than half-truths and evasions. She did not want his blood on her hands, not if it could be helped. "John knows that you brought me a letter. But I do not know how much—if anything—the French king has revealed to him."

She could say no more than that. Nor did Justin expect her to; however worried she was about her son, she'd never choose him as a confidant. So he was not surprised when she said briskly, "Now . . . why do you think you have failed me? You were not able to find any suspects?"

Justin's mouth twisted. "Nay, I found too many. The man's own children had reason to wish him dead. Nor can I rule out his brother. And there will be no help from the law, for the undersheriff may well have the strongest motive of all!"

"You are saying that the killing was personal?" Eleanor's surprise was evident. "That he was not killed because of the letter?"

"I do not know, my lady," he admitted. "I uncovered motives, but no evidence to link any of them to the crime." And he started then to tell her about his suspects, striving to be both fair and concise.

He confessed that he hoped the killer was not Thomas, simply because he did not want to believe that a man could kill for such a perverted purpose. What could be more diabolic than a piety so twisted and profane that it led to murder?

As for Jonet and Miles, he felt sure that neither one could have acted alone. His impression of Miles was that he was one to need a bit of prodding; he couldn't see a murder plot taking root in such shallow soil. The idea would have had to come from Jonet, but she could not have done it on her own. A lass could not prowl the alehouses and taverns in search of cutthroats and brigands for hire. He was about to explain his reasoning to Eleanor when she cut in, saying impatiently:

"You mentioned the under-sheriff. What reason would he have to want the goldsmith dead?"

"Her name is Aldith Talbot. She was Fitz Randolph's concubine, but I am convinced she and the deputy, Luke de Marston, were lovers ere he was slain. And she is a woman a man might well kill over. If he could have her no other way . . ."

Justin shrugged, then concluded grimly, "Who would find it easier to make a deal with outlaws than a sheriff's deputy? He'd know any number of felons, hellspawn who'd kill for a pittance. Sheriffs are not often mistaken for earthly saints, madame. Too many have been caught using their office for ill-gotten gains. If a man is already selling justice and collecting bribes, it may not be so great a leap to murder."

Eleanor did not challenge his jaundiced view of sheriffs. So prevalent were complaints of corruption and abuse of power that her husband had convened an Inquest of Sheriffs, and the investigation results had been so damning that almost all of the sheriffs had been dismissed. That was more than twenty years ago, but she had no reason to assume the current crop of sheriffs were any more ethical or honorable than their predecessors. And if Luke de Marston was corrupt, she did want to know. But she could see that the investigation had gone awry. Rising, she began to pace.

"I am sorry I failed you, madame. But I do not know how to follow the trail any farther, for it goes off in too many directions. I thought if I told you what I'd learned, the sheriff of Hampshire could take it from there. I know you said you did not want to involve him, but I see no other choice . . ."

Justin was talking too much and he knew it, but her continued silence was unnerving. Once his words ebbed away, the only sound was the silken rustle of her skirts as she moved restlessly about the chamber. Justin bit his lip, waiting to be dismissed.

"You have not failed me," she said at last. "If there was any failing, it was mine, for I sent you off into unknown territory without a map. Under the circumstances, you did well, learning a great deal in a brief time. But I ought to have been more forthcoming with you."

Eleanor sat down in a window seat, saying nothing for several more suspenseful moments. "Your actions in Winchester were logical and well thought out. But this is not an ordinary murder investigation. There is more at stake than catching the goldsmith's killers, much more."

Justin was beginning to understand why she'd shown so little interest in his revelations about the goldsmith's kin. "So . . ." he said cautiously, "you are saying that if the guilty are found at the Fitz Randolph hearth, you'd be content to let the sheriff see that justice is done?"

"Yes," she said. "I do want to see the guilty punished. But I have a more urgent need. I must know if the killers were after the letter. You see, I fear that the murder may have been done at the behest of the French king. If that is so, I need to know and as soon as possible. If Philip is desperate enough to set assassins loose in England, it does not bode well for my son. I cannot hope to thwart him unless I have proof of his treachery."

She paused, choosing her words with care. "You must find out for me if the killers were in the pay of the French king. If you can prove that this deputy or one of the Fitz Randolphs is the culprit, well and good. It would ease my mind considerably to have my suspicions refuted. But either way, I must know and soon. Speed is of the essence, for time is not on Richard's side."

She paused again. "I know it is a dangerous mission I've given you. But you're the only one who can recognize the killers. I must rely upon you to serve me well. Do not let me down, Justin."

Her urgency was as compelling as it was daunting. Justin had not bargained upon being entangled in a foreign conspiracy. At that moment, though, he could imagine nothing worse than breaking faith with her.

"I cannot make the same promise as before, my lady. I cannot swear that I will solve this crime for you. But I will do my best, that I vow."

Eleanor needed more than promises. But she'd learned to take what she could get. "Godspeed, Justin. And be wary, watch whom you trust. It is not easy to trap a killer, and for certes, not safe."

After learning that Justin had come straight to her upon his arrival in London, Eleanor had suggested that he seek lodgings for the night at the nearby priory of Holy Trinity, Aldgate. Justin decided to do so, for he need only show the queen's letter to assure himself of a warm welcome, a more appealing prospect than trudging through the city streets in search of an inn.

Having taken his leave of Eleanor, Justin paused on the Tower steps. High above his head, an easterly wind herded flocks of ice clouds across the darkening sky. He'd be racing a storm back to Winchester. It was too cold to linger out in the bailey, and he headed toward the stable to retrieve his horse.

Within, the stable was dim, already sheltering night shadows; torches were not left burning, for fear of fire. The grooms were nowhere in sight. A cat stalked mice up on the rafters, and an aged stable dog gave a halfhearted bark before burrowing back into the straw. Justin's stallion snorted loudly at the sight of him. Entering the stall, he was about to lead Copper out when a hand grasped his shoulder. Spinning around, he found himself face-to-face with Eleanor's son.

"Master de Quincy!" John smiled, his teeth gleaming whitely in the light cast by his lantern. "This is a surprise. I was tarrying out here to see who claimed that chestnut. Had I but known you were the owner, I could have spared myself a wait in this drafty, dark barn."

"How may I serve you, my lord?" There was movement in the shadows behind John. Several men came forward, flanking their lord. They said nothing, watching Justin impassively, showing neither curiosity nor hostility. He suspected that they'd slit his throat with equal indifference should John give the word.

"You can sell me your horse." John reached out, stroking Copper's muzzle. "A right handsome beast. I've always fancied chestnuts. So . . . what say you, de Quincy?"

Justin shifted uneasily. If gossip held true, it was not healthy to possess something that the Lord John wanted, be it a horse, a woman, or a crown. "He is not for sale, my lord count."

"Are you so sure of that? You may name your price."

"I am quite sure," Justin said firmly. "But I am willing to give you the right of first refusal, should I ever change my mind."

John was still smiling. "You are a stubborn one, for certes. Think it over, though."

"I will." Justin was positive that John was lying. As much as he cherished Copper, the chestnut was not likely to tempt a king's son; John would have stables full of finely bred horses. No, this was merely a pretext. Whatever John wanted from him, it was not Copper.

John continued to stroke the stallion's neck. He had Justin's coloring; his lantern's glow revealed hair blacker than midnight. The dark one in a fair family, for his brothers and sisters had all been sun kissed. Richard was said to be lance-tall, towering over other men, with sky-color eyes and hair brighter than molten gold. John was of no more than average height, if even that; Justin topped him by half a foot. Yet he was not a man to pass unnoticed in any company. His intelligence was evident, as formidable a weapon as the finely honed sword at his hip. But if even half of what Justin had heard about John was true, he knew nothing of moral boundaries. Not a comfortable man to encounter in the shadows.

"Have you been in my lady mother's service long?"

"No, not long."

"I understand you delivered an urgent letter about ten days ago. I would be most interested in learning the contents of that letter, Master de Quincy."

Justin swallowed. "I regret that I cannot be of assistance, my lord. I would never dare read a letter meant for the queen's eyes. As for that particular letter, I remember nothing of urgency about it. You must have been misinformed."

"Not likely. Those who serve me know how much I value

accurate information. I hope you change your mind—about the horse. I would naturally make it worth your while."

"I will think upon it," Justin said, as noncommittally as he could.

"It would help if I knew where to reach you—in case you do decide to sell."

"I have no fixed abode, my lord, so it would be difficult for you to find me."

"You'd be surprised how good I am at finding people, Master de Quincy. What of your family? Surely they'd know where you might be?"

Hoping his voice held steady, Justin said, "Alas, I have no family, my lord. But I do know how you can contact me. You need only ask the queen."

There was a silence that seemed endless, and then John laughed. "Now why did I not think of that?" He sounded genuinely amused by Justin's audacity, but Justin's tension did not abate until he signaled to his men. "I daresay our paths will cross again."

"Farewell, my lord count." Justin's throat was still tight. He stood where he was, not moving until long after John had departed the stable. The queen had twice warned him about the perils he was likely to face in Winchester. But what if the greatest dangers were to be found in London?

5

WINCHESTER

January 1193

The alehouse was crowded and it took a while for Justin to attract the attention of the harried serving maid. Ordering two more ales, he watched disapprovingly as his companion gulped his down in several vast swallows. "Are you sure, Torold," he prodded, "that you can remember nothing more about that morning?"

Torold belched, then shrugged. While he was more than willing to drink Justin's ale, he'd been doling out answers in miserly portions. "I already told you, I only remember one man for certes. A swaggering lout with a fine furred mantle and a finer grey stallion, demanding that I open the East Gate early, just for him. He was sorely vexed, too, when I refused, cursing and ranting like he was the missing king! After him, there was a monk . . . I think. But none after Master Fitz Randolph rode out, for by then the snow was coming down thick as pottage."

Draining the last drops in his cup, Torold glanced over to see if Justin seemed inclined to order another round, then got to his feet. "That is all I remember, and what I told the deputy. I do not see why he saw a need to have me go over it again . . ."

Mumbling to himself, Torold headed off in search of the serving maid. Justin had not claimed outright that he was acting on the deputy's behalf, but neither had he corrected the guard's misunderstanding. He suspected that the free ale had done more to loosen Torold's tongue than any hints of legal authority, but he hadn't gotten much for his money. Not that he was even sure what he'd been hoping to find. His assurances to Eleanor notwithstanding, he could not help feeling as if he were fishing without bait.

The guard had confirmed Justin's suspicions, though, that the outlaws had not ridden out of the city before the goldsmith on that last morning of his life. Who knew how many bandit lairs and encampments were hidden away in those woods? No, they were already lying in wait—and for Gervase Fitz Randolph. Not only had they let Justin go by unscathed, they had also ignored that "swaggering lout with a fine furred mantle and a finer grey stallion," surely a tempting target for men with robbery in mind.

Justin reached for his ale cup, trying to decide what to do next. Even if he could track down the overweening lout or Torold's mayhap-monk, what good would it do? What were they likely to have seen? But there had to be some way of finding the bandits, for how else could he hope to prove who'd hired them? If only he did not have so many suspects! Was it the zealot? The disgruntled brother? The illicit lovers? Or that arrogant, cock-sure deputy? Or was it a stranger, elusive and sinister, a spy in the pay of the French king?

"Would you fancy some company?" Without waiting for Justin's response, the woman sat down beside him, staking her claim with good-humored aplomb. It took Justin only a moment or so to decide he'd like to be claimed. It had been too long since he'd lain with a woman, and this one was appealing in an elfin sort of way, fair skin dusted with freckles, small boned and deli-cate. When Justin signaled for more drinks, she smiled and slid closer on the bench, much closer. "I am Eve."

He doubted it; prostitutes often took on a new name for their precarious profession and "Eve" was a popular choice. Unable to resist the obvious jest, he said with a grin, "I am Adam . . . and I would love some company, Eve." There was no need to fret over her price, for never had his money pouch been so healthy, well fed with the queen's coins. He was determined that she'd squander neither her money nor her hopes on him. He could not help with what mattered most to Eleanor—he could do nothing to aid her captive son. But he would find a way to solve this Win-chester killing for her. And when an ironic, inner voice chal-lenged, "How?" he no longer heard it, for by then Eve was sitting on his lap, and the morrow seemed too far away to worry about.

Justin had elected to stay in the guest hall at Hyde Abbey rather than at an inn, hoping that he might be able to learn something useful about Thomas, the aspiring monk. He'd passed two nights at the abbey so far; the third, he'd spent in Eve's bed. The dawn sky was overcast, but it was not as cold, and there was a jauntiness in Justin's step as he crossed the abbey garth, heading for the stables to check on Copper. After that, his plans for the day were still vague. He'd thought about visiting the city's stables in search of Gervase's stolen stallion, but it seemed a waste of time. Surely the outlaws would not be foolish enough to try to sell the horse in the slain goldsmith's own city?

He was so caught up in his musings that he almost collided with a Benedictine brother, laden with an armful of bulky woolen blankets. When Justin sidestepped in time, the monk gave him a smile of recognition. "Good morrow, Master de Quincy. You're either up very early or you're getting to bed very late . . . in which case, the less you tell me, the better!"

Justin grinned. "I promise to save all the depraved details for my confessor!" He liked what he'd so far seen of Brother Paul, an urbane, affable man past his prime, but still possessed of a lively curiosity about the world he'd forsaken, with a caustic humor that sometimes startled Justin, coming as it did from a monk's mouth.

Brother Paul chuckled now, then nodded toward his burden. "I could use a hand with these blankets. Look upon it as penance for those nocturnal sins of yours!"

Justin obligingly relieved the monk of half his load. "Where are we taking them?"

"Across the garth to the almonry. I'm collecting goods to deliver to the lazar house."

Justin stopped abruptly. "Lazar house?"

"The leper hospital of St Mary Magdalen. Why do you look so surprised? It is our Christian duty to do what we can for Christ's poor, the weak and infirm and afflicted . . . and few afflictions are more grievous than leprosy."

"Brother Paul . . . may I fetch the blankets to the lazar house for you?"

The monk was startled, for people rarely volunteered to visit a leper hospital. So pervasive was the fear of the disease that some would not even get downwind of a leper. "If you are truly willing,

Master de Quincy, I would be beholden to you, for I have more tasks to do this day than I have time."

"Well, this is one task you'll not have to bother with," Justin said, but his mind was no longer on the monk. Jesú, how could he have forgotten about the leper?

The leper hospital of St Mary Magdalen was about a mile and a half east of Winchester, on the Alresford Road. It was encircled by a wattle-and-daub fence and had a bleak, foreboding look. Reining in his mount, Justin gazed uneasily upon it, girding himself to ride through that gateway. Never before had he set foot in a lazar house; never had he expected to enter one of his own free will. There was no shortage of theories as to what caused leprosy. Some people insisted it was the result of eating rotten meat or drinking bad wine. Others claimed it could be caught by sharing the bed of a woman who'd lain with a leper. There was talk of infected air. And just about everybody believed that the greatest danger of contagion came from the lepers themselves.

"Ah, Lady Eleanor," Justin muttered, "this road is taking some crooked turns . . ." Nudging Copper forward, he led the abbey's packhorse through the gate and into the hospital precincts.

The first building to meet his eyes was the chapel. Beyond it was the master's hall, and then the refectory, where the lepers ate and slept. There was a barn, a kitchen, a well, and although he could not see one, Justin knew there would be a cemetery, too, for even in death, lepers were shunned. Brother Paul had told him the hospital could accommodate eighteen lepers. That seemed a meagre number to Justin. What of those lepers unable to gain admittance to a lazar house? He already knew the answer to that, though. They'd beg their bread by the roadside or they'd starve. And sometimes they did both.

By the time he dismounted in front of the chapel, Justin had an audience. He was disquieted by the sight of those spectral figures shuffling toward him, muffled in long leper cloaks, the sort of ghostly shadows that were usually banished by the coming of day. "I am here at the behest of Brother Paul," he said loudly. "I wish to speak to the hospital's master, Father Jerome."

"He is not here." It was not the message, but the voice that swiveled Justin's head toward the speaker, for it was high pitched and youthful, utterly out of place in this abode of death.

"I am Simon." The voice had not lied. This smallest leper smiling up at Justin was a child. As the boy's hood fell back, Justin saw that he was in the early stages of the disease, a reddish rash spreading like a blush across his cheekbones. "Father Jerome went into town. Can I pet your horse?"

Justin nodded wordlessly. The other lepers were moving aside to admit a newcomer to the circle. He was tall and thin, stoop shouldered and ungainly in a black cassock that was too short in the sleeves, and worn and patched at the elbows. But he had a rich man's smile, brighter than newly minted silver coins. "Bless Brother Paul," he exclaimed, "and you, too, friend, for bringing us these supplies. Can you help me get them inside?"

"Of course," Justin said reluctantly. "Will you look after my horse, Simon?" The child nodded, eyes widening like moons, and reached eagerly for the reins as soon as Justin swung down from the saddle. Hesitantly at first, Simon began to stroke the stallion's neck. Justin turned away hastily, following after the priest.

They introduced themselves as they carried the blankets toward the refectory. Justin was still shaken by his encounter with the boy, but Father Gregory did not let the conversation lag, chatting away as if they were old friends unexpectedly reunited. He was quite young and seemed amazingly relaxed and genial for a man living daily with death. What would impel one to choose such a path? Justin could only marvel at what he could not understand.

"We get few visitors here, so it is not surprising that your arrival caused such a stir. It does our people good, seeing that all do not shrink from them in dread."

Justin had rarely felt so uncomfortable. "The little lad . . . does he have kin here?"

"No. Simon's family cast him out once his malady was known." The priest sounded neither shocked nor judgmental, but Justin was both. Hissing his breath through his teeth, he shook his head. Father Gregory was not surprised by his silence; there were wrongs that words could not address.

"Do you know what happens once a leper has been detected, Master de Quincy? He is escorted into the church, forced to kneel under a black cloth as Mass is said, and the priest then proclaims him 'dead to the world, reborn to God.' In France, lepers are made to stand in an open grave. We are more merciful than that in England, but here, too, the lepers are driven from our midst, forbidden to enter churches, fairs, markets, taverns, or alehouses, condemned to wander in the wilderness with every man's hand against them . . . or so it must seem. So when you are willing to come amongst us and show kindness to a child of the Lord, it is no small thing and worthy of—"

"No," Justin interrupted, more sharply than he'd intended. "You give me credit I do not deserve, Father Gregory. I had my own reasons for offering to aid Brother Paul, reasons that had naught to do with Christian charity. I came here in hopes of finding a man—a leper—who may be able to help solve a murder."

Justin wasn't sure what reaction he'd been expecting, but certainly not the one he got. The young priest didn't even blink, merely nodded as if this was an everyday occurrence. "And you think this man is here?"

"I do not know," Justin admitted. "I cannot tell you his name. I cannot tell you what he looks like or even how tall he is, for he was squatting by the roadside when I saw him on Epiphany morn, his face hidden by his hood. I suppose I am asking for a miracle, expecting you to identify someone based on so little, but—"

"His name is Job," the priest said, with a triumphant grin that gave way to outright laughter at Justin's astonishment. "Nay . . . no miracle, lad. The answer is simple—you are not the first to seek Job out. The under-sheriff came here, too, in search of him."

"Luke de Marston was looking for him?" Justin asked slowly, and the priest nodded again.

"He knew little more than you, only that Master Fitz Randolph's groom remembered passing a beggar on the road. As soon as he told me it was on Epiphany, I knew it must be Job, for no one else would have ventured out into the snow. No matter how foul the weather, Job begs for alms and then hides the money away ere he returns to us."

By now they'd reached the refectory. Moving up the aisled hall, the priest paused before a large coffer. "We store the blankets here." Once they were neatly folded away, he sat down on the lid and gestured for Justin to join him. "They are supposed to yield up any alms they get, for they are not permitted to own personal property. But Father Jerome turns a blind eye to minor transgressions. He understands why a man like Job needs to have money of his own. Ere a leper can be admitted to a lazar house, he must take vows of chastity, obedience, and poverty. Such vows are not always easy to obey for even the most dedicated of God's servants. Small wonder if some of these poor souls rebel . . ."

Justin was quiet for a moment, pondering what he'd learned. This was the second time that he'd come across the deputy's tracks, and he liked it not. He wished he could take some reassurance from Luke de Marston's endeavors, but he knew they proved naught about the man's guilt or innocence. Even were his hands as bloody as Herod's, he'd still make a show of searching for the goldsmith's killers. "Tell me," he said at last. "His name is not really Job, is it?"

"It is what he calls himself now," the priest said quietly.

Job was squatting by the side of the road, as on that Epiphany morning three weeks ago. Reining in his stallion before the man, Justin asked, "Are you Job?" although he was already sure of the leper's identity.

"Who wants to know?" The voice was hoarse, a leper's rasp. His face was hidden by his hood, but his body's rigid pose communicated both tension and suspicion.

"My name is Justin de Quincy. I need to talk with you about the slaying of Gervase Fitz Randolph. Can you spare me some moments?"

"Why not?" The leper watched as Justin dismounted and hitched Copper and the abbey packhorse, and then slowly and deliberately drew back his hood.

Justin had wondered about his motives in choosing to call himself Job, for it could have been an act of utter faith—or a gesture of embittered defiance. He now had his answer. Job was no longer young, not yet old; it was difficult to guess his age, for he'd suffered the hair loss so common to lepers. Justin found the lack of lashes and eyebrows even more disconcerting than the thickened lips and ulcerated lesions. It was like gazing upon an eerie death mask, for as the disease progressed, those afflicted lost the ability to show expression. But those lashless brown eyes were lucid, offering Justin a harrowing glimpse of the soul trapped within that disintegrating body.

"It is only fair that I pay for your time." Justin dropped coins into Job's alms cup, and then sat down on a fallen log, as close as he dared get. Logic told him that leprosy could not be as contagious as people claimed, else caretakers like Father Gregory could not dwell amongst lepers without being stricken with the malady, too. But fear was instinctive and not always amenable to reason.

Job muttered his thanks, and then startled Justin when he commented, "You were not as openhanded the last time."

"Well . . . my prospects have improved since then. So you remember me?"

"I remember him," Job said, gesturing toward Copper.

"What else do you remember about that morn?"

"The snow started after dawn, and it was colder than a witch's teat. But not as cold as the heart of that hellspawn on a light grey palfrey. For all that he was mantled like a highborn lord, he was as tightfisted as any moneylender. Not only did he refuse to give me so much as a farthing, he turned the air blue with his curses, claiming it was bad luck to encounter 'a stinking leper' when starting out on a journey. Had he a whip, I truly think he would have struck me with it."

"He was no less high handed with the guard at the East Gate," Justin said. "A pity strutting peacocks like that so rarely get their tail feathers plucked as they deserve."

Job's misshapen mouth did not smile, but his eyes held a gleam of mordant amusement. "This peacock did come to grief. He'd not ridden fifty feet after cursing me out when his horse pulled up lame."

Justin frowned, puzzled. "That is odd, for I did not pass him on the road."

"Oh, he did not go all the way back to town. However outraged he was to have 'a stinking leper' cross his path, he was willing enough to turn to us for help. When the snow got too heavy, I returned to the lazar house, and found that Sir High-and-mighty had taken refuge with us. He stayed denned up in the master's quarters till the storm eased, and came back on the morrow for his lamed stallion."

"And let me guess. He showed his gratitude by contributing . . . what? His good wishes?"

"He promised Father Jerome that he'd send us a wagonful of provisions to get us through the winter. Of course," Job added dryly, "he did not specify which winter."

Justin unfastened his wineskin, took a pull, and then offered it to Job. He accepted it with alacrity, and drank deeply before saying, "Next, I remember a Black Monk on a lop-eared mule. From him, I got God's blessings. Then you and your chestnut. At first you seemed like to pass me by, but you changed your mind just in time. I suppose that was why I recognized you again, that and the fact that you were riding a right handsome beast. He must be . . . sixteen hands at least, no?"

"Yes, he is. You know your horses, for certes!"

The corner of Job's mouth curved, ever so slightly. "I ought to," he said, with echoes of an almost forgotten pride, "for I was a farrier, with my own smithy."

Justin did not know what to say. In his mind's eye, he could imagine the farrier in his prime, muscles bulging as he swung his hammer and heated his forge, those once-powerful hands now so maimed that he could barely grip the wineskin.

It was quiet for a moment, and then Job said abruptly, "The last men to ride by that morn were the goldsmith and his groom. May God assoil him, for he had a good heart, did Master Gervase. In all the time I knew him, he never failed to give alms and a cordial 'good morrow,' too. I do not know why you are seeking to track down his killers, but I hope you get them."

"I hope so, too." Job was holding out the wineskin and Justin swiftly shook his head. "Keep it if you like. On a cold day like this, a man needs a little wine to warm his bones."

"Indeed," Job agreed, sounding pleased. But as their eyes met,

Justin saw in the leper's level gaze a cynical understanding: that Justin would never—in this life or the next—have drunk again from that wineskin.

Hyde Abbey lay beyond the city walls, but still within walking distance, and when Justin decided to return to town that evening, he chose to go on foot rather than resaddle Copper. Admitted through the North Gate, he started down Scowrtene Street.

An early winter dusk had long since settled over Winchester, but the morning's cloud cover had been dispersed by a brisk wind and the night sky was salted with stars. Raising his lantern, Justin veered around a rut in the road. He was heading for Edwin's favorite alehouse on High Street, hoping to find the groom had slipped away for a quick ale. Buying Edwin a drink would be an easy way to learn of any new developments in the Fitz Randolph household. He hoped, too, to spur the other man's memory. Mayhap Edwin had seen more than he'd realized at the ambush.

Justin had stopped at the lazar house again on his way back to Winchester, and Father Gregory had confirmed Job's story. He'd even been able to give Justin the name of the grey stallion's ill-tempered owner: Fulk de Chesney. Justin was not sure what use that might be, for the man could have no knowledge of the ambush. Still, he was grateful for any scrap of information he could muster. He'd seen women sew a quilt out of scraps of material. Who was to say that he could not take these random fragments of fact and make of them a discernable pattern? Not a quilt, but a map, one that might lead to a killer.

There were few people out and about, for activity dwindled drastically once the sun set. But one man had been trailing after Justin ever since he'd left the abbey, matching his pace to Justin's, staying a constant twenty feet behind. When Justin began to walk faster, so did he. When Justin stopped to scrape mud from his boot, the man halted abruptly. It did not take long for Justin to become aware of him. Could this be the same man who'd followed him from the alehouse to the Fitz Randolph manor? But that was like being stalked by a shadow. This one was far more clumsy.

Justin was tempted to swing around and confront him, but he wanted to be sure. Better to put his suspicions to the test.

High Street was still a block away, but when he reached the first intersecting street, Justin made a sudden left turn. Soon after, so did his pursuer. Justin deliberately kept his steps unhurried, although his heart had begun to race. There was a tavern up ahead, an alley to his right. He chose the alley. It was narrow and black as pitch. Blowing out his lantern's flame, he flattened himself against a closed door and slid his dagger from its sheath.

He had not long to wait. Footsteps approached the alley, slowed. By now Justin's eyes had adjusted to the darkness and he tensed as a figure filled the entrance. After a moment's hesitation, the shadow entered the alley. As soon as he passed, Justin lunged. The man gave a grunt of alarm, but did not struggle, for Justin's knife was at his throat.

"What . . . what do you want?"

"Answers, but I'll settle for blood if need be. Why were you following me?"

"You're daft! I was not following anybody!"

"Wrong answer. Too bad."

The man yelped. "Christ, you cut me!"

"No, I nicked you. But the next lie will draw blood and a lot of it. So let's start again. What do you want from me?"

"Nothing, I swear it! I was just passing by!"

Justin swore under his breath. But his bluff had been called. He eased his hold and then shoved. The man lurched forward, stumbled, and went down. Swearing and sputtering, he scrambled awkwardly to regain his feet. But Justin had already drawn his sword. Continuing to curse, the man began to back away, then whirled and fled down the alley.

Justin watched the man disappear into the darkness, then turned and hastened back to the street. Up ahead a sudden flare of light spilled out into the night as the tavern door was flung open. Within moments, he was inside. Ordering wine, he found himself a corner table with a view of the door.

He'd been more unnerved by that alley confrontation than he cared to admit. It was the uncertainty that he found most troubling. Had he thwarted a robbery? Or foiled an assassination? A month ago it would never even have occurred to him that he might be a target for murder. Now he found it all too easy to believe.

The candle on Justin's table had burned down to a stub. His wine was almost gone, but he thought it best not to order another one. He'd need his wits about him on that long, lonely walk back to the abbey. How was he going to hunt for a killer if he had to keep looking over his shoulder?

Getting reluctantly to his feet, he was dropping a coin onto the table to pay for his drink when a commotion erupted across the chamber. A tipsy customer had paused in the doorway to bid a friend farewell, blocking someone seeking to enter. There was an angry exchange between the two, and then the dawdler was shoved aside and Luke de Marston stalked into the tavern. Striding toward Justin, he snapped, "You are under arrest!"

Justin stiffened. "What for?"

"I daresay I can think of any number of charges. But we'll start with your attack upon my serjeant!"

"Your serjeant!" Only then did Justin notice the man from the alley, glaring at him from behind Luke's shoulder. "Why was he following me?"

"To find out what you're up to—why do you think? Your conduct could not have been more suspicious!"

"Me?" Justin was incredulous. "What did I do that was suspicious?"

"What did you do that was not suspicious? You return to Winchester after witnessing a murder and you seek out the slain man's family. But not the sheriff—no, you vanish ere I can question you. Then you're back all of a sudden, prowling around, asking about the killing, even lurking out at the lazar house! It surprises you that I know about you and the lepers? This is my town, and you are indeed a fool if you thought your meddling would not get back to me!"

"Since when is it a crime to visit a lazar house? As for your serjeant, he followed me all the way from the abbey into town, even into a dark alley. I thought he meant to rob. What reasonable man would not?"

Luke did not appear impressed with Justin's explanation. "We can discuss what is reasonable and what is not," he said ominously, "back at the castle."

Dropping his hand to the hilt of his sword, the deputy gestured for Justin to surrender his own weapons. He was not about to do so, however. Who was to say what might befall him once he disappeared behind the castle walls with Luke de Marston? The tavern was utterly still, all eyes riveted upon the deputy, his serjeant, and the man they meant to arrest. Justin knew he could expect no help from any of the bystanders. He'd have to take on Luke and the serjeant both, not odds he fancied. The serjeant had a grievance to settle and Luke had the look of a born swordsman.

"Ere you do something you'll regret," he said tautly, "you'd best take a look at this."

"What?" Luke watched suspiciously as Justin drew a letter from his tunic and ordered his serjeant to be on the alert before he reached for it. Justin had a sudden, disturbing thought: what if the deputy could not read? He soon saw that this fear was unfounded. Luke gave him a hard, hostile stare, then picked up a candle from a nearby table and began to scan the parchment.

When he was done, Luke regarded Justin with open astonishment. "Well, well," he drawled, "you are full of surprises!" Turning, he told his serjeant to "Get yourself some wine," ignoring the man's dumbfounded bewilderment. Directing the wide-eyed serving maid to "Fetch us a flagon, sweetheart," he shoved a bench toward Justin's table and settled himself comfortably. Once Justin had done the same, Luke glanced around the tavern, warning the patrons that "The entertainment is over, so cease your gaping and go back to drinking yourselves sodden." Most did, or at least pretended to; Justin noticed that the looks they got after that were surreptitious.

Sliding the queen's letter across the table toward Justin, Luke waited until the serving maid brought them a flagon and two cups and withdrew out of earshot with obvious reluctance. "I suppose there is no point in asking why the Queen of England should be taking such an interest in the murder of a Winchester goldsmith. You're not about to tell me that, are you? But why investigate on your own? Why did you not come to me straightaway?"

Justin said nothing, trying to decide if Luke was in earnest.

Now that he was no longer fuming, his appearance had altered almost as dramatically as his demeanor. He was younger than Justin had initially thought, in his mid- to late twenties, with penetrating grass green eyes, thick, tawny hair, and sharply defined features that gave him the look of a hungry, golden hawk, handsome and predatory. Those unsettling hunter's eyes were fastened intently on Justin's face, questioning at first and then comprehending. "I see," he said evenly. "You think I had a hand in the goldsmith's death?"

"You must admit," Justin said, no less coolly, "that you have a most tempting motive for murder."

Luke regarded Justin impassively, then grinned unexpectedly. "Aldith is that, in truth. You've seen her, so I'll not dispute it. Nor will I claim that I shed any tears for Gervase Fitz Randolph. I did not mourn the man. But I did not murder him, either."

"I will pass your assurances on to the queen," Justin said, with lethal courtesy. He knew full well that this mention of Eleanor was a low blow, but he had the advantage for the moment and meant to make the most of it.

An angry shadow chased across Luke's face, but he showed now that he could rein in his temper when need be. "If not for that letter," he said bluntly, "I'd tell you to stuff your suspicions up your arse. But you are the queen's man and we both know that changes everything. So I'll tell you about Aldith and me. I love the woman. I've been besotted with her since the first day we met. Did I want to share her with Fitz Randolph? Of course I did not. Was I jealous? You know damned well that I was. Did I kill him? No, I did not. Even if I'd been sorely crazed enough to consider murder—and I was not—there was no need. Aldith chose me, not the goldsmith."

Justin did not trouble to hide his skepticism. "It is easy enough to say that now."

Luke smiled thinly. "Because Fitz Randolph is dead and Aldith a suspect witness in your eyes? It is true, nonetheless. You see, I was willing to offer her what the goldsmith could not—marriage."

Justin was taken aback. "You would have married her?"

Luke's head came up sharply. "I *will* marry her," he said, "as soon as we can post the banns." He sounded not so much defensive as defiant, and it was that which convinced Justin he was speaking the truth—at least about wanting to wed Aldith. Luke was gentry. Without knowing anything else about him, Justin did know that much, for only the wellborn were candidates for positions of authority. Aldith was no fit wife for a man with ambitions. Marrying her would not advance Luke's prospects; on the contrary. And for the first time, Justin's distrust of the deputy was tempered by a more positive emotion: a flicker of respect. Still, though, he had to ask. "If you were to wed, why was she still with Gervase?"

"For you to understand, you have to know about Aldith. Her life has not been easy. Her father was a potter at Michelmersh. That is a poor trade at best, and he was poorer than most, with few customers and too many mouths to feed. When Aldith was fifteen, her family married her off to a Winchester baker. The man was nigh on forty years older than she, tightfisted and sour tempered and poorly after their first year, when he was stricken by apoplexy. She was left a widow at twenty, with barely enough to bury him. It was then that she took up with Fitz Randolph."

Luke paused to drain his wine cup. "He was good to her, de Quincy. I do not like saying it, but it happens to be true. He was generous by nature, willing to help out her family. As for Aldith herself . . . well, he saw that she wanted for nothing. And she was grateful. She told me once that the one memory which stays green over the years is of going to bed hungry."

"So you are saying that after all he'd done for her, she was loath to hurt him?"

"Yes . . . that is exactly what I am saying." Luke's eyes met Justin's, challengingly, as if daring him to scoff. But it seemed plausible to Justin and he merely nodded. Somewhat mollified, Luke signaled for more wine before continuing. "She got me to promise that she could tell him in her own time and her own way. Aldith has ever been one for putting off unpleasantness, so I daresay she'd have delayed as long as she could. But she'd have told him. I'd have seen to that."

Justin didn't doubt it. If Aldith had been his woman, he'd have seen to that, too. "I've another question for you," he said, implicitly acknowledging by the change of subject that he believed Luke's account, an admission not lost upon Luke. "How did you know that I was in this tavern?"

Luke's smile was complacent. "My serjeant is not as inept as you think. True, his attempt to follow you was not a rousing success. I gather he could not have been more conspicuous if he'd worn a sack over his head. But he does have a few grains of common sense. Also, he knew I'd skin him alive if he reported that he'd lost you. After that friendly little joust in the alley, Wat was in dire need of an ale, or two or three. It occurred to him that you might have the same urgent thirst, so he crept back up the alley and peered into the tavern to see if he was right. Lucky for you he was no cutthroat or hired assassin."

"Yes, lucky," Justin said tersely, more annoyed with his own carelessness than with Luke's gibe. He still had a lot to learn about self-preservation.

"Do you want to tell me why you think the ambush was not a robbery gone wrong? Or do I have to guess?"

Justin felt a flash of irritation, but Luke's sarcasm notwithstanding, he had a right to know. "I have reason to believe that it was no random robbery. The outlaws were lying in wait for Fitz Randolph." And as concisely as possible, he told Luke why he was sure that was so.

"You're right," Luke agreed, as soon as Justin had concluded. "It does sound like a hired killing. But done at whose behest? Was I your only suspect? Flattering as that might be, where does that leave us now?" He looked quizzically across the table at Justin, and then scowled. "By God, you did not think that Aldith. . . ?"

"Make yourself easy. She was never a suspect." A corner of Justin's mouth quirked. "In truth, I could not imagine any woman wanting you badly enough to commit murder."

"Likewise." The corners of Luke's mouth were twitching, too. "So who else wanted the man dead? Any family squabbles I ought to know about? I seem to remember Aldith telling me that the son was at odds with the old man, wanting to be a priest?"

"A monk. And yes, he is a suspect—one of several. The daughter is in love with Fitz Randolph's journeyman, but he was set upon wedding her to a wellborn widower. And Fitz Randolph's brother argued with him often about money and is now as nervous as a treed cat."

" 'And a man's foes shall be they of his own household.' " Luke shook his head, then smiled ruefully. "I'm not usually one for quoting from Scriptures, but there is nothing usual about any of this, is there? How often do we find the Queen of England somehow linked to a goldsmith? Let's start with the ambush itself and track from there. Do you think you could identify the outlaws?"

"I never got a close look at the man trying to hold onto Fitz Randolph's stallion. He was uncommonly tall and big boned, but that is all I can tell you. I did see the one who did the stabbing, though. I can even give you a name; his partner called him 'Gib.' "

"Gilbert? There are more Gilberts roaming the countryside than we could hope to count. A pity he had not been christened something less popular, like Drogo or Barnabus. What did this 'Gib' look like?"

"Of middle height and build, with brown hair. I never got close enough to tell eye color for certes, but I'd say dark. As for age, I'd guess closer to thirty than forty. And he was Saxon, not Norman. They both were, for they were speaking English."

"You've a sharp eye," Luke said approvingly. "But is there anything you might have forgotten?" All business now, he leaned across the table. Justin had seen such single-minded intensity before, usually on the hunting field. "Sometimes a witness will overlook a small detail," Luke explained, "thinking it insignificant. Most often it is, but every now and then . . . I once solved a murder because the killer dropped a key near the body. Is there anything else that you've not told me?"

That was an awkward question, for there was a great deal Justin was concealing: that blood-stained letter, a royal captive in Austria, the shadow cast by the French king. "Well," he said finally, "there was something. It sounds foolish and most likely means nothing, but I thought I saw a snake."

Luke's hand froze on the flagon. "A snake?"

Justin nodded. "I know what you're thinking. Snakes den up

during the winter months. So why would one be slithering about on the Alresford Road? But it sure as hellfire looked like a snake!"

"It was. I can tell you that for certes. I can also tell you who killed Gervase Fitz Randolph—a misbegotten whoreson known as Gilbert the Fleming."

Luke smiled grimly at the expression of amazement on Justin's face. "This is not the first time he has made use of that snake trick, so I can even tell you how he did it. He found a snake's burrow, dug it out, put it in a sack, and then flung it out into the road as the goldsmith and groom rode by. Nothing spooks horses as much as snakes do—it's an almost foolproof way to get a man thrown."

"That would explain why their horses bolted without warning. What do you know about this man?"

"That hanging is too good for him," Luke said harshly. "Gilbert is a local lad, although he long since moved on to London; better pickings there, I suppose. But he comes back to visit his kinfolk, and last summer he was implicated in a brutal double murder here. He ambushed a merchant and his wife on the Southampton Road, he and another devil's whelp. The man, they killed outright. After raping the woman, Gilbert took his blade to her, and left her to bleed to death by the side of the road. Our Gib does not believe in leaving witnesses behind; so much tidier that way. But the merchant's wife did not die, not right away. She lived long enough to tell about the snake and the ambush and to put a rope about Gilbert's wretched neck."

"Christ have pity," Justin said softly.

"I spent every waking hour hunting them down. We caught his partner, tried him, and then hanged him out on Andover Road. But Gilbert had the devil's own luck and somehow got away. I heard that he'd gone back to London and I warned the sheriffs there to keep an eye out for him, but London is a big enough log to hide any number of maggots. I suppose Gilbert decided enough time had gone by for him to risk returning. God rot him, but he has never lacked for nerve."

"Why is he called Gilbert the Fleming? You said he is Winchester born and bred; did his family come over from Flanders?"

"They call him that," Luke said, "because he is so handy with a knife. Have you not heard men say that there is nothing sharper than a Fleming's blade?"

Justin nodded somberly, chilled to think what would have happened to Edwin had he not gone back in answer to that cry for help. "Do you think you can find him?"

"If I do not, it'll not be for want of trying. At first light, I'll get the word out on the street, and we'll keep his family so closely watched that they'll not be able to burp without one of my men hearing." With that, Luke pushed the bench out and stood up. "I have to get back to the castle. I was in the midst of an interrogation when Wat came bursting in. I'll let you know what I find out about Gilbert. Meanwhile, de Quincy, stay out of alleys." He grinned, then signaled to the tavern owner. "Rayner, put his drinks on my account."

Collecting Wat, the deputy swaggered out, the focal point of all eyes. Justin caught the tavern owner's glowering in his direction and transformed the man's frown to a grateful smile by deliberately dropping some coins onto the table. He knew very well that Luke never paid for the bills he ran up in taverns and alehouses; he'd see free drinks as one of the many perquisites of his office.

After Luke's departure, the tavern patrons settled back to their drinks and their draughts games and their gossip. Justin slouched down in his seat, trying to ignore the curious looks being aimed his way. He needed solitude to assess what the deputy had told him. Could he truly trust Luke de Marston? If so, he'd gained an invaluable ally. If not, he might not live to regret it.

6

WINCHESTER

January 1193

Winchester Castle was easy to find; it claimed more than four acres in the southwest corner of the city. Justin was admitted without difficulty, for he had the password—the name of Luke de Marston. The sky above his head looked frozen and foreboding, and there was a threat of snow in the air. It may have been the weather, but Justin felt a distinct chill as he crossed the bailey. He knew the castle was often used as a royal residence, but he found it inhospitable and unwelcoming. Was it because he knew Eleanor had occasionally been confined here during those long years as a captive queen? Or because he still had a few lingering doubts about Luke's good faith?

It was too late to worry about that, though, for Luke had come into view, swerving at sight of Justin. Falling into step beside the deputy, Justin gave him a sideways, curious glance. "So . . . how did the interrogation go? Did the suspect confess?"

"What do you think?"

"You missed your calling, Luke. With your knack for getting men to see the error of their ways, you ought to have been a priest."

Luke fought back a smile. "What brings you here, de Quincy? Any more secrets you forgot to tell me about? Let me guess . . . in your spare time, you spy for the Pope? You're a royal prince incognito? You know the whereabouts of King Richard?"

Justin burst out laughing. If Luke only knew! "Alas, nothing so dramatic. As far as I know, I've not a drop of royal blood. But I may have a way to flush out our killer."

Luke stopped abruptly. "How so?"

"I thought," Justin said, "to put the cat amongst the pigeons."

Luke listened intently, not interrupting until Justin was done. "Well," he said thoughtfully, "it is worth trying. Of course it might make you a target." He paused then, very deliberately. "But I suppose I could live with that."

Justin grinned. "I'll take that," he said, "as your odd way of wishing me good luck!"

From the castle, Justin headed for Gervase Fitz Randolph's goldsmith shop. It was open for business, the unicorn sign swaying precariously in the wind, the shutters thrown back, a sound of hammering coming from within. Miles was working at the anvil, pounding gold into gold leaf. He looked up with a startled smile when Justin said his name.

"You're back, are you? Come on in." Setting the hammer down, he unlatched the little gate in the corner so Justin could enter. Thinking it had been more fun to vault over the counter, Justin stepped inside and came over to watch as Miles smoothed the parchment protecting the gold foil.

"Are you on your own today, Miles?"

"No . . . Guy is in the rear, heating up the forge. Tom was supposed to be in, too, but he has not shown up yet. I guess men of God need not keep regular hours like the rest of us."

Justin found it interesting that Miles seemed far less indulgent of Thomas's erratic work habits than he had at their last meeting. "Thomas is still set, then, upon taking holy vows?"

"More than ever. He is making life so wretched for the household that his mother and uncle will have no choice but to give in." Miles was taking a decidedly protective attitude toward Jonet's family, sounding more like a prospective son-in-law and less like an employee. Before Justin could pursue this further, the door to the rear room swung open.

Guy looked healthier; his color was better. His surprise at seeing Justin was evident. After a conspicuous pause, he mustered up a remote smile. "What brings you back to Winchester, Master de Quincy?"

"Your brother's murder."

"I do not understand," Guy said slowly. "What is there left to do for Gervase but mourn him?"

"How about catching his killers?"

"Naturally I hope the sheriff captures the outlaws. I also hope for an early spring, a good harvest, and that my dolt of a nephew comes to his senses. But I would not wager money on any of those hopes. Outlaws rarely answer for their crimes, at least in this life."

"That may well be, but I was not talking about the outlaws. I meant the ones who paid them."

Guy gasped loudly. "What sort of daft talk is that? My brother was slain by bandits!"

"I know. I was there. But it was no chance robbery. We have reason to believe that the outlaws were hired to ambush your brother."

"I think you've lost your wits! Where would you get such an absurd suspicion?"

"I overheard something in those woods. But it was only later—after I talked to the under-sheriff—that we realized what it meant."

"Luke de Marston believes this lunacy, too?"

"He does, Master Fitz Randolph."

Miles had been listening, openmouthed. "This makes no sense. Who would want Master Gervase dead?"

"That is what we mean to find out . . . and why I am here. I wanted to assure you that we will not stop until we learn the truth, even if we have to poke into every corner of Gervase's life and unearth all his secrets."

Guy had gone very white. "I have never heard anything so preposterous. My brother had no enemies. Why do you suspect a plot? What in Christ's Name did you hear in the woods?"

"I am sorry," Justin said, politely but firmly. "I cannot tell you that."

Guy's pallor was suddenly blotched with hot, hectic color. "You cannot possibly suspect one of us!"

"Did I say that?" Justin asked blandly. "We have no suspects . . . yet. I came here merely to tell you how the investigation is progressing, and to promise you that we will not rest until Gervase Fitz Randolph gets justice."

"I think we ought to talk to the sheriff about this, Master Guy." Miles was frowning, running a hand nervously through his sleek blond hair, for once indifferent to his appearance. "I am not sure that we can trust Luke de Marston. Or this man de Quincy either, if it comes to that. What do we know about him, after all?"

Guy looked at the journeyman blankly, saying nothing. Justin decided it was time to go. He'd planted the seeds; now they needed a chance to sprout.

They watched in silence as he left the shop. But he could feel their eyes boring into his back all the while. Acting on instinct, he turned into the first doorway he came to. He had not long to wait. Within moments, Guy emerged from the shop. Still wearing his leather smith's apron, he crossed the street without even a glance toward oncoming traffic and stumbled through a narrow doorway.

Justin crossed the street, too. A wilting branch drooped from a crooked ale-pole, and the door's paint was peeled and cracked. Inside, the alehouse was no less dingy, dank and foul smelling. Slumped at a corner table, Guy was clutching unsteadily at a large tankard. As Justin watched from the doorway, Gervase's brother drank deeply of the ale, spilling almost as much as he swallowed.

After leaving Guy awash in ale, Justin paid a surreptitious visit to the Fitz Randolph stable, where he briefed Edwin. He did not want to jeopardize the groom's job in any way, and Edwin needed to be warned that his name would echo like an obscenity in Fitz Randolph ears from now on. He'd wondered if he'd have trouble convincing Edwin. Not only did Edwin believe him, he had to talk the groom out of volunteering to spy on his behalf, so appalled was he that a member of the goldsmith's own family might have had a hand in his death. Justin made Edwin promise not to do anything foolhardy and left him pondering suspects.

As he wandered along the Cheapside, Justin noticed a crowd gathering up ahead. Quickening his pace, he saw that the attraction was a peddler's cart. The peddler was unkempt and greying, but he had a glib tongue and a practiced spiel, and for good measure, a small monkey on a chain. Banging on cymbals and turning cartwheels, the monkey soon had the spectators laughing at its antics, and the peddler then launched his hard sell, extolling the virtues of his wares.

The cart was well stocked with wooden combs, razors, needles, vinegar, salt, and the oil of olives, poppies, and almonds. Joking with his customers, the peddler seemed to have a product for every need. Wormwood for fleas. Sage for headache or fever. Green leeches for bloodletting. Agrimony boiled in milk as a restorative for lust. Senna as a purgative. Candied quince for anyone with a sweet tooth. Bantering with the men, flirting with the women, the peddler was soon doing a brisk business.

Justin paused to watch, amused by the haggling. He'd been there a few moments when he caught a whiff of perfume. He'd encountered it only once before, but he recognized it immediately, for Aldith Talbot had burned her way into his memory like a brand. As she came up beside him, he greeted her with a defensive coolness. He had not forgotten how she had used him to make Luke jealous, but his pulse still speeded up at sight of her.

"What a pity," she said, "that the peddler has no apologies for sale, neatly wrapped and ready to go. I owe you at least a dozen, mayhap more."

"In truth," Justin said, "I'd rather have an explanation than an apology."

Aldith's smile was rueful. "I was afraid you'd say that." Linking her arm in his, she drew him away from the crowd surrounding the peddler's cart. "If I tell you, it will be just between us?" When he nodded, she was quiet for a moment, considering her response. "I wanted to make sure that Luke did not get skittish about our wedding."

"Why would you worry about that?"

"I suppose I was being foolish. But I feared that Luke might have second thoughts about the wisdom of marrying me. It is not the most prudent of matches, after all. I am older than he is, my liaison with Gervase was known throughout Winchester, and I may not be the most fertile of wives. I have gotten with child only twice, and both times I miscarried of the babe. How could I blame Luke if he had qualms about the marriage?"

"Wisdom has naught to do with it. The man is besotted with you. He told me so last night."

"Did he . . . truly?" This time her smile was blinding. "He can be sparing with the words . . . except in bed, of course," she added, with a low laugh. "But what you men say in bed is not always gospel, is it?"

Justin laughed, too. "You do not really expect me to answer that?"

She shook her head, still laughing, and Justin found himself hoping that Luke did indeed mean to marry her. He'd sounded sincere, but Justin knew there were men who hunted for the thrill of the chase, losing interest once their quarry was brought to bay. For Aldith's sake, he hoped that Luke was not one of them.

Aldith's moods were as changeable as those blue-green eyes of hers. No longer playful, she was regarding Justin pensively. "Do you truly think that one of Gervase's own family plotted his death?"

Justin was not surprised that Luke had confided in Aldith. From what he'd seen of the deputy in action, Luke followed his instincts, caring little if rules were broken in the process. "I think someone did, but I cannot say if it was a family member, not yet. You probably know them better than I do, Mistress Aldith. If you had to choose, who would seem most likely to you?"

"I cannot say that I know them well. Mainly, I saw them through Gervase's eyes. If I had to pick, though, I'd say Thomas."

"Interesting. Edwin is convinced that Jonet and Miles are the culprits."

"What say you, Justin? Who do you suspect?"

"Guy." Justin smiled, without humor. "I might as well flip a coin. It is all conjecture and suspicion, cobwebs and smoke. Unless I can prove—"

He stopped so abruptly that Aldith looked at him in surprise. He was staring over her shoulder, so intently that she turned to look, too. Seeing nothing out of the ordinary, she started to ask, "Is something wrong?" But by then Justin was gone.

Justin shoved his way through the crowd, heedless of the complaints and curses trailing in his wake. His quarry had darted around the peddler's cart. Hearing the footsteps behind him, he

ducked into an alley and turned his back, like a man seeking a
place to relieve himself. Justin followed, grabbed his shoulder,
and swung him around.

Durand showed an aplomb that was glazed in ice; he didn't
even blink. "What do you want?" His lip curled. "If you're begging, I have nothing to spare. A man able bodied ought to work
for his bread or do without. And if you've robbery in mind, you'd
best be ready to die unshriven."

"My mistake," Justin said, stepping aside. With the most dis-
agreeable smile he had ever seen, Durand brushed past him. Justin waited until he'd reached the alley entrance. "My mistake,"
he repeated, with a disdainful smile of his own. "I confused you
with a blustering knave called Durand."

The other man's sangfroid was capable of being shaken, after
all, at least briefly, for the look he gave Justin was murderous.
After he'd gone, Justin slowly unclenched his fist from the hilt of
his sword. He'd acted on impulse and was beginning to regret it.
Durand had been spying on him, but why? He could think of
only one person who'd have put the knight on his trail. It was that
troubling realization which had fueled his anger; he'd turned on
Durand the fury he could not let loose upon the queen's son.

He'd not deny the confrontation had given him some satisfaction. For a few moments, he'd not felt like a pawn, a cat's-paw in
a conspiracy of kings. Now, though, he wondered if he'd been
too rash. Was it ever wise to challenge John outright?

Starting back toward High Street, he felt as if he'd blundered
into a labyrinth, murky and serpentine, for that was how he envisioned the workings of John's brain. What was Durand's mission? Could it be more sinister than mere spying? And what
would John do now that his man had been found out? But was
Durand likely to tell John that he'd been outwitted?

The peddler was no longer selling his wares. Instead, he was
embroiled in a shouting match with an angry youth, surrounded
by an interested audience. Aldith was standing on the edge of the
crowd and moved quickly to intercept Justin as he drew near.
"What happened? Where in the world did you go?"

"I thought I saw someone I knew." To head off further questions, Justin pointed toward the men. "What is that all about . . . a disgruntled customer?"

"No, a rival. The lad is from the apothecary shop across the way and wants the peddler to move on ere they lose all their customers."

Justin had no interest in a territorial dispute between merchants. "May I escort you home, Mistress Aldith?" he offered. "It is the least I can do after dashing off with nary a word to you."

She smiled and let him take her arm. He suspected that she'd be flirting with the priest on her deathbed; in that, she reminded him of the dark-eyed Claudine. They were threading their way through the crowd when people began to move aside in haste. Pointing toward the approaching horsemen, the apothecary's apprentice cried out triumphantly, "We sent to the castle to fetch the under-sheriff. You'll be on your way soon enough now, old man, with your tail tucked between your legs!"

The peddler spat an obscenity, then elbowed the youth aside so he could be the first to tell his side to the sheriff's deputy. Luke was mounted on a sorrel stallion. Reining in, he signaled a halt to his flanking serjeants, his eyes taking in the scene, lingering longest upon Justin and Aldith, standing together in the street.

Dismounting, Luke was assailed by competing voices, all eager to enlighten him about the cause of this public disturbance. The noise did not abate until he shouted for silence. It did not take him long to resolve the dispute, finding in the apothecary's favor. The peddler was resentful, but shrewd enough to realize this was a fight he could not win, and he agreed to move on. Luke wasted no further time on them, striding over to Aldith and Justin.

He greeted Aldith by pressing a quick kiss into her palm. It was a simple act, but done in public, it took on symbolic significance, and Aldith glowed. When he suggested that she buy him some candied quince before the peddler packed up, she tactfully pretended to believe he had a sudden craving for sweets. Luke then jerked his head away from the peddler's customers and Justin followed.

"Well?" the deputy demanded. "What happened at the

goldsmithy? Did they buzz about when you jabbed your stick into their hive?"

"They took it badly, which was to be expected. Were they all as innocent as God's own angels, they'd still be dismayed by the news I brought. By the time I was done speaking, they'd gone from bereaved to suspect. Even Miles saw that quick enough. But Guy seemed well and truly stricken. When I said we'd be digging into Gervase's past, he turned the color of curdled milk and fled to the closest alehouse."

"Did he now? Men who try to drink away their troubles can drown in them, too. And when they start flailing about, they give up the truth more often than not. I think I'll pay a visit to Master Guy this noon."

Justin nodded approvingly. "How goes the hunt for Gilbert the Fleming? Have you had any luck yet?"

"I might have a lead later this afternoon. But I can deal with only one crime at a time. Murder or poaching—which shall it be, de Quincy?"

Justin was not surprised; he'd seen flashes of the deputy's jealousy before. "You need not worry about poaching, Luke. I'm not one for hunting in another man's woods."

Luke's smile was almost too fleeting to catch. "I'm reassured to hear that you're so law abiding." Adding, "Stop by the cottage tonight after Compline and I'll let you know what I found out."

The snow had never materialized and stars were beginning to glimmer in the sky as Justin emerged from the abbey guest hall that evening. He'd taken only a few steps when he was accosted by a hooded, mantled figure. He knew this wasn't Durand—not tall enough—and assumed it was one of the monks. But when he raised his lantern, the candle's wavering light illuminated the angry face of Gervase Fitz Randolph's son.

"What sort of crazed quest are you on? Why are you meddling like this in my father's death?"

"You do not want your father's killers to be found?"

"Damn you, do not twist my words!" Thomas was almost incoherent with rage, his mouth contorted, eyes bulging and bloodshot. "My father was slain in a robbery. All this talk of hired killers is utter nonsense. But it is the sort of gossip that people will be eager to spread about, and some fools might even believe it. Let it be, you hear me! Let it be!"

"I can do nothing for you, Thomas. If you have a complaint, I suggest that you take it up with Luke de Marston."

Thomas would have argued further, but Justin was already brushing past him. "I am warning you, de Quincy!" he shouted. "If you jeopardize my chances of being admitted to the Benedictine order, you'll regret it till your dying day!"

"I'll keep that in mind," Justin promised and walked on. He'd not have been surprised if Thomas had followed him. But the goldsmith's son stayed where he was, watching as Justin crossed the garth. When he reached the gatehouse, Thomas suddenly shouted again. By that time, though, Justin was too far away to hear.

A stew simmered upon the hearth, and Aldith was busy stirring and tasting, assuring the men that it would soon be on the table. She'd insisted that Justin stay for supper, delighted by this opportunity to play the role of Luke's wife, not merely his bedmate. The two men retired to the settle with cups of malmsey and Aldith's gigantic Jezebel. Watching with amusement as Luke was overwhelmed by a display of slobbering mastiff affection, Justin told the deputy about his abbey encounter with Thomas Fitz Randolph.

Luke finally managed to shove the adoring mastiff off the settle. "I'll not need a bath for a week," he said, grimacing. "The more I learn about our little monk, the better he looks as a suspect in the goldsmith's killing."

"What about the brother? If ever I've met an unquiet soul, it is his. No one could be that fretful and uneasy and not be guilty of something!"

Luke grinned. "As it happens, you're right. After we spoke in Cheapside, I went looking for Guy. I found him still at that alehouse, sodden and wallowing in self-pity. It was almost too easy to bluff him into believing I knew all. He cracked like an egg, no sport whatsoever. He was indeed guilty as you suspected, but of embezzlement, not murder."

"So that was it!"

Luke nodded. "He took care of their accounts and kept the records, whilst Gervase sought to attract wealthy customers like the Archbishop of Rouen. A few months ago, Guy began to divert some of their funds to his own use and altered the accounts to hide his pilfering. His defense was that Gervase was a hopeless spendthrift and he was just putting aside money so they'd not fall deeply in debt. But somehow or other, the money got spent and all he's got left is a tattered conscience. The poor sot had convinced himself that he was going to Hell and gaol, not necessarily in that order."

"What did you do, Luke? Did you arrest him?"

"Worse—I turned him over to his sister-in-law! I took him home to Dame Ella and made him confess to her, too. She reacted as I expected, with dismay and disbelief and then righteous indignation, watered with a few tears. But when I asked if she wanted him hauled off to gaol, she ruffled up her feathers like a hen defending her chicks. Indeed not, this was a family matter, no concern of the law, and she'd thank me not to meddle further."

"You knew she'd not want him arrested."

"Of course I did. And not just because of the scandal it would cause. With her husband dead and her son set upon taking holy vows, she needs Guy more than ever. She'll make peace with him, for she has no choice. But Guy's guilt will give her the upper hand, and for a widow, that's not a bad thing to have."

Justin took a swallow of the malmsey, found it too sweet for his taste. "What of the Fleming? You said you had a lead?"

"I might. My men spent the day rousting Gilbert's kin and lowlife friends, warning that none of them will have any peace until we get the Fleming. I think one of his cousins may be willing to give him up, for there is no love lost between them. When I saw Kenrick this morn, he claimed to know nothing about Gilbert's whereabouts. But he said he might be able to find out and would send me word if he did. He will expect to be paid, though. Since the queen's coffers are far deeper than the sheriff's, this will be your debt, de Quincy."

"Fair enough," Justin agreed. "What of Gilbert's partner? He might be easier to track down. From what you've told me about the Fleming, that one is more slippery than those snakes of his."

"I've put the word out that I'll pay for the man's name. And most felons and brigands would sell their own mothers for the price of an ale. It may take time, but someone will offer up Gilbert's accomplice."

Justin hoped he was right. Only the outlaws could give him the answers he needed, and Gilbert did not sound like a man who'd be cooperative even if he was caught. They might have better luck with the partner. "Spread some money around," he said. "I'll pay for the bait."

They deferred further discussion of the Fleming until the meal was done; talk of bloody killings was no fit seasoning for Aldith's stew. She had just served wafers drizzled with honey when her mastiff began to growl.

The knock was soft, tentative. When Luke unbarred the door, the lantern light revealed a thin youngster of twelve or thirteen, his shoulders hunched against the cold. Aldith took one look at his patched mantle and ushered him into the cottage, toward the hearth. His teeth were chattering, and when he stretched his hands toward the fire, they were swollen with chilblains. "My papa sent me," he whispered, looking everywhere but at Luke's face. "He said he'll meet you at the mill tonight after Compline."

Luke grabbed for his mantle. "This is Kenrick's eldest," he told Justin. "Come on, lad, we'll get you home first."

The boy shrank back. "Nay . . . my papa said I'm not to be seen with you. He said it was not safe." When Aldith offered him a wafer, he crammed it into his mouth, seeming to inhale it rather than eat it, so fast did it disappear. He remembered to thank her, though, before disappearing into the night again.

They traveled on foot, in the shadow of the city's north wall. In the distance, church bells had begun to chime. Justin tilted his head, hearing their echoes on the wind. "Compline is being rung. We'll be late."

"He'll wait for us. But if I'd hitched my stallion outside the mill, he'd have bolted for certes. No one can know about this, not if Kenrick hopes to make old bones. It is not only the Fleming he must worry about. If it becomes known that he's given Gilbert up, the rest of his family will make his life utter misery. Their Eleventh Commandment is 'Thou shalt never talk to the law.' "

"Why did he pick this mill for the meeting?"

"It lies beyond the city walls and no one will be around at this late hour. And in case he is seen, he has an excuse for being there; he works for the Durngate miller. Likely as not, you'll find him as skittish as an unbroken colt. But I do not blame him for being scared, de Quincy."

Neither did Justin. It would take a brave man to betray Gilbert the Fleming. Or a desperate one, he thought, remembering the boy's ragged mantle. Well, he'd see that Kenrick was generously rewarded. The queen would not begrudge a few shillings. She'd willingly pay that a hundredfold to resolve her suspicions about the French king.

They exited the city through the Durn Gate, tucked away in the northeast corner of the wall, and headed for the mill. They soon saw the gleam of water ahead. It was a clear, cloudless night and the River Itchen looked silvered and serene in the moonlight, but very cold. Not far from the bridge, it had been channeled into a millrace, and as the men drew nearer, they could see the waterwheel. It was motionless, for the sluice gate was down. It seemed strange to Justin not to hear the familiar creaking and splashing. The silence was eerie; all he could hear was the faint gurgling of the millrace. It was dark, too; not a flicker of light shone through the mill's shuttered windows.

"So Kenrick waited, did he?" he gibed softly.

"He'd not have gone off," Luke insisted, "no matter how late I was. He must be inside." Scowling over his shoulder at Justin, he strode toward the door. His knocking went unanswered. When he pushed the latch, though, the door swung inward.

They exchanged glances and, by common consent, loosened their swords in their scabbards before stepping inside. Justin was getting a bad feeling about this, and he could see that Luke was edgy, too. But their lantern light revealed nothing out of order. The floor was dirty: flour and chaff were everywhere and the hulls of spilled grain crunched underfoot as they moved cautiously into the room. The inner wheel took up most of the space, attached to a spindle that disappeared up into a hole in the ceiling. The overhead chamber put Justin in mind of a barn hayloft; a ladder in the corner provided access, and during working hours, Kenrick could peer over the edge to make sure the wheel was functioning properly. But now it was like gazing up into a vast, black cave. Even when Luke raised the lantern high, it could not penetrate the shadows above them.

Luke swore under his breath. "Where did he go? This makes no sense."

Justin shrugged. "Mayhap he is late, too?" He at once saw the problem with that explanation, though. Then why was the door unlatched? One of the ladder rungs seemed muddied. When he got closer, he saw that it was dry, days old. He was turning toward Luke when he felt something wet drip onto his hand. His breath caught. Backing away from the ladder, he looked up as another dribble of blood splattered onto the floor at his feet.

Luke had not yet noticed the blood, but he was alerted by Justin's body language. When he crossed the room, Justin held out his hand so that the lantern's gleam fell upon that glistening red droplet. Luke's eyes flew upward. For unmeasured moments, neither man moved, straining to hear. But no sound came from the loft. No creaking of the floorboards, no giveaway gasps of pent-up breath, nothing. Justin's thoughts were racing as fast as his pulse. Should one of them go get a torch? But that might be leaving the other one alone with a killer.

Luke had reached the same conclusion. Using hand signals, he communicated to Justin that he was going partway up the ladder so he could get a look into the interior of the loft. That did not strike Justin as the best idea he'd ever heard, but he had no better one to offer. Nodding tensely, he brushed back his mantle so he could draw his sword swiftly if need be. Luke simply unfastened his mantle, letting it drop to the floor. Justin was impressed by his coolness, until he noticed Luke's white-knuckled grip on the lantern. Luke paused and then, one slow rung at a time, began to climb toward the loft.

Luke paused again at the halfway point and held the lantern up as high as he could reach. Glancing down at Justin, he mouthed the word "Nothing." It was then that a man erupted from the darkness above, lunged forward to grab the ladder, and shoved. Luke yelled as the ladder started to tip and Justin managed to catch hold of a lower rung. For several desperate seconds, he struggled to keep the ladder upright. But it was swaying like a tree in a high wind, and before Luke could jump free, it went over backward. Justin dived out of the way in the nick of time. There was a thud, a gasp from Luke, and then darkness as the lantern light died.

The silence was broken almost at once by Luke. He did not sound as if his injuries were serious, not by the way he was cursing. Groping about blindly, Justin was trying to untangle the deputy from the ladder when new noises came from the loft. "Christ," Luke cried hoarsely, "he's going out the window! Go after him!" But Justin had also recognized the sound—shutters being flung open—and he was already lurching to his feet. Memory serving him better than eyesight, he plunged toward the door.

It was a relief to get outside, where he had stars for candles. He halted long enough to draw his sword, for he knew his enemy. It was Gilbert the Fleming whom they'd cornered in the loft; when he'd pushed the ladder, he'd been exposed to the lantern's flaring light. It was a brief glimpse, but for Justin, enough. The face of evil had never looked so familiar.

Running around the side of the mill, Justin was half expecting to find the Fleming crumpled on the ground under the window, for the snow was days old and hard packed. But when he rounded the corner, there was no broken body, no blood, only churned-up snow and footprints leading toward a copse of trees.

Justin slowed as he neared the trees, for never had he hunted such a dangerous quarry, capable of turning at bay the way a wild boar would. But nothing mattered more to him at that moment than catching this man. He moved into the shelter of a massive oak, his ears echoing with an odd, muffled drumbeat, the accelerated pounding of his own heart. Was the Fleming lying in wait behind one of these trees? Or fleeing in panic into the deeper snowdrifts? Did he ever feel panic—like other men?

The outlaw's footprints were still visible, scuffed in the moonlight, and Justin followed them. He thought he heard Luke's voice behind him, but he dared not answer, for he did not know how close the Fleming was. He stopped to listen again, and then he was running, caution forgotten.

But he was too late. Coming to a halt, he stood watching as a horseman broke free of the trees ahead. Justin was still standing there when Luke finally came panting into view.

"He got away?"

"He had a horse tethered amongst the trees."

Luke was quiet for a moment, then said savagely, "God rot him!"

Justin heartily concurred. They walked back in silence. Luke was limping, but he shrugged off Justin's query with a brusque "No bones broken."

They were almost upon the mill when they saw a light bobbing off to their left. A man was standing on the other side of the millrace, holding a lantern aloft. "What is going on?" he challenged, managing to sound both truculent and ill at ease.

"You live hereabouts?"

He nodded, bridling at Luke's peremptory tone, and gestured vaguely over his shoulder. When Luke demanded that he yield his lantern, he started to protest—until the deputy identified himself, tersely but profanely.

Trailing after them as they approached the mill, he kept asking questions neither one answered. Justin crossed the threshold with a leaden step. Luke blocked the doorway, instructing the anxious neighbor to wait outside. Glancing then at Justin, he said, "Let's get this over with."

After Justin righted the ladder, Luke crossed the room, still limping, and began to climb. Justin followed, and scrambled up into the loft to find Luke standing beside a man's body. Blood was spattered on both millstones, soaking into the floor. Gilbert's cousin lay upon his back, eyes open, mouth contorted. As Justin moved closer, he saw that Kenrick had been stabbed in the chest, a knife thrust up under his ribs—like Gervase Fitz Randolph. But when Luke shifted the lantern, they saw that his throat had also been cut.

7

WINCHESTER

January 1193

The sky had begun to lighten toward the east, mother-of-pearl faintly tinged with rose. Justin kept his eyes on that brightening horizon. Rarely had he been so glad to see a night end. He was exhausted, for the hours after the discovery of Kenrick's body had been filled with activity, much of it unpleasant.

Luke had raised the hue and cry in Winnal, the hamlet north-east of the city walls, to make sure none of the householders had given Gilbert shelter, willingly or otherwise. The body had to be removed, taken to St John's, the closest church. The mill had to be searched and then put under guard. And Kenrick's wife and children had to be told of his death.

That had been as painful a duty as any Justin had ever undertaken. He'd counted six children, most too young to comprehend their mother's stunned, stifled grieving. He and Luke had escorted her to the church, for she would have no hand but hers wash her husband and make him ready for burial. Having found neighboring women to tend the sleepy, bewildered children, they were now returning to the scene of the Fleming's latest killing, arriving back at the mill soon after daybreak.

As early as it was, there was a large, curious crowd gathered outside, for word of the murder had spread like wood smoke. They found Luke's serjeant Wat arguing heatedly with a portly, red-faced man who turned out to be the Durngate miller. He seemed to be taking the death of his hired man in stride, but he was furious that he'd not be able to open his mill, and began to argue with Luke as soon as they'd dismounted, complaining that he'd lose money if he had to turn away customers.

Luke pushed past the miller as if he weren't there. When he

106

started to follow, the deputy swung around. "It would be a great pity, Abel, if you were to trip and fall into the millrace. Of course if you did, we'd fish you out—eventually." The miller looked outraged, but he showed that he was not an utter fool by backing off. Leaving his serjeant to deal with Abel, Luke entered the mill, with Justin a step behind.

In the light of day, the mill was even dirtier. Luke glanced around with distaste, then made for the ladder. Justin followed reluctantly. There was more blood than he remembered. Abel would have a hard time scrubbing those millstones clean, if indeed he bothered. "What I do not understand," he said, "is how the killing took place up here. Did Gilbert force him into the loft at knifepoint, and if so, why?"

"Kenrick was already up here," Luke said, beckoning Justin toward a far corner of the loft. "See that napkin? The bread crumbs and grease stains on it? This was Kenrick's last meal. He brought along his supper to eat whilst he waited for me. But the Fleming got here first."

"How did Gilbert get in?"

"Kenrick may have left the door unbarred for me. Or more likely, Gilbert forced it. Take a look at the latch ere we leave. It was half rusted off. Abel is not one for making repairs."

A vivid imagination could be a burden. Justin was able to envision all too well how it must have been for Kenrick, trapped in the loft, looking down and seeing his cousin below. "Why did he not knock the ladder down, yell for help, fight back?"

"Have you ever seen a cornered rabbit? They freeze sometimes; fear can do that. Or it may be that Gilbert was friendly at first. Since most people are good at believing what they want to be true, Kenrick may have convinced himself that Gilbert's visit was pure chance—and not because he'd learned that Kenrick had been asking too many questions. With Gilbert, a man need only let down his guard for the blink of an eye. Nothing strikes faster than a snake, de Quincy."

The shutters were still open. Crossing to the window, Luke looked out. "Come here," he said, "and look at this tree. See that broken branch? I was wondering how that whoreson got out without breaking his wretched neck. I think he leaped toward the tree; it is almost close enough to reach. He caught hold of that branch and then dropped down to the ground."

One glance at that sagging tree branch was enough to convince Justin that Luke's conjecture was very plausible. "Is that man's luck never going to run out? How often does he get—"

A sudden uproar below drowned out the rest of Justin's words. The door banged and a man burst into the mill, shaking off Wat's restraining hold. "Tell this fool I can enter, de Marston," he demanded. "I've a right to be here!" He was a stranger to Justin, a man in his sixties, grizzled and gaunt, with hollowed eyes rimmed in red, a mouth not shaped for smiling. "I want to see," he said harshly, "where my son died."

"Let him go, Wat." Luke moved to the edge of the loft. "Come on up, Ivo."

Ivo climbed the ladder with difficulty, glaring at Justin when he offered a hand. He halted before the millstones, staring down at the bloodstains. "You had to meddle," he said, "and look what you caused. You got my boy killed!"

Luke's mouth twisted. "I was not the one wielding the knife. This was your nephew's doing, not mine."

"Gib did not do it. He'd not kill one of his own."

"That must be a great comfort to Kenrick."

"Damn you!" His voice shaking, Ivo looked at the deputy with loathing. "You're lying."

"Why do you think he cut Kenrick's throat? He was sending a message to the rest of Winchester, and you know it, Ivo. What will it take to make your family face the truth about him? Killing comes easy to Gilbert. Yesterday it was Kenrick. Tomorrow it could be you if he starts to wonder how trustworthy you are."

"He said you'd try to blame him for Kenrick's death. But he swore he did not do it, and I believe him."

"No," Luke said, "you do not," and the older man flinched, his shoulders sagging. "If the lot of you had not kept lying for him and protecting him, Kenrick would still be alive. So would the goldsmith and that poor woman he murdered out on the Southampton Road. I know you do not grieve for them, but I will give you the benefit of the doubt and assume you do grieve for your son. Tell me the truth, Ivo. You owe Kenrick that much."

Ivo started to turn away, but Luke caught his arm. "I did not see Gib," he said hoarsely. "He talked to my brother. He said . . . said you were falsely blaming him for Kenrick's killing and it would be too dangerous for him to stay around Winchester."

Luke's grip tightened. "Where was he going?"

"London. He told my brother he was going back to London."

After buying sausages and bread from a street vendor, Luke and Justin withdrew to eat them in a tavern across the road from the castle. "Do you believe Ivo?" Justin asked between bites of sausage. "You think Gilbert is heading for London?"

"It makes sense. He did not expect to be caught in the act, after all. A weasel always goes back to its burrow, and this particular weasel has any number of London lairs to hide away in."

"You think the partner has taken flight, too?"

"Do I look like a soothsayer?" Luke finished one sausage, reached for another. "Sorry, lack of sleep is making me testy."

"No more than usual." Justin was quite willing to indulge Luke's short temper, impressed by the deputy's ability to reconstruct the crime scene and by the reckless courage that had sent him up the ladder, not knowing if a killer lay in wait. A pity he would have to go without Luke's help in London. "Have tales ever gotten back to Winchester about Gilbert's London crimes? Anything at all that might prove useful in tracking him down?"

"I've been thinking about that, too. For reasons you're not likely to reveal, the queen seems to want this killing investigated on the quiet. Even so, the London sheriffs need not be kept out of it.

"Wait—hear me out, de Quincy. I know one of the sheriffs from a past visit to London, a man named Roger Fitz Alan. He seems to be a good sort, and he knows how to stay afloat in political currents, for he is the mayor's nephew. Let me write to him, reminding him that Gilbert is wanted in Winchester for those two killings last summer and now for two more. I'll make it sound like a local matter, tell him we're very keen on hanging Gilbert and ask his help in your hunt for the man. There is nothing odd about a request like that, and I can assure you he'll not take it amiss."

"Well . . . I'll have to get the queen's consent first. But the idea does have merit. I could use some help, for I'm not that familiar with London."

"You'll not get as much help as you ought, for the sheriffs are likely to have few men to spare in a hunt for a Winchester killer. Without a royal command to nudge them along, they'll give priority to their own slayings, and I cannot fault them for it; I'd do the same. So if the man is to be found, you'll have to do it. But if you're lucky enough to locate him, do not try to capture him on your own. Let the sheriff send men to arrest him. Gilbert the Fleming is a worthless devil's whelp, but he is also extremely dangerous, as coldhearted a knave as I've ever come across."

"Have a care, Luke," Justin said, grinning, "for you're beginning to sound as if you're worried about me!"

Luke snorted. "When cows fly!" But after a moment, he said, with unwonted gravity, "Just remember *why* he is called Gilbert the Fleming. Even a queen's letter is no shield against so sharp a blade."

Luke had the letter waiting for Justin when he stopped by the castle early the next morning. Justin tucked it away with the queen's letter, hoping that Eleanor would be receptive to its use. He'd decided that there was a lot to be said for having a sheriff as ally.

He then made a quick side trip to the Fitz Randolph stable, wanting to tell Edwin that he was departing for London. After extracting another promise from Edwin to be circumspect about his suspicions, he rode away with the groom's "Good hunting!" echoing in his ears.

He'd planned to leave the city straightaway, but as the priory of St Swithun came into sight, he reined in, and on impulse, turned into the cemetery. Row after row of weathered, flat tombstones met his eye, like an army lining up in battle array, making ready to fight a war already lost. He'd never passed a cemetery without thinking of his mother, wondering where she was buried, if there was anyone to tend her grave, if there had been anyone to mourn her.

Hitching Copper, he got directions from one of the monks. Making his way among the tombstones, he had almost reached the Fitz Randolph plot when he saw the woman kneeling by the grave. Her back was to him, but he recognized Ella Fitz Randolph at once, looking frail and forlorn in her drab widow's garb.

Justin stopped abruptly, unwilling to intrude. Even at a distance, he could hear the sounds of her sobbing, stirring a sharp pang of pity. And yet he found an odd sort of comfort in her tears, too. At least there was one to weep for the slain goldsmith.

Retrieving Copper, he was heading for the East Gate when he remembered that he'd forgotten to tell Luke that he planned to stay at the Holy Trinity priory once he got to London. It was vexing, but there was no help for it; he'd have to go back. Luke had promised to let him know if he found out anything about Gilbert's partner, and he was beginning to put a great deal of stock in Luke's word.

Returning to the castle, he was told that Luke had gone off to get breakfast across the street. The tavern was the same one where they'd eaten their sausage the day before. Justin pushed the door open, peering inside. He soon saw Luke, seated with another man at a corner table. But then he froze in disbelief. Very slowly he backed out, taking care not to be noticed. Swinging up into the saddle, he urged his stallion into a brisk canter, and he was soon on the road to London. But his thoughts were still in the tavern with Luke and his companion—Durand, John's spy.

8

WESTMINSTER

February 1193

Justin reached London in late afternoon four days later, after a journey plagued by mishaps—a broken rein, a lost horseshoe—and unease. He'd been more shaken by the sight of Luke and Durand together than he cared to admit. Their confrontation with the Fleming had dispelled any last doubts about the deputy's good faith. He was still sure that Luke was not involved in the goldsmith's death. But was he in the pay of the queen's son? John would see an under-sheriff as a useful ally. Was Luke de Marston John's man?

Justin did not want to believe that, and it was not at all difficult to find innocent explanations for Luke's breakfast colloquy with Durand. But each time he'd convinced himself that his suspicions were groundless, he'd hear again the unsettling echoes of Eleanor's warning: *Be wary, watch whom you trust.*

He went straight to the Tower, only to be told that Eleanor was at Westminster for the day. Reclaiming Copper from the stable, he wearily headed west again. There was less than an hour of daylight remaining by the time he rode into the New Palace Yard. After hitching his stallion, he started for the great hall. But the bailey was thronged with people, and he was soon caught up in the crowd, being swept along in spite of himself. "What is happening?" he asked the nearest onlooker. "Where is everyone going?"

"To see the prisoners submit to the ordeal. The sheriff's men will be bringing them out any moment. You'd best hurry if you want to get close enough to watch."

Justin had seen a trial by ordeal once before, years ago in Shrewsbury. A man accused of arson had been taken to the abbey's mill pond, bound hand and foot, and thrown into the water to see if he sank, proof of innocence, or floated, proof of guilt. The man had gone under and was therefore adjudged innocent, although he was half-drowned by the time he'd been pulled out. But the nearest body of water here at Westminster was the river.

"What sort of ordeal?"

"See for yourself." The other man pointed up ahead, where a large iron cauldron had been brought to a boil over an open fire.

Justin was not sure that was something he wanted to watch, but the crowd's momentum carried him forward. People were jockeying for position near the cauldron. Justin's neighbor explained that the men had been charged with the murder of an elderly widow, but others claimed the crime was robbery and one stubborn soul kept insisting it was heresy. Midst all this misinformation, Justin did learn that Londoners could not be forced to undergo the ordeal, having been granted a royal exemption. So either the prisoners were not citizens of London or they'd chosen to submit to the ordeal, preferring that judgment be rendered by Almighty God and not a jury of their peers. Staring at that churning cauldron, Justin winced and made a quick sign of the cross.

The sheriff's serjeants were escorting the prisoners out now and the crowd pressed forward, eager to see. Both men looked young and very frightened. One was shivering noticeably as holy water was sprinkled on his bared forearm and when he was urged to drink he needed help to hold the holy water cup steady. A priest had stepped forward and, signaling for quiet, began to intone a prayer.

"If these men be innocent, do Thou, O God, save them as Thou did save Shadrach, Meshach, and Abednego from the fiery furnace. But if they be guilty and dare plunge their hands into the boiling water because the Devil has hardened their hearts, let thy Holy Justice be done. Amen."

The noise had been considerable, but suddenly it was utterly still. The crowd seemed to be holding its collective breath as the priest dropped a smooth white stone into the depths of the cauldron and then ordered the first prisoner to come forward. By now he was shaking so badly that he seemed on the verge of collapse.

Shutting his eyes tightly, he leaned over the cauldron, but recoiled as soon as he breathed in the cloud of steam rising from the
water. Twice he tried to grope for the stone, but each time his
courage failed and he pulled back. After the third failed attempt,
he began to sob and the serjeants stepped in, dragging him away
from the cauldron.

A murmur ran through the crowd, almost like a sigh. God's
Judgment had been passed; the man would hang. Now it was his
partner's turn. He had gone ashen, biting his lips until they bled.
But he advanced resolutely, peering through the steam to find the
stone. He hesitated so long that people began to fear that he, too,
would balk, and mutters of disappointment and disapproval
began to be heard. But then he lunged forward and thrust his arm
into the cauldron. Staggering back, he held up the stone for all to
see, and some of the spectators cheered.

They were at once rebuked by the priest, who reminded them
that the Almighty's verdict had not yet been rendered. The prisoner was instructed to extend his arm and a serjeant wrapped it
in thick linen. While it was being sealed with the sheriff's signet
to ensure there'd be no tampering, the priest declared that the
man would be returned to gaol. In three days, the bandage would
be unwrapped. If his skin was blistered and scalded, he would
hang. If not, he would go free.

The crowd was slow to disperse and Justin found himself still
walled in by bodies. He was waiting for a path to open up when
he glanced toward his right and saw John and Durand standing
together on the other side of the cauldron.

Recognition was mutual. As their eyes met, Justin's own
dismay was mirrored on Durand's face. Justin was not surprised
that Durand had beaten him back to London; he'd lost half a day
finding a saddler to repair his broken rein. Durand would still
have had to leave Winchester right after he did, though, further
proof—if it were needed—that the knight had been in the city to
spy on him.

Durand quickly recovered his equilibrium. But that brief flash
of alarm had been very telling; so he hadn't admitted to John that
he'd been caught in the act. Justin relished having the upper
hand, but before he could decide what he wanted to do, John

turned and saw him. Justin had to admire the other man's equanimity, for he showed not even a flicker of surprise. Instead, he smiled and beckoned Justin over.

"There is nothing like Judgment Day to bring out a crowd," John said dryly, "especially when the sins being judged are not ours. What did you think of the ordeal, Master de Quincy?"

Justin shrugged. "I'd rather take my chances with a jury."

John laughed. "So would I. It is a lot easier to bribe a jury member than the Almighty. But on to more important matters. Have you decided to sell me that horse?"

"Not yet, my lord count."

"Do not wait too long. I might lose interest."

"Somehow I doubt that, my lord." Sparring with John had a certain edgy appeal, like venturing out onto a frozen lake with no way of knowing when the ice might start to crack underfoot. But with Durand, hostility need not be muted, and Justin gave the knight a cold smile. "You do keep turning up unexpectedly, Sir Durand. If I had a suspicious nature, I might wonder if you were following me."

"Passing strange," Durand jeered, "for I was thinking the same about you."

Dislike surged between the two men, all but sending up sparks, and John looked from one to the other, his eyes narrowing. "I suppose you're in search of my lady mother, Master de Quincy. You'll find her in the great hall."

It was obviously a dismissal, and Justin took his leave. As soon as he'd been swallowed up in the crowd, he doubled back. He moved fast, treading on a few toes in the process, but coming up behind John in time to hear him say in a low, angry voice, "Why did you not tell me he knows you, Durand? I'll have to look elsewhere now."

Justin had never seen a hall as huge as the eleventh-century great hall at Westminster; he guessed its length to be well over two hundred feet, almost a third as wide, with a soaring roof supported by heavy wooden columns. People were milling about, and it took him a few moments to spot the queen. Eleanor and a companion were ensconced in a window seat at the far end of the hall, engaged in what was obviously an intense discussion. Justin started toward her, planning to let her see him and then withdraw, awaiting her summons.

As he drew closer, his step faltered, for the man with Eleanor was a bishop. The sight of that white alb and richly decorated cope was unsettling, calling up unwelcome memories of his father. How often he'd seen Aubrey clad in those same ecclesiastical vestments, never dreaming that this prideful prince of the Church was his own flesh and blood. The man in the alcove was too short and stocky to be Aubrey; at least he need not fear coming face to face with his father. But at that moment the bishop shifted in his seat, and for the first time Justin saw his profile.

Justin recognized him at once. The Bishop of Coventry had visited his father frequently over the years, although he did not think that Aubrey considered Hugh de Nonant to be a friend. Coming to a halt, he stared at the bishop, trying to remember if Hugh had been present when he'd burst into the Bishop's Palace to confront his father. His emotions had been in such turmoil that he could not trust his memories of that night. But he did seem to have a hazy recollection of Hugh de Nonant seated on the dais at Aubrey's side. Better safe than sorry, he decided, and retreated as inconspicuously as possible.

"Who are you trying to avoid, Master de Quincy?" He'd not heard Claudine's approach and started so visibly that she laughed. "You must indeed have a guilty conscience," she teased, "if your nerves are that raw! Are you seeking the queen?"

"I was," Justin said, "but I did not want to interrupt her conversation with the Bishop of Coventry."

"Conversation? Is that what you think they are doing? No . . . what you are watching is a verbal chess game between two master players, each one probing the other's weaknesses, poised to take advantage of any unguarded move, check and mate."

"Why would the queen be so wary of Bishop Hugh?" Justin asked curiously and got an answer that was anything but reassuring.

"You do not know?" Claudine asked, sounding surprised. "The queen has good reason to be cautious, for Hugh de Nonant and John are long-time allies." Lowering her voice, she confided, "If truth be told, the pair of them are thick as thieves, and that means the good bishop is no friend to King Richard."

Justin was quiet for a moment, as he sought to come to terms with the realization that John's shadow might reach as far as Chester. Taking Claudine by the arm, he led her toward the nearest window alcove. "I want to thank you, demoiselle, for warning me that the queen's son was showing too much interest in my activities. Forewarned is forearmed."

"With John, that is always wise," she agreed.

"You know him better than I, demoiselle. In all candor, what manner of man is he?"

"A complicated one, Master de Quincy, with more layers than an onion and undercurrents deep enough to drown in. I think he is twice as clever as Richard, and dangerously charming when he chooses to be, just plain dangerous when he does not." They were standing very close, for he'd not released his hold upon her arm. The look she gave him now was both amused and intimate. "Do you want to know my own private name for John?" she murmured. "The Prince of Darkness."

A chilling wind had sprung up and the last light of day was fast ebbing away. Justin glanced protectively at the queen as they walked. But she'd chosen the cloisters of St Stephen's for their meeting, and he sensed that she'd not welcome his suggestion that they talk indoors. She seemed indifferent to the cold, but he could not help noticing how very tired she looked. There was a distance between them that he'd not felt before. It was as if the inner Eleanor had withdrawn where he could not follow, leaving the queen behind to defend the barricades.

Her first question took him by surprise. "I saw you earlier in the hall. You shied away from the Bishop of Coventry as if he were a leper. Why?"

"He knows my father, madame, and it might arouse his curiosity to see me here, especially if he learned I am using the name de Quincy." That was true as far as it went. He did not want his kinship to Aubrey to be revealed. But it was not his father's reputation that concerned him. Who knew what John might do with information like that? He could not admit to Eleanor, though, that he harbored such suspicions about her son, and he hoped she'd not probe further.

She did not. "Why are you back in London, Justin? I trust you are not going to tell me that the trail has gone cold?"

"No, my lady. I learned that one of the hired killers, a man known as Gilbert the Fleming, has fled Winchester for London."

"Gilbert the Fleming? You were actually able to find out the man's name? Very good work, indeed!"

Justin flushed with pleasure. "I wish I could claim all the credit, madame, but I had help. Luke de Marston was able to identify the man once I told him that I'd seen a snake at the ambush. Gilbert thinks snakes make good partners in crime, for they can be relied upon to spook most horses and keep their mouths shut afterward."

Eleanor's curiosity was as healthy in her twilight years as it had been in her sunlit youth, and she still took delight in the novel and unexpected. "A snake accomplice?" she marveled and then laughed aloud. "Well, why not? A snake was Lucifer's ally back in Eden, after all. Speaking of allies, what changed your mind about Luke de Marston? The last time we spoke, you seemed ready to fit him for a hangman's noose."

"I was too hasty, my lady. I judged the man ere I had all the facts," Justin said carefully, and reminded himself that Luke deserved the benefit of the doubt, too, with respect to any suspicions Durand had stirred up. And he told her then of what he'd learned during his latest foray into the world of the slain goldsmith.

Eleanor listened without interruption. When he was done, he drew out Luke's letter to the sheriff of London. Holding her lantern for her as she read, he silently willed her to agree, to let the sheriff assist in the hunt for Gervase's killer. If she balked, he'd forge on alone, without complaint, for pride would keep him quiet. But he'd be constantly aware of an uneasy prickling at the back of his neck, be seeing a dagger's glint from the corner of his eye. For Luke was right: Gilbert the Fleming was not a foe to hold cheaply.

"A wise precaution," Eleanor agreed, much to his relief. "De

Marston would do well at court, for he knows how to dance around the truth and still avoid an outright lie. It is a cleverly worded letter. By all means, deliver it to the sheriff. Once the man is tracked down, we can decide then how best to get the truth from him. So you are convinced then that this was a family killing and not the doing of the French king?"

"No, not entirely," Justin said reluctantly.

"Why not? From what you've told me, the Fitz Randolph household is awash in secrets, and the only one to lack a motive is the stable cat!"

"I do not dispute that, my lady. But I keep remembering what I overheard during the ambush. Whilst the Fleming was searching Fitz Randolph, the other outlaw shouted out, 'Did you find it?' That puzzles me, madame, for Gilbert already had the money pouch. So what were they looking for?"

Neither one said "the letter," but the words seemed to echo on the air between them. After a few moments of silence, Eleanor said, "I've summoned a Great Council meeting in Oxford at the end of the month. We will decide then what measures to take on Richard's behalf. We're running out of time, Justin. You must catch this Fleming and find out if he was in the pay of the Fitz Randolphs—or the French."

"I will do my best, madame." Justin took back Luke's letter and tucked it away within his tunic. "My lady . . . there is something else you ought to know. I have reason to believe one of your household knights followed me to Winchester."

Eleanor had been turning to reenter the great hall. Swinging around, she studied Justin intently. "One of my men? You know his name?"

"I do, my lady. Durand." Justin did not insist that Durand was John's spy. There was no need to accuse the queen's son. Who else could it be?

Eleanor frowned and he was sorry that he must give her more worries when she already had so many. "I'll see to Durand," she said. "You see to this Fleming."

It was fully dark. Half an hour had gone by since Justin had escorted Eleanor back into the hall. But he'd then lingered outside, heedless of the dropping temperature and the passing time. In the stillness, he seemed to hear again John's impatient words: *I'll have to look elsewhere now. See to the Fleming,* the queen had said. But who was going to see to John?

After a while, he wandered out of the cloisters and into the royal gardens, desolate and deserted now, the ground rock-hard and barren, shrubs withered by killing frosts. The locale matched his mood, and he began to walk along pathways lit only by remote, pinpoint stars. The garden held no maze, but his life had become one, entangling him in half-truths, suspicions, false tracks, and trails that went nowhere.

He soon heard the river, splashing against the garden wall. Leaning into one of the embrasures, he was watching a passing ferry when barking erupted behind him. A brindle greyhound was loping up the path, trailed by a man in a grey mantle trimmed in fox fur. Justin tensed instinctively, for there was something about the man's walk that reminded him somewhat of John. But as the intruder came closer, he relaxed, recognizing Will Longsword.

"Down, Cinder!" The command came in the nick of time; the greyhound was about to launch herself at Justin. "We did not expect to find anyone out in the gardens at this hour, or I'd have kept her on a leash. All she'd do, though, would be to lick you to death—Justin de Quincy! When did you get back from Winchester?"

"A few hours ago, my lord. So you knew that I was in Winchester?"

Will set his lantern on the garden wall, then bent over to attach a leather lead to his dog's collar. "The queen told me. She said you've been hunting the goldsmith's killers. Any luck so far?"

Justin felt a surge of relief that Will knew about his mission. John's half-brother had a well-deserved reputation for integrity and honor, and he very much needed someone he could trust. He felt an odd sort of kinship with the other man, too, for they were both bastard born. Of course the similarities stopped there; Will's father had openly acknowledged him, even raised him with Eleanor's children. But Will still remained an outsider, albeit a respected and prosperous one, and Justin could speak to him with a candor that would have been unthinkable with Eleanor.

He briefed Will about his search for Gilbert the Fleming and was pleased when the older man offered generous praise for his efforts. After a moment's reflection, he told Will about Durand. While he did not doubt that Eleanor was quite capable of dealing with her treacherous knight, it could not hurt to keep Durand under another pair of eyes.

Will showed no surprise at the revelation. "Damn him," he said softly, more to himself than Justin. "The queen confided not long ago that she suspected Durand of conniving with John. More fool I, for turning a blind eye to his double-dealing!"

Justin wondered which man he meant—Durand or John. But now that Will had brought John's name out into the open, he seized his chance, one that might not come again. "My lord . . . may I speak frankly? Lord John has been showing great interest in me, more than I am comfortable with. Like you, I think Durand was in Winchester at his behest. I am at a disadvantage in this hunt, for I do not know what he is seeking from me. Do you?"

That was blunt speaking, but Will struck him as a man who'd appreciate bluntness. John's brother was regarding him pensively. "I can tell you what I suspect," he said slowly. "This can go no further than the two of us, though. I'd not have words of mine used to discredit John, especially since I have no proof, only suspicions. Have I your oath on that?"

"You do, my lord."

Reaching down, Will stroked his dog's silky head, and Justin thought he sighed. "It is no secret that John covets his brother's crown. And if he is as deeply ensnared in the French king's web as we fear, it is likely that he knows of Richard's capture, for that is news Philip would be sure to share. I think he does know and is trying to find out if the queen knows, too."

"Why would that matter so to him?"

"As long as Richard's whereabouts remain a mystery, John can sow rumors with impunity and find ready believers. So far he has been relying upon his agents and spies to spread these stories of Richard's death. Soon he must start making these claims himself. But it would be very awkward—to say the least—if Queen Eleanor could then offer proof that Richard is still alive. I am sure that is why he is so curious about that letter you delivered and your subsequent missions for the queen."

"Thank you, my lord, for being so forthright."

"You had a right to know," Will said simply. Snapping his fingers at the greyhound, he turned to go. "I am afraid you are caught in the middle of two separate hunts, lad, one for a killer and the other for a throne."

Justin stayed by the river wall, watching as the glow from Will's lantern grew fainter and fainter. There were too many players in this game—the Fleming, the queen's son, the queen herself, possibly even the King of France—and the rules kept changing. It was a sobering thought, that a mistake of his might prolong the English Lionheart's captivity.

9

LONDON

February 1193

Early the next morning, Justin set out to find Roger Fitz Alan. He
tried the Tower first, but the sheriff had already departed for the
Guildhall. Mounting Copper again, he headed for Aldermanbury
Street. Upon his arrival at the Guildhall, though, he learned that
the sheriff had been there and gone. Feeling as if he were chasing
down a will-o'-the-wisp, he rode west toward the city gaol.

The Thames was the lifeblood of London, but it was not the
city's only river. The Fleet began as a stream on Hampstead's
hill, and had various names as it wound its way south. By the
time it flowed into the Thames, it had widened and deepened
enough to be navigated by barges and fishing boats, and was
known as the River Fleet. It was here that the gaol of London
was located, a massive, moated building of slate-colored stone
set within a barren prison bailey, as desolate and depressing a
sight as Justin had ever seen.

His visit proved to be as futile as it was unsettling. Once again
he'd missed the sheriff, and this time the trail had gone cold.
Roger Fitz Alan had said nothing about where he was going
next. Muttering a few choice swear words to himself, Justin un-
hitched Copper and tried to decide what to do.

It was difficult to concentrate, though, for his senses were still
being assailed by the sounds and stenches of prison life. The
moat was filled with stagnant water from the river, fetid and
murky. Justin would rather not know what lay hidden in its disgusting depths. The prison itself had an offensive odor, too, a
rancid mingling of urine, unwashed bodies, sweat, and fear.
Even out in the bailey, the air seemed tainted.

The noise had not abated, either, for the gaol had an iron grate, giving prisoners a narrow window to the world. Manacled hands thrust through the rusted apertures, and voices echoed after Justin, entreating alms, for Christ's pity. He'd already dropped a handful of small coins into outstretched palms, for Luke had told him something startling about a prisoner's lot.

According to the deputy, King Henry had provided his sheriffs with funds to feed the imprisoned. But the practice had become sporadic under King Richard, and more and more, prisoners were left to fend for themselves. Those who could not afford to pay for meals, bedding, firewood, candles, or clothing did without— unless they could prevail upon the charity of passersby like Justin.

Now, as Justin watched, a man was dragged out into the bailey and wrestled into the stocks. Two other prisoners were already being punished this way. Yet they greeted the newcomer with no sympathy, only mockery and taunts. Even after his wrists and ankles had been immobilized within the wooden frame, the man continued to struggle, to the amusement of his guards and fellow prisoners. His defiance would not last long, for his tunic was threadbare and ragged and the day blustery and raw, February at its worst. Justin had seen enough. Swinging up into the saddle, he rode out of the bailey, not looking back.

He had decided to return to the Tower, for the sheriff was sure to turn up there sooner or later. But it was past the dinner hour. He'd often seen vendors selling mutton or eel pies in the city streets. Thinking that he'd be most likely to find one midst the bustle of the wharves, he rode south, intending to follow the Fleet down to the Thames waterfront.

The sun had begun to tease the winter-weary Londoners, offering them tantalizingly brief glimpses of brightness through breaks in the cloud cover. Justin had passed the Fleet Bridge when a child's stricken wail interrupted his musings about the whereabouts of Gilbert the Fleming. A small boy, no more than five, was gesturing in panic toward the river, entreating his mother to "Save him, Mama!"

Justin reined in, scanning the river in vain for signs of a drowning victim. "What is amiss?" he asked the closest spectator, a man who had the look of a sailor, for his skin was as weathered and browned as saddle leather. "Did someone fall in the river?"

The sailor shook his head. "Two louts threw a dog off the bridge, and the little lad saw." He sounded regretful, although it was not clear whether his sympathy was for the child or the dog. When life was so hard for people, not many worried about cruelty to animals. There were those with a fondness for dogs, of course, and the sailor might be one. He confirmed that a moment later by saying indignantly, "The pup never had a chance, for they weighed him down with a sackful of rocks."

Justin felt equally indignant. He still remembered how desperately he'd wanted a dog during those lonely childhood years. On the bridge, the young men were laughing and joking, while below them, a little boy was sobbing as if his heart would break. Coming as it did so soon after his disquieting visit to the gaol, the dog's drowning stirred a sharp-edged anger in Justin. Had the smirking youths up on the bridge come down, he'd have been sorely tempted to exact a rough justice of his own. But they were safely out of reach. He was nudging his stallion on when the child cried shrilly, "Look, Mama! There he is!"

A dark head had broken the surface of the water. Struggling desperately against the weight dragging him down, the dog lunged for the light, frantically gulping air before he went under again. It was a gallant effort, and a doomed one. Battling two foes—the river current and that sackful of stones—the dog would soon be too fatigued to fight on. Those watching knew that the animal was going to drown.

Only the small child and the young dog would not surrender hope. Resisting his mother's attempts to pull him away, the boy wept and pleaded, and the adults shifted awkwardly under his imploring gaze. Very few people knew how to swim, and only a madman would jump into an icy river to save a dog, no matter how good a swimmer he was. There were murmurings in the crowd, and even some anger. Why must the wretched beast prolong his agony—and their discomfort?

Casting common sense to the winds, Justin dismounted and handed his reins to the most trustworthy of the bystanders, an elderly Cluniac monk. "I'd be obliged if you'd watch my horse, Brother."

Striding out onto the wharf, he looked in vain for a small boat tied up to one of the pilings; he supposed that would have been too much to hope for. But he did find a rusty grappling hook. Feeling like a fool, he knelt at the end of the pier and urged the terrified animal to swim toward him. Only the dog's muzzle and eyes were visible now, but those eyes were going to haunt his peace; he well knew it. Try as he might, though, he could not get close enough even to attempt a rescue. "It is no use," he muttered, not sure whether he was talking to himself or the dog, "no use . . ."

"I'll hold you steady, lad," a voice offered behind him, and he glanced up to discover that he'd been followed by the sailor and most of the onlookers. Praying that he'd not plunge headfirst into the river, he unbuckled his sword and then let the sailor lower him over the edge of the wharf.

The dog was still beyond reach, and Justin knew they were running out of time. "Lady Mary, smile upon us," he whispered. Dipping the grapnel into the water, he coaxed, "Come on, boy, over here!" The dog swam closer, passed over the grappling hook, and circled back. And then the chain jerked in Justin's grip.

"Jesú, I snared it!" Justin had not truly expected to succeed, but the dog's head and shoulders suddenly popped out of the water, proof that he had indeed managed to snag the rope. A cheer rose from the crowd and the sailor let out a triumphant whoop. But Justin's elation soon ebbed. What now?

"If I pass the grappling hook to you," he told the sailor, "I might be able to cut the rope with my sword. But how do we get him out of the river? He'll never make it to shore on his own; the bank is too steep for him to climb."

"Do you think you can lift the rope up high enough for me to get a grip on it?"

"I can try," Justin said dubiously, and slowly began to maneuver the grappling hook toward the surface. It was heavy and he suddenly realized that he hadn't caught the rope at all; it was the sack itself. By the Rood, what luck! The Blessed Mother Mary truly had favored them. A moment later the sack came into view, neatly speared on one of the grappling claws. "Pull me up," he directed, and then it was the sailor's turn to lean out recklessly into space. As Justin reeled in the grappling hook, the sailor snatched at it and grinned when his fist closed tightly around the rope.

"I'm going to hoist him up," he said. "Better to hurt him than to let him drown."

Justin nodded, then swung his sword and sliced through the rope, above the knot. The sack sank back into the river with a splash, and he reached over to help the sailor haul the dog up onto the wharf. A sharp tug, a yelp, and it was done. The spectators at once recoiled, not wanting to be sprayed. But the dog was too weak to shake himself and lay motionless on the wooden planks, his sides heaving. Bending down, Justin cut the rope away from his neck. For some suspenseful moments, the animal lay still, limp and sodden. Then he gagged and began to retch.

The tension eased and people started to laugh and talk. Justin and the sailor found themselves encircled by approving men and women. Even those who'd normally have been indifferent to a dog's death had been caught up in the drama of the rescue, and all were well pleased by the outcome—save only the two youths on the bridge.

They'd been hooting and jeering, but Justin had been too preoccupied to pay them any heed. Now his anger came back in a rush, and when one of them began to curse him for "meddling with our dog," he shouted a defiant challenge. "Come down and claim him then—if you dare!"

The crowd liked that, and a few men spoke loudly of thrashings and worse. The youths continued to rant, but prudently stayed where they were. Someone found Justin a hemp sack and he dried the shivering dog as best he could. By now the dog's first champion had squirmed through the throng of onlookers. Kneeling by the animal, the child took the wet head into his lap, looking up at Justin and the sailor with a smile of purest joy.

A peddler drawn by the crowd had begun to boast about his "hot, savory pies." They were neither hot nor savory, baked hours ago and flecked with grease, but he was soon selling them at a rapid rate. Justin bought two, and offered one to the dog, whose protruding ribs testified to a constant hunger. So, too, did the way he wolfed the pie down, and Justin ended up feeding him the second one, too. The excitement over, people were beginning to drift away. When the little boy's mother pulled him to his feet, Justin suggested that "This would make a fine pet for your lad."

The boy's face lit up, but the woman gave Justin an irate look, snapping, "Indeed not! Come along, Ned." Still glaring over her shoulder at Justin, she hustled her small son off the pier.

Justin and the sailor exchanged smiles. Their partnership had been highly satisfactory, but it was done. Retrieving his stallion from the patiently waiting monk, Justin mounted and started to ease Copper out into the road. He was followed by a ripple of laughter. Glancing back in puzzlement, he soon saw the cause of the crowd's amusement. The dog had lurched to his feet and was trailing after him.

Justin had planned to follow Thames Street east to the Tower. The traffic was heavy, the street crowded with horsemen, lumbering carts, pedestrians, and stray animals. But as he neared the new bridge, the street became so congested that movement ceased altogether. Peering impatiently ahead, he sought the cause for this disruption. As soon as he saw the man riding backward, forced to face his horse's tail, hands and feet tied and drenched in wine, he understood. A baker who tampered with his scales, a vintner who watered down his wine, any merchant who cheated customers, could expect the same derisory treatment: paraded through the city so all could bear witness to his disgrace. Justin approved of the punishment, but he had no time to watch this day, and he turned off onto Bridge Street, planning to detour around the procession.

He still had not lost his canine shadow. At first he'd tried halfheartedly to discourage the dog. But he'd then decided that it might be best for the poor creature to get as far away as possible from his tormentors. Who was to say that they might not try again once the pup's protectors were gone?

Encountering another peddler, Justin remembered that he hadn't eaten yet and beckoned the man over. A hopeful whimper earned the young dog a pork pie of his own. Tossing a coin to the vendor, Justin was soon on his way again. He'd not gone far, though, before his mount's gait changed. Frowning, he swung from the saddle. A close inspection of Copper's left forefoot revealed the problem—a pebble wedged between the frog and inner rim of the shoe. But try as he might, he could not dislodge the stone. Straightening up, he stood by his lamed stallion in the busy city street and cursed his bad luck. It didn't help.

Justin fidgeted, waiting anxiously for the verdict. But the farrier would not be hurried. A lean, greying man in his forties, sparing with words, he went about his tasks calmly and methodically, first winning the stallion's trust and only then examining the foot and extracting the pebble with a pair of pinchers.

"The hoof is badly bruised," he announced at last. "But I do not think the injury is a crippling one. I can make up a poultice now, if you like. You'll not be able to ride him for a few days, though, as he'll need time to heal."

When Justin readily agreed, saying he'd never put the stallion at risk, the farrier nodded approvingly, for not all of his customers were so solicitous of their mounts. They soon reached a mutually acceptable price for boarding and treating Copper, and when Justin asked about nearby lodgings, the smith suggested that he try the alehouse on Gracechurch Street.

"The owner of the alehouse no longer lives above-stairs and rents the rooms out. Ask for Nell. Tell her that Gunter the smith sent you."

The alehouse was just a stone's throw from the farrier's smithy, a two-story, overhanging timber building that had seen better days; its whitewash was grey, its shutters warped, and its ale-pole sagged out into the street at a drunken angle. Inside, it was dark and smelled strongly of spilt ale. A drunken customer was slumped over a corner table, snoring. Two other men were playing draughts and flirting with a bored serving maid. She looked toward Justin without noticeable interest. "What can I get for you, friend?"

"I would like to speak to Nell."

"You already are," she said, and Justin gave her a startled

reappraisal. Managing an alehouse was a demanding job for anyone, especially a woman, and he had instinctively envisioned Nell as a formidable, no-nonsense beldame, well armored in years and flesh. Instead, he found himself staring at a wood sprite. She was young, not much older than Justin himself, and tiny, barely five feet, with a summer cloudburst of curly hair pouring out of its pins, a sprinkling of freckles, and bright blue eyes fringed with golden lashes. At first glance, she seemed like a rabbit among foxes; Justin could not imagine a more alien environment for her than this squalid alehouse. But those blue eyes were neither guileless nor trustful, and when he asked to rent a room, she studied him with a skeptical smile.

"Why would you want to stay in a hovel like this?"

Justin was amused by her bluntness. "I commend your honesty—if not your hospitality. I've a lamed horse across the street at the smithy, and I need a place close at hand till he is fit to ride again. Gunter said you'd probably be able to rent me a room. Now . . . can you or not?"

"Gunter vouches for you? Why did you not say so?" This time her smile was real, although her eyes remained guarded. "My daughter and I share one of the rooms, so I'm particular about who I rent to. If Gunter thinks you're trustworthy, that is good enough for me. If you are willing to pay a half-penny a night, the room is yours. But no dogs."

"I do not have a—oh, no." Glancing around, Justin discovered that the pup had followed him into the alehouse and was sitting placidly at his feet. "He is not mine."

Nell's skeptical smile came back. "Does he know that?"

Justin smiled ruefully. "Well . . . I'm doing my best to convince him. He truly is not mine, but I am trying to find a home for him. He'd be here a day or so, no more—"

"Indeed not. We get enough fleas from our regular customers. I do not need a mangy cur bringing more in, too."

"If he had any fleas, they all drowned in the Fleet."

Nell scowled, but curiosity won out. "What was he doing in the river? It's a cold day for a swim."

"A couple of misbegotten dolts threw him off the bridge. I fished him out and then made the mistake of feeding him. The

poor beast has not known much kindness in his life, for certes—
or much luck, either. You can change that, lass. Just give me a
day to find him a home."

"I never had a man try to seduce me for a dog before," Nell
said tartly. "One day and that is all!"

Picking up one of the sputtering tallow candles, she led him
into the stairwell. The dog frisked along after them, determined
not to let Justin out of his sight. The room was small, containing
only a stool and a pallet. Justin could not help laughing when the
dog immediately hopped onto the bed. Trying to sound stern, he
ordered, "Shadow, off!"

Setting the candle down on the stool, Nell headed for the door.
The last word was hers. "Not your dog—hah!"

After buying parchment, a quill pen, and ink at the Eastcheap
market, Justin wrote Luke a brief letter, informing the deputy
that he could be reached at the alehouse. If Luke discovered the
identity of the Fleming's partner, that would be a message too
important to miss. He could only hope that he was not also informing John where he could be found. He set out then for the
Tower, occasionally glancing over his shoulder to see if the dog
was still following; he was. They reached the Tower in late afternoon, and this time Justin's luck had changed; the sheriff was in.

Roger Fitz Alan could not have been more unlike Luke de
Marston. He was smooth and polished and bland—no sharp
edges, no hidden depths, no salt. Justin would not have needed to
be told that his was a political appointment. Fitz Alan admitted
somewhat reluctantly that he had no personal knowledge of this
Gilbert the Fleming. But he readily promised to do what he
could to apprehend the man. "One of my serjeants may be able
to help you. He knows all the ratholes in London, and most of
the rats. I'll have him seek you out at that alehouse . . . on
Gracechurch Street, you said?"

Justin thanked the sheriff politely, but without either enthusiasm
or optimism. It sounded as if he was on his own. Masking his disappointment as best he could, he bade the sheriff farewell, and exited out into the Tower bailey. Almost at once, his mood—and his

day—took a turn for the better. A throaty female voice murmured his name, and he turned to greet Claudine de Loudun.

"Who is your furry friend?"

Justin was more than willing to relate the story of the dog's rescue, for he knew that was the sort of exploit likely to win favor with most women, and this was one woman whose favor he very much wanted to win. By the time he was done, he thought he was making progress, too, for Claudine had listened with rapt attention and a smile that hinted at any number of intriguing possibilities.

"You have a good heart, Master de Quincy."

"I also have a dog, demoiselle, one I cannot keep. You could, though. Wait . . . hear me out. Just look at this handsome beast."

He was playing fast and loose with the truth now, for Shadow was bedraggled, gaunt, and dirty, his long black fur matted, his hip protruding at an odd angle. Justin guessed his age to be about five or six months, and if those massive, bearlike paws were an accurate indicator of size, he'd eventually be a large dog, indeed. He seemed to have some alaunt in his ancestry, for there was a wolflike slope to his spine and one ear pricked at an alert angle. But the other one flopped over, giving him a somewhat comical aspect, as did the white ring around his left eye, looking as if he'd been splattered with whitewash. All in all, Justin could not imagine a more unlikely candidate for a royal adoption, but he persevered, insisting that "If ever a dog was born to be a beautiful woman's pet, surely it is this one!"

Claudine laughed, shaking her head. "Very handsome, indeed," she agreed, keeping her eyes on Justin all the while. "But dogs are not as fickle as men, and he has already chosen his master. In good conscience, how could I come betwixt you?"

As if on cue, the pup whined and gave Justin the sort of melting, starry-eyed look he'd have loved to have gotten from Claudine. He surrendered with a smile and a shrug. "You cannot blame a man for trying, demoiselle."

"I never do, Master de Quincy," she assured him with a provocative, sidelong glance through improbably long lashes, and they fell in step together, heading toward the White Tower and the royal apartments. "I am glad we chanced to meet like this,"

Claudine confided, "for there is a question I've been wanting to put to you. Would you be offended if I were to ask you something very personal?"

Justin had never been shy with women, but never had he courted a woman like this one, a queen's confidante. It was like aiming an arrow at the moon. But as their eyes met and held, the moon suddenly seemed much closer than he'd have dared to hope. "Please do, demoiselle."

"Well . . . I was wondering if you were one of the old king's out-of-wedlock sons?"

Justin gave a sputter of startled laughter. "Good Lord, no! Whatever put a notion like that in your head?"

"The queen—indirectly. When I asked her about you—I did warn you about my curiosity—she would tell me nothing, saying only that you had a right interesting family tree, one rooted in hallowed soil. I admit I do not understand what she meant. But I thought she might be hinting that you had a highborn sire . . . and King Henry then sprang to mind. Do stop laughing, for it is not as ludicrous as all that. You seem to have won the queen's trust with remarkable ease—a stranger one day, a confidential emissary the next—and you do have smoke-grey eyes like King Henry, and there is a secret betwixt you and the queen, for certes. Moreover, you are without doubt the most mysterious man I've ever met!"

Still laughing, Justin caught her hand in his and brought it up to his mouth. "Get to know me better," he said, "and I'll share all my guilty secrets with you, demoiselle."

Claudine was no novice to courtly campaigns; she knew exactly when to advance, when to retreat, and when to hold her own ground. "I'll keep that in mind," she said nonchalantly, but she allowed her fingers to rest a moment longer in Justin's grip. By now they had reached the Tower keep, and their flirtation was—if not forgotten—put aside until a more opportune time. "Are you here to see the queen, Master de Quincy?"

Justin nodded. "I wanted to let Her Grace know that I will no longer be staying at Holy Trinity priory. For the foreseeable future, I'll be at the alehouse on Gracechurch Street. My stallion went lame this afternoon and I had to leave him with a farrier till he heals. I also have a letter for the under-sheriff of Hampshire."

He hesitated, loath to admit that he did not know how to go about engaging a courier; he'd never had reason to send a letter before. "I hoped that the queen's clerk might know of a man who is Winchester bound."

"There is no need to wait for a traveler heading that way. The queen will dispatch a royal courier with your letter. And I will tell her that you are now lodging on Gracechurch Street, if you wish. Unless you need to see her yourself . . . ?"

Justin shook his head. "I have no such need." The very fact that Eleanor would admit him without question was reason enough not to abuse so rare a privilege.

"She will see you if you ask. But I suspect she craves no company this day but her own," Claudine said. "You see, we had troubling news this noon . . . about her son."

"Richard? Or John?"

"Not the king." The corners of Claudine's mouth curved, ever so slightly. "The Prince of Darkness. John has left London without a word to the queen and apparently in great haste."

Justin blinked. "Where did he go?"

"As yet, no one knows. I can only tell you what the queen fears—the worst. It is always dangerous when John is close at hand. But it is even more dangerous when he is not."

10

LONDON

February 1193

London was too noisy for late sleepers, and Justin awoke early the next morning. Dressing hastily, for the room was frigid, he then opened the shutters to see what sort of day awaited him. The sky was the color of pewter and clogged with clouds. But there was some brightness to be found below in the yard, where a small child was playing with Shadow. Justin assumed this was Lucy, Nell's little girl, and he watched their antics with a smile. Mayhap he was closer to finding a home for Shadow than he'd first thought.

He was in the stairwell when he heard an odd sound, a sharp cry, cut off too soon. The common room was empty, still claimed by night shadows. But the kitchen door was ajar and as he approached it, there was a thud and another muffled cry. Quickening his step, Justin pushed the door open.

A stack of firewood had been dumped onto the floor, a chair overturned. Across the kitchen, a man had Nell pinned against the wall, one hand clamped over her mouth, the other tearing at her gown. Nell was all but hidden by his bulk, for he was strapping and beefy, not overly tall but as broad as a barrel. Overpowered and half smothered against his massive chest, she continued to struggle, squirming and kicking as he sought to pull up her skirt. His back was to the door, and he was so intent upon subduing Nell that he'd not yet realized they were no longer alone.

Justin was reaching for his sword hilt when his gaze fell upon a sack of flour, half full, on a nearby table. Snatching it up, he was upon the man before he could sense his danger, yanking the sack down over his head and shoulders. Blinded and choking, the man released Nell and reeled backward. Before he was able

135

to free himself of the sack, Justin kneed him in the groin and he went down as if he'd been poleaxed, writhing in the floor rushes at Justin's feet.

Nell had sagged against the wall, gasping for breath. Her veil was gone, her hair in wild disarray, her face and gown streaked with flour. But she recovered with remarkable speed. Grabbing a heavy frying pan from its trivet, she was about to bring it down upon her assailant's skull when Justin caught her arm, blocking the blow.

"He is not worth hanging for, lass!"

She was not easily convinced and he had to take the pan away from her. When he did, she kicked the prostrate man in the ribs, called him a slimy toad, and kicked him again. Drawing his sword, Justin leveled it at the man's heaving chest, then reached down and jerked off the sack. Nell's attacker moaned in pain and pawed at his eyes, blinking and sneezing and then cowering at sight of that menacing steel blade. "If you fetch a rope," Justin said, "I'll tie him up and go for the sheriff."

Nell glared at the cringing man. "No," she said. "Just get him out of here."

Justin was not surprised, for an accusation of rape was not easy to prove. "Are you sure? I'd testify to what I saw." But when she shook her head, he did not argue, prodding the man to his feet with the point of his sword. He encountered no resistance, and within moments, shoved the man through the ale-house door and out into the street.

People turned to stare at this apparition and began to laugh, for not only did he look as if he'd fallen, headfirst, into a vat of whitewash, he was bent over at an odd angle, scuttling sideways like a crab. Already an object of ridicule, he was then made one of scorn, too, when Nell yelled after him, "If I ever see you again on Gracechurch Street, whoreson, I'll geld you with a dull spoon!"

Midst hoots and jeers, the man fled. Nell continued to rage, cursing her assailant with imaginative invective, fuming over the ripped sleeve of her gown. But she'd begun to tremble, and did not protest when Justin urged her to come back inside. Settling her before the hearth, he prowled about the kitchen in search of a restorative.

"It is too early for ale and there is no wine. So cider will have to do," he said, pouring her a full cup.

Nell gulped it gratefully, entwining her fingers around the stem to steady them. But then the cup jerked in her hand, splattering cider onto her torn sleeve. "Lucy!"

"She saw nothing," Justin assured her. "She is outside, playing with the dog."

"Thank God," she said softly. But after a moment, her anger came back, this time directed against herself. "How could I have been so careless? I'd bought firewood from that swine twice before, and each time he was sniffing about my skirts like a dog in rut. But I just took him for the usual prattling fool, paid him no mind. I ought to have known better . . ." She shook her head so vehemently that the last of her hair pins escaped into the floor rushes. "Most men are ones for taking what they want, and God rot them, but they get away with it, too!"

"Not this time."

She stopped in midtirade to stare at Justin. After a long pause, she nodded slowly. "No," she agreed, "not this time. I suppose I owe you."

Justin shrugged, pouring himself some cider. "I do not mean to meddle," he said, "but surely there must be safer work for a woman—"

"Truly?" Nell fluttered her eyelashes in mock surprise. "And here I thought it was either this or starve!" She relented then and gave Justin a quick, forced smile. "I do not have much practice in saying thank you. I am grateful for what you did. But do you really think I need to have the dangers pointed out to me? If you live with polecats, friend, you are bound to notice the stink!"

She rose before he could respond, crossed to the window, and unlatched the shutter. "I want to make sure," she said, "that my girl is in no need of care."

He joined her at the window. "She is right taken with that pup, Nell. It seems a shame to separate them . . ."

Nell turned to look at him, and then grinned. "I owe you, but not that much!" she said, and Justin grinned back, for the first time getting a glimpse of a woman he could like.

"Lucy's father . . . he cannot help you?"

"Not likely. He is dead." She sounded quite matter-of-fact; if this was a wound, it was an old one. Pulling the shutter back in place, she sat down at the table and picked up her cider again. When he followed, she said, "My man and I were properly wed, had the vows said over us at the church door." She raised her chin, as if challenging him to doubt her. "I insisted upon it. I may be no saint, but I am no slut. I'd have no one ever call my child a bastard, for that is a word heavy as any stone and bitter as gall. I ought to know."

"So should I," Justin said, and saw her flicker of surprise. "What happened to your husband?"

"Will was a raker." Seeing his puzzlement, she explained, "That is what Londoners call the men who clean the city streets. It did not pay much and God knows, it was a miserable way to earn his bread. But Will had no trade and he was no thief. Good-hearted, he was, but not one for planning for the morrow. He took his fun where he could find it, and more and more, he found it in alehouses. He liked to stop for an ale after work, and sometimes during work, too. The day came when he stopped once too often, and he fell off his cart. If he'd been sober, mayhap he could have rolled clear. Instead, the wheels ran over his chest." Setting her cider down, she said, without irony, "He was lucky. He died quick."

Justin offered no sympathy, for it was clear she neither expected nor wanted it. "You had no family to turn to, Nell?"

"Money and family—I never had much of either. Most are dead, like Will. So I took in laundry and did sewing and a few times, what I did is better left betwixt me and God. None of it was enough to pay the rent on our house. Here at least we have a bed of our own, my girl and me . . . and that is no small thing, Master de Quincy."

"Make it Justin," he said. "How did you end up here?"

"I have not 'ended up' anywhere, not yet! I admit the Lord's plan for me seems right murky at times, and trying to find my way can be like looking for a black cat at midnight. For now, the road has led me and Lucy here. A cousin on my mother's side is wed to Godfrey, who owns this pigsty. He is old and soured and crippled by gout, and he's come to depend on me more than he'd ever admit. I started by helping out, but now I do the ordering and hiring and firing and in return for all that, I get a bed above-stairs, a weekly wage, and the fun of fending off dolts like the one you tossed out on his ear. But I hope to—"

Nell flinched at the sound of a sudden, loud pounding, showing that her nerves were not as steady as she'd have Justin believe. "Shall I tell them that the alehouse is not open yet?" he offered, and when she nodded, he headed for the door.

The pounding had continued, unabated. Lifting the bolt, Justin opened the door and scowled at the intruder. "You'll have to come back later."

"I think not," the intruder said, and Justin braced for trouble. The man's appearance was no more reassuring than his words. He was of medium height, well muscled and well armed, his mantle swept back to reveal both a scabbard and a sheathed dagger. It was hard to estimate his age. Somewhere, Justin guessed, between thirty and death, and when death did come, it was not likely to be a peaceful one. A black eyepatch, a thin slash of a mouth, contorted at one corner into a sinister parody of a smile by a jagged scar that could have been inflicted only by a knife's blade—no, not a man to die in bed, full of years and honors. Not a man Justin would have wanted to meet in a dark alley. Nor was he happy to have to deal with him here and now, and he said curtly:

"We are closed. You'll have to get your ale elsewhere."

"I am not here for an ale. I'm looking for a man named de Quincy."

"Why?" Justin asked warily, and the man gave him a daunting stare, his one eye as black and fathomless as polished jet.

"Are you de Quincy? If not, why should I be answering to you?"

"Yes . . . I am. Now it is your turn. Who are you?"

"Jonas." When Justin still looked uncomprehending, the man said impatiently, "Did Fitz Alan not tell you that his serjeant would be seeking you out?"

"You're the serjeant?" Justin's smile was both apologetic and relieved. "Sorry—the sheriff did not give me your name. Come on in."

It took a while before they were able to talk, for Justin had to reassure Nell that this formidable stranger was trustworthy, and then fetch candles and cider. The serjeant was still standing. When Justin gestured toward a table, he noticed that Jonas picked the seat facing out into the room. He'd wager it had been years since the serjeant had sat with his back to any door. Pushing a cider cup across the table, he said, "Do you know Gilbert the Fleming?"

The serjeant nodded. "He is the worst of a bad lot. I know of at least three robberies and two killings I want to question him about. But he is not an easy man to track down . . . as you're finding out."

"He has unholy luck," Justin admitted. "If ever there was a man deserving to hang, it is this one. But he somehow slides through every noose. Can you help me change that luck of his? Can you help me find him?"

Jonas shoved his cider aside. "If it were up to me, I'd forswear food and sleep and even whores to hunt that hellspawn down. But the sheriff says he cannot spare me, not until we find out who set the Lime Street fire. Half a dozen houses burned, including one belonging to an alderman, and he has been harrying the sheriff every damned day since, out for blood. The fire must come first, whether I like it or not."

"I understand." And Justin did. The fear of fire stalked every city, dreaded even more than plagues, for it was far more common. But understanding did little to dilute his disappointment. "Can you at least suggest where I ought to start looking?"

"I can do better than that. I can give you a name—a sometime informant of mine. He is a craven little gutter rat, with less sense than God gave a sheep. But he has an uncanny knack for sniffing out other men's secrets. He might be able to help you, as long as you make it worth his while."

"That I can do. What is his name? And how do I find him?"

Jonas grinned. "His name is Pepper Clem, and yes, there is a story behind it. Clem does not have enough backbone to rob a man face-to-face, but he used to be a clumsy cutpurse. He was not very good at it, and more often than not, his victim caught him in the act. So he had an idea. He would bump into his target and surreptitiously spill pepper on the man's clothes, which would cause him to sneeze. And whilst he was sneezing away, Clem's partner would steal his money pouch."

He grinned again at the look of incredulity on Justin's face. "I never said our boy was all that bright, did I? Needless to say, his pepper scheme went awry. The victim was so enraged that he punched Clem in the mouth and knocked out a tooth. And the accomplice spread the story all over London, making sure that he'd be known as Pepper Clem to his dying day!"

This Pepper Clem did not sound like the ideal ally to Justin, but he was not in a position to be choosy. "How do I find him?" he repeated, and the serjeant gave him a description and then the names of several Southwark alehouses that Clem liked to frequent.

Their business done, Jonas got to his feet. "If I think of something else, I'll be back." At the door, he paused, his gaze sweeping over Justin, coolly appraising. "Good luck, lad." That solitary black eye gleamed. "I expect you'll be needing it."

The rest of that Thursday and the day that followed were as frustrating as they were exhausting. Returning, weary and dispirited, each night to Gracechurch Street, Justin felt as if he'd walked down every street and alley and byway that London had to offer, and he'd long since lost count of the alehouses and taverns he'd visited. All to no avail. He'd concocted several different stories: that he was a cousin of Pepper Clem's, that he had a job offer for Clem, even—in desperation—that he was seeking to pay an old debt. No matter how creative he was, no matter how he embellished or elaborated, the result was always the same. Silence and shrugs, indifference and suspicion.

Did they think he was one of the sheriff's men? An informant? Tossing restlessly on his narrow, straw-filled pallet, he had no answers. But since what he'd been doing was not working, he'd have to find a new approach. What had Jonas called Pepper Clem . . . a craven little gutter rat? Would a man like that have many friends—any friends? Mayhap that was the road to follow.

* * *

Southwark lay just across the river from London, and was notorious for its brothels and its brawling and its dangerous sins. Pepper Clem's favorite tavern was on the Bankside, in the disreputable neighborhood known as the stews. Justin had been there twice already, and when he walked through the doorway on Saturday morning, the tavern's hired man signaled his recognition with a raised eyebrow, a cynical smile.

"Back again, are you? Still looking for that *lost* cousin of yours?"

Justin ordered a flagon of red wine. On his last visit, he'd heard a customer call the man by name, and now he said casually, "Rauf, is it not? Put out another cup and I'll buy you a drink."

Rauf's brow arched even higher. But he'd have accepted a drink from the Devil. "Why not?" Pulling up a stool, he watched Justin pour two cups from the flagon. "I see you still have the cur."

By now Justin was getting used to having a faithful, four-legged companion. At least the dog looked less bedraggled today, having been given—unwillingly—the first bath of his young life. Justin could not help smiling at the memory, for he and Lucy had ended up wetter than Shadow, with the kitchen flooded and Nell scolding them nonstop. "This is no cur," he joked. "He has at least a thimbleful of royal alaunt blood. Rauf . . . I have a confession of sorts. I was not entirely truthful with you the other day."

"Does this look like a church? Do I look like a priest? Of course you lied to me, man. People always lie in taverns. The only ones who hear more falsehoods are whores. But your lie was particularly pitiful, I'll admit. Long-lost cousin, indeed! No one kin to that little weasel would ever admit to it, except at knifepoint."

"You're right. That was not very clever of me. The real reason I am looking for 'that little weasel' is the one you've probably guessed. He owes me a debt."

"Money . . . or blood?" Rauf had a high-pitched laugh, almost like a cackle. "You need not answer that. It is enough to know you'll be giving him some grief." Peering into his cup, he then glanced pointedly at the flagon. Taking the hint, Justin filled the cup again.

"Now . . . where would you be most likely to corner Pepper Clem?" Rauf puckered his forehead in thought. "You might try the churchyard at St Paul's. He sometimes lurks there, trying to peddle vials of blood from Canterbury's holy martyr, St Thomas. Every now and then he even finds someone simple enough to believe it! Or he hovers around the Cheapside, selling cat fur as rabbit pelts. You might try the Cock, too, one of the bawdy-houses up Bankside. He runs errands for the whores and offers potions to their customers."

"What kind of potion?"

"The kind that is supposed to fire a man's blood—from gelding to stallion in just one swallow. Men buy it, too . . . at least once." Rauf cackled again. "Clem might be dumb as a post, but he has plenty of company, and that's God's Truth!"

Justin had gotten what he'd come for. He could only hope the hunt's end would be worth all the trouble of the chase. So far, nothing he'd heard about Pepper Clem inspired much confidence.

Justin decided to try the Cock first, since it was so close. All the bawdy-houses were whitewashed, meant to lure potential customers across the river. The symbols of their names—the Crane, the Bell, the Half Moon—were painted above their doors, and he located the Cock without difficulty. He was surprised to find the common room half full, despite the early hour. Apparently sinning was a neverending activity in Southwark. He was accosted by a plump redhead as soon as he walked through the doorway, and disentangled himself with some difficulty. He fended off the next prostitute by feigning shyness, and she went to order wine, hoping that would dispel his nervousness. Justin took advantage of her absence to head toward the far corner of the room, for he'd spotted his quarry.

Pepper Clem was easy to recognize. Jonas had described him as a "chinless wonder," and he did indeed have a receding jawline, poorly camouflaged by a skimpy ginger beard. Everything about the man was meagre: a narrow chest, a small, pursed mouth, sparse, lank hair. His pallor was unhealthy, even for February; he put Justin in mind of a mushroom, grown in a damp cellar far from the sun's warmth. He squinted up uneasily as Justin approached, wavering between alarm and interest at the sound of his own name.

Without waiting to be asked, Justin took a seat opposite the thief. "I've been looking all over Southwark for you, Clem."

"I know you?"

"No, but you know someone I need to find."

"I've never been one for doing favors for strangers."

"Who said anything about favors? You get me the information I want and I'll pay. Play false with me, though, and you'll pay."

Clem digested this. "Who are you looking for?"

"A man named Gilbert the Fleming." Justin saw at once that his arrow had hit its target dead center. Clem shifted in his seat, pulling back like a turtle retreating into its shell.

"What . . . what makes you think I know him?"

"Jonas says so." Clem's reaction to the serjeant's name was unmistakable. Justin watched the emotions battle across Clem's face, his fear of Gilbert the Fleming warring with his fear of Jonas. "I said I'd pay you," he reminded the thief. "Find out the man's whereabouts for me and you'll be the richer by a half-shilling." That was a generous sum and Clem lunged for the bait like a starving trout, heedless of the hook.

"One shilling," he insisted, and looked as if he could not believe his luck when Justin nodded, for he had no way of knowing that was the sum Justin had always intended to pay. "Half now," he bargained, emboldened by his success, but this time Justin shook his head.

"Do not insult me, Clem," he said coldly.

Clem accepted defeat with a shrug; he'd had a lot of practice at it. "I'll see what I can find out," he promised. "Do you know the tavern on the Bankside, the one next to the public bathhouse? Suppose I meet you there on the morrow, the third hour past noon?"

The deal being struck, Justin pushed away from the table. "Wait," Clem protested. "I do not know your name."

"No, you do not," Justin agreed. "The only name that matters is Gilbert the Fleming's."

* * *

"You cannot stay away, can you?" Grinning, Rauf filled a flagon from one of the massive wine casks behind him and set it down, unasked, in front of Justin. He looked disappointed when Justin did not offer to share, but Justin did not want to be distracted by the other's cheerful chatter. Now that the hunt might be nearing an end, he was becoming edgy and tense. Once he found Gilbert the Fleming, what then? Surely the sheriff would agree to make the arrest? Lime Street fire or not, the man was a murderer. Mayhap it would be best to contact Jonas first. Assuming that the sheriff cooperated fully and the Fleming was seized, could he be made to talk? Justin did not doubt that Jonas knew any number of ways to loosen a man's tongue. But the queen would not be wanting Gilbert to unburden himself to anyone but Justin. It was a twisted coil, for certes.

Justin did not expect Clem to be a stickler for punctuality, and he was not concerned at first by his lateness. But as the afternoon dragged by and the shadows started to lengthen, he grew increasingly restless. Where was that wretched little cutpurse? Even if he'd had nothing useful to report yet, he ought to be here, vowing by all the saints to make good his promise. With a shilling at stake, he'd want to keep Justin's trust. Had he gotten drunk and overslept?

Justin waited two hours before giving up. If Clem was coming, he'd have been here by now. He'd have to try again on the morrow. Paying Rauf for his flagon, he whistled for Shadow. Out in the street, he ducked into the doorway of the bathhouse to see if anyone sought to follow him. No one else left the tavern, though. Justin had not truly suspected any of the other customers, but he was determined to take no chances, not with a man like the Fleming. His memories of that bloodstained mill were still too fresh.

Dusk was obscuring Southwark by the time Justin reached the bridge. Torches had begun to bob on the river. He lingered to watch a boat pass underneath, steering between the huge wooden pilings in a dangerous maneuver known as "shooting the bridge." He usually paused on the bridge to watch the ongoing construction of the new stone bridge nearby, begun by

King Henry more than fifteen years earlier. The pile drivers were silent, though, the masons and carpenters being ferried back to shore, and he continued on into London.

He was angry and disappointed and troubled, too, by Pepper Clem's failure to show up at the tavern, but he was also hungry, and headed for the cookshop down by the river. It was crowded with customers, and he had a lengthy wait before he could be served. Nor was the fare particularly appetizing; they'd run out of mutton and pork and he had to settle for an eel pie. That did not improve his mood any, for he had no great liking for fish, and in a few days Lent would be upon them, six long weeks of fasting and salted herring.

Shadow was much more enthusiastic about the meal; he bolted his own pie with comical gusto and begged for more, making Justin laugh in spite of himself. "I'll have to find you a rich master, lad," he said, "for who else could afford to feed you?" In better spirits, he started back toward Gracechurch Street. Clem would surface sooner or later, for he'd never forfeit a chance to earn a shilling.

Vespers was being rung in the city's churches. Justin's step had begun to slow. Like most horsemen, he was not accustomed to walking great distances, and he was glad to spot a familiar cockeyed ale-pole, jutting out into the street like a flag at half-mast. Shadow was already ranging ahead of him, and Justin felt a twinge of pity for the dog. It had taken only four days for the alehouse to become home, doubtless his first ever.

He was opposite Gunter's smithy by now, and Justin decided to stop there first, for he wanted to check on Copper. "Gunter?" Getting no response, he tried the door. It wasn't locked and swung inward when he pushed it. Within, all was quiet. The furnace had been doused for the night, or until the smith returned. But an oil lamp still burned, so he would not be long away. The smithy was well kept; Gunter was obviously a man who believed neatness to be one of God's virtues. A heavy iron anvil dominated the chamber, mounted on a large oak stump, and assorted hammers and mallets and chisels were aligned on a wooden bench. A pair of tongs still sizzled in the water trough, proof that Gunter had just stopped working, for he was too meticulous not to have put the tongs away once they'd cooled. Most likely he was across the street at the alehouse, Justin decided, remembering that Nell had said the farrier liked to come by for an ale in the evenings.

The rear of the smithy opened onto the stable. It held only four stalls, two of them occupied. Copper had thrust his head over the stall door. When Justin stroked his neck, he nuzzled his master's mantle, searching in vain for a hidden treat. The other horse was a newcomer, and even in the gloom of the stable, he caught Justin's eye, for white was an uncommon, highly prized color for mounts. But when Justin came closer, he saw that the horse was not white, after all. A pale roan, he was well past his prime, swaybacked and spavined. Justin continued to stare at him, though. A white horse which turned out to be a roan. Why was that significant? What was his memory trying to tell him?

He heard nothing, the step muffled in the straw. If not for his stallion, he'd have died within moments, almost before he knew what was happening. But when the horse snorted, he started to turn, and the noose did not slip cleanly around his neck, snagging part of his mantle hood, too.

Before Justin could react, the thong tightened, cutting off his air. Instinctively, he clutched at the cord, and the snared material gave him the seconds he so desperately needed—time to get his fingers under the noose. The leather was biting into his throat, but he'd managed to slow the strangulation. Knowing that if he did not break the man's hold now, he never would, he stopped clawing at the noose and flung himself backward. He heard his assailant grunt in pain as they crashed into the stable wall, and he twisted sideways, pulling free.

"Kill him!" his attacker cried, and it was only then that Justin realized there were two of them. A second man emerged from the shadows, the lamp's meagre light glinting upon a drawn dagger. Justin recognized him at once, this man who had become his nemesis, who intended to be his executioner. With no time to unsheathe his sword, he threw up his arm to ward off the blade. Gasping as pain seared from his wrist to elbow, he pivoted to evade the second thrust and grabbed for the killer's knife hand. The Fleming's lips were peeled back from his teeth in a grimace oddly like a smile, and Justin found himself looking into eyes that reflected all the horrors of Hell, so devoid were they of pity or conscience or even humanity.

"Kill him quick," Gilbert's partner urged, "ere someone hears!" He had his dagger drawn, too, and was circling around to stab Justin from behind. By now their struggle had carried them into the smithy. As they grappled together, they lurched against the forge and then reeled into Gunter's work bench. It hit the Fleming at the back of the knees, and already off balance, he could not catch himself, tumbling over the bench into the floor rushes, dragging Justin down with him.

Justin hit the ground hard, and when he tried to get up, the room seemed to tilt. By the time his vision cleared, the killers were both on their feet, closing in. But before they could strike, the door banged and they whirled to face the farrier.

Gunter's eyes cut from Justin, dazed and bleeding, to the two men, daggers drawn. They expected him to flee. Instead, he continued to advance boldly until he was well into the room. Their surprise was evident, but they were quick to meet this new threat, and Gilbert shifted to block Gunter's retreat.

"You ought to have stayed out of this, old man," he jeered, "for now you're dead, too—" He got no further, for Gunter had darted forward, snatching up something from the stable shadows. They recoiled at sight of his weapon, a lethal-looking pitchfork. By then Justin had stumbled to his feet and was struggling to get his sword out of its scabbard.

"Ware!" Gunter shouted suddenly, "ware! Robbers!" At the same time, he moved menacingly toward them. Shutters and doors banged, and they could hear other voices, rising on the evening air. The outlaws hesitated no longer, turned, and plunged for the door.

Justin's memories of what happened next would remain blurred. As the men fled, Gunter chased after them, raising the hue and cry so effectively that fully a dozen citizens were soon in pursuit, with more and more joining in the hunt. Within moments, the smithy was overflowing with people, bombarding Justin with questions. He was grateful when Nell took charge, for he was still shaken.

"Mother Mary, look at the blood!" she exclaimed, and propelled him toward the newly righted bench. "Sit down ere you fall down. And hold your arm up; that'll slow the bleeding. What happened to your head?"

Justin didn't know. "Nothing," he mumbled, but when he brought his hand up to his hair, it came away sticky with blood. "I guess I hit it . . ."

Nell stooped abruptly, running her fingers over a corner of the bench. "I'd wager you banged your head right here," she announced triumphantly. "See this blood?"

Justin leaned over to look and pulled back in alarm, for his head had begun to swim again. Nell saw him lose color and reached over, feeling his forehead. "You're as cold and clammy as the grave! I think we ought to get you back to the alehouse straightaway, so I can put a proper bandage on that arm. Did anyone send for the Watch yet? Blessed Lady, must I do everything around here? You go, Osborn, away with you! Ellis, help me get the man on his feet. And for pity's sake, will someone let that dog in?"

Justin was feeling worse by the moment, fighting waves of queasiness. When Shadow catapulted into the smithy and launched himself at Justin, he staggered and nearly went down. "Shadow, no!"

"Do not yell at that poor beast," Nell chided. "It was his barking that brought Gunter back. Running up and down the street he was, like a mad creature, barking to wake the dead. Gunter thought it strange, and went out to see if anything was amiss . . ."

But Justin heard no more. With his first step, he sagged against the arm holding him upright. Colors were flaming suddenly before his eyes, hot and hazy. After that, there was only darkness.

11

LONDON

February 1193

The dagger slashed the air, grazing Justin's cheek. The next thrust would not miss—he was backed into a corner, with no weapon and nowhere to run. "No!" With a hoarse cry, he jerked upright in the bed. His dream's horror quickly faded, to be replaced by bewilderment. This was not his room at the alehouse. Where was he?

"Glory to God Eternal!" The voice was as unfamiliar as his surroundings. Someone was approaching the bed. The wavering flame of an oil lamp did nothing to resolve his puzzlement, for the face it revealed was a stranger's. The woman was plump and matronly, her eyes crinkling at the corners, a grey braid swinging across her shoulder as she leaned over. "The doctor said you'd likely recover if you soon came to your senses, and bless you, lad, you have!"

No woman had ever smiled at Justin like this, as a mother might. "Who . . . ?" His mouth was dry and his tongue had trouble forming the words, but she seemed to understand.

"I am Agnes, wife to Odo the barber. Lie still, lad, for you are safe here."

Justin wanted to ask where "here" was, but he was too groggy to keep the conversation going. He was not accustomed to using a pillow, and its seductive softness lulled him back into sleep within moments of closing his eyes. When he awoke again, he could see glimmerings of light through the chinks in the shutters and the woman tending to him was Nell.

As soon as he stirred, she hastened toward the bed. "How are you feeling? It was a right nasty crack on the head you took, which could've killed you as easily as that whoreson's dagger.

When you swooned away like that, it scared us enough to fetch a doctor, and then he scared us even more. He said a contusion of the skull ought to heal, but a contusion of the brain was almost always fatal, and all we could do was wait, that either you'd remain senseless till you died or you'd come around on your own."

Nell at last paused for breath. "But when I told him that you'd be the one paying him for his services, that seemed to give him a greater interest in your recovery! He cleaned your wound with honey and then made up a yarrow poultice to stop the bleeding, and promised to come back today."

Justin managed a flicker of a smile. Nell was tilting a cup to his lips and he swallowed without questioning or tasting, sure only that it was wet. His eyes were roaming the chamber as he drank. It still looked totally unfamiliar, although it did remind him of Aldith's cottage. The walls were whitewashed, a fire burned in the hearth, and his bed was piled with clean, neatly mended coverlets. But there was an oddly empty feel to the place, a layering of dust, and the musty scent of vacancy. "Where am I, Nell?"

"Did Agnes not tell you? This is Gunter's cottage."

None of this made sense to Justin. Nell saw his confusion and reached over to retrieve the cup. "The doctor said you ought not to be left alone, so we took turns sitting up with you, me and Agnes and Ursula, the apothecary's widow. We brought you here because we thought you'd be safer. Gunter said those men looked like they were set upon murder, not robbery, and we worried that they might know you'd been staying at the alehouse." She paused again, giving Justin a speculative, challenging look. "Was Gunter right? Were they out to kill you?"

"Yes," Justin admitted, "they were." He was relieved when she asked no further questions, although he knew his reprieve would be brief. She would not interrogate him while he was so weak, but she'd soon be demanding answers, and she'd have a right to them. Nell had moved over to the hearth, announcing that she'd cooked up a pottage for him and hoped he liked onions and cabbage. He had never been less hungry, but he dutifully ate a few spoonfuls of the thick soup before saying:

"I cannot go back to the alehouse, for I'd never put you and

Lucy at risk. But I cannot stay here. I'd not turn Gunter out of his own bed."

Nell handed him a chunk of barley bread, thickly smeared with butter. "You need not fret about that. Gunter beds down at his smithy, has not slept here for months, not since his wife died."

Shadow was nudging Justin's arm, eyes locked hungrily upon the bread tempting inches from his nose. Breaking off a piece, Justin dipped it in the soup and tossed it to the dog. "Passing strange," he said softly. "Gunter saved my life, and yet I know next to nothing about him. When did his wife die?"

"Nigh on a year ago. I do not remember the exact date, but I know it was during Lent. Maude had always been frail, and she'd been sickly for years. But Gunter doted on her. You'd have thought she was the Queen of England, the way he looked after her."

A ghost of a smile flitted across Nell's lips. Sounding faintly wistful, she said, "I never knew a man could be so gentle, not till I saw him cradling her in his arms, pleading with her to eat. She just wasted away, poor woman. And after he buried her, Gunter moved out of the house. We all thought he'd move back once his grieving was done. And when he did not, some people were indignant, calling it a scandalous waste to let a house sit empty. No one dared say it to Gunter's face, though, for he is a quiet one, rarely riled, and yet . . . yet people give him space, if you know what I mean."

"Yes, I do know what you mean," Justin agreed, for he'd not soon forget the image of Gunter whirling around to confront the killers, pitchfork in hand.

"The neighbors did what they could to comfort him. We try to look out for our own here on Gracechurch Street. Of course some of the women had more in mind than comfort, for Gunter would be a good catch: a God-fearing Christian with a kind heart and a thriving trade. But all the pies and newly baked bread they brought to the smithy availed them naught. Gunter had always been ready to offer a hand to anyone in need, but he'd always kept to himself, too. And since Maude's death, he's become even more of a . . . what is the word for those holy men, the ones who shun the company of others and live as hermits?"

"A recluse?"

"Yes, a recluse!" Nell nodded vigorously. "I watch Gunter sometimes, drinking his ale. So sad he looks, like he's forgotten how to smile. But a man chooses his own path, does he not?"

"Gunter and Maude . . . they had no children?"

"Several babes stillborn. Only one survived, a son they christened Thomas, after the saint. People say they thought the sun rose and set in that lad's eyes."

"What happened to him?" Justin asked, already sure there was no happy ending to the farrier's story.

"He drowned when he was thirteen. He'd been playing with friends down by the river and fell in. This was long ere I moved to the street, of course. Tom would have been about your age, I reckon, had he lived."

Nell had related the farrier's sorrows as matter-of-factly as she'd recounted her own. She accepted grief as she accepted January's cold or July's parched heat. "Let me get you some more soup," she offered, and ignoring his refusal, she bustled over to the hearth, began to ladle out another bowl.

"I almost forgot!" She spun around so hastily that she nearly spilled the soup. "That serjeant came by. I cannot remember his name, the one who looks like he escaped from Hell when the Devil's back was turned. We all told him what we could, and he said he'd return on the morrow—on the off chance that you were still alive! I have to tell you, Justin, that I do not care much for the company you keep!"

"Neither do I, Nell." Justin's head had begun to throb. He lay back against the pillow, closing his eyes, and fell asleep almost at once. But within moments, he was jarred into wakefulness by Gunter's entrance.

"You look a lot better than you did the last time I saw you," the farrier said, with a slight smile, and Justin felt a surge of gratitude so intense that his throat tightened.

"If not for you, I'd look a lot worse, for I'd be a corpse. I owe you my life, Gunter. I do not know how a man repays a debt like that. If there is ever anything I can do for you—accompany you on pilgrimage to the Holy Land, hunt down any of your enemies, help you muck out your stalls—I am your man."

"I might take you up on the stall-mucking offer." Although he was striving for a light tone, Gunter's dark eyes were somber. "Did Nell tell you those knaves got away? That is why I felt such unease this afternoon when a man came into the alehouse asking for you. He said his name is Nicholas de Mydden. Do you know him?"

Justin frowned. "No, the name means nothing to me."

"Did Ellis remember what I told him to say if anyone came asking for Justin?" Turning toward Justin, Nell explained, "Ellis is a local lad who helps out at the alehouse when I have need of him. He did not let me down, Gunter?"

"No, he insisted he'd never heard of a Justin de Quincy. But the man then sought me out at the smithy. He knew all about your lamed stallion, Justin, so I could hardly play the fool like Ellis. I told him to try the other alehouse on Gracechurch Street."

"I did not know there was a second alehouse on this street," Justin said in surprise, and Gunter looked at him with a glint of unexpected humor.

"There is not. But de Mydden will eventually learn that for himself and he'll be back. So we'd best decide now what we want to do about him."

Justin was baffled. Neither Gilbert the Fleming nor Pepper Clem could have known about Copper's lameness. "This de Mydden . . . what does he look like, Gunter?"

"Sleek, like a cat he is. God forbid he should ever get mud splattered on his fine mantle or muck on his shoes. Not so tall as you, with hair and beard the color of sun-dried straw, and the kind of courtesy that can be hard to tell from an insult. Wellborn, I daresay, but also a born liar, for he claimed you were to meet him at the Tower this forenoon—"

"Jesú!" Justin sat up too abruptly, wincing at the sudden pain. When he'd met with the queen at Westminster on Candlemas, he'd promised to report back to her on the following Monday— today. "The Tower—I forgot!"

Gunter studied him closely. "So . . . you'll be wanting to see him, after all?"

"Yes." Justin hesitated, torn between the silence he owed to Eleanor and the honesty he owed to Gunter and Nell. "I do not know the man," he said at last, "but I do need to see him. He is one of the queen's household knights. I would tell you more if I could. Later, I hope I can. Till then, I must ask you to trust me—and to fetch him here."

Gunter's face was unrevealing. "Then I'd best go find him," he said evenly, and turned toward the door.

Unlike the farrier, Nell made no attempt to conceal her curiosity. She was staring openly at Justin. " 'The queen's household,' " she echoed incredulously. "Who *are* you, Justin de Quincy?"

Nicholas de Mydden reminded Justin of a cat, too, well groomed and aloof and self-contained. If his fur had been ruffled by the wild goose chase he'd been sent upon, it did not show either in his demeanor or his countenance. He'd followed Gunter back to the cottage with no recriminations, and once there, he'd waited composedly for Justin to offer an explanation.

He proved to be a good listener, hearing Justin out with no interruptions. Only then did he say, "When you did not appear at the Tower this forenoon as agreed upon, the queen feared that something was amiss. Queens are not left waiting, after all, because a man overslept or stopped off at a tavern on his way. I know nothing of your mission for the queen," he continued judiciously, "only what I needed to know to find you. But I assume this attack on you was no random robbery?"

"You can safely assume that," Justin said grimly. "It was good of Her Grace to send you out on my behalf. Tell her that for me, if you will, and that I'll report as soon as I'm on my feet again, in a day or two."

Nicholas nodded. "Anything else?"

"Yes." Justin looked up at the other man. "Tell her that I was careless. But tell her, too, that it will not happen again."

The doctor arrived as Nicholas de Mydden departed, pronounced Justin to be on the mend, and asked for his fee. Nell flitted in and out all afternoon, whenever she could take time away from her duties at the alehouse. Gunter paid another brief visit, as did Dame Agnes and the Widow Ursula, Justin's neighborly nurses, and a few of the alehouse's regular customers who'd taken part in the hue and cry after his attackers. By the end of the day, he was exhausted, and finally fell asleep with a roomful of people milling about.

His dreams were still troubled, filled with foreboding. Turning and tossing, he awoke with a start, sweat trickling into his eyes and his heart thudding against his ribs. "Be easy," a low female voice soothed. "It was but a bad dream."

"Nell . . ." he murmured hazily, and would have drifted off to sleep again had she not spoken up quickly.

"No . . . it is Claudine."

Justin's eyes snapped open. "Claudine!"

She was amused by his obvious astonishment. "I coaxed Nicholas into bringing me here; he is waiting over at the alehouse to take me back. I wanted to see for myself that you were not on your deathbed." Reaching out, she touched her fingers to his beard and then the red welts on his throat. "Are you thirsty?"

When he nodded, she returned with a cup of watered-down wine and watched as he drank, then reclaimed the cup. "This Nell . . . is she your woman?"

"No," he said, and she smiled.

"Good." Leaning over, she kissed him on the forehead. "Rest now," she urged. "I'll stay until you sleep."

The next morning, Justin remembered her remarkable bedside vigil very vividly, although he could not be sure if he was recalling reality or another feverish dream. But not even Claudine could exorcise Gilbert the Fleming's hold, and the day that followed was a dismal one for him. His head ached, his injured arm throbbed, and his nerves were stretched tauter than any bowstring. He saw enemies in the shadows and shadows everywhere.

The doctor had told Justin to stay abed, but neither his temperament nor his circumstances allowed for a lengthy convalescence. He forced himself to get up by midmorning, ignoring the silent protesting of his sore and stiffening muscles, and dressed clumsily in one of Nell's brief absences.

Much to his frustration, just moving around the cottage exhausted him. How could he defend himself when he felt as limp and weak as a melted candle? He soon had to contend with Nell, too, for she was highly indignant to find him out of bed. Out of sheer stubbornness, he balked at heeding her scolding and stayed on his feet until she returned to the alehouse. As so on as she was gone, he cast pride aside and collapsed onto the bed. But he'd barely gotten to sleep when he was roused by an insistent demand for admittance. Stumbling blearily across the chamber, he opened the door to Jonas.

After one glance at Justin's ashen face, the serjeant unhooked a wineskin from his belt. "You look like a man who badly needs a drink." Tossing the wineskin casually in Justin's direction, he straddled the cottage's only chair. "I hear you found Gilbert the Fleming."

"I suppose that is one way of putting it." Justin sat down on the bed and took a swig from the serjeant's wineskin; he suspected he was going to need it.

"Of course it would be more accurate to say he found you." Jonas gestured and caught the wineskin deftly when Justin sent it spinning toward him. Taking a deep swallow, he said, "I've been trying to decide what I ought to marvel at the most—your remarkable luck or your astounding recklessness."

That was the nastiest sort of barb, the kind that held too much truth to shrug off. "When you're tallying up my mistakes," Justin snapped, "be sure to include my listening to your advice to seek out Pepper Clem!"

"Pepper Clem can wait. Let's start with the Fleming and that bloodletting in the stable. The farrier said there were two of them. Could you identify Gilbert's murderous friend?"

"I am not sure," Justin admitted. "He was the one who slipped the noose around my neck, and I was too busy after that to get a good look at him. He was young and sturdy and he had curly brown hair. But that is about all I can tell you. At the time, I was devoting all of my attention to Gilbert's dagger."

"That description could fit half the cutthroats in London," Jonas said regretfully. "So . . . back to Gilbert. Suppose you tell me how he tracked you to that smithy."

"I'd agreed to meet Pepper Clem at a Southwark tavern, but he never came. They must have been lying in wait. Not in the tavern itself; I'd have recognized Gilbert for certes. Mayhap across the street or at the bathhouse. When I gave up on Clem, they just followed me back into London. The streets were crowded at that hour and they knew what they were about. I never saw them, not until it was too late."

"I figured as much." Jonas flipped the wineskin back toward the bed. "You were a bloody fool to let your guard down. But you already know that. In your favor, you were able to keep them from killing you straightaway, which is more than most of Gilbert's victims could say."

"What puzzles me is why they bothered with the noose." Justin's fingers crept up to his throat, tracing the bruises left by that leather thong. "Would it not have been easier to thrust a dagger up under my ribs?"

"I can tell you why. They wanted answers from you first, and the noose is a most effective way of getting them. Cut off a man's air until he passes out, and when he comes around, tighten the cord again until he'll beg to tell you whatever you want to know. If you miscalculate and kill him in the struggle, no matter, for you'd have killed him afterward, anyway."

"A friendly town, this London of yours," Justin said sourly, and Jonas smiled mirthlessly.

"Be thankful you had information Gilbert wanted, or you'd have been carved up like a Michaelmas goose ere you even knew what was happening. Do you know what he wanted to find out from you?"

"I was a witness to a murder he committed, and he might well have decided to make sure I'd not be able to testify against him. But first he'd want to know why I was hunting for him."

"I'd not mind knowing that myself. Your connection to that sheriff's deputy seems sort of murky to me. But I do not suppose you'll be telling me. For now, it is enough that we both want to see Gilbert hanged. So we'd best start planning how we're going to bring that about."

"You're going to help me? But what of the Lime Street fire and that aggrieved alderman?"

"There is not a sheriff in Christendom who'd heed an alderman over a queen. It seems you forgot to mention that you have friends at court. The sheriff was summoned to the queen's presence last night, and she made it very clear, indeed, that she wants Gilbert the Fleming caught as soon as possible—preferably yesterday. So . . . it looks like you and I will be going a-hunting."

Justin was grateful for Eleanor's intercession. Jonas might be more prickly than a hedgehog, but he welcomed the serjeant as an ally. Send a wolf to catch a wolf. "I suggest we start this hunt by tracking down Pepper Clem."

"That is just what I had in mind." Jonas caught his wineskin again, took a final pull, and then got to his feet. "Whilst you are healing, I'll see what I can dig up."

"Good hunting. Pepper Clem has a lot of explaining to do."

Jonas had reached the door. Glancing back over his shoulder, he said with chilling certainty, "If he has the answers we want, he'll give them up." But then he chilled Justin even more by adding, "Assuming, of course, that he is still alive."

12

LONDON
February 1193

Eleanor beckoned Justin toward the closest light, a tall, spiked candelabra. "Come here so I can get a better look at you. Ought you to be up and about so soon? What did the doctor say?"

"I thank you for your concern, madame, but I am truly on the mend. It has been nigh on a week, after all. As for the doctor, we had a falling-out. He wanted to bleed me and I thought I'd been bled more than enough already. In truth, my lady, I've never understood the logic behind bloodletting. How does losing blood make a man stronger? It seems to go against common sense, does it not?"

"It has been my experience, Justin, that when the doctor comes in the door, common sense goes out the window. I always thought it fortunate that doctors are barred from the birthing chamber, else mankind might have died out centuries ago. But if you say you are well enough to be on your feet, I shall take your word for it. Where are you staying now? Are you still at that farrier's cottage?"

"Yes, madame, I am. I told Gunter—the smith—that I'd not feel comfortable staying at his house unless I could pay him, and he reluctantly agreed. I had no other choice, for I did not want to go back to the alehouse, not until we've caught the Fleming."

"That cutpurse you were supposed to meet . . . do you think he betrayed you to the Fleming?"

Justin had been pondering that very question all week long. "I do not know, my lady. He may have. Or it may be that he was clumsy, too heavy-handed in his search for the Fleming. And if Gilbert did hear he was sniffing about and confronted him, we can be sure that he'd blurt out all he knew—and much he did not!"

"And has the sheriff been helping you to track this man down, as I instructed?"

"He was heedful of your wishes, madame, and dispatched his best man to assist in my hunt."

A frown shadowed Eleanor's brow. "Just one?"

"This particular one is more than enough, madame. He is a very—"

There had been several interruptions in the course of their conversation, but they'd been circumspect; a squeak of the door hinges, a light step in the rushes, and a retreat. This time the door banged jarringly, and without waiting to be announced, Will Longsword burst into the chamber. Will looked far more disheveled and agitated than the last time Justin had seen him, in the gardens at Westminster. His bright hair was wind whipped and dusted with melting snow, his face so reddened and chapped by the cold that his freckles seemed to have disappeared. Moving hastily toward Eleanor, he dropped to his knees before her.

"Madame, I was too late. By the time I reached Southampton, John had already sailed."

Eleanor half rose from her seat, then sank back again. "I know you did your best, Will."

Justin glanced at Will, then at the queen. "My lady . . . where did Lord John go?"

"To France," Eleanor said, and although her voice was dispassionate, a muscle twitched faintly in her cheek. "To the court of the French king."

Justin followed Will from the queen's great chamber out into the hall. Heading for the hearth, Will began to warm his hands over the flames. "Mayhap gloves are not such a foppish, newfangled fashion, after all," he conceded. "Jesú, how I hated to bring her more bad news!"

"What happened?"

"You know about John's disappearance on Candlemas Night? Well, when we got word that he'd been spotted on the Winchester Road, I took out after him. I suppose he could have been bound for the West Country or a sojourn in Wales. But Winchester is just twelve miles from the coast, so I rode for Southampton like my horse's tail was on fire—to no avail. He was already halfway across the Channel by the time I got there."

"What did you have in mind?" Justin asked curiously, and Will gave him a rueful smile.

"Damned if I know! Try to talk some sense into him, I guess. Not that I've ever gotten him to listen in the past. I had to try, though, even if I got nothing out of it but saddle sores and frostbite."

Justin knew—along with most of Christendom—that John and Richard had a brotherly bond in the tradition of Cain and Abel. He found himself seeing John in a new light now, for if he could inspire such loyalty in a man like Will, he could not be utterly beyond redemption. "I agree with the queen," he said. "You did your best and what more can a man do than that?"

Will shrugged. "The trouble is, lad," he said, "that the French king is doing his best, too, and if he has his way, King Richard will never see England again."

Bidding Will farewell, Justin crossed the hall and entered the stairwell. It was quite dark, for a wall rush light had gone out, and he started down slowly. His mind upon the hunt for the Fleming, he did not hear the footsteps below, light and hurried. He was not aware of the woman hastening up the stairs, not until she turned the corner and they collided. When she stumbled, he reached out to steady her and breathed in a familiar perfume.

"Oh!" Her voice was low, startled. "I am so sorry!"

"I'm not."

Claudine smiled in the shadows, recognizing the voice. "Justin de Quincy, you are the most unpredictable man I've ever met. Why are you lurking out here in the stairwell?"

"Hoping to run into you, demoiselle."

"Well," she said softly, "here I am."

Justin might not have been involved with a woman like Claudine before, but he was still experienced enough to know an invitation when he heard one. Shifting so there was no longer space between them, he slid his fingers under her chin, then tilted her face so he could claim her mouth with his own. Her response was all he could have hoped for; her lips parted, her arms going up around his neck.

Eventually the sound of an opening door above them intruded, breaking the erotic spell, and they moved apart. "Come on," Claudine whispered. "That might be the queen's chaplain!"

They fled hand in hand down the stairs and out into the bailey. It had been snowing intermittently all morning, and lacy flakes were drifting down lazily around them, so soft and gentle to the touch that it was like a shower of delicate winter flowers. When Claudine caught one on the tip of her tongue, Justin began to laugh. "Do that again and I'll not answer for the consequences!"

"I've never given a fig for consequences," she said airily, pretending to lick another snowflake from her lower lip. "I've been meaning to ask you, Justin, if you found my mantle brooch, a silver crescent? I may have lost it at your cottage, for I missed it after I visited you that night."

"I'll take a look for it," Justin said, and brought her hand up to his mouth, kissing her palm and then the inside of her wrist. "We'd probably have a better chance of finding it, though, if we looked for it together."

"What are we waiting for?" When she slipped her arm through his, he decided that if Eve had a smile half as bewitching as Claudine's, no wonder Adam had been so willing to taste that forbidden fruit.

The cottage was cold, for they'd not taken the time to build a fire in the hearth, lighting one in bed, instead. Afterward, they burrowed under the covers for warmth and shared a meal Justin scrounged up from his bare larders. He apologized for the plain fare, but Claudine merely laughed, assuring him that he was an ideal host in the ways that mattered. He'd never known a woman who was so playful and provocative, too, and, watching as she ate heartily of his brown bread and goat cheese, he felt a prickling of unease. It would be so easy to fall in love with her, so dangerously easy.

She had hair as soft as silk and as dark as a summer midnight. When he wrapped a long strand around his throat, she smiled and nipped his earlobe with teeth like small, perfect pearls. Pillowing her head against his shoulder, she asked, "What are you thinking about? Me, I hope . . ."

He could not very well tell her what he was really thinking— that she was far too beguiling for his own good. Instead, he said lightly, "I was thinking there ought to be a law against any woman being so beautiful. Not only is it unfair to other women, but you must be a hazard to city traffic. Men riding by are likely to watch you instead of the road, dropping their reins and losing their stirrups and getting themselves thrown into the street at your feet."

She laughed softly. "How very true. The mayor even asked me not to venture out into the city during the daytime, for they cannot cope with the chaos I cause. Will you mind if I confine my visits to those hours after dark?"

He propped himself up on his elbow. "I'll have to give that some thought. Ought I to worry that you might be a succubus? They only come out after dark, too."

She blinked. "A what?"

"A succubus—a sultry female spirit who comes in the night to steal a man's seed whilst he sleeps."

"You caught me out," she confessed. "I am indeed a succu . . . whatever, and a very successful one, too. I've stolen your seed twice already this afternoon and you did not offer even token resistance!"

Justin grinned. "The laws of war stipulate unconditional surrender to succubi. How could you not know that, Claudine?"

"Alas," she said, "my education has been lacking. Yours, however, seems to have been very thorough. Are you sure you are not one of King Henry's out-of-wedlock sons, after all? Who are you, Justin—truly?"

"I'm a man bedazzled by your dark eyes," he parried, "a man getting thirsty again for your wine-sweet kisses." She'd been as generous with her history as she'd been with her body, talking freely of her late husband and her brothers back in Aquitaine, telling him about a sun-drenched childhood that seemed worlds away from the solitary years of his own youth. What could he tell her in return? About the taunts of "Bastard" and "Devil's whelp" and Aubrey's stubborn denial of paternity?

She twisted around so she could see his face. "You want to remain a man of mystery, then? As you wish. But I ought to warn you that I'm very good, indeed, at solving puzzles. First things first, though . . ." Leaning over, she gave him a "wine-sweet" kiss. Drawing back then, she studied him pensively. "I know little of Latin," she said, "no more than the responses to the Mass and a few odd phrases . . . like 'Carpe diem.' Do you know the meaning, Justin?"

"Yes," he said slowly, "I do. 'Seize the day.' "

She nodded. "It is a fine thought, is it not?" When he nodded, too, she smiled and kissed him again.

Justin understood more than the Latin translation. He comprehended what she was trying to tell him, as tactfully as possible—that they could have no future together. That he already knew. She was a child of privilege, with dower estates in Aquitaine and a distant kinship to the queen. Whereas he was a child of sin, with no land of his own, not even enough soil to be buried in, all that he possessed able to fit into his saddle bags. They could share a bed, but no tomorrows, make love but not plans. He was glad of her gentle warning. For both their sakes, he must not ask for more than she could give.

"Seize the day," he echoed, and drew her down into his arms. But within moments, they were startled by hammering at the door. Wrapping himself in a blanket, Justin unsheathed his sword before sliding the bolt back and opening the door a crack.

The man outside was a stranger. "Master de Quincy? My serjeant sent me."

Justin opened the door a little wider. "Jonas?"

"Aye. He said I was to fetch you."

"Why?"

"Master Jonas is not one for explaining. He says 'Do it,' and we do, or Christ pity us. He wants you to meet him out at Moorfields straightaway."

Justin was still learning London's byways and contours and boundaries. "Where is Moorfields?"

The man looked at him with the utter amazement of a native Londoner. "Why, everybody knows Moorfields, the meadows north of the city walls. You want me to wait?" When Justin shook his head, he started off on his own, then glanced back over his shoulder. "I think," he said, "that he wants to see you about a body."

Moorfields was a playing ground for London's young and adventuresome. As soon as the waters froze each winter, crowds flocked to the marshlands, sliding and swooping across the ice, the more daring propelling themselves along with the shinbones of horses strapped to their feet, using iron-tipped staffs to gain speed and leverage. It was usually a lively and cheerful site, echoing with shouts and laughter. Now it was somber and hushed, youths clustered in small knots along the shore, watching solemnly as Jonas and his men circled cautiously around a large, gaping hole in the ice, probing the frigid, murky water with long, wooden poles.

Although he seemed to be directing all of his attention to the search, Jonas was still aware of peripheral sounds and sights. When Justin reined Copper in at the water's edge, the serjeant ordered his men to continue the hunt, and then strode over, as surefooted on the ice as he was on solid ground. "How did you come, by way of Dover?"

Justin was not about to explain that he'd had to see Claudine safely back to the Tower first. Quickly dismounting, he ignored Jonas's irritation. "What is going on?"

"Some young fools were sporting out on the ice when it cracked under their weight. Their friends managed to save one, but the other lad drowned. We've been trying to recover the body."

"May God assoil him." Justin sketched a quick cross on the icy afternoon air, all the while wondering why Jonas would want him to see this poor drowned youth. "Do you ever get used to this? It cannot be easy, having to deal with death day after day."

"Nothing about this work is easy," Jonas said, then spat into the snow. "Come over here where we cannot be overheard, for I've news for you."

Hitching his stallion to a nearby bush, Justin followed Jonas across the snow. The serjeant shouted further instructions to the men on the ice, and then turned back to face Justin. "We snagged the body almost at once. But as we started to maneuver it within grabbing range, it slipped off the hook and went under again."

Justin still did not understand why this sad death warranted such an urgent summons. "Bad luck."

Jonas nodded. "It was that. It was also the wrong body."

"What do you mean?"

"It was not the lad. I think it was Pepper Clem."

Justin drew a sharp breath. "Can you be sure?"

"Not until we fish him out. But I got a look at the face ere the body sank and it looked like him to me."

Justin was still dubious. "I saw a body pulled from the River Severn once. He'd only been in the water two days, but not even God could have recognized him, Jonas."

The serjeant pointed impatiently toward the lake. "I'd hate to think all that ice escaped your notice." He remembered then, though, that Justin could not be expected to have his specialized knowledge of dead bodies. "Cold water keeps a corpse from decaying," he explained brusquely, and was about to go into grisly detail when his men began to shout. "They've got one," he said. "Let's go see who it is."

Following Jonas out onto the ice, Justin saw that the men had been using poles with crooks on the end, like shepherds' staffs. One of these hooks had snared the victim's mantle, enabling them to drag him to the surface. By the time he and Jonas reached them, the men had pulled the body up onto the ice. When they turned him over, Justin felt a sickened pity, for he was very young, sixteen at most.

Jonas showed no emotion, gazing down at the drowned youth so impassively that Justin felt a chill; did the man never grieve for the dead? With a few terse commands, Jonas set two of his men to dragging the corpse across the ice toward the shore, where his stunned companions still waited. "Ask those cubs if they know where the lad lived. Someone will have to break the news to his kin, and like as not, it'll be me. And keep looking. We've got another body to bring up."

Justin moved aside, watching as the men continued the search. When Jonas rejoined him, he said quietly, "I get the feeling it did not surprise you to find Clem floating under that ice."

"He was not floating, not when the water's that cold. But you're right. I was expecting Clem to turn up dead. The fool tried to—" As they talked, Jonas had continued to scan the activities of his men, and reacted even before the first outcry. "They've hooked him. This better be Clem. We find a third body out here and I'm heading for the nearest alehouse."

The men soon had the corpse out of the water. He was sprawled on his stomach, his face hidden from view, but Justin thought the limp ginger hair did resemble the thief's. At first glance, his hands seemed to have been dipped in whitewash, and were queerly wrinkled; one of his feet had lost its shoe and it, too, showed that same chalky puckering. Justin braced himself as they shoved the body over onto his back. The face was so bloodless it seemed more like wax than flesh; the eyes were wide and staring, sand trickling from his open mouth, his skin scraped and abraded. But Jonas had been right; Pepper Clem's features were still easily recognizable.

The other men had gathered around and they stared down in silence at the body. There was no need to ask if he'd drowned. The cause of death was painfully obvious, and Justin was not the only one to avert his eyes from that gashed, mutilated throat. Jonas showed no such aversion and knelt by the body, studying Clem's wrists and then his ankles.

"Best to do this quick," he said, "for he'll start to bloat up now that he's out of the water, and in no time at all the stink will put a polecat to shame. I'm looking for rope burns, but it does not seem that he was weighted down. I suppose Gilbert did not think it was worth the trouble." No one else spoke, and he continued his examination of the corpse. "He's been in the water awhile; see all this sand in the seams of his tunic? My guess is he died last Saturday eve and took his final swim that same night, for the lake had not frozen over completely yet."

Justin swallowed with difficulty. "Was he . . . was he hit on the head first?"

"Possibly. Oh . . . you mean this?" Jonas asked, pointing

toward the raw-looking wound that spread from Clem's right eyebrow up into his hairline. "That is not the Fleming's doing. You do not think the fish and crabs would pass up a meal like this, do you?" Glancing over his shoulder at Justin, he bit back a smile. "You're looking a little greensick, lad. I hope you're not going to feed the fish, too?"

Justin shook his head mutely. Those sightless eyes seemed to be staring up accusingly at him. First Kenrick and now Clem. How many more? The other men had retreated, for Jonas had been right in this, too; a foul, fishy odor was becoming discernable. Justin swallowed again. "I got him killed, didn't I?"

Jonas washed his hands in the snow, drying them on his mantle. "You have that backward. He almost got you killed."

"What are you saying?"

"I told you that I'd put the word out on the streets. What I learned was that I'd misjudged the little cheat. As craven as he was, Clem was even more greedy. You probably offered him too much, for he concluded that if you'd pay to find Gilbert the Fleming, mayhap he'd pay more to know you were on his trail. I found two witnesses who saw him meet Gilbert at a tavern in Cripplegate on Saturday eve a week ago. They talked briefly and then left together. That is the last time Clem was seen alive. And when you turned up at the alehouse the next day as agreed upon, Gilbert was waiting."

Involuntarily, Justin's fingers cradled his slashed arm. It was still sore and somewhat stiff, but how much worse it could have been. That deadly blade could have lodged in his gut or stabbed through to his heart. "Clem told him what he wanted to know, how to find me. So why, then, did Gilbert kill him?"

"I'll tell you something about killing. Until a man has done it, he shrinks from it, makes of it more than it is. The first killing comes hard for most men. After that, it gets easier, a lot easier. For some, it gets to be a habit, or worse."

Jonas broke off to give orders concerning the disposition of Clem's corpse. There was a lot to be done and it was a while before he turned his attention again to Justin.

"You asked why the Fleming murdered that worthless little thief? Because it pleasured him. And that's also why there were men willing to talk to me about it. Not because they cared a rat's arse about Pepper Clem. Even a mother'd not mourn his loss. But it scares other men when they find one who takes too much joy in killing." That lone black eye held Justin's gaze, unwavering and unblinking. "As well it should."

13

LONDON

February 1193

Sleep did not come easily to Justin that night. His bedsheets were still scented with Claudine's perfume. But the cottage's other spirit was not as welcome, for Clem's meagre ghost had followed him from Moorfields, and watched reproachfully from the shadows. When he finally slept, though, he did not dream of Clem or even Claudine. He was back in the Durngate Mill, feeling Kenrick's blood splatter upon his skin, and then the mill became Gunter's smithy and he was fighting again for his life, struggling to stave off the Fleming's thrusting blade. He awoke well before dawn to a cold hearth, ice skimmed over the water in his washing laver, and sweat on his brow.

The snow had continued during the night and was still spiralling down slowly from low-hanging grey clouds, large, fat flakes that seemed almost benign, an innocuous cousin of the snow that clogged roads and collapsed roofs and made winter travel so treacherous. Justin dropped Shadow off at the alehouse to play with Lucy, saddled Copper, and rode over to St Clement's Church on Candle-wright Street where he heard Mass and prayed for the souls of all the Fleming's victims. It occurred to him that his was probably the only prayer to be offered up for Pepper Clem, and that seemed the saddest possible epitaph for a man's misspent life.

Afterward, he arranged with the priest to give Clem a Christian burial and then left word for Jonas that he would pay for the little thief's funeral. He was still in a somber, reflective mood when he finally returned to Gracechurch Street, and he decided to leave Shadow with Lucy for a while longer. Gunter had gone off on an errand and the smithy was being watched by young

Ellis, the neighbor lad who helped Nell out. Giving the boy a coin to unsaddle and feed Copper, Justin crossed to the back door and went out into the pasture behind the smithy.

Gunter's cottage did not seem like a city dwelling, for it was set apart on its own, surrounded by the fenced-in field and sheltered by several bare-branched apple trees. The garden once tended by Gunter's dead wife had long since shriveled under the neglect born of a long illness, but the holly she'd planted still thrived, bright splashes of green against the softly drifted snow. It was the snow, not the holly, that caught Justin's eye now. His tracks were still visible, not yet filled in. Beside them was a new set of footprints, leading straight to the cottage door.

Justin came to an abrupt halt. Gunter's cottage did not have a lock and key, for he'd never seen the need for such expensive protection. Instead, he'd fitted his door with a simple latch, a small bar which pivoted at one end and could be lifted from the outside by a latchstring. When Justin had left that morning, he'd taken the precaution of snagging the latchstring around a nail he'd driven into the wood. Now it dangled free, further proof that someone had lifted the bar and entered the cottage.

Justin was motionless for a long moment, considering. There was but one set of footprints. And the shutters were still in place, so whoever was within could not see his approach. He slid his sword from its scabbard. In one swift motion, he jerked up the latchstring and hit the door with his shoulder, shoving inward.

He came in fast and low, sword drawn. An oil lamp had been lit, its flame shivering in the sudden draft. A man was kneeling by the hearth, striking flint to tinder. He recoiled with a startled oath as the door banged open. "Jesú! Most men are content to open a door and just walk in. Leave it to you, de Quincy, to blow in like an ill wind and bounce off the walls!"

Justin was now the one to swear. "Hellfire and damnation! What are you doing here, Luke?"

"I happened to be passing by. What do you think?"

"I think that you nearly got yourself run through, and who'd have blamed me?"

They glared at each other, but their glowering gave way then to sheepish grins. Shutting the door, Justin dropped the bar back into place and carefully drew in the latchstring. "I'll confess that I'm glad to see you, Luke. At least now the Fleming will have a choice of targets."

"It sounds like you got somewhat confused, de Quincy. You were supposed to be the hunter and Gilbert the hunted, remember?"

"Good of you to point that out to me." Moving to the hearth, Justin helped Luke to get the fire going. "How did you find out where I was? The entire street is in a conspiracy to keep my whereabouts secret—and there are none more stubborn or suspicious than Londoners!"

"You need not tell me that, for I've already met the hellcat over at the alehouse. I might as well have been speaking Welsh, for all the good it did me. 'Justin who? Never heard of the man.' And the chill got even worse when I admitted to being an undersheriff. They do not fancy the law much hereabouts, do they?"

Justin laughed. "I'd love to have seen that, you and Nell locking horns. So how did you win her over?"

"By sheer perseverance. I would not go away, kept insisting that we were allies. I even stretched the truth enough to claim we were friends. Finally it occurred to me to show her your letter, proof that I could be trusted. But then I had to wait whilst she sent for the priest, since he is the only man on the street who can read, and she was not about to take my word for the letter's contents. If they protect you half as well from Gilbert the Fleming as they did from me, you've nothing to worry about!"

Justin was looking around the cottage in vain for food or drink to offer Luke; they'd have to go over to the alehouse and coax Nell into cooking a meal. But that would have to wait, for he'd been doing some rapid mental math. "Today is the fourteenth, only ten days since I sent that letter. You must have ridden for London as soon as you got it. Why?"

Luke's smile was triumphant, and a trifle smug. "Whilst you were playing cat-and-mouse with the Fleming, I was having better luck. Remember Gilbert's unknown partner? Well, he is unknown no longer. We're looking for a lout named Sampson, one of Winchester's least-loved sons. I daresay the entire town heaved a great sigh of relief when he fled with Gilbert. Unfortunately, we never lack for felons, but at least Sampson is London's worry now—and ours."

"Good work, Luke. But are you sure this is the man? I doubt that I could identify him."

"From what you told me about him, he is young and strong and stupid, no? Well, Sampson has an ox's strength and an ox's brains, powerful enough to hold onto a terrified stallion and dumb enough to call out Gilbert's name. Moreover, he is known to have worked with Gilbert in the past, and he disappeared from Winchester at the same time as Gilbert did. I have no doubts that he is our man. Do you think he could also have been in on your London ambush? The hellcat told me—very grudgingly—about that attack on you in the smithy last week. I assume one was our friend the Fleming. Was Sampson the other?"

"No, I think not. The man in the smithy was nowhere near as tall and strapping as this Sampson. Also, he had a London accent, and you say Sampson is a Winchester lad. But you are right about Gilbert. He did indeed come calling, knife in hand."

"That is the third time you've encountered the Fleming in one of his killing moods and lived to tell about it. Your guardian angel must be putting in very long hours these days." Scorning the sole rickety chair, Luke seated himself cross-legged on the foot of the bed. "Do you think that means Gilbert and Sampson have parted company?"

"Well . . . you say Sampson is none too clever. But we know Gilbert is, for certes. He might well have decided Sampson was too risky a partner and cut him loose. Gilbert knows London, would have no need for Sampson here. He swims in these waters with ease, one more shark amongst the rest. I'd wager they went their separate ways once they reached the city."

"That makes sense," Luke agreed. "Of course Sampson could be dead, then. People around Gilbert do seem to die at an alarming rate."

"Possibly. But you say Sampson is big and mean spirited and knows Gilbert's ready way with a knife. He'd not be that easy to kill. It might have been simpler for Gilbert just to let him go off on his own."

Luke nodded thoughtfully. "What sort of help are you getting from the sheriff?"

"He agreed to let one of his serjeants assist me, a man named Jonas. Are you familiar with him?"

"I'm not sure. I met several of the sheriff's men on past visits to London. He might be one of them, I suppose."

"Believe me, Jonas is not a man to be forgotten. If you'd met, you'd remember. In his own way, he is as formidable as the Fleming. So you and he will probably take to each other like long-lost brothers," Justin added wryly. But almost at once, his smile faded. "Luke, there is another death to be charged to Gilbert's account. A wretched little thief and cutpurse named Pepper Clem. No one grieves that he is gone. But his murder ought not to be forgotten. Even the least of us deserves justice."

After experiencing Jonas's indifference, Justin half expected Luke either to shrug or scoff. But the deputy merely nodded again. "I seem to remember Scriptures saying something about birds: that not even a sparrow falls to earth without the Almighty's knowing. If that holds true for sparrows, it must hold true, too, for 'a wretched little thief and cutpurse.'"

Justin studied the other man for signs of mockery, did not find them. "You could have sent me a letter about Sampson. You did not need to come on your own. Why did you, Luke?"

"I could say I fancied a trip to London. Or that I knew you'd get yourself into trouble on your own. Or that I've always been one for being there at the end of a hunt. Why do my reasons matter?"

"They do not," Justin said, but it was a lie. Luke's reasons mattered very much, indeed, to him. There could be a less innocent explanation for the deputy's sudden appearance here. John had passed through Winchester on his way to the port of Southampton. Had he sent Luke back to London to be his eyes? As little as Justin wanted to believe that, he could not dismiss the suspicion out of hand. He dared not. He'd made some mistakes so far, but the greatest mistake of all would be to underrate John.

Smithfield was a large open area just northwest of the city walls, a popular gathering place for Londoners. Weekly horse fairs were held there, and, weather permitting, rowdy games of camp-ball, archery, wrestling matches, and mock jousts.

Luke had visited the horse fair during a previous stay in London, and it was his idea that they go out to Smithfield, question the dealers to see if one of them had been offered a pale roan stallion of high calibre in the past month. Justin was skeptical, but Luke insisted. It was a longshot, he admitted, for even if they could find a buyer who remembered Gervase Fitz Randolph's stolen palfrey, the chances were slim that it would lead them to Gilbert the Fleming. But they had to follow up every lead, he argued, and if they did not go this afternoon, they'd have to wait a full week for the next horse fair. Since Justin could not refute the logic of that, Luke prevailed.

Upon their arrival at Smithfield, however, they discovered that Luke's memory was flawed; the horse fairs were held on Fridays, not Mondays. The fields were empty except for a few reckless youths who'd shown up to joust despite the weather and a handful of hardy spectators, for it was not a day to be outdoors by choice. The temperature had risen during the night, turning Sunday's snowfall into a muddy slush, and the wind was unrelenting, with an edge, Luke grumbled, that not even the Fleming's blade could equal.

Luke was taking the setback with poor grace. "This was madness, de Quincy. Even if the horse fair had been held today, that blasted stallion was likely sold off weeks ago."

Justin grabbed the other man's arm, stopped him in time from stepping into a pile of freshly deposited manure. "Need I remind you that this was your idea, Luke?"

"So? Why did you not talk me out of it? Devil take the horse and the weather and Gilbert, too. If we do not get inside soon, I'm in danger of freezing body parts I can ill afford to lose!"

Turning on his heel then, Luke started back to retrieve their horses. "I cannot believe I dragged us out here on such a fool's errand. But I was bone-weary of going from one tavern to the next all morning, hoping against hope that Sampson would be drinking himself sodden within. If we have to depend upon happenchance to find the man, we may be wandering about London's seedier neighborhoods for years. Yet what other choice do we have? It's not as if that friend of yours was much help!"

"I'd not call Jonas a friend. But he did have a point. He does not know Sampson from Adam, would not recognize him if he fell over the man. You're the one who knows him on sight, not us. And Jonas might have been more cooperative had you not been so high handed with him." Justin was cold and irritable, too, and the look he gave the deputy was not friendly. "You cannot always demand, Luke. Sometimes it is wiser to ask."

"What is that, the gospel according to Justin de Quincy?" But after a few moments of mutually annoyed silence, Luke thawed first. "Bear with me; I am out of sorts today. I've come so close to catching Gilbert in the past. Yet each time he has somehow managed to elude me. I am not willing to let that happen again, by Corpus, I am not."

"We'll find him," Justin said, hoping he sounded more certain than he felt, for he'd begun to wonder if the Fleming's ungodly luck would ever run out.

"We'd better . . . and soon, ere I start to ask myself what I'm doing here, sleeping on your floor instead of snug in Aldith's bed. And speaking of beds, think you that we can borrow some extra blankets from the hellcat? That pallet was harder than a landlord's heart."

They soon reached the hitching post where they'd tethered Copper and Luke's temperamental sorrel. "I cannot believe I got the day wrong," Luke said glumly. "Now we'll have to come back at week's end. They hold races there, too, on Fridays, and that might lure Sampson out, for he has a fondness for gambling. I hear tell he is not very good at it, but he is always keen for making a wager."

That sounded like a promising lead to Justin. "We need not wait for the Friday races then. If we can find out from Jonas where the high-stakes dicing games are played, we could keep watch for Sampson."

Luke at once swung up into the saddle. "I ought to have thought of this sooner. Most men have a weakness of some sort, be it for drink or whores or high living."

Justin mounted, too. "A pity the Fleming only lusts after dead bodies and not whores. I'd much rather track him through bawdy-houses than cemeteries."

"Christ on the Cross!" Luke reined in his stallion so hastily that the horse reared up. "How could I have forgotten about the woman?"

Justin's hopes kindled. "Which woman?"

By the time Luke had gotten his horse under control again, he had reined in his excitement, as well. "I do not want to make more of this than I ought," he said cautiously. "It is only a comment Kenrick made last summer, when we were hunting the Fleming for the murders of that merchant and his wife. He told me he was sure Gilbert had gone back to London, back to his 'Irish whore.' He said his cousin had been boasting about how hot she was in bed. When I wrote to the London sheriffs about Gilbert, I passed on what Kenrick had said, but he could not remember the woman's name, so they must not have thought it worth pursuing."

"Why do you think Kenrick called her that? Because he had contempt for any woman who'd take up with the likes of Gilbert? Or could she really be a whore?"

Luke did not answer immediately, considering. "I know of at least one whore he was bedding back in Winchester. Rumor had it that she'd send him word when she got a customer worth robbing."

"Well, that gives us a place to start—the Southwark stews. Let's go find Jonas again."

"A hunt for an unnamed whore who may or may not know the Fleming?" Luke was grinning. "Who could resist a mad quest like that?"

Jonas was not very enthusiastic about their conjecture. Justin doubted, though, if the serjeant was ever enthusiastic about much of anything. But he did agree to try to find out if there was a whore in the Southwark stews who happened to be Irish. Justin and Luke spent the rest of the day checking out alehouses and taverns that were known to be frequented by gamblers, to no avail. There was no sign of Sampson.

It was evening when they got back. As soon as they entered

the alehouse, Justin was hailed from several corners of the common room, and he paused to exchange greetings with Odo the barber, young Ellis, and Roland the wainwright, who'd been the first to join in Gunter's hue and cry against the Fleming. By then, Luke had already claimed a table for them and ordered a flagon of ale. "You seem to be settling right in."

"I suppose I am," Justin agreed, realizing in surprise how comfortable he did feel here on Gracechurch Street. "They are right curious about you, of course, wanting to know if it is true that you are a sheriff of some sort. I said you were, but not to hold it against you."

Luke shoved the flagon across the table. "Help yourself, for you're paying for it. I told the hellcat to put it on your account."

Justin poured himself a drink. "When we talked earlier about the Fitz Randolphs, you said they were faring poorly, stalked by rumors and gossip. You would not have spread those rumors, by any chance?"

"Sometimes it helps to sow some suspicion about. But in this case, the rumors were already springing up. Their neighbors are looking askance at the family, and there is a lot of talk in the alehouses, much of it unkind. Have you ever noticed how eager people are to believe the worst? But because of all the gossip and speculation, the abbot of Hyde Abbey has told Thomas Fitz Randolph that it would be for the best if he did not seek admission to their order just yet. I believe he used such soothing phrases as 'in God's good time' and 'once the dust has begun to settle.' But we both know—and so does Thomas—that he really meant, 'Come back once we're sure you're not a murderer.'"

"I daresay Thomas took that with his usual grace and good-will."

Luke grimaced. "He accosted me at high noon in the Cheapside, accusing me of ruining his life and putting his immortal soul at peril. I lost my temper, too, and threatened to shove him into a horse trough if he did not go home. If he ever does end up as a Benedictine brother, God help his brethren!"

"What of the others? No wedding plans announced yet for Jonet and Miles?"

"I think they are still seeking to win the mother over. They'd have to wait anyway, for the same reason that Aldith and I do, since no marriages can be performed during Lent. But when I stopped by the Fitz Randolph house ere I left for London, Miles was there, breaking bread with the rest of the family, so I expect that he and Jonet will have their way in the end. Assuming, of course, that they are not implicated in her father's murder. I doubt that they are guilty, though. I'd put my money on our lovable little monk if I had to choose between them."

"At least we were able to eliminate Guy as a suspect. But it sounds as if the goldsmithy will be in for some rough times. Gervase was the wind behind those sails. And if we cannot solve the murder, it might well go under." Until now, Justin had thought only of providing answers for Eleanor. But Ella needed them, too, mayhap even more than the queen did. Suspicions could blot out the sun for all the Fitz Randolphs, the guilty and innocent alike.

"I do not truly think it was Thomas, either," Luke said suddenly. "I suspect the man was slain for reasons I can only guess at. His groom told me that he was on an urgent mission to London, and that might well explain the inexplicable interest of the Queen of England in this killing. How much do you know, de Quincy? More than I do, for certes. Do you not think it is about time you shared some of that knowledge with me?"

Justin stiffened. "What do you mean?"

Luke set his cup down with a thud. "You're the queen's man, I've not forgotten. But we are on the same side in this fight. I think I've earned the right to ask some questions."

Justin thought so, too. But was Luke asking for himself? Or for John? "What do you want to know?"

"Was the goldsmith carrying a letter for the queen?"

Justin had not expected such a bold challenge. "Why would you think that?"

Luke scowled. "The goldsmith had just delivered a chalice to the Archbishop of Rouen, who also happens to be the king's justiciar and a known ally of the queen. He arrived home on Epiphany Eve, and then set out the very next morning for London, in a snowstorm. It does not take a mastermind to wonder if there is a connection between those two facts, de Quincy."

It sounded plausible. Luke was certainly clever enough to draw such conclusions on his own. But were they his own conclusions? "I have no answers for you, Luke. I am sorry."

Luke's eyes darkened. "So am I," he said tersely.

Justin swallowed the last of his ale, silently damning the queen's son to the deepest recesses of Hell Everlasting. At that moment, there was a stir at the door. Gunter found himself greeted heartily by virtually every man in the alehouse, for his courageous rescue had turned him into a neighborhood hero, at least for a fortnight or so. Looking both bemused and shyly pleased by all the attention, he mumbled greetings in turn, and then headed across the room when Justin beckoned.

"Join us, Gunter. You've met Luke de Marston, have you not?" Both men nodded and Luke signaled for more ale.

"This flagon's on me," he insisted. "Any man who'd take on Gilbert the Fleming with a pitchfork is someone I'd be proud to drink with."

Gunter shrugged self-consciously. "I'm glad the lad here had such a hard head," he said, glancing sideways at Justin. "Where is the pup tonight?"

"Shadow? Under the table," Justin said, and felt the dog's tail thump against his leg. "I'm sure you've heard that Luke is Hampshire's under-sheriff. He is here to help me track down Gilbert the Fleming. I wish I could tell you more," he said, and although the words were addressed to Gunter, he looked straight at Luke. "But I cannot—"

He got no further, for the alehouse had suddenly gone quiet. Puzzled, Justin shifted in his seat, seeking the cause. He saw at once the reason for the odd hush; Jonas stood framed in the doorway. When he started toward them, a path rapidly cleared for him, men stumbling to get out of his way. Justin and Luke exchanged startled, speculative glances, for they'd not expected to see the serjeant again today.

Jonas halted in front of their table. "There is an Irish whore working at the Bull over in Southwark."

Luke and Justin were impressed that he'd been so successful

so soon. But when they began to offer up praise, Jonas cut them off. "It gets better. One of my informants claims he has seen her in the past with our man. It looks," he said, with the glint of a grim smile, "as if we've found the Fleming's woman."

14

LONDON

February 1193

Rain had begun to fall at dawn, mixing with sleet by midday. Hastening into the alehouse, Luke shoved a table as close to the hearth as he could get without being singed and shed his sodden mantle. From a hemp sack, he withdrew his purchases: several parchment sheets, an inkhorn, and a goose-feather quill pen. Coaxing a tallow candle from Nell, he was soon laboring over his task, gnawing his lower lip in concentration, occasionally swearing when the ink ran and he had to scrape the skin clean with the edge of his knife. He lacked a goat's tooth to smooth the surface afterward, but he was still satisfied with the final result, a letter that was both concise and reasonably legible. Only then did he look up and discover he'd attracted a curious audience, for writing was a mysterious and arcane skill to the residents of Gracechurch Street, most of whom knew no more about books than they did about the black arts.

A few of the bolder ones began asking questions about writing. Almost before he knew what had happened, Luke found himself surrounded, spelling out their names for them on one of his costly parchment skins. At first he'd enjoyed being the center of such awed attention, but the novelty soon wore off, and he was relieved when Justin's entrance put an end to the impromptu lesson.

Trailed by Shadow, Justin pulled up a stool and rid himself of his wet mantle. "I see you're keeping busy," he said, glancing at the parchment. "But I think Thomas is spelled with an *h*."

"Why? Next you'll be telling me I need to stick an *h* in Justin, too!"

Justin grinned. "I do not believe it. You do know my name, after all!"

Luke shook his head. "You're odiously cheerful for a cold, wretchedly wet day in Lent. Usually when a man is this good humored, he's just come from some woman's bed."

Justin laughed outright, for when he'd gone to the Tower to inform Eleanor about the latest developments, he'd had a brief but ardent encounter with Claudine in the stairwell and she'd promised to meet him as soon as she had a free afternoon.

Luke was still regarding him curiously. "Was I right about the woman? Or is that another one of your secrets?"

Justin shrugged. "I've good reason for cheer. The queen is pleased with our progress and this Irish whore may be the lure we need to draw the Fleming out of hiding. That is more luck than I've had in a long time, Luke."

"If you were truly lucky, you'd have found some poor fool willing to take in that mangy beast. Or have you decided to keep him? I notice you have stopped trying to foist him off onto innocent passersby."

Justin was embarrassed to admit he'd become so fond of Shadow. "No," he insisted, "I'm still looking to find him a home. I thought, though, that I'd have a better chance if I taught him some manners first."

Luke's smile was skeptical. "So . . . you have the fun of teaching him not to piss in the house or chew on table legs or eat a candle and then spit it up on the bed like he did yesterday, and once the dog is tolerable, you give him away? Makes perfect sense to me. But I'm not one for meddling betwixt a man and his dog. Here . . . I want you to do me a favor. The next time one of the queen's couriers is passing through Winchester, will you see that he takes my letter? It'd be too costly to hire a messenger on my own."

"My luck must be starting to rub off onto you, for there's a man riding west on the morrow. Hand it over and I'll see that it goes with him. Whom is it for—Aldith?"

"Eventually. First it goes to the sheriff, explaining that I've been detained in London. I imply that it's at the queen's request, so I trust I can rely upon you for corroboration if need be. I asked him to send the letter on to Aldith once he's read it. I've penned a message for her, too, down below."

When Luke pointed, Justin saw that there were indeed a few lines scrawled at the bottom of the page. After scanning them, he glanced up at Luke in amused disbelief. "You tell her you expect to be back in a fortnight or so and that you hope she is well and that is it? You're a romantic devil, in truth!"

"I told her what was important, when I'd be back," Luke protested. "What else am I supposed to say?"

"It would not have hurt to say you missed her. You might even have told her that she holds your heart. What do I have to do, write your love letters for you?"

"Jesú forfend! I might say that in bed, but not in the light of day, and for certes, I'm not about to put it down in writing. I'd feel like the world's greatest fool. Not to mention how the priest would feel when Aldith brought him the letter to read!"

Justin couldn't help laughing. "I suggest, then, that you teach Aldith to read. Now . . . what of Gilbert's whore? Were you able to find out anything more about her?"

"Jonas is seeing to that. He said he'd meet us here this afternoon with whatever he'd learned. But I'll be astonished if that road leads anywhere."

"Are all sheriffs so miserly about doling out hope?" Justin gibed, although hope had always been a scarce commodity in his own life, too—until now.

"Hope and whores rarely go together," Luke countered, and with that, Justin could not argue. Instead, he borrowed a pair of dice from another alehouse customer and ordered a flagon from Nell. If they had to wait for Jonas, they might as well enjoy themselves.

They had not long to wait, for Jonas arrived within the hour. He was accompanied by a tall, gangling youth, towheaded and freckle faced, who looked as if he belonged behind a plough in the Kent countryside, not braving the urban perils of London. Signaling to Nell for drinks, Jonas pulled up a bench.

Almost at once, Nell materialized by the table. Ostensibly, she was there with two more cups and a brimming flagon. She made no move to withdraw after serving them, though, hovering nearby with unabashed curiosity. But the men were so focused upon Jonas and his news that they did not even notice her eavesdropping.

"This is Aldred. We have to speak English, for he knows no French. Aldred is the one I sent to the Bull. All my men wanted to go," Jonas said with a sly smile. "It was the first time I can remember them actually volunteering for a duty. But Aldred did right well. Being in a bawdy-house seems to've sharpened his wits, for he was able to follow Nóra home afterward without getting caught. I've a man watching now in case the Fleming comes calling on her."

Justin was surprised. "She does not live at the bawdy-house? I thought that was the usual practice?"

Jonas shook his head. "The Southwark stews are different from whorehouses in other cities, for the old king set forth laws to govern them, laws meant to confine sinning to one specific area and keep public disorder to a minimum."

"They have all kinds of rules," Aldred chimed in eagerly. He had a rustic's way of speaking, lacking the distinctive East Saxon accent of the native Londoner. But the blue eyes meeting Justin's gaze were bright and clear. He might be green; he was not dull. "Women married or with child cannot work in the stews," he continued. "Nor can nuns."

Luke interjected a wry "I would hope to God not!"

But Aldred was intent upon sharing his newfound knowledge and plunged in. "Nóra—that be her name—told me all about the laws. They're right interesting and I think fair, too. No woman can be held there against her will. The whores are to live elsewhere and pay rent for their rooms to the stew-master. He is not supposed to lend them money, not over sixpence, lest they get so deeply in debt that they end up working for nothing. They must be seen by a doctor every three months, so men can be sure they are free of the pox. They are not allowed to have lovers, are punished if they do. They're not to whore during holy days, and the last man with a whore must stay with her all night long."

"Why?" The other regulations seemed self-explanatory to

Justin, but that one puzzled him; he very much doubted that the Crown was concerned with making sure a man got his money's worth.

"That is easy," Luke explained. "It is to thwart river crossings. Once curfew is rung, the city gates are closed. But if men could hire a ferryman on the Southwark side of the river, they could then roam the streets as they pleased, up to no good."

Aldred started to speak, stopped abruptly as Nell approached with another flagon. As soon as she withdrew, he seized control of the conversation again. "I suppose that is why they are forbidden to sell ale or wine in the stews—to keep drunken brawls from breaking out. But some of the bawdy-houses still offer it on the sly," he confided. "Nóra had wine sent up to her room. She said they are not supposed to sell food either, and I see no reason for that rule. Do you, my lords?"

Luke was about to venture a guess that it was to keep the customers from tarrying once they'd gotten what they paid for above-stairs. But Jonas forestalled him. "I daresay we could pass the rest of the day talking about whores. We ought to be talking, though, about one whore in particular. Tell us about the Fleming's Irish wench, Aldred."

"Well . . . she is young and pretty. Her hair is a pale yellow color, like new-churned butter. She has a little waist and . . ." Aldred hesitated, for Nell was still nearby, and he did not know how to describe Nóra's physical charms in polite terms. "She'd make a good wet nurse," he finally blurted out, gesturing with his hands to indicate the ampleness of Nóra's breasts, and flushing then when Luke and Justin laughed.

Jonas did not. "I already know she's good in bed, lad," he said impatiently, "for you came back grinning from ear to ear. That's not what we need to know. Is she clever? Featherbrained? A bitch? A talker? You must have formed some opinion of the woman, Aldred!"

Aldred squirmed on the bench; up until now, Jonas had called upon him to provide brawn, not brains. "She . . . she talks easy enough, but she says little, in truth. She's not one for chattering, like most women. She was sweet as honey at first." His flush deepened; he could hear again that soft Irish lilt, calling him "darlin' lad" and "lover." "But she was different afterward, once she had the money. Then she became right practical. I think she is a woman with secrets, not easy to read." This last phrase was said self-consciously, for Aldred had never so much as opened a book. "Looking into her eyes was like looking into the eyes of our barn cat back home. Does that make any sense?" To his relief, they were nodding, so it must.

"Very good, lad," Luke said, and Aldred grinned widely. Picking up his ale cup, he drank, eyeing Nell all the while. She was cleaning spilt ale from a nearby table, but Aldred had enough experience in eavesdropping to recognize another practitioner of that useful skill. When Nell glanced his way, he winked, and was delighted when she gave him an impish half-smile before turning aside. She did not go far, though, staying within earshot. Aldred did not give her away, and as the men talked, planning their strategy, she listened intently, and she, too, made plans.

Six nights later, Justin, Luke, and Jonas were back, seated at the same table. Nell was giving them such good service that the other customers noticed and marveled. But her efforts were in vain. They were not talking much, and when they did, it was in French. Nell was growing increasingly frustrated. Her spirits lifted, though, when the door banged and Gunter strolled in. A man who valued order and took comfort in routine, he was expecting only his usual evening ale. But he'd taken just a few steps before he was accosted by Nell, pulled aside for an urgent conference.

"Am I glad to see you! Go over and talk to Justin straightaway!"

"Why? Is something wrong?"

"I want to hear what they're saying. If you're there, they'll talk English." Gunter was starting to shake his head, for he did not want to get involved in one of Nell's schemes. He liked her well enough, but he did not fully approve of her; he was somewhat alarmed by her headstrong ways and quick temper. But then she entreated softly, "For me, Gunter? Please?" And he found himself crossing the chamber, as if propelled by the sheer force of her will. As she'd predicted, he was welcomed warmly by Justin and Luke, succinctly by Jonas, and was soon pulling up a stool to join them, feeling uncomfortably like a spy in their midst.

They were quite willing to share their disappointment with him, for his pitchfork attack upon Gilbert the Fleming had earned him the right to participate in their hunt, if only vicariously. They'd had no luck whatsoever, they informed him glumly. For six days now, they'd kept Nóra under watch. They'd rented a room across the street from the house Nóra shared with three other prostitutes, and took turns keeping her lodgings under surveillance. They'd put the Bull under close watch, too, and whenever she ventured out, she was trailed at a discreet distance. All to no avail.

Justin was not as downcast as his companions, for he'd managed to find some free time to spend with Claudine. He'd escorted her to the leper hospital of St Giles, where she'd distributed alms at the queen's behest, and later in the week he'd taken her skating at Moorfields; both times, they'd ended up in bed back at Gunter's cottage.

But neither Luke nor Jonas had a Claudine to make the waiting bearable, even pleasurable. As the days dragged by without results, Luke was becoming as edgy and ill tempered as a wet cat. Nor was Jonas in the best of moods, either. He listened morosely as Luke complained about the futility of their efforts and did not argue with the deputy's pessimistic conclusion: that Nóra was poor bait to catch a killer.

"The truth is," Luke said grimly, "the Fleming is not a man to lose his head over any woman. However much he enjoys rutting with this whore, he is not about to put himself at risk for her."

Jonas grunted a sour assent, and Justin shrugged. "What will you do now?" Gunter asked, trying to ignore Nell, who was industriously sweeping the floor rushes near their table.

"That is what we've been arguing about," Justin admitted. "I think we ought to give it more time. But Luke says we've squandered nigh on a week as it is, a week he can ill afford to lose. He thinks we have to take more drastic measures."

Luke nodded vigorously. "I'm getting bone-weary of sleeping on the floor of your cottage, Gunter. And it's becoming obvious to me that we can watch this woman from now till the spring thaw with no results. So Jonas is going to arrest her, see if we cannot get her to reveal the Fleming's whereabouts—"

"No! You cannot do that!"

The men were staring at Nell as if she'd lost her senses, but she didn't let that daunt her. "You must not do this," she insisted. "Once you arrest her, you lose any chance of catching Gilbert off guard. And if you cannot get her to talk, what then? You cannot even be sure she has anything to tell you!"

Luke was frowning. "I do not mean to be rude, Nell, but this is none of your concern."

"Be thankful that I'm here to keep you from making a great mistake. What do you know about this woman? Whores are not supposed to take lovers, can be fined and even put in gaol for a few weeks. So why is she sharing her bed with Gilbert? Is she too scared to tell him nay? From what I've heard about the man, that is not far fetched. Or she might like having such a dangerous lover. Some women do. Or she might want the protection of being known as the Fleming's woman. Or she could be his accomplice as well as his bedmate, for whores often hear useful information. Who's to say she's not passing it on to him? She could even fancy herself in love with him. As unlikely as that sounds, the world is full of fools. Could she be one of them? You do not know, do you? You cannot answer any of those questions. And until you can, arresting her would be lunacy!"

"What you say makes some sense," Luke conceded. "I'll not deny that. But how are we supposed to find out those answers? Hide under her bed? None of us can approach her, for we're all known on sight to Gilbert. So who could we send . . . Aldred? A lamb to the slaughter, for certes!"

Glancing toward Justin, Nell saw that he'd guessed where she was going with this conversation, and she said hastily, before he could object, "I doubt that any man alive would have much luck with Nóra. She'll take men into her bed, not into her confidence. Most whores do not trust men, as plain and simple as that. To get the answers you need, it'll take a woman."

Luke leaned back in his seat, the hint of a smile hovering

in the corners of his mouth. "Do you have any particular woman in mind, Nell?"

"Well . . . I thought Justin could ask the queen if she had a free afternoon. Who do you think I meant? Me, of course!"

15

LONDON

February 1193

"No!" Justin slammed his cup down with such force that ale sloshed over onto the table. "Have you lost your senses, Nell? I'd not let you get within a mile of Gilbert the Fleming, not even if he were six months dead and six feet deep!"

Nell arched a brow. "Need I remind you that you are not my husband? For certes, you are not my father. So unless you are one of the Almighty's own angels in disguise, what right have you to forbid me to do anything?"

Justin frowned, but her argument was incontrovertible. "No right," he conceded. "But I am not meddling in your life, Nell, merely trying to save it! I do not think you realize how dangerous a man the Fleming is—"

"No? And who patched you up after your own encounter with the Fleming?" Arms akimbo, Nell glowered at Justin. Almost at once, though, she relented. "I know you mean well, Justin. But you need not fret on my behalf. I'll not be matching wits with the Fleming, or even crossing paths with him. It is his whore I seek to cozen, and I fully expect all of you to be close at hand."

"You can rely upon that, lass," Luke said, so heartily that Justin realized he'd embraced Nell's idea as his own. As for Jonas, Justin never doubted that he'd be one for staking out a lamb to catch a wolf. Finding himself outnumbered and outvoted, Justin could only say grimly, "I like it not," while vowing silently not to let Nell out of his sight, come what may.

Gunter was no less dismayed than Justin, troubled enough to forsake his usual reticence. "I have no say in this. But I must voice my misgivings, nonetheless. Nell, I urge you to think again. This Fleming is an evil, godless man, who kills for the sport of it. Why ever would you take such a risk?"

"For the money, of course." Nell smiled patiently at Gunter. "They pay informants, after all. They even offer rewards for the capture of some felons. Is that not so?" she demanded of Jonas and Luke, her eyes narrowing until they both nodded. "So you see, Gunter, it will be a profitable partnership for us all. They get what they want—to see Gilbert the Fleming hanged—and I get the money I need for my Lucy. Can there be a more worthy aim than that?"

Gunter shook his head somberly. "Any good mother wants what is best for her child. But what if this plan goes awry? What if you find yourself facing down the Fleming? What would happen to Lucy then?"

Despite her iron-edged resolve, Nell was chilled by his words. What if evil did befall her? An orphan's lot was not an easy one. Could her cousin be relied upon to do right by Lucy? For a moment or so, Nell wavered, and then turned a deliberately deaf ear to these insidious eleventh-hour qualms.

"I'll not deny there is some risk. But risk is as much a part of life as the air we breathe. I could step on a rusty nail this very night, have it fester, and be dead ere the week was out. I trust these men to see to my safety. Is that trust misplaced?" she challenged, and got the response she expected, immediate assurances from Justin and Luke and even Jonas that her faith in them was utterly justified.

Luke then went on to promise recklessly that she'd be in no danger whatsoever. But neither Justin nor Jonas echoed his avowal, for the former could not shake off a sense of foreboding and the latter knew that even the most heartfelt of promises could be reduced to tatters by the slashings of a sharp knife.

During those hours when Masses were not being said, St Paul's Cathedral was used for more secular activities. Known as Paul's Walk, the nave was a favorite gathering place for citizens in search of bargains, gossip, and respite from the bitter winter weather. Although it was frowned upon by Church officials, who made sporadic attempts to discourage people from displaying their wares for sale and trade, on this bleak Tuesday morn in late February, the cathedral was crowded with peddlers and their customers. By the "serving man's pillar," bored youths were loitering in hopes of finding employment. Nearby, lawyers conferred with prospective clients, while boisterous youngsters played tag in the aisles, trailed by the vexed curses of their irritated elders.

Justin's gaze kept straying toward the west end of the nave, where scribes sat at small wooden tables, hiring out their quill pens as soldiers did their swords. Had he not blundered into that killing on the Alresford Road, he could have been at one of those tables, too, laboring to earn his bread by writing letters and wills.

"I feel I've got blinders on," Luke complained, but he kept his hood prudently in place, shadowing his face. Glancing at Justin's equally shrouded profile, he gibed, "I hate to say this, de Quincy, but you look like you escaped from a lazar house."

Justin agreed with him, for the only hooded cloak he could find on such short notice was a drab, over-sized garment of rough burrell, coarse and scratchy. "You're one to talk," he retorted, "for you look like you ought to be prowling about cemeteries after midnight." Scanning the nave again, he shook his head in frustration. "Where the devil is Jonas? What if he does not get here in time?"

"If need be, we'll set it up for another day. But I do not think it'll go wrong. We were lucky that Aldred overheard Nóra say she'd be at St Paul's this morn. I think we'll be lucky again. You ought to—"

Luke broke off in midsentence. "I see Jonas," he announced. "Over there . . . coming in the Si Quis door." But then he swore softly. "Damnation, he's alone!"

Swathed in a dark cloak of his own, Jonas elbowed his way toward them, responding to their anxious queries with composure. "I sent word that he was to meet me at St Paul's. He'll be here."

Justin did not share his confidence. "I ought to have locked Nell in the root cellar and have done with it," he muttered, glancing gloomily across the nave toward Nell, who was bargaining zestfully with a peddler over a bolt of linen. She was not ten feet from their target, but Justin had not caught her stealing so much as a glance at Nóra. He had to admit that Nell was better at this than he'd dared hope.

His eyes kept coming back to Nóra, for she was not at all what he had expected. He'd envisioned a woman whose appearance brazenly proclaimed her profession, overly lush and voluptuous and heavily rouged and powdered, like a fruit ripened past its prime. Instead, she was as Aldred had described: quite pretty, with fashionable fair coloring and dimples. Justin would never have taken her for a Southwark whore. Still less could he imagine her coupling with the brutal, ice-blooded Fleming. It would be like matching a snake and a summer songbird.

Luke was looking admiringly toward Nóra, too. "I never thought that the Fleming and I could fancy the same sort of woman. I was sure he'd be one for rutting in pigsties!" Turning back to Jonas, he said dubiously, "This man of yours, Jonas . . . are you sure he'll not botch it?"

"Philip the Fox is the best cutpurse I've ever seen. Nimble fingered enough to pluck any pigeon clean without leaving so much as a telltale feather, and sharp witted enough to see that his skill was like to get him hanged sooner or later. These days he rides in the Friday races out at Smithfield and wins often enough to be in demand. If he strays from time to time, I've yet to catch him at it. When he gets an itch, I daresay he scratches it across the river in Southwark, where the sheriff's writ does not run."

"A pity all of London's felons could not be so accommodating," Luke said dryly, and Jonas shrugged.

"You've heard it said that a bird does not foul its own nest? Well, Philip the Fox is wise enough not to foul mine. And speaking of Philip, here he comes, just as I said. By now you both ought to know that I never promise what I cannot deliver."

For a fleeting moment, Justin felt as if he were watching an unlikely ghost flit across the nave toward them, for Philip the Fox had the same ginger coloring and slight build as the double-crossing informant, Pepper Clem. But as Philip drew closer, he saw that any resemblance was superficial at best. Philip was much younger than Clem, possibly even younger than Justin himself. Although small in stature like Clem, he had none of the little thief's slackness, nor the drooping, flaccid posture of one accustomed to defeat. Philip was lean and fit, as alert and agile as the woodland creature whose name he bore. His tumbled thatch of reddish hair resembled a fox's plumed tail, and his eyes—a light golden brown, slanted at the corners—were oddly compelling, intent and unwavering. If the hapless, slow-witted Clem had been nature's prey, this wiry, watchful youth was unmistakably a predator.

Justin was impressed when Philip made none of the uneasy protestations of innocence that a summons from Jonas would be likely to unleash, confining himself to a wary "You wanted to see me?"

Jonas jerked his head and Philip followed them toward the greater privacy of the closest bay. "This is Luke de Marston, the under-sheriff of Hampshire." Glancing toward Justin, Jonas added, with the trace of a smile, "And Justin de Quincy, who answers only to the queen and God. I want you both to meet Philip of Aldgate, also known as Philip the Fox, London's best cutpurse."

"Not anymore," Philip demurred calmly. "I'm a law-abiding citizen these days."

"As glad as I am to hear that, it would still be a pity to let your skills rust from lack of use. So I suggest you ply them on behalf of the Crown. You see that woman yonder, the one in the blue mantle? I want you to steal her money purse."

Justin suspected that Philip wasn't easily startled, but Jonas had managed it. Those golden eyes opened wide. "You are jesting . . . right?"

"Am I noted for my humor? When she moves, you can see the money pouch swinging from her belt. After you filch it, I want you to give it to that young woman over there."

Philip's gaze swept from face to face. Satisfying himself that they were in earnest, he was quiet for several moments. "It is very kind of you to want to include me in this interesting enterprise of yours. But I think I'd rather not join in the fun."

"Think again," Jonas said coolly. "Do this for me and I'll owe you a favor. Do you truly want to turn that down?"

Philip smiled faintly. "No, I suppose I do not." When he looked over at Nóra again, it was with a calculating, professional eye. "You want only the purse?"

When Jonas nodded, Philip turned to go. Luke quickly caught his arm. "Do you not want one of us to cause a distraction?"

"That will not be necessary," Philip said, too politely for Justin and Luke's liking, for they detected the hidden amusement in his voice, the utter assurance that was so closely akin to arrogance. As they watched, he strolled across the nave toward Nóra. Justin expected that he'd bump into her, then make his move in the ensuing confusion. But they seemed barely to brush, their contact so brief and inconsequential that no apologies were even required. Justin felt a stinging sense of disappointment. Philip had bungled his first try. How many tries did he get ere he aroused Nóra's suspicions?

"He shied away like a spooked horse," Luke hissed. "This is your master thief, Jonas?"

"Indeed he is," Jonas said complacently, and as Justin and Luke looked on in astonishment, Philip ambled over to Nell, squeezed past her, and moved on. He looked back once, grinned triumphantly, and then vanished into the crowd, leaving them to marvel at a sleight-of-hand so deft that they'd neither seen it done nor were able to explain exactly how it had been accomplished, even though they'd been watching him as intently as cats at a mouse hole.

Neither Justin nor Luke had seen Philip pass the purse to Nell, either. But now she bent down, straightening up with the pouch in her hand and a puzzled look on her face. She glanced about at the people closest to her and then approached Nóra. For the men, it was like watching a play without dialogue. But it was easy to follow the plot.

At sight of the proferred purse, Nóra gasped, hastily fumbling under her mantle. Nell gestured toward the spot where she'd purportedly found the pouch. Within moments, they were both smiling, both talking, with considerable animation. And when Nóra at last turned back to the impatient peddler, she held out his cloth for Nell's inspection. Nell shook her head emphatically, pointing toward a bolt of russet wool. For a moment, she looked in the men's direction. Although he could not be sure, Justin thought she winked.

*   *   *

They flipped a coin to see who'd follow Nell and Nóra. Luke won, and Jonas went off to tend to other duties. Justin eventually went back to Gracechurch Street. Gunter was keeping an eye on Lucy and Shadow, and Justin passed a restless hour in their company, eventually wandering over to the alehouse to await word.

Nell returned in late afternoon, flushed with cold and excitement. She'd already shared all she'd learned with Luke, but she was quite happy to recount it for Justin's benefit. The alehouse was crowded, but instead of taking over from the harried Ellis, she ordered ale and then launched enthusiastically into her narration.

She and Nóra had spent the afternoon together, browsing in the shops along Cheapside, stopping for a meal at the cookshop down by the river. They'd gotten along right well, she reported jubilantly, and had agreed to meet again in two days. No, of course she'd learned nothing yet of the Fleming. What did Justin expect of her—miracles? She must tread cautiously at first, do nothing to stir up Nóra's suspicions. For that much she had learned this day: Nóra was no fool.

"Aldred was right. This is a woman with secrets. She was most grateful that I'd recovered her purse and did not seem to be weighing her words with me. Nevertheless, she told me very little about herself. It will take time to gain her trust."

That was not what Luke wanted to hear, for it seemed to him as if his London days were slipping by like the sand in an hourglass. "You say she told you nothing useful. But from what I could see, the two of you never ran out of words, chattering away like magpies. Just what did you find to talk about, then?"

"We talked mainly about men, God love them, about what fools they can be." Nell smiled at them then, so blandly that they could not be sure if she'd been joking or not.

The days that followed were a severe test of patience for Luke and Justin. They took turns trailing after Nell, as she and Nóra explored the city and the perimeters of their newfound friendship. In Nóra's free time, the women met for dinner at the cookshop, watched the Friday horse races at Smithfield, visited the

Eastcheap market, even a cockfight. And they began, with exasperating slowness, to exchange confidences.

Nell had been forthright from the first in talking about the life she'd concocted for herself, with the help of her male partners. "Bella" claimed to be the wife of an overbearing, older man, a well-to-do chandler who supplied candles to half the churches in London. It was not a happy match; she'd dropped enough hints to make sure Nóra picked up on her discontent. Unfortunately for Nell and her fellow conspirators, Nóra was much more sparing with intimate details of her own life. It was fully a week before Nell learned anything at all of the other woman's past.

"She has not had an easy time of it," Nell related to a very attentive audience. "At fifteen, she was seduced by an English merchant in Dublin on business. When he returned home, he took her with him to London. He'd promised to marry her, but he'd neglected to mention that he already had a wife. So he set Nóra up in a cottage, whilst she sought to convince herself that in time, he'd leave his wife for her. Instead, she got with child, and he stopped paying the rent. Cast out into the streets, she miscarried of the babe. She did not tell me the rest of it. In fact, she has yet to admit she whores for a living."

Justin found himself feeling great sympathy for that young Irish girl, on her own in a foreign city, with neither kin nor friends to turn to for help. "That poor lass," he said. "Little wonder she became a whore. What else did she have to barter except her body?"

"And then she had to get herself entangled in that hellspawn Fleming's web." Luke shook his head. "If not for bad luck, she'd have no luck at all, would she?"

Nell leaned back in her seat, regarding them with bright, mocking eyes. "Are the two of you always so tender toward whores? Or just the ones with flaxen hair and fluttering eyelashes?"

Luke and Justin exchanged puzzled glances. "You said yourself, Nell," Justin protested, "that Nóra has had a hard time. It surprises me, in truth, that you seem to have so little pity for the lass."

"Well, it does not surprise me that you have so much pity to spare, Justin. But I did not expect *you* to be so trusting, Luke. I know many men retain a touching belief in whores with hearts of gold. I'd not have thought to find a sheriff's deputy amongst them, though. Can it be that some of these fabled creatures can truly be found in Winchester?"

Jonas gave a guffaw of laughter, nearly choking on his ale. But Justin and Luke both bristled, Luke denying vehemently that he was "trusting," and Justin demanding to know why Nell was so lacking in charity. "The woman had been badly used. How can you be so unmoved by her story?"

"Mayhap because I did not take it as gospel."

The two men traded looks again. "You think it was all a lie?"

"No . . . not all of it. She might well have been abandoned by her London lover. But even at fifteen, I doubt that she was the utter innocent she claims to've been. And if she miscarried of her babe, I think it's probably because she found a midwife who knew which herbs can end a pregnancy. As for being cast out penniless, I doubt that, too. Our Nóra could teach a cat about landing on her feet."

"Why do you judge the girl so harshly, Nell? Do you truly find whoring to be such an unforgivable sin?"

"No, I do not," she insisted. "For too many women, there is no other way to feed themselves and their children. Justin, you are usually so quick. So why are you so slow now to grasp what I am saying? I do not mistrust Nóra because she is a Southwark whore. I'd not trust her were she the mayor's wife. When I said she'd not had an easy time, I meant it. But rain falls on the good and the ungodly alike, does it not?"

"And Nóra is one of the ungodly?"

"Yes," she said firmly, "I believe she is. She may have an angelic smile and a soft, honeyed voice, but she has flint where her heart ought to be. After a week in her company, I can tell you this about your 'poor lass,' that she puts Nóra first and foremost. Remember how we were guessing why she'd take up with a killer like the Fleming? Well, I'd say it is for whatever she can get from him."

Justin lapsed into a troubled silence. If Nell was right about Nóra's selfish, unscrupulous nature, that meant her danger was twofold: from both the Fleming and his whore.

* * *

Justin arrived at the alehouse in midmorning, for Nell had agreed to meet Nóra at the Westcheap market at noon. He would accompany her partway, then follow the women at a circumspect distance, muffled in one of the nondescript hooded cloaks he'd bought for their surveillance.

Justin was in better spirits this morn, for Nell's reconnaissance finally seemed to be paying off. Nóra had begun to mention a mysterious, as yet unnamed lover, bragging about his generous gifts, boasting that he doted on her every whim. He was away on business, she claimed, but she hoped he'd soon be returning.

Jonas had stopped the official hunt for Gilbert. No longer did his men roust the ale-keepers and stew-masters in search of the Fleming, and he'd put the rumor out on the streets that they believed Gilbert had fled London. They were heartened, therefore, by Nóra's offhand remarks about her lover's return. Did this mean their ruse had worked? Did the Fleming now think it was safe to venture out and about again?

At sight of Nell, Justin's mouth dropped open. "Good God, what happened to you?"

"It looks dreadful, does it not?" Nell lifted a candle up to give him a better look at her blackened eye. "You'd swear a man's fist did the damage," she said proudly. "Do you want to know how I did it? First I smudged kohl around my eye, and then I smeared on cinders, ever so lightly. Lastly, I powdered it over heavily, the way a woman would do to try to hide it."

"Very convincing," Justin agreed. "But we never talked of this, Nell. What are you up to?"

"I've grown weary of the waiting, too. When I stumbled on the stairs yesterday and bruised my wrist, it gave me an idea. Now that we've found the fishing hole, it is time we baited the hook."

Nell and Nóra were sitting at a trestle table in a tavern just off Watling Street. It was poorly lit by pungent tallow candles, its once whitewashed walls smoke blackened, its matted floor rushes filthy with mud and mouse droppings. Nóra had suggested it, though, because they served meals. The women had ordered a hot eel pie with their wine, and the aroma was appealing. But Nell was too nervous to have much of an appetite, and Nóra was absorbed in her scrutiny of Nell's blackened eye and bruised wrist.

"Your husband did this?"

Nell nodded, averting her eyes. For an unsettling moment, she could not recall what his name was supposed to be. Justin had chosen the name, that of a tightfisted miller back in Winchester. Adam? No . . . Abel. "He can be foul tempered when he's drinking," she mumbled, taking a deep swallow of her wine. Should she say more? No, she'd done enough complaining already about his sour nature and miserly ways. Let the bruises speak for themselves.

Nóra was frowning, on the verge of speech. But they were interrupted again by another customer, this one shy, not brash, clutching his woolen cap between work-roughened hands as he offered diffidently to buy them more wine. While it was not unusual for women to frequent their neighborhood alehouses and taverns, Nóra and Nell were too young and attractive not to draw unwanted attention. Nóra now sent the man away with a stinging, expletive-laden dismissal. For all that she looked as demure as any virgin bride, she had a command of invective that even fishmongers or sailors might well envy. As the man slunk off in embarrassment, Nell could not help feeling sorry for him. But at least they'd not be bothered again; Nóra's scornful tongue-lashing had echoed throughout the tavern.

"Does this happen often, Bella?"

Nell shrugged. "Abel likes his ale, and he's hard enough to please even when he's sober . . ." For the first time, she felt vaguely uncomfortable about feigning friendship like this; Nóra's sympathy seemed quite genuine. "The worst of it," she said, "is that he maltreats me in front of others, calling me 'slut' and 'dull-witted cow,' not caring at all if the servants or Joel can hear."

"Joel? You've not mentioned him before."

"Oh . . . did I not?" Nell fiddled with her napkin. "Joel is Abel's journeyman. Lord knows why he stays, for Abel pays him only a pittance and takes out his vile temper on Joel, too. A pity, for Joel would do right well for himself, if only he had the means. It was his idea to add perfume to the French soap. I did tell you Abel sells soap as well as candles? Well, French soap is made by boiling mutton fat with wood ash and caustic soda. After Joel talked Abel into scenting it with rosewater, sales were much better . . . I'll try to remember to bring you some when we next meet."

"Thank you," Nóra said absently. The blue eyes Justin and Luke had so admired were too shrewd and knowing for Nell's liking, and she continued to stare down at the warped tabletop. "Is he young . . . this Joel?" When Nell nodded, a cynical smile played about Nóra's mouth. "So you fancy him, do you?"

Nell raised her head. "What if I do?"

"Smooth your feathers, girl. I am not blaming you for having a wayward eye. What woman would not prefer a young ram to an old goat? But what do you mean to do about it?"

"What can I do? I cannot run away with Joel, for we'd both starve. On the days that Abel goes to his guild, we steal some time together in his shop, in the back room. We make do with what we can. But if Abel ever caught us . . ." It was easy enough to fake a shiver. Nell had always had an overly active imagination, and she could even summon up a dash of pity for poor, foolish Bella, trapped in a miserable marriage and about to leap from the frying pan into the fire.

"So why wait for the roof to fall in on you?"

"I already told you why we cannot run away together, Nóra! Or are you one of those fools who think people can live on love?"

Nóra laughed. "When it rains pea soup! It seems to me that Abel is your problem. Get rid of him and your problem is solved, as simple as that."

Nell drew her mantle more closely around her shoulders, for she suddenly felt chilled to the bone. She thought she'd taken Nóra's measure, but she still hadn't expected the other woman to suggest murder as casually as if she were ordering more wine. "And how do I do that, Nóra?" she said, with all the sarcasm she could muster. "Smother him with a pillow whilst he sleeps?"

Nóra reached for her wine cup. "I think we can do better than that."

Nell's pulse was racing. "Nóra . . . you're not serious?"

Nóra sipped her wine, smiling. "That depends. Do you want me to be?"

"I . . . I might. If I did, could you help me?"

"No. But I know someone who can. Giles is very good at solving problems like Abel. But you'd have to make it worth his while. Can you do that, Bella?"

Nell cast her eyes down hastily, lest Nóra see their exultant gleam. Giles, was it? Just as she'd deliberately chosen a name very like her own, so had Nóra. Snatching at her napkin, she brought it up to conceal her smile. "I think I could," she said slowly. "As I told you, Abel does a profitable trade, and hoards nigh on every penny he earns. But this is happening too fast for me. I need to know more."

Nóra's smile was cold enough to cause frostbite. "All you need to know," she said, "is that Giles can do for you what you dare not do yourself—if you're willing to pay his price. Are you, Bella?"

Nell drew a deep breath. "Yes," she said, "I am."

"She took the bait!" Nell flung her arms around Justin's neck, hugging him joyfully. "She proposed murder, right over the eel pie!"

Although Justin had waited until Nóra was long out of sight before approaching Nell, he was still uneasy about her acknowledging him so openly in public. Catching her arm, he drew her into the shelter of a nearby alley. "She mentioned Gilbert by name?"

"She called him 'Giles,' but who else could it be? How many killers on the run is the woman sharing her bed with, after all!"

"She knows where he is, then?"

Some of Nell's elation faded. "Alas, she does not. She explained that he has been 'lying low, waiting for the storm to blow over,' and so she has not seen him for several weeks. But he got word to her that he thought 'the pot was no longer on the boil,' so she expects he'll soon be seeking her out."

Nell paused for breath. "So it would indeed have been a mistake for Jonas and Luke to arrest her. I'll try to resist the temptation to say I told them so, but I can make no promises!"

"Did she reveal how he got a message to her, Nell?"

"No, she did not, and I thought it would've seemed suspicious had I asked. I suspect that he sent a man to the bawdy house. But she'd not be likely to tell me that, for she's led me to believe she is Giles's kept woman. I daresay that is why she's never invited me home. You said she shares it with three other whores, hardly the lavish love nest she's been bragging about. But I think that prideful lie of hers worked to our advantage. Since she had something to hide, too, mayhap that's why she did not question my excuse for not inviting her to my own home: that my husband is so jealous he begrudges me even women friends and sets his servants to spying on me."

"What happens now?"

"She says she'll talk to Giles on my behalf, see if he is willing to 'help' me. We agreed to meet again on Sunday at that same tavern. If he is still in hiding, all we can do is set up another meeting. After that . . ." She shrugged, and Justin finished the thought for her.

"We wait," he said. "God help us, we wait."

Nell's Sunday meeting with Nóra proved to be an exercise in futility, for Nóra had not been contacted by her fugitive lover. They fumed in vain, and Luke sent a second letter to Winchester, putting off his departure from London, hoping that he'd convinced the sheriff and Aldith of the need for another delay. Nóra and Nell agreed to meet again on Wednesday afternoon, this time at Paul's Cross in the churchyard of the great cathedral.

That Wednesday morning, Justin rode to the Tower, welcoming Eleanor back from the Great Council meeting at Oxford and luring Claudine into the keep stairwell for some sweet, stolen kisses. He'd missed her much more than he'd expected—or wanted. His clandestine love affair with Claudine had given him greater pleasure—in bed and out—than he'd experienced with any other woman. But he never let himself forget that for lovers with no future, time was the enemy.

After leaving the Tower, Justin headed for the alehouse. Jonas had drawn Nell's bodyguard duty, so he passed the time with Luke, playing tables and draughts and arm wrestling, growing more and more restless as the hours dragged by. Luke was in a pessimistic mood, and he wagered Justin an extravagant sum that this, too, would prove to be a dry well. The deputy had never been so happy, though, to lose a bet as when Nell and Jonas returned at dusk, triumphant.

Steering Nell toward an empty table, they hovered over her so eagerly that she complained they put her in mind of hungry vultures ready to pounce. "Sit," she insisted, so adamantly that Shadow promptly did. "I promise to tell you all, to leave nothing out. The Fleming has emerged from his burrow. Nóra found him in her house when she got home yesterday from the market."

She quickly held up her hand, fending off any interruptions. "I just want to say that I know Aldred botched it, for he was supposed to be watching Nóra's house. But I hope you'll help me convince Jonas that it was not entirely his fault. Gilbert had a key and—"

"The Devil take Aldred!" Luke leaned across the table. "What did Gilbert say?"

Nell sighed, abandoning Aldred to his fate. "Nóra says she told him about my 'problem,' and he thinks he can help me out—his words, not mine." She glanced covertly at Justin, knowing he'd not like what would be coming next. "He has agreed to meet with me on Friday, at the Smithfield horse fair."

"No! That was never part of the deal. I'll not let you get within range of the Fleming's knife!"

To Justin's surprise, he got some unexpected support now from Luke. "I'd have misgivings about that, too," the deputy confessed. "The risk is too great, Nell. There has to be another way."

"There is not," Jonas said flatly. "Nell can lure him out into the open. This may be our only chance. Nell understands that and is willing to take the risk."

Nell had been secretly hoping that Justin or Luke could come up with another plan, one that would keep her far away from the Fleming and his well-honed blade. But her pride prevented her from backing out, and when Jonas looked toward her for confirmation, she nodded slowly. "I do not see what choice we have."

Neither did the men. Justin was not yet ready to acknowledge that, though. "Why does Nell have to be the one to meet him? What if we could find someone else to play the role of Bella? Jonas, do you not know a youth small enough to pass for a woman?"

"I might, but you're forgetting how wary the Fleming is. Nóra is to accompany Nell to Smithfield. So unless you can suggest a way to fool Nóra, too, with this substitute Bella, I say we have to go with the genuine article."

Justin's silence was a concession of defeat. Luke turned sideways and hit him on the arm. "We'll stay closer to the lass than her own shadow," he vowed. "Between us and Jonas, I daresay we could keep her safe from the Devil himself!"

Justin reached across the table and caught hold of Nell's hand. "Are you sure you want to do this, lass?"

"Yes," she lied, "very sure."

"We'd best start making plans, then," Luke pointed out, "for Friday is just a day away. That hellspawn would pick the horse market. Half of London is likely to be there. Where exactly are you to meet him, Nell?"

"By the horse pool, whilst the races are being run. He'll be leading a bay gelding and I'm to pretend I want to buy . . ." Nell stopped, for she'd caught the look of dismay that flashed between Justin and Luke. "What is it? I've a right to know!"

"You do," Justin agreed, "and we'll keep nothing from you. That crafty whoreson is as slick as a greased pig and about as hard to corner. The crowds will have thinned out by then, with most people watching the races. And there he'll be at the horse pool, holding the reins of a fast horse, ready to bolt if he sees anything at all suspicious. Damn him to Hell and back!"

Nell bit her lower lip. "Will you be able to get close enough to seize him?"

"If we cannot," Justin said, "we're not letting you anywhere near the horse pool."

Luke nodded, his eyes meeting Justin's across the table. They had one day and two nights to come up with a strategy to outwit a man who'd so far seemed blessed with the Devil's own luck, or once again, he'd slip through their snare.

Justin awoke with a start. The room was unfamiliar and it took him a moment to remember where he was. Beside him, Claudine slept peacefully, her hair cascading over them both like a sable mantle. This was the first full night they'd had together, all Claudine's doing. She'd fabricated an excuse to explain her absence to the queen, then engaged a room in a secluded riverside inn on the outskirts of London. With their trap for the Fleming to be sprung on the morrow, Justin had tried to beg off. But she had persisted and when she confided that she wanted to be able to fall asleep in his arms at least once, he could think only of how much he wanted that, too.

Although he'd taken care not to disturb Claudine, when he lay back, her eyes opened, dark and drowsy. Stifling a yawn, she snuggled closer. "You're having a very restless night, love."

"Sorry," he murmured, kissing the corner of her mouth. "It probably would have been better for us to do this on another night. For certes, you'd have gotten more sleep."

"I'm not complaining. But it would have been easier if we'd been able to spend the night at your cottage. Will that friend of yours be staying with you much longer?"

"That depends," he said, "on what happens tomorrow."

She rolled over in his arms, looking up searchingly into his face. "What was it you said the other day, Justin—that my curiosity would put a cat to shame? And you were right. I am too inquisitive for my own good, I love to discover secrets, and I like to gossip. Whereas you, my darling, are as closemouthed as a clam!"

"I'm not as bad as all that," he protested, and she reached up, tracing the curve of his mouth with the tip of her finger.

"Oh, indeed you are. There is much I would like to know about you. Where you were born. If you have brothers or sisters. How you got this scar on your shoulder. Your favorite food, your favorite color. Why you are so evasive about your past. But I have never asked you—not once—how you came to be the queen's man or what you've been doing on her behalf. Have I?"

"No . . . you have not."

"Nor am I going to ask now. But I know you are involved in something dangerous. Justin, I fear for you. I cannot help myself, I do."

He'd never had someone to worry about him before, and his arms tightened, drawing her into a more intimate embrace. "On the morrow," he said, "we are going to catch a killer. I cannot tell you more than that, Claudine, not yet. But the danger will not be all that great, at least not for me."

"I hope you are telling me the truth," she said, and never had he heard her sound so serious. "But if you will not be at risk tomorrow, what is stealing your sleep tonight? Whom are you fretting about, if not yourself?"

"A woman."

"A woman?" she echoed. "Justin de Quincy, are you cheating on me so soon? You're not supposed to develop a roving eye until much later in the love affair!"

"You need not worry, lass. Whatever the game, I always abide by the rules."

His heart was not in his banter, though, and it showed. Turning her head, she kissed his chest. "I ought not to have been teasing you," she said contritely, "not when you're so troubled. Tell me about this woman, love. Why are you afraid for her?"

"She is a friend," he said softly, "who wanted to help us trap a killer. But to do that, she must be the bait. And if harm comes to her, Claudine, I'll never forgive myself."

16

LONDON

March 1193

March had been indistinguishable so far from February, the days cold and damp more often than not. But there was a sudden shift in the weather on the 12th. Bright sunlight and much milder temperatures offered the winter-battered Londoners a beguiling hint of coming spring. They knew it would not last, for March was the most untrustworthy of months. And so they flocked outside to make the most of this brief respite, large numbers deciding to take in the Friday horse fair at Smithfield, just north of the city walls—thus providing even greater cover for the Fleming.

Nell had another reason to rue the unseasonably balmy weather. Any man bundled up in a hooded cloak would be all too conspicuous today, sure to attract Gilbert's ever-suspicious eye. She was thankful, therefore, that Justin and Luke had come up with another disguise. Pray God that it worked!

She was grateful that at least she was spared the need to make conversation, for she and Nóra had walked in silence for most of the way. Now that their deal had been struck, Nóra was utterly single minded, brisk and businesslike. Nell had begun to wonder if the Fleming's whore had seen her as prey from the very first. She had talked freely of her unhappy home life, after all. Long ere they had that candid talk over eel pie, had Nóra concluded it might be profitable to befriend her? The bored young wife of a respectable merchant might well be a promising target for extortion. That would explain why Nóra had responded so warmly to her overtures; usually friendships did not flower so fast.

The more she thought about it, the more sense it made to Nell, for she was convinced by now that the Fleming and the Irishwoman were partners as well as bedmates, linked as much by greed as lust. Glancing uneasily at Nóra's delicately drawn profile, Nell marveled anew that a woman could have such an innocent, lovely face and such an ugly soul.

The horse market was in full swing, would-be buyers mingling with browsers and those who'd come out to gamble on the afternoon races. Nóra paid no heed to the activities going on around them, ignoring the admiring and lascivious comments hurled her way. Nell followed mutely behind. Now that she was so close to confronting Gilbert the Fleming, she felt as if she'd swallowed a butterfly, an entire flock of butterflies, so unsettled was her stomach. *Sweet Lucy, what has your mama gotten herself into?*

By the time they reached the horse pool, they'd left the crowds behind. Nell understood now how perfectly Gilbert had chosen his ground; midst all this open space, no one could take him unaware. The slightest shadow falling across his path and he'd be in the saddle, spurring his mount for the open fields and freedom. He was waiting by the water's edge, holding the reins of a rangy bay horse, watching intently as the women approached. From a distance, he seemed quite ordinary—no tail, no cloven hooves. But Nell knew better; she did not doubt that she was about to double-cross one of Lucifer's own.

But at least she'd not be venturing into the netherworld alone. All was in readiness. Off to her right, she could see a carefully positioned cart, covered with canvas. A slovenly dressed stranger was watering his animals at the pool. Although Nell had never seen him before, she knew he was one of Jonas's men, for she'd recognized Justin's chestnut and Luke's sorrel among his string. He was haggling with two monks about the price of a white mule. Nell dared not look in their direction; it was enough that they were there, her guardian angels clad in the stark black of the Benedictines. She had not been forsaken. She had friends. Lifting her chin, she squared her shoulders and walked toward Gilbert the Fleming.

Nóra made the introductions. Nell waited tensely then to see what the other woman would do. They'd gambled that she'd not want to linger. The Fleming was a wanted felon, after all, and Nóra had so far shown a very healthy concern for her own welfare. But if they'd guessed wrong about her, the next part of their plan could be imperiled. What if Nóra remembered Aldred? Nell held her breath, exhaling it in an audible sigh as Nóra kissed Gilbert casually on the cheek, waved nonchalantly, and sauntered away, not looking back.

Gilbert was appraising Nell quite openly, and when she began to fidget under his scrutiny, he said coolly, "You seem nervous, Bella."

"Nervous? I'm scared half to death, and who could blame me? It is not as if I've had any practice at this!"

He seemed amused by her outburst. "You mean this is the first husband you've plotted to kill?"

Nell flinched, for she'd gotten back into character by now, and Bella would have been offended by that. "Must you put it so . . . so crudely? It is not the way you make it sound. Did Nóra not tell you how he maltreated me and—"

"What makes you think I care? Your reasons for doing this are between you and God. Justify it to Him if you can, but not to me. I need only know if you can meet my price. You told Nóra you could. Suppose you tell me how."

Nell's mouth had gone very dry. She'd never seen eyes like his. Dark and flat and glittering, they seemed dead to her, like the eyes of the snakes Justin said he used in his crimes. "I do not have any money of my own," she said hoarsely. "But my husband has a lot of money. He must, for he spends almost none of it. He keeps it in an iron coffer at his shop. I suppose he thinks it is safer there than at home, for he'll not trust me with the key, either. But I've seen him open it, and there are coins in there beyond counting, mayhap as much as twenty-five shillings. So . . . I thought we could split the money. Half for you and half for me. That . . . that seems fair."

The corner of his mouth twitched. "Very fair."

Nell knew full well why he'd agreed so readily; he had every intention of keeping all the money for himself. But silly little Bella would have believed him, and so she smiled and nodded, as if relieved that they'd come to terms so quickly.

"The easiest way," he said, "would be to make it look as if

your husband was slain during a robbery of his shop. But what of the journeyman? Does he sleep there at night?"

"No. Abel insisted upon charging him rent and he preferred to find a room of his own elsewhere. Nóra . . . told you about Joel?"

His eyes gleamed knowingly, so salaciously that Nell found it easy to blush. "I know you've been creeping into his bed every chance you get, if that is what you mean. But what puzzles me is why you did not turn to him instead of to me. Why not ask him to help get rid of the inconvenient husband?"

"I could never do that!" Nell did her best to sound appalled. "Joel would never take part in a killing, no matter how much he loves me. It is just not in his nature." She saw the outlaw's smug half-smile and suppressed a smile of her own, one of victory, for this was the last nail driven into the Fleming's coffin. He'd be keen to do her killing, for now he knew she could be bled white afterward. Whenever he and Nóra wanted extra money, they need only threaten to reveal the truth to Joel and she'd pay to keep them quiet.

"I want to do it soon," he said, "for I've been inactive of late and I need some fast money. Where is his shop?"

Nell was prepared for this question. "On Candle-wright Street, opposite St Clement's Church." She yearned to turn her head, to see if Justin and Luke were closing in yet, but she dared not. They had agreed beforehand on the need for extreme caution, for with a man like Gilbert, they could not afford the slightest misstep.

"I'll want to check it out for myself. In the meantime, you are to get me a copy of his money box key. Do not argue, woman, just do it! The man does take a bath occasionally, does he not? Whilst he bathes, you press the key into warm wax and make an impression. I know a locksmith who'll ask no awkward questions."

"I . . . I will try," Nell said hesitantly. "I must—Jesú!" Gasping, she clapped her hand to her mouth. "It is my husband's cousin! And he's seen me, is coming this way! What will I say, what—"

"Get hold of yourself," he snapped. Grabbing her arm, he dug his fingers into her wrist, causing her to gasp again, this time in pain. "Tell him you're looking for a horse on your husband's behalf."

Aldred was already bearing down upon them. "Bella! What are you doing here? Where is Cousin Abel?" He was overly hearty in his greetings, but he was bound to be nervous, desperate to get back into Jonas's good graces after botching his surveillance of Nóra's house.

"Abel is not with me. This . . . this is going to be a surprise. I want him to buy a horse, and I thought if I got the prices and such beforehand, I might persuade him. It would make his deliveries so much easier . . ."

"It would, indeed," Aldred agreed enthusiastically. "It is lucky for you that I happened along, for I know all about horses and can help you pick out a sound one." Brushing past the Fleming, Aldred began to run his hands down the bay's forelegs. Nell looked over at Gilbert and shrugged helplessly. He was scowling, but there was nothing he could do except play the charade out. Aldred was on the other side of the horse by now, talking about the need to look out for "splints" and to make sure the horse was not "touched in the wind." Nell thought he sounded quite convincing. Just having him beside her was a comfort. She no longer felt quite so vulnerable, so exposed to the outlaw's malice and blade.

Shifting so she could survey the field, she thought all looked perfectly normal and deceptively peaceful, given what was about to happen. Having rejected the white mule, the Black Monks were pacing sedately in their direction, their cowls shadowing their faces. The disappointed vendor was trailing after them, offering to drop the mule's price. Two dogs were romping near the cart, and a fair-haired man was leading his horse toward the pond's edge. When Nell would later replay the scene in her memory, she could not recall anything that seemed amiss, out of order.

And so she was utterly unprepared for the Fleming's action. She would never know what had spooked him. He'd often shown himself to have a sixth sense, an eerie ability to scent danger in the wind, and it was clearly in play now. "I'll get back to you about this," he said abruptly and grabbed for the reins.

"Wait, we're not done talking!"

Aldred's protest was more effective than Nell's. As Gilbert swung up into the saddle, he caught the outlaw's arm and tried to pull him off. Pandemonium followed. Justin and Luke sprinted toward them. So did the mule vendor. The canvas was flung into the air as Jonas erupted from the cart. The only innocent bystander, the man watering his horse, turned to stare and the dogs began to bark. Stunned by the swiftness of it all, Nell stood frozen. Gilbert was cursing, trying to shake Aldred off as his horse skidded sideways on the muddy ground. And then there was a metallic flash in the sunlight, a choked cry from Aldred, and as blood splattered her face and upraised hands, Nell began to scream.

Aldred slumped to the ground at her feet, and she dropped to her knees beside him, tearing off her veil. His neck was covered in blood, and she tried frantically to staunch the flow. But she was acting instinctively, for none of this seemed real to her, not the moaning youth nor the struggle now going on just a few feet away. Luke had reached them, lunging for the Fleming's reins. But Gilbert lashed out with his foot, kicking viciously at the deputy's head. Luke swerved and the boot caught him on the shoulder, with enough force to send him reeling. Jabbing his spurs into his mount's sides, Gilbert wheeled the horse toward the distant woods.

Nell could only watch helplessly. Jonas was still some distance away, but Justin was almost upon them. When he saw the Fleming send Luke sprawling, he whirled and whistled shrilly. Copper's head came up and then he loped over, reins dangling free. Nell might have marveled at that—a horse better trained than most dogs—but now she had thoughts only for Aldred, terrified that he might be bleeding to death in her lap.

To her amazement, though, he was soon trying to sit up. For all the bleeding, the wound was not life threatening; the Fleming's knife had mercifully missed any veins or arteries. Luke had gotten the wind knocked out of him. Lurching to his feet, he swore hotly and then spun around to get his own horse as Justin shot past them, Copper's flying hooves churning up a shower of mud.

"Dear God, no!" Nell cried out in horror as the realization struck her: the Fleming was going to escape. Justin was in pursuit, but Gilbert's horse had a daylight lead. As for the others, they were out of the game: Luke about to mount his stallion, Jonas on foot and fuming. The closest horse belonged to the gaping bystander. Running toward him, Jonas shoved the astonished man aside and snatched up the reins. But Nell knew it was too late. Once again Gilbert the Fleming would elude capture, free to keep on killing, even to track her down and take his vengeance for her trickery.

"He's getting away!" she screamed, her words breaking on a sob.

Holding her bloodied veil to his slashed neck, Aldred staggered to his feet. "No," he panted, "he is not. Justin told me to cut the knots on his saddle girth."

Nell stared at him, and then swung back toward the chase. Nothing seemed to have changed. Justin had cut into Gilbert's lead somewhat, but not enough. And then it happened. The bay seemed to shorten stride, and suddenly Gilbert was grabbing for the mane, desperately trying to retain his balance as the saddle started to slip. Within moments, he'd been overtaken by the big chestnut. Kicking his feet free of the stirrups, Justin flung himself onto the other man and they crashed heavily to the ground. Aldred shouted and then began to run unsteadily toward them. Lifting up her skirts, so did Nell.

She could tell that Justin was in trouble, for he was hampered by his long monk's habit, unable to get to his weapons. They were rolling about in the mud, in what looked to be a no-holds-barred battle for survival, far more savage than any alehouse brawl she'd ever seen. Breaking free, the Fleming actually smiled, the threatening, feral grin of a man with nothing left to lose. Seeing the dagger glinting in his fist, Nell would have screamed again, but her breath was gone. Justin evaded the first thrust. The second slashed through his sleeve, and the Fleming closed in.

But by then, Luke was there. Jumping from his horse before the animal had come to a full stop, he began to circle the outlaw, driving him back toward Justin. All three men were soon on the ground. But Gilbert continued to resist fiercely, with such frenzied rage and fear that they were having difficulty subduing him, for they were seeking to keep him alive and he sought only to kill. The fight did not end until Jonas galloped up on his commandeered horse. Unlike Justin and Luke, he dismounted without haste, then strode over to the struggling men and kicked the Fleming in the face. He went limp, and at long last, it was over.

Aldred seemed remarkably cheerful to Nell for a man who'd almost had his throat cut. But as she watched him tag along after Jonas like a puppy eager to please, she understood why. Not only had he redeemed himself for his earlier blunder, he'd have a scar well worth boasting about, grisly proof of his heroic confrontation with the murderous Fleming. As far as she was concerned, his money would be no good back at her alehouse. She figured he'd earned himself at least a month's worth of free drinks.

Luke and Justin were still sprawled on the ground, chests heaving, gulping air as greedily as they did the ale they were sharing from Luke's leather flask. Sinking down beside them, heedless of the mud, Nell gestured wordlessly and Justin passed her the flask. She knew neither would ever admit it, but both men had been shaken by that brutal, lethal mêlée. They'd soon be joking about it, she never doubted. But not yet.

Jonas had sent someone for a rope and he was roughly binding the hands and feet of the captured bandit. Gilbert had yet to stir, and Nell wondered if he could be dead. With a savagery that surprised her, she found herself fervently hoping so. Men had been known to escape the gallows. But not even one of the Devil's brood could cheat Death. Passing the flask back to Justin, she was surprised to discover that they had drawn a large, curious audience. Off to the right, she caught a glimpse of color, the same shade of bright blue as Nóra's mantle. But when she looked again, she saw nothing.

Ablaze with righteous indignation, the bystander was jogging toward them. "That was my horse!"

Jonas ignored him until he'd completed his task. Giving the Fleming's ropes a final tug, he stared up at the man. "Then you'd best go catch him."

The man flushed deeply; even the tips of his ears darkened. He sputtered, but the words seemed to catch in his throat. Turning aside, he trudged off in pursuit of his horse, now galloping aimlessly at the far end of the field.

Luke and Justin looked at each other and then burst into laughter. Luke was the first to sober up. "Look at this," he demanded, holding up a bloodied palm. "That weasel bit me!"

Justin got stiffly to his feet, moving like a man much older than twenty. Reaching down, he helped Nell to rise. His face was bloody, but so muddy, too, that she couldn't tell if it was his blood or the bandit's. He then grasped Luke's hand and pulled him up, too. Ridding themselves of their camouflage cowls and habits, they walked over and together stood staring down at Gilbert the Fleming.

"He seems to be breathing," Luke observed. "We could always drop him in the pond to bring him around."

But the outlaw's lashes were flickering. Opening his eyes, he gave an involuntary groan of pain, and then focused hazily upon a familiar face floating above him. With recognition came a surge of hot, helpless rage, hatred so scalding it all but burned his throat as he spat out the words of defiance, a diatribe that ended only when Jonas forced him to his feet, none too gently.

Luke had listened impassively to the Fleming's raving, envenomed tirade. But when he at last fell silent, his invective exhausted, the deputy smiled. "We'll have a long ride back to Winchester, Gib. It would be a pity if I forgot to feed you on the way."

Gilbert's lip curled. He was about to retort when he noticed Nell, who'd come up to stand beside the men. Snarling like a wolf, he turned on her in a fury. "You treacherous bitch! You'll pay for this, and you'll beg for death ere I'm done with you, I swear—"

Nell had gone very pale, and Justin backhanded the Fleming across the mouth, hard enough to draw blood. "You so much as look at her," he warned, "and you'll be the one begging for death!" He would not have believed he could get so much satisfaction from striking a man unable to hit back. Putting his arm around Nell's shoulders, he said, "Come on, lass. Pay his rantings no mind. A doomed man can do you no harm."

But before they could move away, the outlaw cried out, "Wait!" When Justin turned back, he said, "It is you again, the man on the Alresford Road. I know why that accursed deputy followed me to London. But why you? I've a right to know. Who are you?"

Justin looked at him, thinking back to their chance meeting on that snowy Epiphany morn. It seemed so random, and yet it had changed both of their lives dramatically, setting them upon a road that would lead to the queen's court and the gallows. "I am a friend," he said, "of Gervase Fitz Randolph."

"You say that as if it is supposed to mean something to me."

Justin was outraged. "You murder a man and then forget about it?"

The Fleming's mouth was bruised and bleeding, but his smile was chilling. "Why would I bother," he said, "to remember all their names?"

17

GAOL OF LONDON

March 1193

The lantern's light was unsparing, exposing a face that would have been unrecognizable even to those who knew the Fleming well. One eye had puffed shut and his jaw was grotesquely swollen, blackened with bruises. Those were injuries he'd suffered in the struggle out at Smithfield. But the blood gushing from his nose was fresh, for Jonas had just hit him. It took him a moment to get his breath back, and when he did, he spat out another obscenity. Jonas stepped forward again, but this time Luke pulled him away.

"Let the whoreson bleed," he said, "whilst we talk." Keeping hold of Jonas's arm, he steered him across the dungeon. Retrieving the lantern, Justin followed.

Jonas was not pleased. "Why did you stop me?" he demanded.

"If you want to hit him for the fun of it, that is fine by me. But if you are still trying to get him to talk, it's a waste of time." Luke glanced down at his own skinned, scraped knuckles and grimaced. "It is painfully obvious by now that we'll get nothing from him."

"Give me an hour alone with him and we'll see about that."

It was the first time that Justin had heard Jonas resort to bravado, but as their interrogation had foundered, cracks had begun to show in the serjeant's usually dispassionate demeanor. His anger was understandable; Justin felt equally frustrated. It was as if they'd been engaged in a prolonged and bloody castle siege, scaling the outer walls and finally fighting their way into the inner bailey, only to discover that the keep was impregnable, impervious to assault.

"I do not doubt your powers of persuasion, Jonas," Luke said, smiling grimly. "I can be rather persuasive, too, so I've been told. But there are men—thankfully few of them—who cannot be broken. They'll die, but that's all they'll do for you. Do not tell me you've never encountered one of them, for I'd not believe you. We might as well face it. We can beat the Fleming bloody. We can turn his remaining days into the Hell on earth he so richly deserves. And eventually we can hang him. But what we cannot do is make him talk."

Justin had already reached that same bleak conclusion. Glancing over at Jonas, he saw that the serjeant knew it, too, even if he was not yet ready to admit it. "Ere we concede defeat," he said, "let's try one more time."

Shackled to iron rings in the wall, Gilbert was sagging so badly that the manacles were cutting into his wrists. He was still bleeding from Jonas's last blow, and his breath was coming in labored, wheezing pants. When Justin let the lantern's light play over that battered, bloated face, he could not summon up even a pinprick of pity. What pity had Gilbert shown Kenrick, cornered in the mill loft?

"You're making it needlessly hard on yourself, Gilbert. You know you're going to hang. So why ask for more pain in the brief time you've got left? Why not tell us what we want to know? Give us some answers and we'll go away and let you be."

The Fleming raised his head. When he spoke, his voice emerged as a croak, raspy and harsh, throbbing with hatred. "Rot in Hell . . ."

Justin had dreaded telling Eleanor, but she took it better than he'd expected. Apparently she, too, had known a few men in her life who could not be broken, for she did not seem surprised by the Fleming's refusal to cooperate. And when Justin had completed his report, she said something that would later strike him as odd, reminding him of his earlier suspicions about her motives.

"Well," she said softly, "mayhap it was not meant that the truth come out . . ."

"Madame?"

"No matter. I was but thinking aloud, wondering if this means the Fleming's secret will die with him. Was he our last hope? What of his woman?"

"So far Nóra has eluded us, my lady. When the serjeant's men arrived to arrest her, she was gone and some of her belongings were, too. They've been out scouring the city for her, with no luck so far. But even if she is caught, I doubt that she'd be of much help. I cannot see why the Fleming would tell her about a killing in Winchester. He's not the sort to be boasting in bed about his crimes, to give away any secrets that might be used against him later."

"What of the man's partner?"

"He is not likely to be as hard a nut to crack, madame." Justin was striving to sound confident, but he could not help adding a pessimistic qualifier, ". . . if we can find him."

Eleanor gave him a penetrating look. "You ought not to be so downcast, Justin. At least this Fleming will be doing no more killings. You said he is known to have slain five people, did you not? The true tally of his victims is probably twice that many. You may not have been able to get the answers we were seeking, but you undoubtedly saved some lives."

Justin nodded somberly. "But I wanted the answers, too."

Their eyes caught and held. "So did I," she said. "So keep on the trail. The hunt is not over yet."

Justin's chagrin was not eased by Eleanor's praise; her generosity only made him feel even more disheartened. He'd let her down. No matter how he rationalized their failure to get the Fleming to talk, it always came back to that. She'd relied upon him and he'd disappointed her. And unless they could find the missing Sampson, no one but Gilbert would ever know if he'd been in the pay of the French king.

Claudine was waiting when he emerged from the queen's great chamber. "You look wretched!"

He smiled wryly. "I know. But I spent most of the night over at the gaol, going home only to wash up."

She touched her fingers to the bruise spreading across his

cheekbone. "Did the killer do this? Did you catch him?" When he nodded, she slipped her arm in his, drawing him toward the comparative privacy of a window alcove. "Then why are you not happier about it?"

"It is a long and troubling story," he said evasively. "No need to burden you with it."

Claudine shook her head reproachfully. "Now why am I thinking of clams?" Her fingers again sought his bruised cheek. "Do you know what I think you need? Me. Is there a chance you can get rid of that inconvenient friend?"

"I suppose he could always bed down in the smithy with Gunter. But what about the queen?"

"I'll get her to agree," Claudine said and then grinned. "Surely you've noticed that I am very good at getting what I want?"

Justin grinned, too, his spirits beginning to soar. "I can right gladly attest to that," he said, "and I'd like nothing better than to do more attesting, the sooner the better."

Claudine winked. "Wait here, then, whilst I talk to the queen. I'll be right back."

Justin sat down in the window seat to await Claudine's return. But no sooner had she disappeared into the queen's chamber than the door to the great hall was flung open and Durand strode in. Justin stiffened. This was the first time he'd seen Durand at court since confiding his suspicions to Eleanor. He had no idea how she had chosen to discipline her false knight, for she'd said nothing further. But it was obvious that Durand had lost the queen's favor. Nothing else could explain the look of fury that crossed his face now.

Justin got slowly to his feet as the other man stalked toward him. These past weeks had taught him that all wars were not fought on the battlefield, and one of the lessons he'd learned was to strike first and fast. "I'm surprised to see you, Sir Durand. I assumed that you had sailed for France with Lord John."

Durand's eyes were a brittle Viking blue, fathomless and frigid. "You'd do well to consider a sojourn in France yourself, de Quincy. If I were you, I'd ride for the nearest port as if my very life depended upon it."

"That sounds almost like a threat. But I am sure you meant it as a friendly warning, did you not?"

"Of course. You've given me such good reason to feel friendly toward you, after all," Durand said, with a menacing smile. "If not for you, the queen would have continued to see me as just another of her knights, one amongst many. That is all changed now, though—because of you."

"The pleasure was all mine," Justin said, and Durand's sarcastic civility splintered into shards of sheer ice.

"Some pleasures can be hazardous to a man's health," he said, "and some can even be fatal." He got the last word, for he turned on his heel then, not waiting for Justin's retort.

"Justin?" Claudine's eyes were wide, her brows arching upward toward her hairline. "What was that all about? I did not realize that you even knew Durand. What happened to cause such bad blood between you?"

"I accused him of being John's lackey—more or less—and he liked it not."

"You do enjoy courting danger, for certes! Luckily for you," she added, "I find madness to be well nigh irresistible in a man."

Justin smiled, but kept his eyes upon Durand's retreating figure. "You warned me about John, and with cause. But why should I accord the Prince of Darkness and one of his minions the same respect?"

"You're wrong," she said, with such vehemence that he looked at her in surprise. "John is indeed dangerous. Yet there are still occasional flashes of brightness in the dark depths of his soul." Her lips curved slightly then, hinting at a smile, for she could never be serious for long. "Lucifer was a fallen angel, after all. But you'll look in vain for any sparks in Durand's darkness, Justin. He is not a man you want as an enemy."

"Want him or not, I have him." Justin was touched by her concern, but he did not take Durand's threats as seriously as she did. How could the knight be a more dangerous foe than the Fleming?

Shaking her hair over her shoulders, Claudine stretched so sensuously that Justin paused in the act of pouring wine. "You have more in common with cats than an overactive curiosity," he said admiringly. "You move like a cat, too."

"I hope you mean that as a compliment. Most people think cats are good only for catching mice and serving witches. But I fancy them myself, so I thank you." When he handed her a wine cup, she settled back comfortably in his arms. "I've been known to purr, too . . ."

"And to scratch."

She smiled into the wine cup. "I hope you're not complaining?"

"No . . . I think I was boasting," he said, and she laughed, then offered him the cup.

"Drink up, darling," she urged. "You're going to be needing your strength tonight."

He began to laugh, too. "You are a shameless wench. I like that."

Reclaiming the cup, she deliberately dribbled wine onto his chest, and in the tussle that followed, the rest of the wine was spilt. After squabbling playfully over who ought to fetch the flagon, Justin dived, shivering, from the bed, for the hearth was not giving off much heat. "It is lucky the cup went into the floor rushes," he said with mock severity, "for I have but the one sheet."

Claudine pretended to pout. "If you had not started squirming about like an eel, I'd have licked it off!" Lifting the covers, she patted the bed invitingly. "Hurry, I'm getting cold. I want you to warm—Jesú!"

"What?" He glanced around the cottage, puzzled, seeing no reason for her outcry.

She was staring at the huge mottled bruise on his left hip. "Surely I did not do that? Was it the man you captured yesterday? The killer?"

He nodded and climbed hastily back into bed, handing her the refilled cup. Sipping the wine, she explored his bruises with gentle fingers, a faint frown creasing her brow. "Forget what I said about your courting danger. You've taken her right into your bed!"

"So danger is a woman, then? I've always thought so, too."

She continued to survey his contusions, unsmiling. "I am not joking. You could have been killed, Justin. And it is not over, is it?"

"No," he admitted, "it is not." The afterglow of their love-making had begun to fade and reality was once more intruding. How were they going to find Sampson? And even if they did, could he be made to talk?

"That wretched letter had blood on it," Claudine said suddenly, and scowled at his look of surprise. "Of course I've figured out that the letter is at the heart of this, Justin! It is so obvious. You did not know the queen yet, for I had to help get you in to see her, remember? So whatever was in that letter had to be important, indeed, since she then took you into her service. You are not going to insult me now with a false denial, are you?"

"No," he said, "I am not."

"Good," she said, sounding mollified. "That was an easy guess. But I do not understand how the letter is linked to your hunt for this killer?"

Her voice had risen questioningly and he brought her hand up to his mouth, kissing her fingers. "I cannot tell you that, love."

"Why not? You could pretend this is a church and I am your confessor," she suggested impishly. "Anything you told me would not go beyond this bed, for I'd never betray the sanctity of the confessional!"

Justin was laughing again. "Listen, my beautiful blasphemer, I'd tell you if I could. But these are not my secrets, so I have not the right to reveal them, even to you."

"Yes, I am prying," she conceded. "And I'll not deny that I am curious, for who would not be? They are a most unlikely couple, after all: the Queen of England and a Winchester cutthroat! Of course I wonder about such an odd pairing. But it is more than curiosity."

Her eyes lingered for a moment on the bruise under his eye. "Justin, I am worried about you. You were ambushed once already, and the next time you might not be so lucky. I do not know what information you hoped to gain from that outlaw, but I do know you did not get it. You admitted as much when you said it was 'not over.' What are you going to do now? I need to know if your life will be at risk. Surely you can tell me that much?"

Justin's feelings for Claudine had been veering between passion and protection, between wanting to take care of her and take her to bed. His emotions were complicated now by a great surge of tenderness, a sentiment he'd had little experience with. Reaching over, he caressed her cheek, and she closed her eyes, her lips parting temptingly.

He did not kiss her, though, for in that moment the significance of her words sank in. She'd called Gilbert a "Winchester cutthroat." He'd never told her that, had never even mentioned the Fleming's name. So how had she known?

His fingers slid from her cheek, came to rest upon her throat. She smiled without opening her eyes, a dimple flashing. Fumbling for the wine cup, he drank deeply, but the cold continued to seep into his body, through marrow to the very bone. Only a handful of people had known of Gilbert's Winchester roots. Eleanor. Will Longsword. Luke and Jonas. Nell. And John. John would know, for Durand would have told him all that he'd gleaned from those spying missions to Winchester.

I'll have to look elsewhere. John's words seemed to echo in the stillness. He'd harbored suspicions about Luke. Ought he to have looked closer at hand? Could Claudine be John's spy?

Until that moment, he'd not known that the worst sort of pain need not be physical, utterly unrelated to broken bones or bleeding. Had she bedded him at John's bidding? All those questions about his past, so gently insistent, questions that a woman would naturally want to know about her lover. Jesus God. Had she been playing him for a fool from the first?

"Are you retreating into that clamlike silence again?" Claudine chided. "I do not expect you to betray the queen's confidence, no more than I would. But I can see how troubled you are. Keep back what you must, but do not shut me out entirely. Let me help, Justin."

She sounded very sincere. Those lovely dark eyes did not waver, her gaze as trusting and innocent as a fawn's. Could he be sure that he'd not let something slip about the Fleming? Was he doing her a terrible wrong? But it explained so much, too much. He had to know the truth. He *had* to know.

"You are right, Claudine," he said, and wondered if his voice sounded as strained to her ears as it did to his own. "Mayhap it might help to talk about it, and . . . and whom can I trust if not you? But I must have your word that you'll keep secret whatever I tell you. There is more at stake than I think you realize."

"I promise," she said readily. "Of course I do."

"I'll tell you, then, about the contents of that letter. It concerned the queen's son. It is very likely, Claudine, that King Richard is dead."

Her gasp was audible. "Oh, no! What happened to him?"

"He was shipwrecked on the way home from the Holy Land. The letter was from one of his shipmates. He claims there were but few survivors and the king was not amongst them."

"Dear God!" She seemed genuinely shaken. "Nothing could give the queen greater grief. Richard has always been the dearest of all her children. How could she keep pain like that bottled up within? She's acted as if nothing was wrong . . ."

"She is not willing to believe it, not yet. That is one reason why she is keeping it quiet. She is waiting for confirmation, whilst hoping that it will be disproved. But I read that letter and I have no doubts that the man was telling the truth."

He drained the cup, the wine tasting like vinegar. "Do you see now why I was so loath to speak of this, Claudine, and why I had to swear you to secrecy?"

"By the Rood, yes! Justin, this will . . . will change everything!"

"Yes . . . it will." He knew his story would not bear close scrutiny, but it was so sensational that no one would think to question it, at least not on first hearing. Setting the cup down in the floor rushes, he lay back wearily against the pillow. Claudine curled up beside him, continuing to express her astonishment, to sympathize with Eleanor, to speculate how Richard's death would affect the succession. Finally becoming aware of his silence, she poked him in the ribs. "You're not falling asleep, are you?"

"Sorry," he mumbled. "But I was up all night . . ."

"I'd forgotten about that." Leaning over, she kissed him on the cheek. "Get some sleep, then, love. Mayhap I will, too . . ."

Turning his head on the pillow, Justin found himself breathing in the rain-sweet scent of her hair. He was exhausted, but sleep would not come. What if he was wrong about Claudine? How could he ever expect her forgiveness? But if he was not wrong? What, then?

He was never to know how long he lay there. He was lost in time, trapped behind enemy lines in a foreign country, with no familiar landmarks in sight. "Justin?" Claudine was shaking his arm. "Love, wake up."

"What is wrong?"

"I am feeling poorly," she said, mustering up a wan smile. "Sometimes I get these severe headaches. They come upon me without warning, like a storm out of a cloudless sky . . ."

Justin sat up. "There is an apothecary shop across the street. I'll see if it is still open."

She shook her head, then winced. "It is sweet of you to offer. But that will not help." Rubbing her temples, she winced again, and gave him another apologetic smile. "The only remedy that does is a tisane made up for me in Aquitaine. I'm not even sure what is in it, feverfew and betony and other herbs I could not name. When one of these bad headaches hits, all I can do is take the tisane and keep to bed until the storm passes. Would you mind taking me back to the Tower?"

"No, I'd not mind."

"No wonder I am so smitten with you," she said, groping for his hand. "I am truly sorry, love, to spoil our night together."

Justin stared down at the delicate fingers entwined in his. "It is all right, Claudine," he said softly. "I understand."

They parted on the steps leading up into the Tower's great keep, for Claudine insisted that he need not accompany her any farther. She did not kiss him, for it was too public a place for that. Instead she squeezed his hand, her fingers stroking his palm in a clandestine caress. "I am so sorry, Justin."

"I'll take your mare over to the stables," he said. But he did not move away at once, stood watching until she'd disappeared into the forebuilding of the keep.

"That is a fine horse." A youth had come whistling by, pausing long enough to cast a covetous glance toward Copper. He looked vaguely familiar to Justin, was most likely a squire to one of Eleanor's household knights.

"Wait," Justin said. "I'd like a word with you, lad. Do you know the Lady Claudine?"

"I do. Why?"

"I just escorted her back to the Tower. She was taken ill this afternoon and I am worried about her. It will ease my mind if I know she's gone right up to the queen's chambers and to bed. It would be worth a half-penny to me if you could find out for sure?"

"A half-penny just for that? Consider it done!" By the time the words were out of his mouth, the boy was heading for the stairs. "I'll meet you at the stables," he called over his shoulder, "in two shakes of a cat's tail!"

Justin had told the groom he'd unsaddle Claudine's mount himself, and set about it with meticulous care, trying to keep his thoughts only upon the task at hand. He was removing the mare's sweat pad when the squire came loping in, a blur of elbows and knees and adolescent enthusiasm.

"Well," he announced, "I did it. Can I have my money?" When Justin tossed him a coin, he caught it deftly. "I thought I'd best get it first," he said with a cheeky grin, "for you're not going to like what I have to tell you."

He was only about fourteen or so, but already with a worldly understanding of court intrigues and the perversities of adult love affairs. "If Lady Claudine was ailing, she recovered right fast. I found her downstairs with the chaplain. She was asking if he knew the whereabouts of one of the queen's knights. It was urgent, she said, that she find him straightaway."

"Did you hear the man's name?" Justin asked tonelessly, already knowing what the youth would say.

The squire nodded. "Sir Durand de Curzon."

It was dusk by the time Justin got back to Gracechurch Street. Gunter and Ellis were inside the smithy, shoeing a horse. Shadow was sprawled in an empty stall and greeted Justin with a burst of riotous barking as he led Copper into the stable.

Ellis gaped at sight of Justin. "I sure did not expect to see you here," he blurted. "Luke said you'd kicked him out so you could have a tryst with some mystery woman!"

"That is none of our concern, Ellis." Gunter was using a rasp to file down a front hoof and looked up from his work to deliver a mild rebuke. "If you're looking for Luke," he told Justin, "he's across the street at the alehouse."

"The whole neighborhood is over there, celebrating the capture of that killer." Ellis gazed reproachfully at the farrier. "Except for us."

"You know we have to finish the shoeing ere it gets full dark," Gunter said patiently. "Smiths are not allowed to work within the city walls unless they forbear from heavy hammering and pounding at night."

Ellis's shoulders sagged and he turned to tend the forge with an air of martyred resignation. He cheered up considerably, though, when Justin gave him a coin to take care of the chestnut. Bidding them a terse farewell, Justin whistled to the dog and stepped out into the soft lavender twilight.

The day had been chilly; the night promised to be downright cold. Justin's steps slowed as he neared the cottage door. He reached for the latchstring, but his fingers clenched, instead, into a tight fist. He could not cross that threshold. He could not face the ghosts that waited within, not yet, not tonight.

Justin had never seen the alehouse so crowded; in claiming that the entire street had turned out, Ellis had not exaggerated by much. His entrance passed unnoticed at first, for most of the customers were watching an arm-wrestling contest between Luke and Aldred. Nell was attracting a fair amount of attention herself, perched on the edge of a table and gesturing so expansively that her ale cup was sloshing about like a storm at sea. "And so I told him, 'Abel has twenty-five shillings hoarded away, which we can split after you do the murder,'" she declared, with such tipsy verve that she drew admiring murmurs from her audience.

In the midst of all this boisterous, chaotic commotion, Jonas seemed like an island of calm, watching the festivities from a corner table with a full flagon of ale and a sardonic half-smile.

Justin was not surprised that he was alone. The alehouse regulars had come to accept Luke, for his powers were vested more than seventy miles away. But Jonas was the local law and thus posed a more immediate threat. Even those with an unsullied conscience grew uneasy whenever the serjeant intruded into their world.

Weaving his way between customers, Justin picked up an empty cup from a nearby table and headed in Jonas's direction. If Ellis knew about Claudine, that meant all of Gracechurch Street did, too. But Justin was sure that Jonas cared little about gossip, no matter how lurid. Jonas proved him right by showing no surprise when he materialized at the serjeant's table.

"I need to talk to you, Jonas." Justin caught the flagon as the serjeant slid it over and poured himself a generous portion. "We cannot wait for Sampson to surface on his own. We have to flush him out of hiding ourselves, and we have to do it as soon as possible. Any ideas?"

Jonas shrugged. "The sheriff does not pay me enough to have ideas."

"Do not do that!" Justin leaned angrily across the table. "Do not act as if you do not care, for I know better. You do not want Sampson prowling the London streets any more than I do. So how are we going to find him?"

Jonas leaned back in his seat, regarding Justin with a gleam of amused approval. "Whoever put a burr under your saddle, I ought to thank. It's always useful to have such single-minded allies. We can start by putting out the word that we'll pay for information about Sampson. Next we can—"

"What are you doing here, de Quincy?" Lurching into the table, Luke dropped, laughing, into the closest seat. "Why are you not back at the cottage, stoking your fire?"

Justin gave the deputy a look of such hostility that Luke blinked and then pretended to flinch. "Oh, ho, so that's the way the wind blows, is it? Well, I've got the cure right here for what ails you. Drink up, lad. You may not be able to drown your troubles, but you can damned well get them drunk!"

"I do not remember asking you for advice, Luke," Justin said, so curtly that the deputy's smile vanished. Before he could decide whether he ought to take offense, Jonas made that decision for him.

"If I wanted to watch a couple of young roosters go at it, I'd find a cockfight. We were talking about ways to track down Sampson, Luke. You have any suggestions?"

"Not offhand, no. You two are gluttons for punishment, so dedicated to duty it is truly disgusting. Would it kill you to spare one night for celebrating? Now the Fleming was a real challenge. But Sampson? He could not outwit that moon-mad dog of yours, de Quincy. Trust me, it is only a matter of time until he trips himself up. Have some patience. As for me, I'd rather have some ale."

"Take mine," Justin said, shoving the cup toward the deputy. "You might be onto something, Luke. Let's consider what we know about the man. He is on his own in a strange city, his money running out. He is not one to go looking for work, now is he?"

Luke hooted. "That lout has never done a day's honest labor in his life. All he knows how to do is steal."

"Exactly. But is a slow-thinking stranger going to thrive in a city like London? Or is he more likely to blunder and run afoul of the law? Mayhap we've been looking for him in the wrong places. Instead of searching the streets, what about the gaols?"

Luke stared at him, a slow grin spreading across his face. "Now why did I not think of that myself? Let's give the Devil his due, Jonas, for de Quincy's idea is downright brilliant!"

"I'd not go that far," the serjeant said, laconic as always. "But it does sound promising." And coming from Jonas, Justin knew that was high praise, indeed.

His ale-drenched sleep had given Justin a brief respite. But he awoke in the morning to a hangover and an onslaught of memories, mercilessly vivid, of Claudine's treachery.

His other memories of the night were much hazier, though. He did remember becoming the unwelcome center of attention. Once his presence had become known, everyone had wanted to congratulate him. But they'd wanted to joke, too, about the woman he had hidden away at Gunter's cottage, and their good-natured raillery had lacerated a wound still raw and bleeding.

It was Luke who'd come unexpectedly to his rescue, diverting the conversation away from bedmates to murder and mayhem. Justin's last clear memories were of the deputy holding court to the entire alehouse, all listening avidly to his riveting and gory recounting of the Fleming's bloody career. After that, Justin had set about drinking himself into oblivion, with some success.

Sitting up in bed, Justin discovered that he was still fully dressed, even to his boots. A groan from the pallet on the floor told him that Luke was stirring, and a hoarse "Christ Jesus!" that the deputy was too weak to fend off Shadow. Getting stiffly to his feet, Justin stumbled toward the table, only to find that his water pitcher had frozen solid in the night, for he and Luke had been too drunk to light a fire.

"My mouth," he said, "feels like five miles of bad road. And we have got nothing to drink in the entire cottage. We'll have to go across the street . . ."

"You go," Luke muttered, keeping his arm firmly crooked over his eyes to ward off daylight. "I'll just open a vein . . ."

Justin was searching for his mantle, finally finding it crumpled up on the floor, Shadow's bed for the night. "When I come back from the privy," he said, "I'll go get us some more ale. That is supposed to help . . ." But the bed was beckoning again and since it was much closer than the latrine or the alehouse, it won out.

When he awoke again, his head seemed to be pounding like a drum. It took him a befuddled moment to realize it was the door. Groping his way across the room, he shoved the bolt back and let in such a blaze of bright sunlight that he was half blinded.

"Still abed?" Sauntering past Justin, Jonas looked down at Luke's prostrate body and shook his head. "Mayhap you lads ought to stick to milk from now on."

"Most people do not come calling until past dawn, Jonas." Justin leaned against the wall, wondering how the serjeant could have drunk so much ale himself and show so few aftereffects. It hardly seemed fair.

"Dawn? It is nigh on noon." Jonas nudged Luke with the tip of his boot. "You have any water to throw on him?"

"Do that and you're a dead man," Luke warned, although his threat might have carried more weight if he were not so entangled in the blankets, looking as if he were cocooned in his own burial shroud. "Go away, Jonas . . ."

"So . . . you do not want to hear about Sampson, then?"

Jonas got the reaction he was aiming for. Luke sat up so abruptly that he cracked his head on a table leg and Justin lunged forward, grabbing for the serjeant's arm as if it were a lifeline. "What did you find out?"

Jonas smiled triumphantly. "Your hunt is done. Sampson is being held in Newgate Gaol, waiting to hang."

18

LONDON

March 1193

A bleary-eyed Ellis reluctantly let them in, arguing feebly that the alehouse was not open yet. Inside, it was as dark and silent as a tomb, and there was even a body stretched out on one of the tables. "Nell said to let him sleep it off," Ellis mumbled, wincing as Jonas reached out and tipped the table over, dumping Aldred into the floor rushes.

The crash was followed by a startled yelp from Aldred and an immediate cry of "Ellis?" coming from above-stairs. "What was that noise?"

Jonas strode over to the stairwell. "I've got some drunkards down here who need sobering up, Nell, and I could use your help."

"What is that?" Luke was staring suspiciously into the depths of his cup. "It looks like swamp water."

"Just drink it down," Nell insisted. "You'd think I was asking you to swill hemlock! If you must know, it is saffron in barley water, with a few other herbs mixed in. I've had a lot of practice at this, for my husband liked his ale more than he ought."

Setting a platter in the middle of the table, she said, "Try to eat some bread. I'll be back after I see what I can brew up for Aldred's headache." Aldred moaned his thanks, then slumped down in his seat, as boneless as one of Lucy's rag dolls. Nell rolled her eyes, muttered something about men that did not sound complimentary, and disappeared into the kitchen.

Jonas poured himself a brimming cup of ale and began to smear honey on a large chunk of bread. "If you have any salted herring left," he called after Nell, "I could eat one or two." At that, Aldred moaned again and bolted for the privy, much to Jonas's amusement. "I hope you two do not have such delicate stomachs."

"Sorry to disappoint you, but no." Justin broke off a piece of bread and forced himself to take a few bites. "Tell us what you found out about Sampson."

"He seems to have squandered his money right fast, for his first robbery was committed on Shrove Tuesday. He was a busy lad, for he struck at least three times. His method was simple. He'd prowl the alehouses and taverns after dark, pick his victim—a lone drunkard—and then follow the man out, pouncing as soon as they were alone. Unfortunately for him, he was not a man to pass unnoticed: as huge and hulking as a bear, with a gap where his front tooth ought to have been and a scar over one eye."

Luke nodded. "Yes, that is Sampson. But you said back at the cottage that he is in Newgate Gaol. How was he caught?"

"He blundered, like Justin here guessed he would. The third robbery went wrong at the outset, for his intended target was not as drunk as he'd thought. When Sampson jumped him, he fought back. That misjudgment was Sampson's first mistake. His second was that he'd been too eager, for curfew had not rung yet. A Requiem Mass was ending at St Andrew's Cornhill and parishioners were soon spilling out into Aldgate to see what all the commotion was about."

Jonas drank deeply, then wiped his mouth with the back of his hand. "By then, Sampson had overpowered his quarry and was straddling him whilst he groped for the man's money pouch. But ere he could get away, he was confronted by one of the parishioners. They struggled, and when Sampson could not break free, he stabbed the Good Samaritan in the throat."

Justin swallowed with difficulty, washing the crust down with barley water. But it was not the bread which left such a bitter taste in his mouth. They killed so casually, the Sampsons and Gilberts of this world. And they left so much grieving in their wake. Hanging such men only kept them from killing again. It did nothing to ease the pain they'd brought to so many on their descent into Hell. Glancing around the table, he saw his own frustration and fury mirrored on Luke's face. Jonas, as ever, was inscrutable. He paused to drink again before picking up the bloody threads of his story.

"Sampson then fled, with the parishioners in pursuit. But his size and that bloody dagger would have kept most of them at a safe distance. I daresay he'd have gotten away if he'd not had the bad luck to turn onto Lime Street. By chance, he ran right into the Watch. It took fully four men to subdue him, and then they had to protect him from the crowd, who were all for hanging him from the nearest tree. But the priest from St Andrew's was able to shame them into backing down, and Sampson was dragged off to gaol. His reprieve will be a brief one, though. I'd wager the court will convict him ere the trial even begins!"

"I wish I could be so certain of that," Luke said morosely, for he had learned the hard way that it was not easy to get a man sentenced to the gallows. He'd often pondered why juries were so loath to see a man hang, and had finally concluded that the notorious leniency of juries was paradoxically linked to the harshness of their laws. Whether a man killed by accident or in self-defense or with calculated and cold-blooded intent, he was charged with murder. He could argue "mischance" or "justification," but he had to prove that in court, and many men fled rather than risk submitting themselves to the king's justice. A man could be hanged, too, for theft, could pay with his life for a crime of hunger or desperation. The result was that juries often refused to indict, even when the evidence seemed to demand it.

Justin looked puzzled by Luke's skepticism, but Jonas understood all too well. "We've both seen men walk away from the gallows when we knew they were as guilty as Cain," he explained to Justin. "But not this time. That fool Sampson murdered a man in full sight of more than a dozen witnesses, including the victim's own wife and a parish priest. No, this is one knave who'll get exactly what is coming to him—a short dance at the end of a long rope."

"When can we question him?" Justin asked. A pity they could not wait until after the trial. Sampson might be more inclined to talk once he knew there was no hope. But if he was tried and found guilty, it would be too late then, for executions were almost always carried out immediately. Only pregnant women could count upon a delay. If convicted, Sampson would be taken at once to the gallows.

"We can go to the gaol this afternoon." Jonas then gave voice to Justin's own unease, saying, "But he may not be willing to talk with you. Why should he? He can always hope for a miracle—a jury so blind, deaf, and dumb that they might not indict him. Or he could balk out of sheer spite. So it may well be that you'll have no better luck with him than we did with the Fleming."

Justin felt a chill of foreboding, for this was his last chance to learn the truth about the goldsmith's murder. But Luke was shaking his head. "Leave that to me," he said, "for I know Sampson. I'll get him to talk." And when Justin asked how, he would say only, "You'll see," with an enigmatic smile.

Newgate was one of London's most strategic gatehouses, guarding the approach from the west. It was an impressive stone structure, several stories high, tracing its origin back to a time when London was known as Londinium and under the rule of ancient Rome. Newgate had been rebuilt five years ago, and was now used as a city gaol. It did not have a sordid history like the prison by the River Fleet, did not hold as many ghosts or echoes of past pain. But it, too, was a bleak, sad place, at once formidable and forlorn. And the stench was the same. It hit Justin in the face as soon as they were escorted inside. Familiar odors of confinement and crowding, and that most pervasive stink of all—fear.

The more fortunate prisoners were kept in the upper chambers; the lower a man's status, the lower down he was lodged. The worst and most dangerous of the lot were held in the underground dungeon called "the pit," and when Sampson was shoved into the guards' chamber, it was obvious that he'd come from there, for he was blinking and squinting even in the subdued lamplight.

Sampson was as broad as he was tall, heavy in the torso, but not sloppy fat. He would be a nasty foe in any alehouse brawl, and an even deadlier one on a dark, deserted street. This was Justin's first close encounter with Sampson, and he found himself marveling at the reckless courage of the slain Good Samaritan. Sampson was younger than he had expected, not more than five and twenty. But the pale blue eyes were ageless. They darted around the chamber, drawn irresistibly to the shuttered and barred windows. Only after Sampson had satisfied himself that the room offered no opportunities for escape did he turn his attention to the men. His gaze moved from Justin to Jonas with indifference. But hostile recognition blazed across his face at sight of Luke.

"What are you doing here?" His voice was low pitched, so hoarse and guttural that the words emerged almost as a growl.

Luke smiled blandly. "I decided to treat myself, Sampson. I'm here to watch you hang."

Sampson gave the deputy as lethal a look as Justin had ever seen. Reaching for a chair, he settled himself as comfortably as his irons would allow, tilting the chair back until he could prop his feet upon the table. The obscenity he then flung at Luke was a common one, but he invested it with enough venom to overcome his lack of imagination. Luke glanced across at Jonas, and nodded, almost imperceptibly. Jonas said nothing, and Justin was not sure if he'd caught Luke's signal. The serjeant had been leaning against the wall, arms folded. But suddenly he was in motion, lunging forward and, with one well-aimed kick, sending Sampson's chair crashing over backwards.

The outlaw went down, sprawling in the floor rushes in a tangle of chains, for he was both manacled at the wrists and shackled at the ankles. Spitting curses, he struggled to regain his feet, and for a moment, Justin thought he would launch himself at Jonas. But as their eyes met, he changed his mind, and instead righted the chair with what dignity he could muster.

"Why'd you do that?" Sampson protested, sounding more querulous than defiant.

Jonas did not bother to respond, resuming his stance against the wall. Justin had never seen a man look so relaxed and yet so redoubtable, too. This was uncharted territory for him, and he was content for the time being to watch, to let Luke and Jonas blaze the trail.

Luke claimed a chair for himself. "I was not totally honest

with you, Sampson, when I said I was here to see you hang. Mind you, I plan to stay for the hanging. I'd not miss that for all the wine in France. But your arrest was an unexpected bounty. What actually brought me to London was that cutthroat friend of yours, Gilbert the Fleming."

"Who?" Sampson started to tip his chair again, glanced over at Jonas, and thought better of it. "Who?" he repeated, smiling as if pleased by his own cleverness.

Luke was smiling, too, a smile shot through with mockery. "Do not waste your time with such pitiful denials, Sampson. You have so little time left, after all. We know all about you and Gilbert. He confessed to the killing out on the Alresford Road."

"Did he now?" Sampson scoffed. "When was that, over drinks at the local alehouse?"

"No . . . I believe it was in the city gaol, after a long night's interrogation. You look taken aback. Did I forget to tell you that, Sampson? We caught Gilbert on Friday out at the Smithfield horse fair. Mayhap we can work it so that you both are hanged on the same day, for old times' sake."

"You're lying," Sampson said, but he did not sound at all certain of that.

"Why are you so surprised? Sooner or later, the Fleming's luck was bound to run out . . . just as yours did. Of course you tripped yourself up, whereas Gilbert was done in by a woman, but both roads still lead to the gallows."

"A woman?" Sampson's jaw dropped. "I told him he could not trust that Irish whore, I told him!"

Luke's eyes shone in the lamplight, cat green and gleaming. "He ought to have listened to you."

Sampson was quiet for a moment, mulling over his partner's ill luck. "What a fool," he said, with a notable lack of sympathy. "I'd never have let a slut hoodwink me."

"No," Luke agreed, "you needed no woman to foul yourself up. You managed that all on your own."

Sampson glared balefully at the deputy. "You never got a word out of the Fleming about any killings. Let me tell you about Gib. If you were drowning, he'd throw you an anchor. If you were dying of thirst, he'd not even spare you a cup of warm piss. Gib would never talk to the law, never. He'd save his confession for the Devil and his best curses for the likes of you."

Justin exhaled a breath held too long. His disappointment was all the keener because he'd let himself hope that Luke's bluff might succeed. Glancing toward the deputy, he was startled by the other man's aplomb. Far from being flustered by Sampson's challenge, Luke was grinning.

"Well, you cannot blame a man for trying," he said, so cheerfully that Justin realized he'd never expected to dupe Sampson with this concocted confession of Gilbert's. Reassured and curious, Justin settled back in his seat to watch the rest of the performance.

Sampson was caught off balance by Luke's candor; in his experience, sheriffs were rarely so forthright. "You admit you lied?"

"I thought it was worth a try." Reaching under his mantle, Luke drew out a wineskin. "We do not need confessions, for we have enough evidence without them to hang both of you higher than Haman. Master de Quincy there was a witness to that killing out on the Alresford Road. His testimony alone will be enough to send Gilbert to the gallows. And there are so many people eager to testify against you that they'll have to hold the trial in St Paul's churchyard to accommodate them all. No, the verdicts are a foregone conclusion. I was merely seeking to tie up loose ends."

"How?" Sampson said with a sneer. "By having me make my peace with God?"

Luke shrugged. "Some men find it a comfort to go to their deaths with a clear conscience," he said, and appeared quite unfazed when Sampson responded with a burst of profanity. "It cannot be easy, lying down there in the pit day after day, just waiting to die. What man jack amongst us is not afraid of death, especially a death by hanging?" Tilting the flask up, he drank with apparent relish, seeming not to notice how Sampson's eyes followed the wineskin. "If it were me, I'd want a priest, for certes."

"Well, you are not me," Sampson snapped and added a "bleeding whoreson" for punctuation.

Luke was no longer smiling. "No . . . I am not the one who is going to be hanged by the neck until dead, and right glad I am of it. That is a wretched, slow way to die. I'd rather take a knife in the gut than face a noose."

Sampson had slouched down in his seat, but he still kept his eyes upon the wineskin. "Who's to say that I'll hang?"

"Oh, you'll hang, Sampson. You killed a man in full view of half of Aldgate and then got caught in the act. Christ, man, the blood had not even dried on your dagger! One of God's own angels could come down to speak out in court in your behalf and it would avail you naught. The day you go to trial is the day you go to the gallows."

Luke passed the wineskin to Justin, then tossed it to Jonas. "I suppose you can always hope that the rope might break. That happened to a prisoner back in my first year as under-sheriff, and the king pardoned him."

"I'll see to it that we use a sturdy new one, just for him," Jonas promised and laughed as if he'd made a joke.

Luke caught the wineskin deftly in midair, then set it down without drinking. "I know you've seen men die, Sampson. But have you ever seen a man hanged? It is not a sight to be forgotten, believe me. It is not quick, takes a long while for a man to strangle. His hands are tied behind his back, so he cannot free himself. Helpless, he just dangles there, feet kicking desperately to reach the ground, face turning blue and then black, gasping for air, willing to barter anything for one more breath. Sometimes a man even swallows his own tongue—"

"God curse you!" Sampson was on his feet, his manacled fists raised in a futile threat. "I've had enough of this, I do not want to hear any more!"

"You think I care what you want?" Luke said coldly. "Sit back down."

Justin doubted that Sampson would obey the command, but after a moment, the man slumped back in his chair. His face was blotched with heat, his eyes red rimmed and puffy, and when Luke suddenly tossed the wineskin, he snatched at it with hands that shook. He gulped the wine as if he could never get enough, uncaring when it ran into his beard and splattered on his dirty, torn tunic.

"What do you want of me?" he asked, clutching the wineskin to his chest. "Why are you here?"

"I want the truth. We have questions to put to you about other killings and we need answers. I want to be able to bury these cases with you."

"Why should I?" Sampson asked, with a trace of his earlier bravado. "What do I get out of it?"

When Luke leaned forward, Justin knew this was the question he'd been waiting for Sampson to ask. "You are going to die. I cannot change that, would not if I could. But I can make your last days more tolerable. If I were facing the noose, I'd want to make my peace with God. And then I'd want to get drunk, so drunk I'd not care when they came for me. You tell us what we want to know, Sampson, and I'll see that you get enough wine or ale to go to the gallows as drunk as a blind minstrel's bitch."

Sampson started to speak, stopped himself. Twisting around in his seat, he looked over at Jonas, then back at Luke. "If I agree, how do I know you'll keep your part of the bargain?"

Luke reached under his mantle again, this time drawing out a money pouch. "Answer our questions and you'll earn money to buy all the ale you want from the guards. Not to mention food or blankets. For enough money, a man might even be able to buy himself some female company. Am I right, Jonas?"

"It has been known to happen," the serjeant said laconically.

Luke balanced the pouch in the palm of his hand. "So . . . what say you, Sampson? Do we have a deal?"

"Let me count it first." Sampson fumbled the catch, made clumsy by his manacles. Scooping the pouch up from the floor, he fingered the coins before saying gruffly, "What do you want to know?"

Luke permitted himself a quick glint of triumph in Justin's direction. "Let's start with London. I know Jonas is right curious about all you've been up to in his city."

"You already know about that lackwit in Aldgate."

"Overcome with remorse, are you?" Luke said sardonically, and Sampson looked at him blankly.

"Why should I feel sorry for him? He brought it upon himself, meddling like he did. He gave me no choice. I do not know what else to tell you."

"How many robberies?" Jonas asked impatiently. "I know about the man you robbed in Southwark, near the bridge. And the drunkard you dragged into an alley off Cheapside. Any more?"

Sampson screwed up his face, trying to concentrate. "Well . . . I took a money pouch away from a stripling over in the stews. Green as grass he was, boasting that he was there to 'buy some tail,' and waving his money about like he was begging to be robbed. Then I got into a brawl in an alehouse near Cripplegate, took the man's rings and dagger for my trouble. That is all, I think. Oh, I also broke a woman's jaw, but she was just a whore, trying to cheat me. And Gib and me robbed a man on the Watling Street Road. Since we'd not reached London yet, does that count?"

"Gilbert was getting careless, letting a witness live. Or was he feeling charitable that day?"

Luke's sarcasm was wasted upon Sampson. "Gib meant to kill him, but he ran off into the woods and we decided it was not worth chasing after him." Shaking the wineskin, he discovered that there was enough for one more swig and gulped it down. "What else do you want to know?"

They'd been conversing in English, but Luke now switched to French, effectively shutting Sampson out. "I suppose you want to take over from here, de Quincy? He's in no hurry to go back to the pit, ought to tell you whatever you need to know about the goldsmith's murder. I hope you will share it with me afterward, for I want to solve Fitz Randolph's murder as much as you do. But I expect you'll have to get the queen's consent first?"

"Yes, I will," Justin admitted. "But I'll tell the queen that if not for you, we'd not have gotten Sampson to talk."

Luke grinned. "If you want to praise me to the queen, I'd not object. But you'll still owe me for the money I gave that swine!" Standing up abruptly, he aimed a hard, quelling stare at Sampson. "The serjeant and I have an errand to take care of. Master de Quincy will ask the questions whilst we're gone. Answer them well and I might bring back a wineskin for you. Lie to him and you'll pass the night out in the stocks, stripped down to your braies."

With that, he started for the door. Jonas followed, leaving Justin alone with the prisoner. The other man was regarding him incuriously. He showed no antagonism, but neither did he display any of the grudging wariness he'd accorded Luke and Jonas. Justin was not troubled, though, for Luke had taught him how Sampson could be tamed.

"Here," he said, and pitched his own wineskin toward the burly outlaw, waiting while Sampson drank greedily. He'd felt an involuntary twinge of pity, watching Luke break the man's spirit with such brutal expertise. But it had dissipated as soon as Sampson had begun his nonchalant confession. Listening to that unemotional litany, he'd soon concluded that the dim-witted Sampson was no less loathsome than the more murderous Fleming.

Sampson took another long swig from the wineskin. "So you're the one who spoiled our ambush on the Alresford Road. I thought you looked familiar. What do you want?"

"I want to hear about that killing. How it came about and why."

"Why do you think? We were paid to lie in wait for him. Why else would we be freezing our tails off out in the woods? No man with any sense goes robbing in the midst of a snowstorm, not unless he knows it'll be well worth his while."

Justin felt sudden excitement, realizing that he was but one question away from solving the mystery of the goldsmith's murder. "Who paid you?"

"A friend of Gib's."

Justin went cold. Christ Jesus! What if Sampson did not know who had hired them? What if Gilbert had been the one to make the deal? Taking another tack, he said, "Why was he to be killed? What had he done?"

The answer he got was completely unexpected. "You need not waste your pity, for he had it coming to him. Lord Harald swore the dice had been tampered with, and I believe him. I'd never seen him in such a tearing rage. He said he'd split the money with us, but he had to know we'd keep most of it. I suppose it was enough for him to get his revenge . . . and the ring back. He set quite a store by it. I was sorry the coxcomb did not have it on him, for I'd always fancied it myself. Silver, it was, with a reddish stone, mayhap a garnet or—"

"What in blazes are you talking about?" None of this made any sense whatsoever to Justin. "Who is Lord Harald?"

Sampson smiled scornfully, amazed at such ignorance. "All of Winchester knows Lord Harald. For certes, that poxy deputy does! Not that he is a real lord, for all that he gives himself airs like one. He salts his speech with words no one else can understand and struts about in his fine clothes like a preening peacock. Slick as ice, he is, though, the best cutpurse I've ever seen. He is right clever with the dice, too, and those games with walnut shells and dried peas. He's always prided himself on his gambling skills, so I guess that's why he took losing so badly. Not as I blame him, for I hear the whoreson kept crowing about it afterward, bragging how—"

"What dice game are you talking about? When did it take place?" Justin demanded, so sharply that Sampson looked at him in surprise.

"How do I know? What does it matter?"

"It matters," Justin said grimly. "The killing happened on Epiphany morn. But when was the dice game played? I need to know!"

"I am trying to remember," Sampson complained, "so ease up! Epiphany was a Wednesday, right? We met with Harald the day before, on Tuesday. He'd found out that the man was leaving Winchester on the morrow and he was in a sweat to make sure we'd be lying in wait for him. Ah . . . I recall now. The game was on Sunday. Harald said he ought to have known better than to play games of chance on God's Day, that it was an ill omen. And Gib laughed at him, saying it was indeed a sin to gamble on Sunday, but lucky to do murder on a holy day like Epiphany."

"That cannot be. Gervase Fitz Randolph was still in France on Sunday. He did not get back to Winchester until that Tuesday eve."

Sampson looked puzzled. "Who is Gervase Fitz Randolph?"

"The man you and Gilbert ambushed and killed!"

Sampson shook his head slowly. "Nay . . . that does not sound right. I do not remember the name, but I doubt that it was Gervase . . ."

"Blood of Christ," Justin whispered, for in that moment, he understood. "You'd never seen him, then?"

"No . . . why? There was no need, for Harald told us how to recognize him. Right prosperous, he said, with brown hair, riding a fine grey palfrey. There were so few travelers on the road that it was easy enough to pick him out. That fool Harald had forgotten to tell us about the servant, but— What? Why are you looking at me like that?"

"Was the man you were to kill named Fulk de Chesney?"

Sampson brightened. "That's the one! But what about the other name? I thought you said he was called Gervase?"

"That was his name," Justin said, through gritted teeth. "At least remember it. You owe him that much, damn you!"

"What are you so vexed about?"

"You murdered the wrong man!"

Sampson continued to look befuddled. "How so?"

"Fulk de Chesney was the one who cheated at dice, the one you were paid to kill. But his horse went lame and he had to turn back. The man you murdered was a Winchester goldsmith. He was riding a roan stallion, and you fools mistook it for de Chesney's grey. The man died for no logical reason whatsoever. God help him, he was in the wrong place at the wrong time . . ."

Justin's voice trailed off. He was more stunned than enraged, overwhelmed by the utter futility of it all. Gervase had not died because his son burned to be a monk or his daughter lusted after his hired man. Nor had the queen's secret letter brought him to ruin. He'd been doomed by a pebble, wedged up into a grey stallion's shoe.

Sampson finally comprehended what Justin was saying. "So the man we ambushed was not Fulk de Chesney? That explains why he did not have the ring then." He thought about it for a moment longer, and then laughed. "The poor bastard, the joke's on him!"

19

LONDON

March 1193

Striding along the Shambles toward Newgate Gaol, Luke and Jonas were surprised to see Justin waiting for them out in the street. One glance at his face and Luke quickened his stride. "What went wrong? Did that whoreson balk at telling you about the goldsmith's killing?"

"No . . . he told me all I needed to know."

"Then why are you not happier about it? I've seen men look more cheerful on their way to the gallows."

"Are you familiar with a Winchester gambler known as Lord Harald?"

"Indeed I am. As smooth as cream, that one, but the milk is soured. What does he have to do with Fitz Randolph's murder?"

"He's the one who paid Gilbert and Sampson to set that ambush."

Luke whistled soundlessly. "But why? What grudge did he bear the goldsmith?"

"None whatsoever," Justin said bitterly. "They killed the wrong man. The intended target was a knave who'd cheated Harald at dice, one Fulk de Chesney—"

"Good God Almighty! The prideful churl on the grey stallion?"

Justin nodded, and then explained, for Jonas's benefit, "De Chesney rode out of Winchester that same morn, but he had to turn back when his horse went lame."

Jonas was quick to comprehend. "So they struck down the goldsmith by mistake. Bad luck for him."

"Yes," Justin agreed, so tersely that Luke gave him a probing, speculative look.

"If I'd been asked to wager that you'd solve the goldsmith's slaying, I'd have called that a fool's gamble. But you did it, de Quincy, by God, you did. So why are you taking so little pleasure in your triumph?"

"I'm not sure. It seems so pointless, Luke. A man ought not to die by . . . by mischance."

Luke considered, then shrugged. "Would you like it better if he'd been murdered at his son's behest? Either way, he is just as dead. At least now Dame Ella need not be told that her little monk plotted a killing for Christ."

"You're right," Justin conceded, and the deputy grinned.

"I usually am. Now let's go inside and finish interrogating Sampson. I've been waiting for a long time to catch Harald with his hand in the honey pot. I want to put it all down in writing and get Sampson to make his mark ere he sobers up." As he started toward the gaol, so did Jonas. But Justin stayed where he was. "What about you, de Quincy? You're not coming with us?"

"No," Justin said. His part in the goldsmith's murder was done. It was over. Or almost over.

Justin had expected to be jubilant in the event that he was fortunate enough to solve Gervase Fitz Randolph's murder. But now he could not summon up even a drop of gladness; the well was bone dry. He was troubled in part by the randomness of the goldsmith's slaying. He was still young enough to think life ought to have coherence and purpose. He'd not yet learned the lesson set forth in Scriptures, that the Judgments of God are unsearchable and His Ways inscrutable to mortal men.

But it was not just the senseless nature of the goldsmith's death. For nigh on ten weeks, he'd been involved in Fitz Randolph's murder, and for fully nine weeks, he'd focused upon nothing else. He'd cared only about keeping faith with the queen, not letting her down. He'd not given any thought as to what he'd do afterward. But once he told Eleanor what he'd learned, she'd have no further need of him. He'd be cast adrift again, with no moorings and no shore in sight. He'd not fully realized how much being the queen's man had meant to him, not until it was about to end.

* * *

Upon his arrival at the Tower, Justin was heading for the keep when he heard his name being called. The voice was an alluring one, redolent of the lush, sun-drenched lands of the South, the seductive accent of Aquitaine. Until yesterday, it had put him in mind of melted honey. Now he could think only of a myth he'd once been told: how fabled Sirens lured sailors to their doom by the sweetness of their songs. He turned around very slowly, waiting as Claudine crossed the bailey toward him.

"You're coming as I'm going," she said, waving a hand toward her saddled mare and waiting companions. "We need to work on our timing, for certes." She smiled up at him, her eyes sparkling in the sunlight, flirtatious and fond and carefree, the most innocent of spies.

Holding out her hand for his kiss, she asked, "Are headaches contagious? You look as if you caught mine!"

"I had too much ale last night."

"You mean you went off to drown your sorrows after taking me back here? That is very flattering, love."

"You think so?"

"Of course. What woman would not want to believe she could drive a man to drink?"

"Well, you need not worry. That, Claudine, you definitely can do."

She laughed, then said regretfully, "I have to go. But I owe you for last night, and I'll not be forgetting."

"Nor will I," he said softly. "Nor will I . . ."

Eleanor looked intently into Justin's face and then rose abruptly. "Follow me," she said, and led the way across the hall toward the privacy of her great chamber. But even that did not satisfy her, and with Justin in tow, she swept through the doorway of St John's Chapel. "Leave us," she commanded the startled priest, and as soon as the door closed behind him, she beckoned Justin forward.

"You found out something."

"How did you know?"

"Yours is an easy face to read, at least to me. Tell me what you've learned, Justin. Hold nothing back."

"I found out," he said, "why Gervase Fitz Randolph died."

"Was it the letter?"

"No, my lady, it was not. He was slain by mischance, mistaken for another man. He died believing that they were after your letter, but it was not so."

Eleanor's eyes searched his face. "Are you sure of that?"

When he said yes, she moved away from him. Crossing to the altar, she leaned forward, resting her hands, palms out, on the embroidered altar cloth. Justin was taken aback; this was the first time that he'd seen her emotions surging so close to the surface. Did the French king pose so great a danger as that?

But then Eleanor turned around. Her face was so radiant with relief that Justin caught his breath sharply, in belated understanding. It was not the French king's involvement she'd feared, it was John's! It had been John all along. She'd been afraid that he'd been forewarned by Philip and hired assassins to make sure the letter never reached her.

Why had he not seen the truth ere this? It was all too plausible. If the Archbishop of Rouen had spies at the French court, why would Philip not have spies of his own? What had Eleanor said about the French king? Ah, yes, that he had more spies than scruples.

This explained so much. *Mayhap it was not meant that the truth come out.* Even that cryptic comment of hers made sense now—if she could not prove that John was innocent, she'd have to settle for keeping his guilt secret. Remembering his own unsettling encounters with John, Justin felt sure that Eleanor's youngest son was quite capable of murder if it served his own interests. The queen's fear had been well founded. Realizing how much had been at stake, he was suddenly very glad that he'd remained in ignorance of that. Had he known how much this mattered to Eleanor, would he have been tempted to tell her what she needed to hear?

"You've brought me welcome news, Justin. Now tell me the rest of it, why the goldsmith died and how you learned the truth."

Justin did, leaving nothing out. The interrogation in Newgate Gaol. The crooked dice game. The embittered gambler out for vengeance. Two horses, one grey and one roan. The outlaws lying in wait, so careless in their killing. "Fulk de Chesney's good luck was lethal for Fitz Randolph," he concluded somberly. "I was outraged at first, that it was so arbitrary, so meaningless a death. But I think his family will care only that they've been cleared of suspicion. At least his widow will be spared any more grieving."

"It is remarkable," Eleanor said, "that you were able to solve this murder with so little to go upon. You've more than justified my faith in you. Now . . . I imagine you incurred expenses in the course of your investigation, no? I'll instruct Peter to reimburse you for whatever you spent on my behalf."

"Thank you, madame." Justin waited expectantly, sure that she would offer extra compensation, a reward for services rendered so successfully.

"I suppose we ought to decide upon an amount," Eleanor said with a smile. "I had two shillings in mind. I think that seems fair."

"Two shillings . . ." Justin had hoped for more, much more than that. Now that he was on his own again, money mattered. But he bit back any words of disappointment or dissatisfaction. Complaints were not made to queens.

His chagrin was so obvious, though, that Eleanor's smile chilled. "Surely you were not expecting more than that? Good Lord, Justin, I pay the knights of my household two shillings a day!"

"A day? Madame . . . you meant wages?"

"Of course," she said impatiently. "What did you think I meant?"

"You want me to remain in your service?"

"Yes, I do. Does that surprise you so much? You've proved yourself to be resourceful and daring and trustworthy." Her smile came back. "I'd be a fool to let you go!"

"What . . . what would I do for you, madame?"

"Whatever I wanted done." Her earlier irritation had fled and her eyes were shimmering with suppressed laughter. "But nothing illegal, lad, at least not blatantly so!"

"Madame, I was not implying that!" Justin said hastily.

"Of course you were." Eleanor was laughing openly now.

"But I took no offense. I've always admired the way cats look ere they leap. So . . . what say you? Is my offer agreeable to you?"

He nodded mutely, still at a loss for words.

"You need not look so bedazzled, Justin, for there will be plenty of hard work involved. I can promise you long hours in the saddle and sleepless nights in my service more often than not."

Eleanor's moods had always been mercurial. As Justin watched, her laughter stilled and those hazel eyes met his with compelling candor. "I can admit now that I feared John might be involved in the goldsmith's murder. You guessed that, I suspect."

Startled, he could only nod again. Her gaze was mesmerizing; he had the eerie sense that she could see right into his soul.

"John was blameless . . . this time. But I know where he has gone and I know what he intends to do. I'd wager the surety of salvation that he is at the French court even as we speak, plotting with Philip to make certain that Richard never sees the light of day again. Troubled times lie ahead for England, for us all. I am going to need men I can trust, utterly and wholeheartedly. Men like you, Justin de Quincy."

"I will not fail you, my lady." But the words rang hollow in his ears, for he was failing her by his silence. He'd meant to tell her of his suspicions, to warn her that Claudine was her son's spy. She needed to know that her kinswoman could not be trusted. And if she dismissed Claudine in disgrace—or worse—it was no more than Claudine deserved. But now that the moment had come, the words caught in his throat.

"Justin?" Eleanor was regarding him quizzically. "You seemed about to speak. Have you more to tell me?"

He swallowed, no longer meeting her eyes. "No, madame," he said, "nothing more . . ."

20

WINCHESTER

March 1193

Winchester had built its gallows beyond the city walls, out on the Andover Road. A crowd had already gathered by the time Justin and his companions arrived. He was not surprised by the throngs of spectators, for public hangings usually drew a large audience, offering both grisly entertainment and reassuring proof that there is always a reckoning for evildoers, a Dies Irae.

For Gilbert the Fleming's Day of Judgment, much of Winchester had turned out: men, women, even a number of children. Justin knew that some people believed this was an effective way to teach impressionable youngsters that Scriptures spoke true: the wages of sin is death. But he could not imagine ever taking a child of his to watch as a man choked to death at the end of a rope.

Aldith obviously agreed with him. "Blessed Mother Mary, look at all the little ones! And over there—a vendor selling hot pies! You'd think this was the St Giles Fair."

"Public hangings are always thus—like a besotted wake where none of the mourners grieve over the dead. Are you sure you want to be here, Aldith?"

"Yes," she insisted, not very convincingly. "This was a great triumph for Luke, catching a merciless cutthroat like the Fleming." Adding as a polite afterthought, "For you, too, Justin."

While Justin admired her loyalty, he still thought that the gallows was no place for her. He kept his opinion to himself, however. Nell insisted that women were much tougher than he realized, and he'd begun to suspect that she was right. Nell and Nóra were capable of looking after themselves, for certes. But was Claudine? What would she have done had the queen been

255

told of her duplicity? Would she have gone home to her family in Aquitaine, shamed and dishonored? Or would she have turned to John?

His mouth twisted, for he'd begun to feel as if his thoughts were no longer his own. Claudine seemed able to lay claim to them at will, despite his best efforts to banish her into limbo. Priests could exorcise evil spirits. A pity there was no exorcism for casting out a faithless lover. But self-mockery was no more effective than anger at vanquishing his ghosts, and it was a moment or so before he realized that Edwin was speaking to him. "Sorry, my thoughts were wandering. You asked . . . what?"

"I was curious," the groom confessed, "about the Fleming's whore. If she'd been caught, could she have been hanged, too?"

"Not likely, since the killing Nóra was helping to set up never happened. But an accomplice to murder can indeed be hanged, and she might well have been involved in some of his other crimes. If so, she could have gotten a death sentence. According to Luke, a court is usually harsh in its judgment upon a woman charged with murder."

Aldith nodded in quick confirmation. "Luke says we expect men to lose their tempers and become violent. But women are supposed to be docile and biddable, and when a woman is not, she is punished for it. This is a double-edged sword, though, for he says indictment and conviction are both more likely when the victim is a woman."

That made sense to Edwin. "That is as it ought to be," he declared, "for it is craven to harm a woman. They cannot fight back, after all." But soon he was muttering, with far less gallantry, "Quick, bow down, for here comes Queen Jonet and her court jester."

As they watched, Jonet and Miles swept through the crowd, intent upon staking out a vantage point as close to the gallows as they could get. Justin was not surprised to see them there, but he was startled at sight of the cowled figure hurrying to catch up with them. "What is Thomas doing here? I doubt that the abbot would give him permission to attend a hanging. Want to wager, Edwin, that our novice monk took off on his own without even asking?"

"Jesú, I hope not," Edwin said, with feeling. "If he gets thrown out of the abbey, he'll come back to Mistress Ella's house, and God help us all then!"

Justin thought it very unlikely that Thomas would ever be allowed to take his final vows. But he saw no reason to burden Edwin with his doubts, for the groom's pessimism was well founded.

Edwin had begun to fidget under the hostile looks aimed in their direction. "Mistress Ella told me I could come to the hanging, and Jonet was right there, heard every word. Yet now she's glowering at me like I sneaked away when Mistress Ella's back was turned."

"It is the company you're keeping, Edwin," Aldith said wryly. "Here you are, after all, consorting openly with me, Winchester's very own Whore of Babylon."

"I'm not in their good graces, either," Justin pointed out. "During the trial, they made it quite clear that they'd sooner break bread with a leper than with me."

"You've got that right," Edwin grumbled. "Even after they learned that you'd solved Master Gervase's slaying, they still blamed you for unfairly casting suspicions upon them, saintly souls that they all are."

"Now why," Justin joked, "does that not surprise me? Naturally their wounded pride would matter more than their father's murder."

A sudden stir in the crowd put a halt to their conversation. Riders had come into view. The spectators surged forward at sight of the lumbering cart. Gilbert the Fleming was standing upright, defiant even in chains. But Aldith had eyes only for Luke. "There he is!"

Luke and his men were riding alongside the cart, keeping the onlookers back. Sometimes a condemned outlaw attained celebrity stature, but too many of the Fleming's crimes had been committed against the men and women of Winchester. He was greeted with a chorus of boos, hisses, and curses, and one man let fly with a rock, poorly aimed, that thudded into the cart. Before he could throw another one, Luke's serjeant shoved his way toward him. Wat remonstrated with the man, but no more than that, and when Justin remarked upon his restraint, not common when dealing with crowd control, Edwin explained that the stone-thrower was a kinsman of the merchant's wife left to die on the Southampton Road.

"I do not believe my eyes!" Aldith sounded astonished, and then indignant. "What is the sheriff doing here? None of this was his doing. How dare he claim credit for Luke's arrest?"

One glance convinced Justin that she was right. The sheriff was indeed acting as if he'd been the one to capture the Fleming: gravely acknowledging the salutations of the crowd, giving needless orders to Luke and the other men, casting bellicose looks toward the outlaw, and generally putting Justin in mind of a barnyard cock crowing over another rooster's hen.

The more Aldith watched his preening and posturing, the angrier she became. But when Luke dismounted and joined them, he seemed philosophical about being relegated to a supporting role in the play about to begin. "You know how the Fleming was caught," he told Aldith, "and so does Queen Eleanor, thanks to de Quincy. So who else matters?"

The shackled and manacled outlaw had been dragged up onto the gallows, where the hangman was waiting impatiently. The sheriff had followed and gestured to indicate he wanted to be the one to put the noose around Gilbert's neck. Luke seemed to guess what was coming, for he said softly, "A bad move." And moments later, he proved prophetic, for when the sheriff approached with the rope, the Fleming spat directly into his face.

There was a mixed reaction from the crowd, gasps interspersed with some tittering. Aldith hid her face in Luke's shoulder to stifle her giggles, but Luke prudently kept his own amusement private. Forgetting his dignity, the outraged sheriff responded with a vituperative tongue-lashing, cut short by the condemned man's scornful laughter. Stepping back, the sheriff signaled abruptly and the Fleming's sneer became a contorted grimace as the hangman obeyed and hoisted him up.

The spectators fell silent. A few surreptitiously made the sign of the cross over the dying man. Aldith soon buried her face again in Luke's mantle. Edwin, too, looked away. But Luke and Justin watched grimly as the outlaw fought a losing battle for breath. It seemed to take a very long time before his struggles ceased and his body went limp.

Luke was the first to break the silence. "Well, he is finally on his way to Hell."

"I doubt," Justin said flatly, "if even the Devil would want him."

Justin approached the Fitz Randolph house with reluctance. Unlike her children, the goldsmith's widow had not attended the Fleming's trial. While he cared nothing for the younger Fitz Randolphs' goodwill, he was not as indifferent to Ella's opinion. She was the only one of the bereaved family whom he'd found sympathetic, and he wanted her to think well of him. But if she did blame him as her children did, he was about to find out.

He was admitted by Edith, the serving maid, and escorted into the hall. Ella did not keep him waiting long. "Master de Quincy, this is a surprise." Ordering Edith to fetch wine, she led Justin over to the hearth. They'd barely seated themselves when the door banged and Jonet hastened into the hall.

She'd evidently been forewarned of Justin's presence, for she showed no surprise, only antagonism. "I cannot believe you have the gall to come calling upon us after the way you slandered our family! You are not welcome here."

"That is not for you to say, Jonet."

"Mother! This man saw us as suspects in Papa's murder!"

"I know that, Jonet. I also know that if not for him, your father's killers would never have been brought to justice."

"That does not excuse——"

"Yes," Ella said firmly, "it does. Nurse a grudge if you will. But I'll not have you be rude to a guest in this house—my house. Is that clear?"

Justin could not help noticing that Jonet was not as pretty when she was angry. Her fair skin splotched with hot color, her eyes slitted, she glared at her mother. But she was the one who backed down, flouncing off in a huff.

Justin found this exchange very interesting. It seemed that Ella was spreading her wings, asserting her authority as the family matriarch. A more satisfying role, for certes, than that of a wronged wife or a grieving widow.

"I apologize for my daughter's bad manners. I am glad that you've come, Master de Quincy, for I've wanted to thank you again for all you did on my husband's behalf."

"I wish I could have saved him, Mistress Fitz Randolph."

"I wish you could have, too," she said quietly. "He had his flaws, as do all men. But he was good-hearted and generous and he did not deserve to die by an outlaw's hand. It pains me to say this, but his death seems to have grieved no one but me. For the others, it was almost . . . convenient."

"Surely that is not so," Justin protested politely, but without much conviction, for that same thought had occurred to him, too.

"I fear that it is. If Gervase were still alive, Thomas would not be Hyde Abbey's newest novice. For certes, Jonet and Miles would not be plight-trothed. Even that wanton woman has benefited from Gervase's death if the gossip is true. Is it? Does Luke de Marston really mean to wed her?" When he nodded, she grimaced. "Men are such fools!"

Justin felt confident that Aldith would understand if he did not try to defend her to her former lover's widow; she was too fair minded to deny that the older woman bore her a genuine grievance. "I have something for you," he said, taking out a sealed parchment. "The Queen's Grace asked me to deliver this to you."

"Why would the queen be writing to me?" she asked in wonderment. When he held the letter toward her, she did not take it. "Gervase insisted that Jonet be taught to read, but my father saw no such need in my girlhood. Will you read it to me?"

"Of course." Breaking the royal seal, he unrolled the parchment and shifted toward the closest light, a cresset lamp suspended from the ceiling by a braided rope.

" 'Eleanor, Queen of England, Duchess of Normandy and Aquitaine, Countess of Poitou, to Ella, Mistress Fitz Randolph of Winchester, greetings. I wish to offer you my condolences upon the death of your husband. From all that I've heard of him, he was a good and brave man. I hope it may comfort you to know that he died in the service of the Crown.' "

When Justin glanced up, he saw that Ella was staring at him in bewilderment. "I . . . I do not understand. What does she mean?"

"You've heard that King Richard was captured by his enemies on his way home from the Holy Land?"

As he expected, Ella nodded, for Eleanor had finally made her son's plight public knowledge, after meeting with the Great Council at Oxford. "When your husband departed for London on Epiphany, he was bearing a letter for the queen, a confidential and urgent message entrusted to him by one who'd learned of the king's abduction. It is my belief that Gervase resisted his attackers so fiercely because he feared they were after the queen's letter."

"I see . . ." she breathed. "Then . . . then he truly did die in the queen's service?"

Gilbert the Fleming had not believed in leaving eyewitnesses to his crimes, and Gervase Fitz Randolph would likely have died whether he'd offered resistance or not. But Justin saw no need to tell that to his widow. "Yes, Mistress Fitz Randolph, he did."

Reaching over, he laid the letter in her lap. She touched the parchment gently, almost reverently, her eyes brimming with tears. He'd viewed the queen's message as a gamble, one that could have done as much harm as good. But he soon saw that Eleanor had guessed correctly, for when Ella looked up, her tear-streaked face was lit by a tremulous smile.

The last time that Justin had looked upon Gervase Fitz Randolph's grave, it was covered with snow. The ground was still bare and brown, but it would not be long until Gervase slept under a blanket of lush, green grass. On this mild, sun-splashed Monday, the day after Easter, the scent of spring and renewal was in the air.

Kneeling by the grave, Aldith closed her eyes, her lips moving in a silent prayer. When she rose, brushing dirt from her skirt, she said, "I wish I could have brought him flowers or a funeral lamp. But that would only have caused his widow's wounds to bleed anew. He does have my prayers, though, and will as long as I have the breath to say them."

Justin joined her beside the grave. "Requiescat in pace, Gervase," he murmured, hoping that the slain goldsmith would indeed rest in peace, and then offered Aldith his arm as they moved away. "I need your advice, Aldith. I want to buy something for Nell, to thank her for taking care of my dog whilst I was gone."

"It will be my pleasure. But if you let me, I can do more. I'd like to help you patch up a lovers' quarrel." She felt his sudden tension, the muscles in his arm constricting under her hand, and she said hastily, "Wait, Justin, hear me out. Luke told me that your courtship of one of the queen's ladies had gone awry, and I would—"

" 'One of the queen's ladies,' " Justin said incredulously. "How in hellfire did Luke learn that?"

"From Nell. They were drinking at the alehouse after the Fleming's capture, gossiping and joking how you'd evicted Luke for a mystery bedmate. They were all curious about her, of course, and someone suggested, half in jest, that Nell ought to invite you and the girl to come over and join the revelries, so they could get a look at her. Nell retorted, right sharplike, that 'She's too grand for the likes of us,' and once the others realized she knew something, they badgered her until she told them: that a 'very elegant lady' had visited you after you'd gotten stabbed, escorted by the queen's knight."

When Justin swore under his breath, Aldith gave his arm a sympathetic squeeze. "It ought not to surprise you so. People love to gossip, especially about bedsport. And you're always going to be talked about on that Gracechurch Street, what with rumors that you serve the queen."

They had stopped on the narrow pathway that wound among the graves, and she raised her hand to shield her eyes from the sun's glare, looking up earnestly into his face. "I do not pretend to know what happened between you or what went wrong. But I think you're still hurting. It might help to talk about it, to get a woman's view—"

"No!" he said, with a sharpness that he at once regretted. "I know you mean well, Aldith, but there is nothing you can do. It is over."

"Are you sure of that, Justin? There are few breaches which cannot be mended—"

"You do not understand. This was far more than a lovers' quarrel. It involved a betrayal."

"I see," she said. "But was it beyond forgiving?"

"Yes," he said, "it was."

They continued on up the path, walking in silence for a time. After giving him several sideways glances, she said, somewhat hesitantly, "When you said her betrayal was unforgivable, you really meant that you had to make a choice: whether to forgive her or not."

He smiled, mirthlessly, for she'd spoken greater truth than she knew. He had indeed been confronted with a choice. "I suppose so."

"I know I'm meddling," she said, "and after this, I'll say no more, I promise. But it seems to me that it is still gnawing at you."

"I suppose so," he said again, much more reluctantly this time.

"Could it be, then," she suggested softly, "that you made the wrong choice?"

When he did not reply, she was content to let the matter drop, hopeful that she'd planted a seed, one which might flower into reconciliation. Taking his arm again, she said, "Come on, let's go spend your money. I think you ought to buy Nell a mirror. I know where you can get one of polished brass at a reasonable price. And some hair ribbons for her little girl. After that, would you mind if we stopped at St Mary's Church over in Tanner Street? Father Antony has been getting up a collection of blankets and clothing for Kenrick's family, and I would like to see how it is faring."

"I'm glad to hear that. But I'd not give Father Antony all the credit for that good deed. I understand he got a nudge or two in the right direction."

"Luke told you, did he? It was the lad, Kenrick's boy. I could not get that pinched little face out of my mind," she confided, "for that was once me . . ."

By now they were back on High Street. Eager to show Justin

the brass mirror, Aldith was tugging at his arm, urging him to hurry. They had not gone far, though, before Justin heard his name being shouted. Aldith heard it, too. "It is Luke!" she exclaimed in surprise. Turning, they saw the deputy striding swiftly toward them.

"Where in blazes have you been, de Quincy? I've been searching all over town for you!"

Justin was startled by the tension crackling in the other man's voice. He'd thought that Luke had gotten over the worst of his jealousy. "Why?"

"I'd sent two of my men to Southampton to fetch a prisoner. They got back this morn, and with news you need to hear. John's ship dropped anchor in the harbor last night."

Justin drew a sharp breath, and Aldith looked from one man to the other in puzzlement. "John? The queen's son?"

"Who else?" Luke said tersely. "You know what this means, de Quincy?"

Justin nodded. "Trouble." Seeing that Aldith still did not comprehend, he said, "If what we heard is true, John has made a Devil's deal with the French king. He did homage to Philip for Normandy and promised to wed Philip's sister, apparently forgetting that he already has a wife. In return, Philip vowed to assist him in claiming the English crown. So you see, Aldith, his sudden return to England does not bode well for the queen or Richard."

"What are you going to do, Justin?"

"I have to let the queen know," he said, "straightaway."

Aldith emerged from her cottage with a package wrapped in hemp. "I packed bread and cheese for you, so you can eat on the road." While Justin put the food away in his saddlebag, she made one final attempt to get him to stay the night. "I do wish you'd wait, Justin, and leave in the morning."

"There are still hours of daylight left, enough for me to reach Alton with luck. That'll put me fifteen miles closer to London on the morrow."

Justin tightened the straps fastening his saddlebag to the crupper, pausing to look across the stallion at the deputy. "I've been curious about something, Luke. Do you know a man named Durand de Curzon?"

"No . . . the name is not familiar."

"He may have used another name. A man in his thirties, taller than most, with dark auburn hair and beard, bright blue eyes, an overbearing manner." Justin was unable to resist adding, "And a sneering sort of smile."

"I do remember a man like that," Luke said thoughtfully. "He claimed to be the sheriff's deputy for Berkshire, on the trail of an escaped felon. As I recall, he asked a lot of questions about crimes hereabouts, saying he had reason to believe his man might be sheltered by local outlaws. Why? Does it matter?"

"No," Justin said, "not anymore."

Aldith slipped her arm through Luke's, and they followed Justin out to the street. "Keep your guard up, de Quincy," Luke said brusquely, "for John could be a more dangerous foe than the Fleming."

"I'll be back for your wedding." Bidding them farewell, Justin turned his horse out into the road. When he glanced over his shoulder, they were still watching, and he waved, then rode on. The streets were thronged with carts and other riders and he had to keep checking Copper to avoid trampling careless passersby. Once he reached the East Gate, though, he left the city's congestion behind. The road ahead was clear and he urged his stallion into a steady gallop. But Luke's warning seemed to float after him on the wind.

It was late and most of London was abed. But lights still blazed in the queen's great chamber. It was quiet after Justin was done speaking. Eleanor was gazing down into her lap, her splendid rings glittering on tightly clasped fingers. "Pour us some wine, Justin," she said at last, "and we'll drink to my son's homecoming."

Her irony was so labored that Justin winced. Crossing to the table, he brought back two cups, but drank sparingly of his, for wine and fatigue could kindle a fire faster than any fuel he knew.

Almost as if reading his mind, Eleanor said, "You look bone

weary. You must have slept in the saddle to get here so fast. Once again you've served me well."

Justin's mouth was dry. He took a quick swallow of the wine, then set the cup down in the floor rushes. "No, madame, the truth is that I have not served you well at all. For more than a fortnight, I have kept something from you, something you needed to know. I have good reason to believe that Lady Claudine is spying for your son."

She continued to sip her wine. "Indeed?"

Justin had been braced for anger, disbelief, even outright denial. But not indifference, never that. "Madame . . . you did hear me?"

He sounded so bewildered that she almost smiled. "Yes, I heard you, Justin. You said that Claudine is John's spy."

His breath quickened. "You already knew!"

She nodded. "Actually, I've known for some time."

Justin was dumbfounded. "But . . . but why?"

"Why did I not expose her double-dealing? Surely you've heard of the adage, 'Better the Devil you know than the one you do not.' Well, that holds even truer for spies. Besides, Claudine's spying was never more than an irritation, for she is not ruthless enough to be truly good at it. And as long as John thinks I trust her, he will not look elsewhere."

Justin decided that he needed a drink, after all. "You seem to accept betrayal so calmly, madame. Why are you not outraged?"

"Outrage is an indulgence of youth. It is not a vice of age . . . or queens."

Before Justin realized it, he had drained his cup. "You know her better than I, madame. Why would she do it?"

Eleanor shrugged. "There are any number of reasons why people are tempted to dance with the Devil. Some do it for money. Some are coerced, some seduced. My son can be very persuasive. But if I had to guess, I'd say Claudine was lured in by the adventure of it."

"The adventure of it?" Justin echoed, so bitterly that the words, innocuous in themselves, took on the sting of savage profanity.

"Yes, adventure," Eleanor insisted, "for that is how she'd see it. I am sure she has convinced herself that no great harm comes from her disclosures. She gives John what he wants, gets what she wants, and no one is truly hurt. It is a game to Claudine, only a game."

Justin shook his head slowly, a gesture as revealing to Eleanor as any outburst could have been. She watched as he returned to the table, poured them more wine. Accepting another cup, she said, "For what it is worth, lad, Claudine seemed to fancy you from the first. I doubt that she would have bedded a man she did not find desirable. She considers herself a spy, not a whore."

To Justin, that was meagre consolation, and he drank again, so quickly that she was moved to caution him to go slower. "I have no intention of getting drunk," he said tautly. "I've already gone down that road." Hearing his own words, he realized that the wine was loosening his tongue more than it ought, and he put the cup aside. "Did you know, madame, that I'd found out about Claudine?"

"Yes, I knew."

"Then why would you want to take me into your service?"

"I felt reasonably confident that you would come to me with the truth. I suppose I was curious to see how long it would take," she said, with a slight smile.

"You were testing me?"

"What do you think?"

"The truth?" he said, with a shaken laugh. "That I'm in over my head!"

She smiled at him over her wine cup. "I think you've been treading water quite well. No . . . you're a better swimmer than you realize, Justin. You proved that by the shipwreck story you concocted to tempt Claudine."

He stared at her. "How could you know about that? It is not as if Claudine would tell you!"

"No . . . but Durand did."

For Justin, this was one shock too many. "I do not understand," he said, in what was the greatest understatement of his life. "Why would Durand tell you? He is John's tame wolf!"

"No," she said, with the faintest glimmer of grim amusement, "he is *my* tame wolf."

"Are you saying that Durand has not been spying for John?"

"No . . . he has been spying for John for months. But what John does not realize is that Durand tells him only what I want him to know."

Justin was still trying to come to terms with this new reality. "But Claudine knew about Gilbert the Fleming. How could John have learned about him if not from Durand?"

"Yes, that came from Durand," she confirmed. "What use would he be to John if he did not deliver valuable information? He gives up just enough to keep John coming back for more."

"So . . . when Durand confronted me in the great hall, that was all an act?"

"No, not entirely. Oh, he was doing what you expected. You'd have been surprised, even suspicious, if he had not blamed you for his supposed fall from grace. But his dislike of you is quite real. He was very vexed at being caught out in Winchester. He rarely makes mistakes like that and does not take failure well. It is obvious that you return his hostility in full measure, and that is one reason why I am telling you this. You are likely to be working with Durand in the future, and I'd not want your suspicions of him to blind you to other dangers."

Justin was regarding Eleanor with awe. If family could indeed be equated with that "castle on a hill" he'd once envisioned, hers was a magnificent structure, luxurious and majestic, but with blood splattered on the walls within. While he marveled that she could face a son's treachery without flinching, he sensed, too, that the queen's needs would always prevail over the mother's. He was not sure if he'd have chosen to be part of her world—so sun blinding and dazzling and dangerous—but he could not imagine walking away. For better or worse, it was too late.

Thinking that Durand must like to ride his stallion along the edge of cliffs and sleep in burning buildings, he said, "I am still puzzled, though, about Durand's role in this . . . you called it a 'Devil's dance,' I believe. Since Durand was not truly John's man, why bother following me all the way to Winchester, not once but twice? Why not simply tell John that he had done so and save himself a lot of needless time in the saddle? Instead, he even went so far as to interrogate Luke de Marston—"

The answer came to him then, in a burst of clarity that took his breath away. "My God . . . he was not in Winchester at John's behest, was he? You sent him after me!"

"I was wondering," she said, "when you'd realize that."

Justin had so many questions that he settled for one, a simple "Why?"

"You alone had seen the killers. That made you the logical choice. But you were still a stranger to me—and if you'll forgive me for saying so—very young. I wanted to make sure that I'd not be throwing a lamb into the lion's den. So I thought it best that you had Durand there to keep an eye on you, at least until you'd demonstrated that you were quite capable of looking after yourself."

"And until you could be sure that I'd not make a botch of it," Justin suggested and Eleanor laughed.

"Yes, that, too. With so much at stake, I needed to know that I could rely upon you. Fortunately, my instincts were right. But then I've always had good judgment where men are concerned." Her lips curved and she added wryly, "Except for husbands, of course!"

Drifting clouds hid the moon and when Justin led Copper from the stables out into the Tower bailey, it was like plunging into a black, silent sea. Swinging up into the saddle, he was almost at the Land Gate when several horsemen rode in. Raising his lantern as they passed by, Justin was jolted to come face to face with Durand de Curzon.

Durand was astride a big-boned black stallion, an ill-tempered beast to judge by the flattened ears and white-rimmed eyes. Spurring the horse forward, he swerved into Justin's path. Justin hastily reined in. Fortunately, his chestnut was of an equable temperament and not easily spooked. He did not doubt that Durand's action had been deliberate, a warning to stay out of his way. The queen's tame wolf was going to make a provoking ally, if not a downright dangerous one.

Justin exhaled a deep breath, wondering what he'd gotten himself into, for in that moment, the future seemed as dark and murky as this moonless spring night. But he glanced up then, saw the lights still burning brightly in the queen's windows, like a shining beacon midst the blackness of the bailey.

"Come on, Copper," he said. "The Devil with Durand and John, too." Leaving the Tower behind, he rode for Gracechurch Street, for home. And each time he looked back, he could still see the glow from Queen Eleanor's chambers, high above the sleeping city.

AUTHOR'S NOTE

My Author's Notes usually begin with a declaration of sorts, an assurance to my readers that all of the improbable events in the book actually did happen. What with solar eclipses and brides kidnapped on the high seas by pirates in the pay of the English king and assassins with poisoned daggers, it is easy to see why a skeptical reader might wonder if I'd gone hopelessly Hollywood. So I've come to view an Author's Note as an essential ingredient in my historical recipes, particularly when dining with Plantagenets. This Author's Note is something of a departure, therefore, as the mystery plot came from my head, not from history.

The Archbishop of Rouen truly did obtain a copy of the letter sent by the Holy Roman Emperor to the French king, and secretly dispatched it to Queen Eleanor. But while the letters—and Richard's plight—were real, the goldsmith's role was not.

Justin's father, Aubrey de Quincy, is a fictional creation; so is his bishopric. Chester lay in the diocese of Coventry and Lichfield, and although the title Bishop of Chester was used during the Middle Ages, it was an unofficial usage. The Bishop of Coventry and Lichfield and Chester in 1193 was Aubrey's nemesis and John's devious ally, Hugh de Nonant.

I used the term *coroner* in the novel, but I was being somewhat premature, as the office of coroner was not established until September, 1194. Prior to that date, the coroner's duties were usually performed by the county justiciar and serjeants or bailiffs.

Some readers might be surprised by the interrogation scene of Gilbert the Fleming, for the very words *medieval dungeons* conjure up lurid images of horror chambers and bloodstained stone walls. But such gruesome instruments of persuasion as the rack were of a later age. Judicial torture was not widely practiced in the twelfth century and was never as common in England as it was on the Continent. Interestingly, it came into greater use after the Church Lateran Council of 1215 prohibited the Trial by Ordeal. Some legal historians have also found a connection between the abolition of the Trial by Ordeal and the rise of the trial jury. But since *The Queen's Man* takes place in 1193, Gilbert the Fleming was fortunate enough to be spared any close encounters with the rack or the Devil's daughter.

S.K.P.
April 1996

ACKNOWLEDGMENTS

In writing *The Queen's Man*, my first mystery, I was venturing into unfamiliar fictional territory, and I strayed off the road from time to time. Fortunately, I did not lack for guides. My parents, as always. Jill and John Davies, my English interpreters. Valerie Ptak LaMont, who is truly the book's godmother. Marian Wood, who has been my editor at Henry Holt and Company for fifteen memorable years. My agents, Molly Friedrich and Sheri Holman of the Aaron M. Priest Literary Agency and Mic Cheetham of the Mic Cheetham Literary Agency, for offering encouragement, moral support, and several first-rate road maps. Susan Watt, my editor at Michael Joseph, Ltd, for helping me to teach Justin how to match wits with Plantagenets, prostitutes, and assorted evildoers. And lastly, Dr. Lyla Perez, the Atlantic County, New Jersey, Medical Examiner, for generously sharing her time and expertise, enabling me to describe Pepper Clem's water-logged body in accurate, if grisly, detail.

A CONVERSATION WITH
SHARON KAY PENMAN

Q: **Why did you choose *The Queen's Man* as the title of this book?**

A: I usually agonize over the titles of my books but this one came very easily because the connection between Queen Eleanor and Justin de Quincy is so strong. In the beginning of the story de Quincy is a man with no identity—the bastard son of a bishop. By the end of the tale he has found a place for himself in Eleanor's world as her operative—in other words, as the Queen's man. The title also has the benefit of attracting anyone with an interest in the Middle Ages. Somehow it just seemed to fit.

Q: ***The Queen's Man* is not the first time that Eleanor of Aquitaine has played a prominent role in one of your novels. What is it about her that appeals to you?**

A: Eleanor has always fascinated me because she was always someone who lived by her own rules. What she accomplished was truly amazing when you consider the fact that she was a woman of the twelfth century. By age fifteen she was the Queen of France. By age thirty-two she was the Queen of England. She paid a price for her success—spending sixteen years in prison when her marriage to Henry failed—but she was a survivor, and by reaching the then vast age of eighty-two, she outlived all of her enemies!

Q: **This story is a bit of a departure for you in that it's your first historical mystery. How does writing such a story differ from writing straight historical fiction?**

A: I had to use much more discipline in writing the mystery. My historical novels are usually eight or nine hundred pages long so there's plenty of time to develop character and plot, and to make frequent digressions. A mystery presents a bit of a challenge because it needs to develop at a much faster pace. In writing a mystery you also have to play fair with your readers by leaving clues for them to pick up so they can solve the crime.

Q: **One reviewer has said, "Penman writes about the medieval world and its people with vigor, compassion, and clarity." What appeals to you about the medieval world?**

A: I find the whole era incredibly interesting. It was raw, vital, and larger than life in so many ways. Emotions seemed much closer to the surface than they are today. It also offers everything from a novelist's standpoint. There's high drama, tragedy, and constant betrayal going on—all very exciting stuff. And the time period offers a marvelous window to explore the position of women in society, or how children or the poor were treated—issues that still resonate in our society today. I guess there's a small part of me that hopes putting a mirror up to the Middle Ages will cast some reflection on our times as well. I don't think human nature has changed over the centuries. The trappings and beliefs of humanity are different but the core of human nature has stayed the same. What I try to do is give my readers a little jolt of recognition so that even though they're reading about something that happened in the twelfth century, they can still identify with the emotions of the people involved.

Q: **Where do the facts end and the fiction begin with this story?**

A: Justin de Quincy, and most of the characters surrounding him, are fictitious. Richard the Lionheart was captured by his enemies while returning home from the crusades. The Archbishop of Rouen truly did obtain a copy of the letter sent by the Holy Roman Emperor to the French king, and secretly dispatched it to Queen Eleanor. But while the letters—and Richard's plight—were real, the goldsmith's role was not.

Q: What do you think will surprise readers of this book the most?

A: I have been told by people who have read it that there are several twists at the end that surprised them. In terms of the overall story I guess that will depend on how knowledgeable they are about the Middle Ages to begin with. Some people might also be surprised to learn that England was bilingual at the time—with many people speaking both English and French.

Q: How did you go about conducting your research for *The Queen's Man*?

A: I tend to do a lot of on-site research and visit the places I write about. In this case, I spent a lot of time in Winchester, where much of the action in *The Queen's Man* takes place. This gives me a sense of time and place when I actually sit down and start writing. As far as general information is concerned, I do a considerable amount of research at Penn State, which has an extensive medieval history collection.

Q: How do you strike a balance that allows characters to deliver dialogue true to the time period in which they live without making their words so antiquated that it's hard for today's readers to understand what the characters are saying?

A: That's the most challenging hurdle that any historical novelist faces. Some writers take an approach in which they do not attempt to make the dialogue even the slightest bit medieval. At the other end of the spectrum is the ghastly parody of medieval speech in which the author throws in a significant number of terms like "gadzooks" and "varlet." Neither of these methods works for me. I try to keep the language relatively simple while using terms that sound medieval and give a flavor to the speech. I also try not to jar the reader with words that sound out of place or that might break the mood.

Q: Has your work as a lawyer influenced your writing?

A: The one thing I really enjoyed about the law was doing research. I loved going to the law library to look for the perfect case. What I do as a writer is an extension of that.

Q: After completing your first novel many years ago, the only copy was stolen from your car. How did you recover from that?

A: It was very difficult. Although I tried, I was unable to write again for almost six years. It was as if the well had gone dry. But I continued researching throughout this barren stretch because I knew I would write again some day. I had finished law school and was already practicing law when the words started to come again. This time they didn't stop.

Q: Do you find writing easy or hard?

A: Writing is rarely effortless. There's a famous quote about the writing process: "Writing is easy, you just sit down at a typewriter and open up a vein." Most of the time, when I sit down to write, it feels like an opening-a-vein type of day. Occasionally, if I'm really caught up in it, the words do seem to flow, but that's the exception rather than the rule.

Q: Do you have a writing routine?

A: I do one chapter at a time. First I get a mental "script" firmly planted in my mind. Then, when I sit down at the computer, I think of myself as a director saying, "Lights, camera, action!" At that point it's just a question of getting it out of my head and onto paper. The one thing I do not do is set specific hours. Some writers work every day from nine in the morning to three in the afternoon, come hell or high water. So far I haven't had to do that.

Q: Do you revise as you write?

A: Some writers will do three, four, or five drafts of a book. That doesn't work for me. I stay with a chapter until I'm satisfied with it and then I move on to the next chapter. I revise it as I'm working on it, but once I decide it's done, I leave it as is.

Q: What would you tell an aspiring writer today about the frustration of where to start?

A: I would tell them that perseverance is the most important quality a writer can have. It's so hard for writers to get published and a lot of it is just dumb luck. I know some very talented writers who have not been able to get a foothold in publishing—not because they have a lack of ability but because they haven't been at the right place at the right time. My best advice to aspiring writers is don't be discouraged about first rejections. Just hang in there. It's also incredibly important for a writer to have an agent. Of course the catch-22 is that it's often harder to find an agent than it is to find a publisher.

Q: *The Queen's Man* is the first in a trilogy of books featuring Justin de Quincy. What's next for de Quincy?

A: The next book will be called *Cruel as the Grave*. Basically I pick up where *The Queen's Man* leaves off, with virtually the same cast of characters. Readers will learn more about John's attempt to usurp his brother's throne while Richard is being held prisoner. As for Justin, he finds himself involved in a murder as he tries to help out a friend.

Q: What do you want readers to get out of this book?

A: I'd like them to finish *The Queen's Man* and think, "I can't wait for Justin de Quincy's next adventure." I'd also like them to come away feeling they've learned something about the Middle Ages, and wanting to know more about that era.

Reading Group Questions and Topics for Discussion

1. Eleanor of Aquitaine was one of the most powerful and accomplished women in history. What other strong female characters (either real or fictional) have you read about recently? What are the similarities and differences between those characters and Eleanor?

2. What sort of confinements did women live within in medieval society? Although the position of women in society has changed dramatically since the Middle Ages, do you feel there are similarities between the way women live in society today and the way they lived then?

3. Did you notice Penman's use of medieval words and phrases in *The Queen's Man*? Did it add to your enjoyment of the story or detract from it?

4. Every once in a while, Penman allows her characters to use modern phrases, such as when Luke—suffering from a hangover—says his mouth "feels like five miles of bad road." Did you notice these flashes of modern phrasing? Did they interfere with or contribute to your understanding of the characters or your enjoyment of the story?

5. In describing the process of working on a mystery, Penman has said it's necessary to leave clues for readers to pick up—should they choose to do so—so they can solve the puzzle. Were you trying to solve the mystery as you read through this story? What clues did you find?

6. Do you see any parallels between the medieval fear of leprosy and the modern fear of AIDS? If so, what are they?

7. What effect did the revelation about the murder of the goldsmith, Gervase Fitz Randolph, have on your feelings about his death?

8. If you had been Justin, would you have stopped to help Gervase? Would you have carried out your promise to deliver his letter?

9. As you read about Gervase's family and their possible motives for murdering him, did you think one of them might have been involved in the killing?

10. After spending some time in the twelfth century with Justin de Quincy and Queen Eleanor, did their world seem surprisingly familiar? Or utterly alien? What were the most striking similarities between their society and ours? The greatest differences?

11. Do you think the changes in society have caused changes in human nature over the centuries?

12. How does this medieval mystery compare to contemporary murder mysteries? Do you prefer one over the other? If so, why?

13. The historical characters central to this story—Eleanor of Aquitaine and her sons Richard and John—have appeared in movies, books, and on television. How does Penman's portrayal of these characters compare to other portrayals you may have encountered?

14. Justin is very angry at his father for failing to acknowledge him as his son, and yet the Bishop of Chester made sure Justin was clothed and fed, that there was a roof over his head, that he received a first-class education, and that he became a squire for a local lord. Considering the bishop's position and the social values of twelfth-century England, do you think Justin was wronged by the bishop? What alternatives did the bishop have?

15. How would you describe the relationship between the bastard youth Justin and the aging Eleanor of Aquitaine? Why do you think she places so much trust in him?